FROSTLINE

Justin Scott is the a_____ _ho Loved the Norman__ _ _of the Sear, HardScape _ _in New York City in 19_

Praise for FrostLine and the Ben Abbott series:

'This novel is a delight! Those of us who've been clamouring for a new Ben Abbott will be ecstatic with his latest adventure among the folk of Newbury. Nobody does a better job that Scott in blending big-book suspense, utterly believable characters and his brilliant – sometimes humorous, sometimes heart-wrenching – insights into small town New England life. And what a stylist – every page is a pleasure to read. We want more!'
JEFFERY DEAVER, author of *The Bone Collector*

'Justin Scott is a writer with such a rich variety of arrows in his quiver that you never know what to expect from him next. This diversity has probably kept him from getting the following he deserves. Ben Abbott should change that. He is a character who has grown and developed with each appearance, and anyone who reads FrostLine will want to sign on for the whole trip. It's the best book in a series that started strong and keeps getting better.'
LAWRENCE BLOCK

'[Ben's] sardonic views ... give this sophisticated series its unexpected and wholly delicious tartness.'
New York Times

By the same author

JUSTIN SCOTT

FrostLine

HarperCollins*Publishers*

HarperCollinsPublishers
77–85 Fulham Palace Road,
Hammersmith, London W6 8JB

This paperback edition 1998

1 3 5 7 9 8 6 4 2

First published in Great Britain by
HarperCollinsPublishers 1997

ISBN 0 00 651004 3

Printed and bound in Great Britain by
Caledonian International Book Manufacturing Ltd, Glasgow

For my sister Alison Scott Skelton
– friend, novelist and telemark champion

FrostLine

We bury footings deep in New England – below
the frost line – and hope that ice won't heave
our walls or wedge water under dams.

1

Picture an angry New England farmer: red face; lantern jaw; grey hair sweeping bony shoulders; arms like braided wire. He roars into his neighbour's motor court, which is paved with Belgian cobbles, and skids his twenty-year-old salt-rotted, bald-tyred pickup truck to a screeching stop beside a fleet of Range Rovers. He's got a shotgun in a rack in the rear window.

Richard Butler owns little on earth but land. Cedars are taking his outer fields. Now and then he earns some cash blasting ledge for a builder surprised to find granite where a cellar was anticipated, and he sells firewood when he finds time to split it. When the VA deposits his monthly cheque, he jokes that the only way a dairy farmer can make a living is get shot serving his country.

His neighbour is a celebrity statesman – Henry King, the 'Silver Fox' – who cut his diplomat teeth negotiating a long, bloody end to the Vietnam War. Retired from public service, King earns millions advising governments and international corporations.

Their lands intersect like crazed pottery. King has named his Fox Trot and enclosed it with an electric deer fence. Mr Butler's hardscrabble acres cap the summit of Morris Mountain and sprawl to boundaries stacked of stone half a century before the American Revolution.

He mounts marble stairs, fails to identify a brass fox head as the bell pull, and bangs on the door. Neither he nor King's morning-coated houseman knows what to make of each other. But when Henry King rushes into the foyer Mr Butler shouts, 'Get those pipes off my land.'

'They're only temporary,' King starts to placate him. 'For drainage while I build my lake.' But it galls King that he has to oblige a hostile neighbour whose net worth is less than he earns in a day, and the statesman blunders: 'As it's not precisely *your* land anyway, I presume you'll accommodate –'

'If you cross my fences again, I'll sue you.'

King flushes darkly, the memory of a stinging defeat in the local court fresh in his mind. 'Show him out.'

The houseman hesitates, unsure whether the farmer's eyes burn with rage or insanity. There's a shotgun in his truck.

That's where I came in.

Although at the very moment they were cementing their feud, I was up a tree – steeple-high in a Main Street elm, trying to rescue the Meeting House cat, who was stuck where the branches got thin. A voice loud enough to hail friends across an interstate boomed up from the frozen ground.

'Hey Ben! Guess who just got out of Somers.'

Somers Correctional, security-five state prison.

Far below, my audience had doubled: Alison Mealy, the skinny eleven-year-old shivering in a hand-me-down ski parka, who had talked me into this mercy mission, had been joined by Scooter MacKay – publisher, editor and ace reporter of the *Newbury Clarion*. Bulky as a bear in Eddie Bauer goosedown, he had brought his Nikon in case I fell.

A gust of wind set the flag thundering over Church Hill. My branch began to sag. I extended a gloved hand to the cat, a brindly calico that looked like a dirty tablecloth.

'Hear me? Guess who just got out of Somers.'

Scooter's family had owned the *Clarion* since the invention of linotype. The weekly earned him an awful lot of money, but few opportunities to wow the town with breaking news.

'Dicky Butler.'

'How the hell did you find out?'

None of Scooter's business.

My reticence provoked explanatory roars: 'Appellate Court threw out the intent-to-sell conviction. He'd already served enough time on the assault.'

'Tell that to the assaulted.'

Dicky Butler was a vicious brawler. He had a screw or two loose that made him violent. But he wasn't stupid, and the possession case had been shaky from the start: Newbury's resident state trooper Oliver Moody had stretched Supreme Court guidelines to lengths that would have raised Stalin's eyebrows; then the jury refused to disregard Dicky's reputation for punching the lights out of innocent Newburians while roaming the town between convictions, and voted that Connecticut would be a safer state with Dicky Butler behind bars.

The cat hissed. I faked a tail yank; and when the dummy fell for it, scooped her off the branch and into the laundry bag I'd tied to my belt.

Horns blared. Brakes screeched. Startled, I slipped off my branch as a speeding caravan of Range Rovers forced Hopkins Septic's tanker off the road. Arrogant DPL-plated sons of bitches from Henry King's Morris Mountain estate. I hung for my life like a three-toed sloth.

'Don't drop her,' screamed Alison, and the Nikon's motor drive began whining eagerly.

Upside down, from elm height, Newbury looked like a Currier and Ives New England miniature enamelled on Grandma's brooch: clapboard churches clustered around the tallest flagpole in Connecticut; snug Colonials; snow-white mansions; barn-red General Store; a sturdy bank; and Town Hall. All crisp in the piercing March sunlight. No one had had the nerve yet to unwrap their winter-burlapped rhododendrons, but a breath of yellow on the willows in the Rams Pasture warned country-house shoppers to buy soon or spend summer in the city. So if I were in my office, instead of up a tree, I'd be answering my telephone with high hopes of business, 'Benjamin Abbott Realty.'

I slothed my way down towards a friendly fork. Scooter, conceding he had lost the photo opportunity of the winter, yelled, 'Dicky's dad says they're going to sue for false arrest.'

'You want to hold the ladder?'

Branch to branch, then down the rungs, a smile ready

11

when Scooter snapped my landing: REALTOR RESCUES CAT — the kind of front-page advertising you just can't buy.

Alison unbagged the animal, which eluded her consoling hug and ran into the road in the path of a pickup truck, survived that somehow, and started up a tree in my Aunt Connie's front yard.

My knees were shaking. 'What does Ollie say?'

'Nothing I can print. He says he'll tear Dicky's head off if he steps out of line.'

'That should be exciting.'

Dicky was like Joe Frazier: he got an adrenalin rush when someone hit him. Trooper Moody enjoyed inflicting pain.

'I thought you'd want to know,' said Scooter. Then he got embarrassed and looked away.

'Thank you. I appreciate it.'

Dicky and I had hung out the summer we were twelve — the summer before Scooter and I were enrolled in Newbury Prep as day students and Dicky was shipped off to the Manson Youth Institute at Cheshire. We'd not seen a lot of each other since.

Except when I was released from Leavenworth Penitentiary — three years for the sins of an overly meteoric yuppie career on Wall Street — and Dicky had stopped by with a six-pack to see how I was adjusting to hometown life. So I owed the man a visit.

Scooter's stage whisper was audible at the flagpole. 'I hear Alison wants a cat.'

'Actually, she wants a dog. But she can't have a dog because it would bark all day while her mother's working and she's in school.' I winked at Alison. She snarled back, braces flashing like razor wire. 'And she can't have a cat because her Mom's allergic.'

They lived in the old stablehand's apartment over my barn, since I'd found them hitchhiking and homeless on Route 7. By logic beyond my grasp, I was in line for a proxy pet.

'Naomi's pregnant, again. Should I reserve a kitten?'

'Send the whole litter. There's a Mongolian hotpot recipe —'

Scooter said goodbye. I carried my ladder back to the barn.

Alison trailed me into the house. I nuked us a couple of mugs of hot apple cider, which we took to my office in the glassed-in front porch.

'A cat would help out by eating scraps.'

'I have a compost heap.'

'You get lonely in this great big empty house.'

I reminded the child that while Abbott House – a Georgian Colonial with ink-black shutters and snow-white clapboards – might dwarf Newbury's older saltboxes, it was modest compared to my Great-aunt Connie's Federal mansion across the street, and the Greek Revival and Second Empire residences that the fast-money crowd had thrown up in the nineteenth century.

Nor did it feel empty, crammed with furniture that frugal Abbotts never threw out. But how to explain to my prepubescent friend that when lonely, I hoped less to connect with a cat than with a fellow human of the warm and feminine persuasion? (Hopes dashed of late.)

The telephone rang, cutting short my hunt for euphemisms and halting an unwelcome lapse into mournful reflection.

'Benjamin Abbott Realty.'

'Mr Abbott,' said a woman who sounded used to being obeyed. 'Henry King wants you to come up to Fox Trot.'

I took my feet off my desk.

Henry King was pouring serious money into the old Zarega place, which he had renovated, rebuilt, and added on to. I had heard that he was trying to run some land deals by his neighbours – 'buying to the horizon', as WASP New Englanders put it.

Not that King was old Connecticut. Far from it, despite elocution and polo lessons. But having cashed in a career in personal diplomacy for Republican presidents, this Harvard-educated son of a Red Hook longshoreman had earned the means to acquire the *accoutrement*.

My aerial photo map indicated several possible sales of unused pastures and woodlots. But the prize was a hundred acres on the summit, which belonged to, of all people, Dicky Butler's father.

My gut told me that's what King wanted. It also told me

that Mr Butler wouldn't sell. And yet, farmers got tired. He had struggled alone for years – no wife to bring in steady cash with a part-time job, no kids to share the chores, Dicky being incarcerated most of the time and raising hell when he wasn't. He just might appreciate a way out. If so, I would earn a handsome commission. But from a buyer I wouldn't be proud to do business with.

I didn't hold with former public servants augmenting their pensions by selling publicly-paid-for contacts. The practice devalues their office and skews their judgement in favour of their future benefactors. By rights, I should tell Henry King to take his business to my competitors.

But face it, I needed the business. Wall Street had down-sized my natural customers. While those still employed were spending differently than they had back in the 1980s. My country-house listings had all the appeal of *ris de veau* in a rib joint.

I weighed a potential good deed for Mr Butler. I reminded myself that I cared more about swinging deals than the money involved – ignoring memories of hot water *that* had landed me in in the past. I told myself I was curious for a peek at King's estate, rumoured to rival Kublai Khan's.

'Mr King has people coming for lunch. Join us at noon.'

Alison was watching, her big eyes guarded.

'Hold on, please.' I covered the phone. 'Is your Mom working?'

'Yeah.'

'"Yes", not "yeah".'

School days, Mrs Mealy cleaned houses; Saturdays, she helped Main Street matrons prepare their dinner parties. 'There's tuna in the fridge. Why not invite Dora and Patty for lunch?'

Dora and Patty were *capo* and *consiglieri* of the girls-only Main Street bicycle gang. Alison, *capo di tutti i capi*.

She pretzelled deeper into her chair and studied the pattern on the worn oriental carpet. 'We're not talking . . . We had a fight.'

'Call a peace conference. Frozen yoghurt for dessert.'

'Can't. They're riding Patty's horse. With Patty's mother.'

14

I'm rarely violent. But if Patty's parents had walked in at that moment I would have slugged them. Alison had enough problems with an abusive drunk for a father – absent, on my orders, until the day world peace was declared and he got sober – and the frightened daughter of a hardscrabble farmer for a mother. She didn't need more grief from social climbers.

'Go on, Ben. I'll watch TV.'

I said to the lady on the phone, 'I'm afraid I'm tied up. I'll be there after lunch.'

'Mr King specifically requested you come to lunch.'

'Please give him my regrets. I'll see him at two.'

'Make it one-thirty.'

A point getter. 'One-thirty it is, Ms – ?'

'Julia Devlin. They'll have your name at the gatehouse, Mr Abbott.'

I hung up thinking, gatehouse? Gates alone were considered a tad pretentious in Newbury, more appropriate to strivers' driveways in commuter towns like Greenwich.

Alison said, 'A compost heap won't curl up in your lap.'

'If Mr King offers me a ride to Washington DC in his helicopter, someday, I won't have to say, "Sorry, Mr King, I have to go home and feed the cat." '

'*I'd* feed her.'

'What if you had band practice? Or stayed late for your computer course? By the time one of us got home we'd be down to compost anyway.'

We settled around the kitchen table for tuna sandwiches, Aunt Connie's bread-and-butter pickles, and a little chat about Dora and Patty. It didn't help much.

Henry King's gatehouse looked like an English country railroad station – a fanciful structure of stone, steep gables and leaded windows. An iron gate sufficiently sturdy to keep locomotives out was guarded by Albert and Dennis Chevalley, rambunctious young cousins of mine from the wrong side of the tracks.

I'd heard they'd found work dynamiting tree stumps for Henry King, until some government killjoy ruled that the argument that Dad and Granddad 'always blew stumps' did not automatically qualify the boys to be state-licensed pyro-technicians. Particularly with explosives borrowed from a highway construction site. Nevertheless, it appeared they had been promoted to full-time Fox Trot retainers: parked by the gatehouse gleamed a jet-black four-by Chevy pickup with FOX TROT emblazoned on the door; the boys themselves were decked out in their first-ever garments from L.L. Bean, 'Scottish tartan' flannel shirts.

Dennis hulked at the gate controls. Albert held a clipboard that looked like a playing card in his large and hairy paw. They were dark-haired and dark-eyed like most Chevalleys, medium-size by clan standards (quite enormous). Albert was of typical intelligence, which made finding his shoes each morning something of a project. Dennis could be more complicated.

'Hi, guys,' I said. 'Neat truck.'

'Name?'

'What?'

'What's your name?'

'You know my name, Albert. You're my cousin, for crissake.'

'We got orders. Gotta ask everybody's name. And check the list.'

Legend has the Chevalley clan founding the Frenchtown district of Newbury around the time of the Revolution, the first arrival variously described as a French army deserter, a runaway indentured servant, or a Hudson Bay trapper way off course. In fact, Chevalleys have been around Newbury almost as long as Abbotts. Borough records locate one Anton 'Chevalier' in Newbury's first stockade. The charge was 'carousing' and not a lot has changed since. My mother's brothers, cousins and nephews are excellent companions in bar brawls, off-season deer hunts, and drag races. Their women learn young to cope.

I stared. Albert stared back.

Dennis lumbered closer. Dennis *seemed* dumb as Albert. But he was a secret watcher – eyes mean and busy – like a pig waiting to see who wandered close enough to eat.

'Security,' he explained.

16

There was plenty of that: motion detectors to turn on the floodlights, laser eyes between the gateposts, a seven-strand electric deer fence that took up where the walls ended. There was even a pressure plate in the driveway, which curved up into the deep woods that blocked any sight of the house. On the gatehouse roof a TV camera panned the approach.

'I'm not going to tell you my name.'

'Then we can't let you in.'

I picked up my cell phone. 'If you don't open that gate I'm going to tell our mutual cousin Pinkerton Chevalley to bring the new wrecker.' (The 'new' wrecker was a 1973 Peterbilt for hauling tandem tractor trailer trucks out of deep ditches.) 'We'll hook that goddammed gate right off the posts and drag it up the driveway and tell Mr King you and Dennis made us do it.'

Cousin Pink was a full-size Chevalley, very large indeed, who set standards of disorganization and wilfully unsocial skills Albert and Dennis could only dream of. The death of his brother had left him in charge of Chevalley Enterprises' seven repair bays, two tow trucks, and a dozen drivers and mechanics. A lot for a man who operated on impulse, which made his short fuse shorter.

I, too, had been known to get wild on occasion – my reputation pegged to a youthful skirmish involving Trooper Moody's state police car and a very long logging chain.

'Aw, come on, Ben, give us your name.'

'Benjamin Constantine Abbott III.'

I helped them spell Constantine. He was the China Trade pirate who had enriched Aunt Connie's branch of the family. I got stuck with it because for two centuries Abbotts of modest means have hoped they couldn't go wrong naming kids after wealthy relatives. (There is no evidence that as much as a penny was ever shifted from one Abbott to another by this manoeuvre, and Connie's will leaves her considerable fortune to charity.)

The gate swung on silent machinery.

'What's with the security?'

Albert tossed a shaggy-minotaur nod towards the Butler

farm, hidden behind the brow of the mountain. 'Old Man Butler's making trouble.'

'What kind of trouble?'

'Neighbour trouble,' said Dennis. When I pressed for details, the brothers got all glowery and said they weren't supposed to talk to the guests. Which was certainly the basis on which I would have hired them.

'Don't get sucked in,' I said. 'Dicky's out.'

Their response to my warning was pure Chevalley: broad, gap-toothed grins at the prospect of a bloody fight.

I drove on through the gate and entered Fox Trot on to land I hadn't seen since I'd snuck over the fence with Dicky Butler back when we were twelve.

2

Henry King had gone private after the Bush gang shut him
out for badmouthing their international tomfoolery. Criticizing his boss publicly had seemed to me a clumsy mistake by
a diplomat so smooth he was known as the Silver Fox. Being
right hadn't helped his cause and the Fox had found himself
out on his silver ear – a disaster he had turned to remarkable
advantage when the Soviet Union's collapse opened half the
planet to American business.

To nervous executives, Henry King, Incorporated offered
top-drawer connections and insights into an often baffling,
always frightening world. When GM wanted to tilt again at
the Japanese market, they hired Henry King to consult them
in matters Japanese, which he was current on because Toyota
hired him to explain matters British and the Brits, et cetera
. . . The *Economist* swore the scam was taking down twenty
million a year.

Add weekly speeches at fifty grand a pop to the tax advan-
tages of paying for pleasantries like the helicopter and the
Georgetown townhouse through the non-profit 'Henry King
Institute of Geopolitics', and the man was accumulating a lot
of money. Much of which he appeared to be spending on
construction.

His estate resembled a war zone. The driveway followed
the same elegant sweep it had before the place got a name,
disappearing up the meadow and into a deep woodlot, but
the meadow had been extended by obliterating several acres
of trees. Cratered where Chevalleys had dynamited stumps,
it looked like a morally outraged Kaiseran Army had barraged
obdurate troops of the Czar.

19

The alterations were subtler inside the woodlot, where tree surgeons had judiciously thinned and pruned. Weed trees had been culled, and dead limbs removed from the stately red oaks. It was unusual to see a managed forest in Newbury and to my eye it looked a trifle too managed, like a CD-Rom version of Robin Hood's Sherwood. But I had to admire the views designed to highlight handsome specimens. Beech and shagbark hickory and sugar maple revelled in the clean new space.

Rounding a curve I ran into more security. The real thing, this time. A spike barrier blocked the driveway – foot-high razor-sharp steel prongs that would make hamburger of my tyres if I didn't stop beside a speaker box and stifle the impulse to order a Whopper and fries.

'Ben Abbott.'

'You may continue,' said the box.

The spikes sank into the macadam.

I continued.

Now hemlock trees began speckling the forest, denser and denser until they formed an impenetrable wall, which opened suddenly on a long view of the main house that hit the eye like a frozen snowball.

I stopped the car and stared. The *new* main house, I realized, a monumental stone and stucco structure built in the neoclassical style the *New York Times* has dubbed 'Corinthian avant-garde'.

Four columns supported a massive pediment over the two-storey entrance. Palladian windows arched heroically. Majestic chimneys dominated an elegant mansard roof. It wasn't ugly. There was too much ordered symmetry for that, too many finely executed details. But it did look like a banker had commanded his architects to build something solid around a pile of money.

The original dwelling, Mr Zarega's 1920s country house – pleasantly shingled, and draped in porches – that had looked so big and sprawling to adolescent eyes, stood dwarfed at some distance. Here, too, construction was in progress and both buildings were surrounded by frozen mud studded with construction trailers. Plank paths criss-crossed the mud, which was thawing stickily in the afternoon sun. I didn't recognize any of the workmen plodding through it, as King's contractors were from down on the coast of the Long Island Sound.

They had finished the motor court. I parked the Olds in a herd of Range Rovers, hobbled across the cobblestones, and mounted an imposing flight of marble stairs. The doorbell played a ragtime tune that Aunt Connie later identified for me as having been composed by Harry Fox, the bandleader who had invented the fox trot when she was a little girl.

King's butler wore a swallowtailed coat and a grimace for the sea of mud. He whisked me inside where it was warm and dry. Perhaps he saw in me a sympathetic spirit, or maybe he'd had a bad day, but he shuddered visibly and said, 'The country,' leaving no doubt where his preferences lay. 'Welcome, Mr Abbott. I'll take you in to Madam, and the others.'

Henry King and fourteen guests were still at the lunch table, in a heated sun porch that overlooked the valleys to the west. The butler led me to an empty chair, slightly below the salt, between a fellow about my age, who looked familiar, and a raven-haired woman who looked lovely.

King, short and broad-shouldered, rose with a charming smile. He greeted me in a low, heavy voice and if he was miffed that I hadn't come as early as Ms Devlin had demanded, no hint escaped the thick brows that hooded his bright, deep-set eyes. Everything in his manner seemed intended to suggest that a splendid lunch had just gotten better because I had arrived.

'Just in time for coffee, Mr Abbott. Let me introduce you.'

His wife, a very nice-looking blonde who hosted a Washington TV interview show, smiled from the foot of the table. Her immediate neighbours, a younger Harvardy-Yalish bunch, looked like King Institute employees. King had kept the big guns for himself.

At his right hand sat former Secretary of State Bertram Wills, whose Connecticut family had staffed the Foreign Service since the XYZ Affair. Even friendly biographers agreed that Henry King had emasculated him during negotiations with the Red Chinese.

To King's left was Josh Wiggens, a blandly handsome gentleman who could have had 'CIA Station Chief' tattooed on his forehead. Another early retiree, unless I missed my bet, probably one of the many sacked for failing to notice turncoat Aldrich Ames driving a Jaguar with KGB vanity plates.

Ex-diplomat Wills and ex-spy Wiggens might have been twins: lean, well-dressed patricians in the classic New England mould of long faces with fine bones, sandy hair (temples greying gracefully), and piercing blue eyes. Both had the big hands you get from a lifetime of horses, tennis and sailing. Both, the genteel cragginess that comes from active leisure out of doors. But where Secretary Wills appeared to be all dignified accommodation, Josh Wiggens looked like a man with a taste for naked force: Wills like a ceremonial sabre, Wiggens a boarding cutlass – metaphors which could be misleading, as neither man, I suspected, was to be trusted in a dark alley.

Way below the salt, down at Mrs King's end, was a writer from *The New Republic* who looked glad to be invited. King Institute staffers surrounded him like kitty litter sopping up an oil spill.

Directly across from me sat an up-and-coming Connecticut Congressman whose career I'd followed with interest. I asked after his father, who had given me my senatorial appointment to Annapolis Naval Academy. A look I knew too well glazed the Congressman's eye as he recalled how Ensign Abbott's post-commission financial career had grounded on the shoals of insider trading.

The fellow who looked familiar turned out to be Gerald Wills, Secretary Bert's son, a gossipy genealogist, and an amazing snob for one so young.

The raven-haired woman who looked lovely was Julia Devlin. She asked if I'd like dessert. The others had finished, so I said coffee would be fine.

Pressed to classify Julia Devlin on a scale of cold to hot beauty, I'd have rated her a cool beauty. I pictured her on horseback five hundred years ago: aide de camp to a Spanish grandee, her father; their army harassing Moors – something about her dark eyebrows.

A pretty velvet vest cinched her waist. A white blouse accented the faintest olive cast to skin I felt a very strong desire to explore.

'Mr Abbott!' King called down the table. 'How do you call the first selectman's primary?'

Faces that had frowned upon the fate of nations turned to me now. I answered, 'Vicky McLachlan is the best first selectman Newbury's ever had.'

'Better than your father?' asked Gerald Wills.

'It was an easier job in my dad's day.'

'Why?' asked King. His brows lifted like the curtain at Radio City Music Hall and when he looked straight at me the intelligence radiating from his eyes was almost blinding. 'I'm told your father was responsible for our beautiful Main Street.'

He'd been told half. Back in the 1950s, when my grandfather was still first selectman, his handpicked zoning board had shown remarkable prescience by banning commercial development on Newbury's historic Main Street. When population pressure hit in the 1960s, Dad was running things. *His* handpicked zoning board zoned modern conveniences out of sight down Church Hill Road. As a result, we are the prettiest town in Northwest Connecticut, unblemished by gas stations, Subways, or McDonald's.

'When my dad served, he could concentrate on local matters because federal and state government still faced up to their responsibilities.'

'I met Ms McLachlan's challenger in his liquor shop. He promised to cut my property taxes. Definitely a candidate with my interests at heart.'

Former Secretary Wills placed a manicured hand firmly against his rib cage and chuckled, without seeming to move his lips or jaw. 'Very funny, Henry. Very funny.'

I said, 'Voters' incomes are falling; they see taxes as their only chance to save a buck. Our discount Ribbentrop knows this and makes promises he cannot keep.'

King raised a bushy grey eyebrow, indicating he

appreciated the reference, and wagged a friendlily mocking finger. 'I wonder if you're biased, Mr Abbott. Haven't I heard that you and the first selectman are an "item"?'

I thought that was a bit intrusive. But he had intruded with a smile. So, wondering how much he'd had me checked out, and why, I answered, 'No such luck. We're only friends.' No longer what Aunt Connie, born of another age, called 'dear friends'.

Wiggens, the CIA guy, who since I had arrived had demolished an after-lunch Scotch and signalled for another, ventured the opinion that Americans were fed up with government and that in most of the countries he had visited – he actually used the word 'visited' – the natives would be burning police stations.

Mrs King deftly changed the subject, and young Gerald Wills said to me in a low voice, 'I've always wondered what your Great-aunt Constance thought when your father married a Chevalley.'

He seemed utterly unaware that an uncharitable soul might invite him outside for such a crude reminder that my mother came from the wrong side of the tracks. I was, in fact, grateful to my parents for bridging the social divide between Frenchtown and Main Street. The boldest act of my father's sober life and my mother's timid acquiescence had allowed me to roam everywhere. (Widowed after half a century, she had fled home to Frenchtown.)

Which put me in mind of Patty's mother excluding little Alison. I resolved then and there to sic Aunt Connie on the woman: a coveted invitation to tea; an icily polite lecture on the obligations of privilege.

King called out to me, again. 'What do you think of Fox Trot, Mr Abbott?'

'Astonishing changes.'

'You've seen it before?'

'Once. Years ago, when I was a kid.'

'Oh, you knew old Zarega?'

'No. He was a recluse. Couple of us snuck over the fence. We had to have a look.'

'What did you expect?' asked Mrs King.

'Probably looting the place,' growled the former spy.

'When I was growing up, it was an article of faith among small boys that Mr Zarega – whom no one had ever seen – owned seven Cadillacs – different colours for every day of the week.'

'Did you see them?'

'Something better.'

'What?'

'He had a bear.'

Julia Devlin looked over at me. 'A bear?'

'A pet bear. Roaming around like he owned the place. Housebroken. Very affectionate. Shook my hand.'

'A very civil bear,' said Julia: a phrase that aroused another memory of earlier times and prompted me to say, 'I think you read my favourite writer.'

'Patrick O'Brian! Isn't he wonderful? I'm trying to get Henry started on *Master and Commander*, but he's so busy –'

She was leaning closer, her eyes bright, when up the table, where people were ohhhing and ahhhing over the bear, things got suddenly loud. King, red in the face, had raised his voice to the butler.

'If I wanted coffee in a filthy cup I'd order coffee in a filthy cup. Get back to the kitchen and bring a clean one!'

There was a shocked silence. The butler, a tall man, stared fixedly down at Henry King and for a second seemed to threaten physical attack. I felt Julia Devlin coil beside me, tensing like she would vault the table to King's defence.

King countered the threat with a pugnacious, '*I'm waiting!*'

The butler took the offending cup and marched stiffly to the door. There he clicked his heels and gave Mrs King a stiff, jerky bow, his eyes cast firmly at the floor. 'Madame, forgive me.' He lifted his gaze to Henry King. 'Sir. You may take this job and shove it.'

King found himself in the untenable position of yelling at his houseman's back. Julia Devlin uncoiled. And Gerald Wills redeemed himself for ever by murmuring, 'Third butler this year and it's only March.'

When King finally shut up, his wife said, 'Oh, Henry.'

King rounded on her. '*You* hired him!'

25

Mrs King lowered her eyes, and slid the smallest glance up the table towards Bertram Wills. For a second I thought he would come to her defence. But instead, his hand fell to his side again and he tried to console King with a lockjawed joke, 'Difficult to find a butler who's a hero to his man, Henry.'

King glared at him like a monkey that had sprung its cage. Then he turned on me. 'Mr Abbott! Would you join me in the library? There's something I'd like to discuss.'

That was what I had come for, so I followed him out of the room, pausing to thank Mrs King for the coffee. She gave me her very soft hand and a bruised up-from-under blue-eyed smile. I hoped to catch a better smile from Julia Devlin, but she had fixed the *New Republic* man with a gimlet stare. *He* was smiling the smile of a writer who had the lead for his story, a smile that faded as Julia advanced on him for what looked like a severe recital of the ground rules under which journalists were invited back to Fox Trot.

King was waiting in the hall. 'Let's go, Abbott.'

'I think I'll come back later.'

'What for?'

'You're a little upset and you've just demoted me from Mr Abbott to Abbott. I have to go see someone. So why don't we connect around four when everyone's calmed down?'

King surprised me with a big laugh. 'They told me you were a pisser.'

'Who told you I was a pisser?'

'Let's talk. I'll behave. You want a drink?'

'Little early for me.'

'Yeah, me too.' As we talked, we walked down a broad hall and into an absolutely exquisite library.

'I'm nuts for this room,' he said. 'You like it?'

'It's about the only one I've ever seen that deserves the phrase, "Would you join me in the library?"'

I wandered for a few minutes, trailed by a proud King pointing out details. 'Wonderful,' I said. 'It looks like it's been here for a hundred years.'

'It was in its last house for *three* hundred years.'

'The books or the wood?'

26

King grinned, utterly happy with his house. His pleasure was so open that it was infectious, and I found myself liking him a lot more than I had expected to. 'The woodwork's from England. The books are mine, since graduate school.'

First I'd heard that graduate students' books were leather-bound.

'My thesis adviser bequeathed his library to me.'

I'd read that somewhere. King had published that thesis before he had his doctorate. It had made him famous and attracted a new mentor – a Texas oil millionaire with ambitions to walk the halls of power and the patience to cultivate the young. I wondered if King still took his calls. The former Secretary of State at his lunch table and the cashiered spy wore the quick-to-please expressions of those permanent house guests the very wealthy keep around for their amusement.

'Sit down.'

We sat at either end of a tufted green leather chesterfield. King pointed an infrared zapper at the fireplace and flames engulfed the birch logs stacked on the grate. 'Do you know why I asked you here?'

'I assume you want to buy some land.'

'No.'

I felt a little adrenalin surge of excitement. Call it greed. If Henry King was *selling* Fox Trot, the commission would take care of a modest man's shelter and transportation needs into the next century. He waited. I said nothing. If he was selling, we had already begun negotiating my percentage, and one thing I had learned on Wall Street was when to be silent.

'Aren't you curious?' he asked.

'Well, if you're not buying, you're selling. Why else would you invite a real-estate broker to lunch?'

'I'm not selling. And I'm not buying. At least not now.'

I keep an affable smile handy for disappointments. 'Why not give me a ring when you decide? In the meantime, if you're looking for a ballpark appraisal, I'd be delighted to look around and give you a number. No charge, of course.'

My free appraisal offer was more sincere than my smile.

27

I'd been hoping for a close look at the place. And once he made up his mind to buy or sell, he might think of me first. Turned out he already knew me – or thought he did.

'I've got a problem,' he said. 'From what I hear you can help me with it.'

'You keep alluding to hearing things about me. What do you hear?'

'I hear that you – shall we say – fix things.'

'That's what I hear about you.'

'I fix things internationally. I hear you fix things locally.'

'You've heard wrong,' I said. 'I sell houses and land.'

'You bring buyers and sellers together.'

'The normal function of a broker,' I said, stressing 'normal'.

King gave me an indulgent smile. 'A broker's connections are his stock in trade. I hear you're connected, that you know everyone worth knowing in Newbury.'

'I've heard you're having a problem with your neighbour. Is that what this is about?'

'That crazy old farmer is a thorn in my side.'

'Most neighbours are. They're worse than relatives; you can't get away from them.'

'He's making threats. He's undermining my sense of security in my own home. I want it stopped.'

'First of all, if we're talking about Mr Butler –'

'We are.'

'First of all, that "crazy old farmer" is younger than you are.' He had fathered Dicky while on R&R from Vietnam when he was only eighteen, which put him early fifties, though you wouldn't know it to look at him. 'Second, if you think he's crazy, you should meet his son.'

'So I've heard. Fortunately, they've locked him up and thrown away the key.'

'They just found it. Appellate Court overturned his conviction.'

'*Why?*'

'Apparently the rule of law took precedence over what had seemed like a good idea at the time. He's probably home by now.'

'Good Christ.'

'Making this an excellent time to resolve your dispute – what is your dispute?'

To my surprise, King looked embarrassed. He couldn't meet my eye. Suddenly I realized what he had done. 'OK. I get it. You want to buy his place, right?'

'It cuts into my property. The old boundaries are so odd. It cuts right into the *heart* of my property.'

'You figured you'd negotiate directly, him being your neighbour and all.'

'Not to save commissions. The money means nothing. Abbott, do I have to spell it out to you? I admit it was ego. I figured any man who could get Reagan and Deng to the same table could persuade some stupid old farmer to sell his farm.'

'I've got to tell you, Mr Butler is not old. The war may have made him crazy. But he's never struck me as stupid.'

'It never occurred to me in a million years I'd need a real-estate agent. Hell, I bought this place direct from Zarega's executor.'

'Ira Roth.'

King winced. 'The way you say "Ira Roth", are you implying I paid too much?'

'You paid market value,' I said, mustering all the tact that is a broker's stock in trade. The price of Fox Trot was public record. Ira was a brilliant criminal lawyer. But the deal he'd cut for Mr Zarega's heirs suggested he had missed his calling. Or maybe Henry King was telling the truth when he claimed that money meant nothing to him. Although in my experience guys who profess not to care about the money are usually too insecure to admit they care very much.

'I got nowhere with Butler. Worse, he got the idea in his head that I'd insulted him. He threatened to shoot me if I stepped on his land.'

'Had you?'

'Had I what?'

'Stepped on his land.'

'I had one of his fences repaired. His cows were getting out.'

29

'People around Newbury are kind of touchy about property lines.'

'*I'm* touchy about property lines. I understand. I was just trying to help.'

'Cows do much damage?'

'They would have if we had the gardens in. They bring flies. The flies follow the herd. You couldn't sit outside last August.'

'That's why they invented screen porches.'

King turned a lot less affable. 'Mr Abbott, I haven't worked my whole life to be trapped indoors on my own property.'

'How do I fit into this?'

'I'm aware that I've poisoned the well with my offer to buy his farm. You're welcome to try as a real-estate agent, but I don't hold much hope.'

'Sounds that way.'

'I'd like you to reason with the man.'

'Why not just ignore him? You won't be the first neighbours who don't talk.'

'I want those cows away from my house.'

'How close are they?'

'Close enough to spread flies that bite me and my guests. I had a Saudi prince here last summer who left with a welt the size of a tennis ball.'

'Could I see a property plan?'

He had it ready, spread out on an antique billiard table in the game room. Clipped to it was a one-page lease notarized in 1985.

'You see the problem?'

The map showed something that wasn't visible on my aerial photos: Mr Zarega had leased a cow pasture to Mr Butler for a dollar a year until Butler died.

'I'm not a lawyer, but this looks solid.' The lease's brevity was exceeded only by its precision.

'It's not even his land.'

'In effect, it is.'

The pasture was long and narrow and cut into Fox Trot like a knife. On days the cows were on it, and took it into their collective heads to bunch at the lower end, they would launch a few flies into Fox Trot's rarefied air. Flies with teeth honed on cowhide.

King said, 'I can't understand why Zarega would have agreed to such an arrangement.'

'They were friends.'

King snorted derisively, offering an unpleasant reminder of the melting pot he'd escaped fifty years earlier: 'A wop from the Bronx and a Connecticut redneck?'

His contempt sounded real, which annoyed me, and I said, 'Our traditional slur is "swamp Yankee". Though, like most slurs, it's evolved into something of a compliment lately.'

'I stand corrected,' King replied icily. 'But you get my point.'

'Your point misses the point. It was a genuine friendship. Mr Zarega really was a recluse and very, very old. Mr Butler had his problems after Vietnam. Somehow they hooked up. And the way I heard it, when the old man was ill Mr Butler would be up here every day.'

'My lawyers say I can't break the lease.'

'Ira Roth drew it up.'

'I feel like a damned fool. It was right there in black and white, but I didn't realize the distances until I'd been here awhile. I'm a city boy.'

I'd seen stranger deals. When ordinary people sought mortgages, the banks demanded zealous title searches. Buying for cash you were on your own.

I said, 'Mr Zarega's house was farther from the fence. At any rate, they're not going to be on this pasture that often. It won't sustain them.'

'Am I supposed to *hope* that he doesn't put his cows in there on days I've got clients visiting? I won't be able to use the goddammed swimming pool. Am I supposed to put screens over my pool? And my tennis courts?'

I had no answer beyond, 'Flies go with farmland.'

'I'm hiring you to reason with Butler. You're local. Maybe he'll listen to you.'

'Who told you I was a pisser?'

King smiled easily. 'I can't reveal my sources.'

'Why'd you ask?'

'Let's get on the same page, Mr Abbott. Do you understand that I regard this as a very serious matter?'

'Do *you* understand that you're in a classic country–city clash? You've got a lovely estate here, cheek by jowl with a cow farm. You pay for all this with money you earn elsewhere. Mr Butler earns his right here. You're a new arrival. He's third-generation. I could go on, but I think you get my point.'

'Exactly why I intend to hire the best-qualified person to resolve it for me. It's beyond the lawyers. I need a local fixer. You're a local fixer – don't interrupt. Not only that, you've worked as a private detective – don't interrupt. I *know* you have no licence and I don't care. I do care that you learned your trade when you served with Naval Intelligence.'

'This is more a job for a psychiatrist.'

'The one I send my staff to charges one hundred and fifty dollars an hour. Would that be sufficient?'

We know that my real-estate business was not exactly booming that March. Although, having experienced first hand the financial markets' ephemerality – evanescence I had contributed to back in the 1980s as an overpaid, underaged Wall Street shark – I had diversified my listings, scouring Newbury for commercial space to rent to the new wave of start-up businesses being founded by the recently fired. So I wasn't starving, yet.

But the Olds was getting old; I had dreams of replacing my dad's message pads with a voice-mail-pager; and if a fresh coat of paint wasn't applied soon to the aforementioned snowy clapboards the word 'shabby' would affix itself to the directions I gave customers: 'The Georgian house near the flagpole.'

I was marvelling how diplomat King had blundered into this clumsy affair, when he reminded me that he was no dummy. 'Look at it this way, Abbott. Not only do you pick up a fat fee for making peace, but you'll get your full commission on any land you can get him to sell me.'

'Would that include your buying the lease?'

'I will buy the lease and every damned acre he'll sell me besides.'

I nodded, tempted by the chance to swing a land deal.

King raved on, 'I'll buy his whole goddammed house. Hell, I'll buy him a mountain he can move to.'

'You're offering to buy him another place?'

'As long as it's on the other side of town.'

'I'll go talk to him,' I said. 'But don't get your hopes up. I was just a friend of his kid.'

'You're *friends* with that criminal?'

I ignored that and said, 'I noticed some heavy security at the gate. Are there any incidents I should know about?'

'This morning, Butler drove in here with a shotgun.'

'Did you call Trooper Moody?'

'Well, he didn't point it at anyone.'

'You mean it was in the rack.'

'In the back window. Very visible, very obviously there.'

'He's not the only man in town with a shotgun in his truck. It doesn't mean anything more than wearing a cap.'

'I found it very threatening. Frightened my staff. What if I had been entertaining clients when he came roaring up my driveway?'

'How'd he get past the gate and the spikes?'

'The place was wide open for my lunch guests. Now, I want something done about him before someone gets hurt.'

'What did he come for?'

'He was yelling to stay off his land.'

'Is this the fence thing?'

'Well . . .' King hesitated.

'Please,' I said. 'I can't talk to him if I don't know what's going on.'

'I'm building a lake – here, I'll show you.' He whipped aside the plot plan, revealing a landscape designer's rendering of a twenty-acre lake to be formed by erecting a fair-size dam across a brook that started up on Butler's farm, cascaded through their adjoining woodlots, and emerged from the leased pasture.

'Fantastic,' I said.

It sported an island, with a Corinthian avant-garde gazebo. One could imagine rowing out to it in the moonlight, with a bottle of Moët and Ms Devlin.

'That's going to be a hell of a dam.'

'It's going to be the biggest dam in the county,' said King. 'But my engineers have to divert the stream to work on it. Run it through a temporary pipe, here.'

'Here' was on Butler's leased pasture. I turned back to the plot plan and traced the topo lines.

'You know you could simplify this by running the pipes here.' I pointed to a gully well on his own land.

'My engineers –'

'Anything else I should know?'

'No. That's pretty much my side of it. Why don't you go hear his?' He took my elbow in a friendly way and walked me back through the library. 'I don't know where the hell your coat is with the goddammed butler quitting.'

'I'll find a closet near the door.'

'Here. Here's something to amuse you.' He plucked a videotape from a shelf that contained a row of them and scribbled his signature on it. 'A&E just shot my biography. It's mostly kind. And fairly accurate.'

I didn't know what to say but thank him, so I did, and hunted up my winter jacket. I looked for Julia Devlin on the way to my car. But the Range Rover herd had migrated to the old house, where King Incorporated had set up offices.

I wondered if Mr Butler could make King so unhappy that he'd sell Fox Trot. The commission would beat amateur diplomacy hands down. Except he would blame me for failing to make peace and list with my competitors.

As I came down the driveway, emerging from Sherwood Forest and crossing the barraged meadow, I saw Mr Butler's rusty Ford pickup parked askew outside the gate. Nearby, Dennis Chevalley was pummelling a man whom Albert was holding in a firm grip.

I stepped on the gas and blew the horn. Mr Butler was a little long in the tooth to be scrapping with twenty-year-olds. But closer, I saw that it wasn't Mr Butler the Chevalleys were beating up. It was Dicky, prison-white, head shaved to a reddish stubble. He'd lost his jacket in the struggle and his bare arms were dark with tattoos.

In the time it took to stop the car and jump out yelling,

the situation changed radically. Dicky Butler flung his head up and back, butting Albert's chin. Albert staggered and lost his grip on Dicky's arms. Dicky buckled him over with an elbow in the gut and tore into Dennis like a stump grinder.

3

Dicky Butler was half a head shorter than the Chevalleys. But he was wide, and lightning-fast. For every punch Dennis threw, Dicky slammed two into his face. The bigger man planted his feet solidly when he swung. Dicky's feet moved like pistons – up-down-up-down – doubling the power of every punch and whisking his body out of range like quicksilver.

Albert roared to his feet and charged his back.

Dicky whirled to him, grinning, and decked him with a roundhouse right whose impact Albert increased by running into it. Before Albert hit the ground, Dicky whirled again and broke Dennis's nose with a crack I heard from twenty feet away.

The gate was closed. I found a man door in the ironwork.

Dicky pivoted towards me. Hot eyes gauged a new threat while tracking Dennis, who was coming at him spitting blood, and Albert writhing on the ground. Before I covered the distance, he sidestepped Dennis – rabbit-punched him off his feet as he lurched by – and kicked Albert in the groin.

'Get out of my way, Ben. Not your fight.'

'Can't. It's family.'

Dicky went up on his toes, again, leading with his left, dropping his right.

'Besides,' I said. 'You won.'

'I'm not done with 'em.'

'It's over.'

'Get out of my way.'

I circled out of earshot of the brothers, to avoid forcing

36

Dicky to defend his honour. 'I can take you, Dicky. You're tired.'

He measured me. He *was* tired. And no one floored two Chevalleys without sustaining damage. He was hunched over to the left where Dennis had landed body blows he'd feel for weeks. I was hoping his mind worked the way it used to. He wasn't afraid of me – he wasn't afraid of anyone – but he hated to lose.

I kept my hands down and my voice conversational. 'Congratulations on getting out. I was just heading up to see you.'

'Oh, yeah?'

'I got a bottle of dago red in the car.' He liked red wine a lot. It was ruining his face, the fair Irish skin veined like a much older man's.

'Oh yeah?' he said at last. I could see the heat fading in his eyes as they filled with the broader surroundings. They settled on my car, which was sitting inside King's gate, like a prisoner. 'Hey, you're still driving the Olds.'

'Pink keeps it going for me. Repairs don't cost much more than leasing a new BMW.'

Dicky's eyes flared towards movement. Dennis was trying to stand up. 'Stay there,' I told him. 'Catch your breath.' And to Dicky I said, 'Can I ride up with you?'

Dicky looked over the carnage as if he would miss it. Finally, as Dennis lay back, holding his face, he shrugged and headed for my car. 'I'll get the wine.'

He came back through the gate with the bottle tucked under his arm, and opened his fly.

Dennis said, 'What the hell's he doing?'

'Reminding you who won the fight.'

'He jumped us.'

'Yeah, I saw. Guy's got no morals.'

Dicky cleared his zipper and pissed on Henry King's wrought iron like a wolf marking territory.

'The son of a –'

I told my cousin to shut up.

Dicky Butler took aim at King's shiny black Chevy truck. Dennis tried to stand. I didn't let him.

Dicky marked the Chevy, zipped up and swaggered to his

37

own truck. Dennis tracked him, eyes burning. The broken nose made him sound whiny as a bitter old man.

'I'm going to get my gun and shoot 'im.'

'If you do you'll go to prison and make your Mom real unhappy. You up to driving?'

'Where?'

'Emergency room. Get your nose taped.'

'I gotta watch the gate.'

'Albert's waking up. He can watch the gate. Take my car. Don't worry, you can tell Mr King you tripped over a stump.'

I checked out Albert's eyes to make sure that they were focusing in unison. Then I climbed into Dicky's pickup. He popped the clutch, scattering mud on King's new four-by, and tore up the road.

'What was that all about?'

'Son of a bitchin' neighbour's bugging my old man.'

I'd have bought deeper into his filial concern if I didn't know the hoops he'd run his father through for the past twenty years.

'I went down to see him. Your cousins tried to stop me.'

'Just doing their job.'

'I fired 'em.'

Blood was trickling from his nose, so I reached out with a handkerchief. 'Here. You're bleeding.'

Dicky recoiled. 'Don't touch me!'

'Easy . . . Easy. You're bleeding. I'm just handing you a handkerchief. Here.' Again I extended my handkerchief. He took it gingerly, and pressed the linen to his nose. Only then did I realize he was wearing deerskin gloves and had been the whole time.

He drove fast, beating the old truck, whipping it through the switchbacks that worked their way up the mountain, skidding the rear end, spinning the tyres on the muddy surface of the frozen ground. A month of this treatment and his father would need a new one he couldn't afford.

'What's the neighbour doing to your father?'

'Trying to force him off our land. Bugging him with lawyers. Said if he didn't sell Pop would be living in a tent. Rich bastard.'

'What were you going to say to him?'

'I *am* going to say it to him: Leave my old man alone or I'll be down there kicking ass and taking names.'

'Dicky, you threaten a guy with his kind of money he'll have lawyers on you like paint. Before you know it you'll be right back inside.'

'Hey, I'm not on parole. I'm clear as you are. They can't touch me.'

'Dicky,' I said very firmly. 'I worked on Wall Street. I know these people. They buy what they want. *They can touch you.*'

'What do you care?'

'King asked me to talk to you and your dad. He doesn't want to keep fighting and I don't think you guys do either, do you?'

'Shit, man, I don't care. But Pop, he just wants to be left alone. Is that too damned much to ask? Man just wants to pay his taxes and be left alone.'

'Is he behind?'

'Behind what?'

'On his land taxes.'

'Ask him.'

Henry King would put the screws to him when he caught wind of that.

'It ain't fair,' Dicky went on. 'Ain't fair a guy reaches that age and gets pushed around. Especially a guy who served his country.'

Some of the most ardent patriots I'd known I'd met in prison. But I heard in Dicky's voice a strange and unexpected note of compassion.

'Pop suffered, Ben. What you and me been through's nothin' compared to the shit he saw in Vietnam. We can't begin to *know* what he went through. You know what I'm saying?'

'I know what you're saying. But I never heard you say it before.'

'Yeah, I never thought it before. Seeing a lot of things different now.'

I had a feeling he was going to tell me next he got religion. It happened. Lots of people inside found God.

'Ben, the shit I put that poor bastard through. And blaming him for my mother cutting out . . . Who the hell knows why she left.'

Now I wondered if the prison shrink had gotten hold of him. But it wasn't that either.

He said, 'I don't even know what happy women are thinking. Who knows what the sad ones want?'

My responses were down to near-silent grunts. Just enough to get him back to his father's land feud.

'I figure my mother was one of the sad ones, right?'

'Couldn't have been happy leaving a little kid.'

'You realize my father raised me all by himself?'

We emerged from the scraggly woods hugging the road. He stomped the brakes. The truck stopped on a little bump of a rise from which we could see the weather-beaten house and barns of the Butler farm. A rare flash of humour lit his face. ''Course Pop had some help from the state.'

'Dicky, you seem a little different.'

He turned off the engine. We sat quietly for awhile, gazing out at the grey monotones of a Connecticut farm in winter. If I ever wondered why farmers moved to town, graphic evidence lay before me. Mud everywhere. Cows bunched unhappily in bare pastures. Rickety buildings scattered like the crash site of a gigantic wooden airplane.

'I got the AIDS, Ben.'

'What?' He had spoken so softly I hoped I'd heard him wrong.

'I got the AIDS.'

'Oh, Jesus . . . I'm sorry. What do you mean? HIV-positive? Or . . .'

'Positive. Ready to roll.'

'Not full-blown?'

'Not yet.'

'Well, that's something. Any luck you got some time.'

'Get it tomorrow. Get it next year.'

'Next year they may get a cure. Already, they're slowing it down. Right?'

'Feel like I swallowed an alarm clock. Wait for that baby to wake me up . . . Wake up and die, 'sucker.'

I didn't ask how he'd got it. We both knew the opportunities inside. Or maybe he'd picked it up years ago between convictions. Either way, it was his business. But there was something that was my business. Mine and everyone else in town.

'You jumped when I reached with the handkerchief. You know it's transmitted by blood.'

'Yeah, I know.'

'You can't go around punching people, Dicky, it's like shooting them with a gun.'

He held up his gloved hands. 'I'm not a goddammed killer, Ben.'

'Yeah, what would have happened if you duked it out with me and I cut a knuckle on your tooth?' I shivered at the thought. 'Jesus Christ, Dicky. You scare the hell out of me.'

'Yeah, well no one's ever knocked out my teeth. I'm too fast. They taught me so good in Cheshire I could have fought pro.'

I looked at him. I was angry. And scared silly by the near miss of potentials and possibilities. 'Dicky, they taught you damned good footwork. And that's a nice fast left you got. Dennis Chevalley hadn't a clue. But you ever fight a real boxer you'll lose a tooth every time you throw a right.'

'Think so?'

'I *know* so. And you'll kill the poor bastard in the process. The gloves aren't enough. You're a weapon. You got to give up the fighting.'

'Hey, I didn't start it. I was just going to talk to that rich son of a bitch running the gears on Pop.'

'Treat fighting like it's booze and you're a drunk. Give it up.'

'Maybe I should get a girlfriend? Kill her instead?'

'You could do worse than a girl who's a friend. Just don't sleep with the poor woman.'

Dicky shrugged. 'I got used to not getting laid inside. Maybe I'll pretend I'm inside . . .' He grinned again, with little humour this time. 'Life's a bitch.'

I had to agree.

'And then I die.'

We stared out the windshield for a while and finally I asked, 'Have you told your dad?'

'Not yet.'

The cows started drifting towards the barn.

'Here he comes.'

Dicky opened the window, leaned into the cracked side-view mirror, and began wiping the blood off his face.

4

Mr Butler – I could never call him by his first name; even in my own maturity, less than twenty years his junior, he would always be Mr Butler – plodded out of the barn with a bale of hay on his shoulder. I couldn't see his face from where Dicky and I sat in the truck, but anyone in Newbury would have recognized him by his long hair swinging in the sun.

The cows closed in on him, their breath white in the cold air.

'Want to give him a hand?'

'Not in that mud.' Dicky held up one of his stitched cowboy boots by way of explanation.

A huge old yellow dog plodded at Mr Butler's heels – DaNang – the last of three golden retrievers named for places Mr Butler had been wounded in the war. 'How the hell old is DaNang?' I asked Dicky.

'Old.'

He finished wiping his face. 'Don't tell Pop what happened.'

'You got a knot on your head.'

He inspected it. Protruding from his bristly hair where he had butted Albert, it looked like a good start on a rhinoceros horn. 'Shit.'

'Tell him you banged it getting out of the truck.'

Dicky stuffed my bloody handkerchief in his pocket and started the engine. As he put it into gear he looked at me with an unspoken question.

I said, 'You can tell who you want. They won't hear it from me.'

'Appreciate it.'

'Do me a favour. Last thing you and your dad need is a war with Henry King. Will you let me see what I can work out?'

Dicky thought it over. 'Just don't bulldoze him, Ben. I won't let nobody do that.'

I promised I wouldn't, and we drove into the farmyard.

Mr Butler opened the hay bale with a wire cutter, scattered it with a few practised kicks as the cows closed in, and climbed through the fence. Dicky's clean-up job didn't fool him for a second. His face fell when he saw the knot.

I said, 'Hello, Mr Butler,' and extended my hand. 'I don't know if you remember me. I'm Ben Abbott.'

'I remember you. Heard you took over your dad's business.'

He took my hand in a work-callused palm and squeezed politely, his eyes drifting to Dicky. 'Whatcha looking at?' asked Dicky.

'What happened to your head?'

'Hit it on your truck.'

I could see he wanted to believe him. And he might have talked himself into it, if Dicky's nose hadn't chosen that moment to resume bleeding. 'You're home three hours and you're in a fight.'

'I was doing it for you.'

'For me? You want to do something for me, see if you can stay out of jail long enough to sue for that false arrest. You think getting locked up again'll help our case?'

Dicky said, 'Tell him, Ben.'

Ordinarily, I excuse myself from family arguments. Entering in is a wonderful way of making mortal enemies of an entire clan. But Henry King had wedged me right into the middle of this one. Still, if I was going to ignore my instincts, the least I could do was cover my back. So I said, 'Dicky, get lost. Let me talk to your dad.'

Dicky grabbed the bottle from the truck and stalked up to the house. His father looked mildly astonished that his son hadn't taken a poke at me for ordering him around.

'I'll explain,' I said.

He watched Dicky until the kitchen door slammed. Then he stared at me a long moment. 'Come on, let's get out of the wind,' he said, and led me into the barn. There was a torn and bent webbed folding chair set in the open wall that faced the corral where the cows were eating. He sat heavily in it and indicated a rusty tractor seat welded to an old milk can for me. I pulled it close and sat beside him where we could watch the animals or turn to face each other.

'What's up?' he said. He leaned over to pick at the hay stalks that had stuck to his muddy boots, and his long hair draped his face. We were looking west, into the sun. It made the grey look almost silver. But when he raised his head, the same light was cruel, exposing hard years. His moustache was grey. Deep lines scored the skin beside his hawk nose. His eyes were dull.

'What are you going to tell me Dicky can't tell me himself?'

'It's not about Dicky. At least not directly.'

'Who'd he fight?'

'Dennis and Albert Chevalley.'

'They're working for King.'

'He went to see King. They tried to stop him.'

'Sons of bitches.'

'They're a couple of dumb kids. They do what they're told.'

Mr Butler's shoulders sagged. 'Ben, I don't want no trouble with Chevalleys. I got my hands full with that 'sucker down the hill.'

'I guarantee you they won't tell a soul that one guy smaller than them kicked both their asses simultaneously.'

Mr Butler smiled. 'No, I guess they won't.'

'So that's not a problem,' I said. 'The problem is King.'

'What's it to you?'

'He asked me to intercede.'

'Intercede?'

'Make peace.'

'Why you?'

'Hell, I don't know, Mr Butler. I thought he wanted to talk real estate. Instead he got this idea in his head that I'm some kind of local fixer.'

Butler smiled again. 'Maybe he heard how you found poor old Uncle Pete.'

'He wasn't that lost.'

'Troopers couldn't find him.'

'I had more time on my hands.'

The Butler family – unduly impressed by my ONI service – had hired me to track down a forgetful elder who had disappeared. 'He had already been found,' I reminded Mr Butler, who was distantly related to Uncle Pete. A waitress from New Milford had found him.

'Heard they got engaged,' said Mr Butler.

'I wouldn't be surprised.'

'Shows there's hope for all of us.'

'Anyhow . . .'

'Anyhow, I don't see what business it is of yours.'

'Hey, I can only help if both sides want me to. I promised King I'd help. Are you interested? Or do you want to keep on fighting?'

'I'm not fighting. He's fighting. I was doing fine till the son of a bitch started throwing his weight around.'

'How do you mean?'

'I bet he told you he didn't understand the pasture lease – said he didn't realize how close it was to the house, because he was a city boy. Did he?'

'That's what he said.'

'Bullshit. He saw it. He just figured he'd plough me under with lawyers. Blow me off. Screw the dumb farmer.'

'Well, he knows now he was wrong about that. I think he feels like a damned fool. Won't be the first time a city guy got his wires crossed.'

'He looks at me and I see in his eyes if I disappeared from the face of the earth, he'd be a happy man. Well, I ain't disappearing. This is my home. Been home to my family since my grandfather bought it.'

Most of Newbury's Butlers had migrated up from Bridgeport after World War One.

'And when I die, it'll be Dicky's home – I know what you're thinking. You think when I die Dicky'll sell. Well, that's his business. When I'm dead and gone I won't give a

46

damn. But I'm not dying and I'm not going anywhere. I'm going to live my life here. And you can tell that son of a bitch down the hill I just passed my VA physical with flying colours. They told me I'll be farming at ninety.'

'Congratulations.'

'Damn straight – Christ, I'm twenty years younger than Uncle Pete. Maybe I'll meet a waitress, too ... Wouldn't mind having a woman around here, again. I been alone a long time ... You're not married, are you?'

'No.'

'Why not?'

'Seem to have a bad habit of falling in love with the wrong woman.'

'Tell me about it. Jeez, Dicky's mother was a looker ... You know, Ben. If that sorry son of a bitch had just come up here, man to man, and asked, neighbour to neighbour, could we work out something with that lease – hell, I wouldn't have spit in his face. But he sent goddammed yuppie lawyers. I set DaNang on 'em. Then he sends a pair of washed-up bureaucrats: Bert Wills from Middlebury? And some jerk spook drummed out of the CIA giving me a song and dance about the lease isn't good. Ira Roth wrote that lease. Goddammed Devil couldn't break it.'

Mr Butler liked Ira because back when he had hope that Dicky would straighten out, Ira had twice had charges thrown out of court.

'Wills and what's-his-name –?'

'Wiggens?'

'Yup, Wiggens. They treated me like garbage. What if I were the sorry 'sucker they thought I was? They'd have scared me into giving up what was mine.'

'How'd you happen to lease it? It's a funny-shaped little piece.'

'I didn't want the damned thing. Crazy old Zarega insisted.'

'Why?'

'Oh, I don't know. The bear died. He wanted cows around.'

'The bear died?'

'Of course he died. Must have been hitting forty. So I leased it, strung some fence, and I made sure to run a few head in. Old Man Zarega would shuffle out on his walker, lean on the fence, watch 'em for hours. He was a neat old guy. Sorry I didn't get to know him sooner. But I was pretty crazy the first ten years I was home. Lived like a goddammed hermit.'

'Tell me if I'm out of line. But it sounds like you wouldn't miss it if you leased it back to King.'

'You looking for a commission?'

'It's how I make my living, Mr Butler. You farm. I broker property.'

'I hope you're doing better than I am.'

'I've seen better years.'

'Thank God I got my disability. Only way a dairy farmer can make a living is get shot for his country. You know people pay more for Perrier water than a quart of milk?'

'I know that people send yuppie lawyers when they should have sent real-estate agents.'

'Bullshit. He should have come himself. But he's always been a guy to make other people do his dirty work —'

He cocked his ear, suddenly tense. A second later I heard it too, the heavy thudding of a helicopter. It got closer and louder until it shook the rafters, screamed over the tin roof, and thundered towards Fox Trot.

Mr Butler sat rigid, hands clasped in double fists, strings of muscle trembling in his neck. When the sound had died entirely, he spoke in a cold and bitter voice.

'They're using you, Ben. I thought you were better than this.'

The helicopter had derailed what had felt like an increasingly cordial conversation. DaNang raised his huge head and gazed at me inquiringly. I asked for both of us, 'How do you mean?'

'Didn't they teach you any history at Annapolis?'

'History? Some. Mostly naval.'

'Ben, I personally knew five guys who wouldn't be dead if that son of a bitch hadn't been grandstanding in Paris. There's *twenty thousand* of us would still be alive today.'

'You mean Vietnam?'

'Yes, I mean Vietnam, you goddammed draft dodger.'

Spit flew. He had screamed the accusation. The dog stood up, and positioned himself close to Mr Butler. Something unpleasant rumbled in his chest.

I shifted my feet to move quickly, and tried to keep it light. 'I was five years old, Mr Butler. I had a kindergarten deferment.'

He worried his moustache with his work-blunted fingers. Then he expelled a whoosh of breath that hung in the cold like a comics balloon. 'Oh, yeah. Yeah, musta been thinking of somebody else. You're Dicky's age, right?'

'Yes, Mr Butler.'

'Lotsa times I still think he's a kid. You guys aren't kids.'

'No, sir.'

'Time blows my mind. Sometimes I don't know what year it is.'

I said, 'My mother's father farmed over in Frenchtown. He used to say seasons count more than years.'

'You know anything about the war?'

'Not a lot.'

Mr Butler stared at his cows, who had demolished the hay. DaNang settled at his master's feet. When Mr Butler finally spoke, in his soft voice, he sounded normal again, almost professorial in his measured statement. 'King egged Nixon on. Who do you think dreamed up, "I'm not going to be the first American president to lose a war"? We'd already lost. Johnson knew it. Goddammed McNamara knew it. Us grunts knew it.

'I was a demo man. That's how I got my licence for blowin' ledge. Want to know what I was blowing up in Nam? Microwave relay towers. *Our* microwave relay towers. The Viet Cong took territory, they left the towers standing, figured they'd use 'em after they won.

'King and Kissinger made their careers at the Paris peace talks. Page-one news every day it dragged on. King encouraged Kissinger's fantasies: you know, their nineteenth-century tin-soldier politics. What did they call it? Had some fancy name for it. Real politics. Something like that. Jesus H. Christ, Ben, we're talking about eighteen-year-old flesh and blood. We weren't tin. Not us, not the poor gooks either.'

And just in case I didn't fully comprehend how the Vietnam War affected the lease, he added, 'So when Henry King sends lawyers, and flunkies, and real-estate agents creeping up my hill, he's just doing what he always did: treating ordinary people like tin soldiers. Tell him no, Ben. Tell him no, I won't lease it back. Tell him I won't sell an acre. Tell him he can't run pipes on my land. And tell Henry King he better stop bugging me or one of these days I'll bug him back.'

'How do you mean, "bugging" you?'

'He's got people spying on me.'

'Spying?'

'They're watching me. I'll be out in the field and get this feeling I used to in the war – when someone's lining a bead on you.'

'Watching you? What for?'

'Saw the sun glint on binoculars – or a sniper scope.'

'Who's watching you?'

'Could've been a sniper scope.'

'Mr Butler, if someone were aiming a sniper scope up here alone on the hill, you'd be dead, wouldn't you?'

'They ever find me with my head blown off, you'll remember I told you.'

'Have you actually seen people on your property?'

'They been tapping my phone. It's clicking.'

I said, 'SNET's lines are pretty old up the hill. I get clicks on Main Street. But these lines gotta be thirty years old. Mr Butler, I think there are two questions here. Who are "they" and why would "they" watch you and tap your phone?'

'Trying to scare me.'

'To make you sell the lease?'

'Tell Henry King the United States Army taught this tin soldier demolition. Tell him if he gives me any more trouble I'll blow his dam and make his fancy new lake look like a crater on the moon.'

As mildly and conciliatorily as I could, I said, 'Mr Butler, I'm not going to repeat that and I don't think you should, either. That's a pretty serious threat.'

'Get off my land.'

He stood up, balling his fists. DaNang lurched purposefully to his feet, menacing as a bitter old prizefighter sunk to dance-club bouncer for drinks and tips.

Finishing-school posture, bright eyes and thick, curly white hair made Great-aunt Connie Abbott look considerably younger than her many years. Days she felt well, it was hard to believe that on a school trip to the White House she had met President Woodrow Wilson. And had asked how he intended to keep his campaign promise to keep America out of the World War while American ships supplied the British, whose island happened to be surrounded by German submarines. (Eight months later she was a volunteer nurse in the trenches.)

I invited her over to watch Henry King's A&E biography, hoping for a historical perspective on how to handle him. It seemed a fairly tame puff piece, with little taste for exposing villainy. Actions that had propelled a significant portion of the population into the streets twenty-five years ago were labelled 'controversial'.

Five minutes into it, Connie was perched like a sparrow-hawk on the edge of her chair. And at the first shot of burning flags, she couldn't contain herself. 'How *dare* they impugn the patriotism of the protesters!'

King had spent his early career lurking. Still young in the Vietnam years, he was ever at the elbows of Kissinger, Haldeman, Erhlichman, Nixon, his bright face alert, body poised like a runner in the blocks. But after the war was over, he stood taller; and now the eager faces were behind him. Of course by then, Connie smiled, his former mentors were all in prison or disgrace.

As the Republicans shuffled off in leg irons, King had finessed himself into the Carter Administration, then bailed out by resigning publicly – 'Sanctimoniously,' Connie snapped – over the Iran hostage crises in time to join the Reagan mob. That's when he began to look like money. His suits became handmade; his transport, corporate jet.

Around that same time, his harsh Brooklyn voice evolved into the vaguely English tones Wall Street guys pick up when they parachute into the London office. He spoke more slowly, too. He was probably trying to concentrate on his new accent, but it made him sound very important, as if, Connie noted acidly, his elocution teacher had painted his larynx with *gravitas*.

By the time President Bush took away his White House pass, the transformation from scholarship student was complete. Henry King sounded as wise and sure as a Harvard professor who published regularly and was endowed with an immense family fortune and friends in the highest places.

Henry King Incorporated hit big and soon he enjoyed all the perks of a top CEO – private jets, personal helicopters, full floors of the best hotels – combined with all the courtesies due a visiting head of state – Third World military salutes, palace luncheons and presidential dinners.

'Have you noticed that young brunette?' asked Connie.

'Julia Devlin. I met her up there.'

'There's something odd about her.'

'There was something about her. I wouldn't call it odd.'

The pleasures of a world-class world-beater included servants, flocks of aides and luscious protégée/personal assistants. Since he had gone into business for himself, Julia Devlin travelled everywhere with him like the Emperor's concubine.

'What do you think?' I asked Connie when the tape ended.

'If a vulgar, self-serving, unprincipled betrayer of the public trust rates a reverent biography on television, then our country has gone to Hades in a handbasket,' she said, and went home without thanking me for the show.

Clues to handle him? Hard to tell. The latter part of the tape, which ballyhooed Henry King Incorporated's contribution to world trade and everlasting peace, showed a man surrounded by admirers who were convinced that if they could only be near him some of his immense power and wisdom might rub off.

People so attended lost their sense of humour. The only way to negotiate with them was to possess something they wanted very much and feared they couldn't steal. Mr Butler did not enjoy that position – a disadvantage of which he was ignorant. That put the local 'fixer' between a fast-moving rock and a grim and bitter hard place.

Henry King declared he was surprised to see me back so soon. I said No thank you to mulled cider, but he insisted. It was the King of Norway's recipe.

It was late afternoon the next day, with a cold night looming. His library was lit splendidly by dying daylight and a bright orange crackling fire of applewood. Josh Wiggens, the CIA man, had brought the cider, which he appeared to have been sampling since lunch, and seemed barely to notice when King dismissed him on the flimsy pretext that so-and-so in Washington was awaiting his call.

Julia Devlin stuck her head in the door. I smiled. She smiled back and said to King, 'Excuse me, shall I sit in with you?'

'I told you, no,' King snapped at her.

She held her face blank, as she closed the door.

Alone at last, cosied up on the chesterfield, he repeated, 'You have come back so soon.'

'It didn't go well.'

'Why not?'

I related my conversation with Mr Butler, minus references to Vietnam on the theory that King, too, might have a sore spot there, and if he didn't, then he wouldn't understand a word Butler had said.

Turned out he didn't understand a word I said either. Angered, he sent the Harvard professor on sabbatical, and I got a taste of what Julia had to work with.

'What the hell did you tell him?'

'I told him,' I repeated patiently, and more politely than his manner deserved, 'that you asked me to intercede to try to make peace between you.'

'What about the lease?' King shot back.

'As I told you a moment ago, the good news is, he doesn't really want the pasture. He only took it to please Mr Zarega.'

'What the hell did Zarega want with a dollar a year?'

'Mr Zarega wanted to look at cows.'

'Are you joking with me?'

53

'When Mr Zarega's bear died,' I explained, evenly, 'he wanted animals around. Mr Butler obliged by shooing some cows into that pasture.'

'I'm next door to a lunatic asylum.'

I smiled, hoping he had a sense of humour after all. But King did not smile back. Instead, he raked me with that laser gleam of intelligence. 'Something's missing, here. What did you leave out?'

'Vietnam. He's a vet. He blames you for the war.'

'He's not the only man who suffered in Vietnam.'

'He blames you for them, too.'

King sighed. 'I did not start the Vietnam War.'

He stood up and walked to a shelf and ran his hand along the books. 'But there are eighty volumes on this shelf that blame me for Vietnam. And my friends in publishing warn me that the revisionists have only begun to stir. Decisions I agonized over twenty-five years ago – and still torment me – have spawned a vigorous cottage industry. So tell me, Ben. If these professors and reporters and memoirists and historians refused to believe that when the United States bombed the North, the enemy came to the table – and when we stopped bombing, they left the table – then how can I convince the farmer next door that I did my best to stop the killing?'

'I can't answer that. All I know is he experienced it up close, and he's not ready for any revisionists.'

'Hundreds of thousands came home and resumed their normal lives. They don't look back. What's different about him?'

'He's not hundreds of thousands. He's just one guy.'

King returned to the couch and sat heavily. 'Is this my penance? I'm supposed to lay back and open my knees?'

'Laying back would be sufficient.'

'It's not fair,' he said. 'I served my country, too. I served it as I knew best.'

'Look, I was five years old. I can't judge either of you. All I know is you'll be neighbours a long time. Maybe, someday, you can agonize together over a drink.'

King did not look convinced. 'What's next?' he demanded. 'What's your next move?'

'I just told you. Sit tight. Let him cool down.'

'How the hell long is that going to take? I want my lake finished by summer. I want my guests here. Do something.'

I stood up to go. 'The sooner you stop pushing him, the sooner he might come around. My advice is leave him alone. No lawyers. No more offers. Just let it lay awhile . . . And you might tell your helicopter pilot to find another landing path. I thought we were getting someplace, until he buzzed the barn.'

'Am I supposed to pay you for this advice?'

'No charge. I didn't deliver.'

'That's for damned sure – I suppose you expect me to call you back when he's cooled down?'

'He set his dog on me, Mr King. I take that as a signal he doesn't want me back.'

'If that damned dog comes around here, I'll have it shot.'

I leaned close and made him look me in the eye. 'Don't shoot his dog or you'll answer to me.'

'To you?'

'And let me give you some more advice.'

'Keep it.'

'Mr Butler is your neighbour. He's not going away. And whatever you do, don't rile his son.'

'I've got people who can handle his son.'

'I wouldn't count on that.'

'I don't mean those bozo cousins of yours.'

So the camera on the gatehouse *had* recorded the fight. 'I still wouldn't count on that. The State of Connecticut has tried and failed for twenty years.'

King tried to have the last word. 'My people aren't bound by their rules.'

By his 'people', I supposed he meant that his retired spy could call up hitters on a per diem basis. Or maybe former national security advisers had Secret Service protection.

'Diplomacy by different means?'

'Every war has a winner, Mr Abbott.'

I went home wishing I'd done a better job.

5

The following Saturday I got a phone call from a frantic Mrs Henry King. I could barely hear her over the noise of a revving chainsaw.

'Mr Abbott – Ben – can you come up here? Henry's really upset. The farmer's sawing trees.'

I said, 'If you're outside on a cell phone, go inside and close the door.'

The racket ceased with a bang. 'Can you hear me, now?'

'Much better. Is he on his leased land?'

'Henry's going crazy. I'm afraid –'

'Where's Josh Wiggens?'

'He took the Chevalley boys shopping.'

'Shopping?'

'For spring work clothes.'

There was a picture: the patrician security man herding those two through the Danbury Fair Mall like bulls in search of china.

'How about Julia Devlin?'

'London.'

'Is Mr Butler's son with him?'

'I don't see him.'

Pray you don't, I thought.

'Please come. He's killing our beautiful trees.'

'Twenty minutes. Open the gate and –'

'Henry, don't,' she cried.

I ran for the car, and made Fox Trot in fifteen. The gate was open, the driveway spikes latent. The motor court and parking area were empty, the offices dark, the workmen off for the weekend.

I jumped out of the car and squished through the mud towards the whining, growling din of Mr Butler's chainsaw. It stopped abruptly. There was a sharp *crack* and, as I rounded the house, a triumphant, 'Timmmmberrrr!'

I saw a beautiful tulip tree, tall and straight as a square rigger's mast, quiver against the sky. It leaned, slowly at first. Then, gathering speed, it fell with a nearly silent rush of leafless limbs and hit the ground with a tremendous *whoommmp*.

King, decked out in a shooting jacket, came running to me. He was red with anger and indignation. 'Stop him!'

'I'll try.'

There was real anguish in his voice. 'We had four beautiful trees in the corner of the wall. You could step inside them. It was like a cathedral.'

I suspected that if DaNang weren't standing guard, he'd have climbed the deer fence and tried to stop Butler with his bare hands. But the big yellow dog *was* standing guard, hackles stiff, ears flat back. Mr Butler sat on the fallen tree and began nonchalantly sharpening his chain with a file.

'Turn off the fence,' I told King. He yelled at Mrs King, who ran up to the house and threw the switch. 'It's off.'

I climbed through the wire. DaNang eyed me. I said, 'Call him off, Mr Butler.'

Butler looked up from his sharpening. '*Stay!*'

DaNang sank reluctantly on his haunches, like a gigantic rat trap set to spring.

'What do you want, Ben?'

'Mrs King called me. They're really upset about the trees.'

'Not their trees.'

'I know that . . . What are you cutting 'em for?'

'Pawloski's paying eight cents a board foot.'

'Sixty bucks a tree?'

'For the poplar. More like a thousand for those oaks.'

'You're kidding.'

'Proper veneer wood in some of 'em.'

They looked more like ordinary piss oak to me. I said, 'Let me sell 'em to King.'

'What's he gonna do with 'em?'

'Pay you the money and leave them standing.'

'Naw, I'd rather sell 'em to Pawloski.'

'Come on, it'll save you snakin' 'em out of here.'

He thought about it awhile. Logging was back-breaking work and no fun at all with a light farm tractor. But if he asked Pawloski to send his dragger truck the price would drop even lower. And no Yankee worth his salt was going to turn his nose up at found money extorted from a city person.

'But King's got to pay me more.'

'Give me a minute, I'll see what I can do.'

I walked back to the fence, climbed through the strands, and spoke to King. The diplomat started trying to negotiate me downwards until I asked, sternly, 'Are you out of your mind?'

At last, I reported back to Mr Butler. 'He's getting his chequebook.'

King came marching stiffly down from the house, across his lawn and through the fence that separated his field from Butler's leased pasture. He shoved the cheque at Mr Butler, but when the farmer reached for it, King snapped it back. 'What guarantee do I have that you won't cut them down when I turn my back?'

Mr Butler regarded him for a long moment, while I tried to think of something to soften the insult. Before I could, he picked up his saw. 'Guarantee? You *would* have had my word, you son of a bitch.'

He reached for his ear protectors.

'Wait!' King yelled. 'What are you doing?'

'Cutting timber.'

'You're destroying beautiful trees.'

'You're lucky I'm not spraying Agent Orange.'

'What?'

'Or napalm.'

'Are you crazy?'

'Nope. My head's fine. Memory, too.' He covered his ears and yanked the starter cord.

'Listen to me. We had a deal.'

Butler crouched beside the thick trunk of another tulip

poplar. Of the original four in the corner clump, the three still standing were an awesome sight. He revved the saw and scored the bark to mark the wedge he would cut to direct where it dropped.

King ran after him and grabbed his shoulder. Butler turned – real anger in his face, and something more, something a little crazy. I moved towards them, thinking, Boy I don't want to get into this.

'Get away from him, Henry.'

I reached for Henry King and tried to pry him loose from Butler's shirt. There was a slurry underfoot of mud and sawdust from the first cut, and all three of us were slipping in it. Mr Butler whipped the saw around.

A chainsaw – for the uninitiated – consists of a motor-driver chain that spins around a flat metal bar. The chain is studded every inch and a half with sharp hooked teeth. You can get a nasty cut just brushing by it with the motor off. Running, it's a circle of moving razors. A plastic surgeon once told me that they 'didn't leave much to work with', and strongly recommended wearing a motorcycle helmet and face shield.

I yanked King out of the way. I didn't know if Butler had slipped or whether he had deliberately aimed for King's face. My problem was, having yanked King aside the saw was now wheeling at my face.

It wasn't the kind of thing you wanted to block with your hand. I tried to fall away from it.

Butler tried to arrest his swing.

But it was Henry King who saved me, inadvertently, or not, swinging his gloved hand between us. His cry mingled with his wife's scream.

He and I tumbled to the ground. Butler choked the motor, and the sudden silence was almost touchable.

King stared in disbelief at the shredded fingertips of his glove. Slowly, fearfully, he pulled it off his hand. 'Oh, God,' cried Mrs King, creeping closer. I braced for the blood. But the chain teeth had miraculously pulled the glove away from his fingers and only cut the leather. There was a single bright red drop on the tip of his index finger.

Mr Butler laughed. Veins were popping in his forehead. 'You're a lucky bastard.'

King's face was white as snow. 'You tried to cut my hand off.'

'You tried to grab a chainsaw,' Mr Butler retorted. 'Damned fool.'

'I'm going to sue you.'

'Get off my land.'

'It's *my* land.'

'Get. Off. My. Land.'

'You f –'

'DaNang!'

'We're outta here,' I said, throwing a firm arm around King and marching him towards the fence. Just as Josh Wiggens came running down the lawn and vaulted the fence with remarkable ease for a man his age. The automatic pistol in his hand didn't seem to unbalance him at all. 'Call off the dog,' he yelled at Butler, 'or I'll shoot him.'

Great. We'd just gone from chainsaws to guns.

I finished pushing King through the strands. 'You want to put that away before someone gets hurt?'

Wiggens wasted no words. Without warning, and without taking his eyes from the dog, he flicked the gun at my temple as if he were swatting a fly.

I was still wired from dodging the chainsaw and not in a charitable mood.

I caught his wrist behind the gun, separated him and it, and tossed him on his back. He bounced like he had landed on a trampoline and tossed *me* on my back. Which surprised me, but not enough to keep me from getting to the gun first. I snatched it off the grass and threw it as far as I could on to King's lawn.

Wiggens came at me, moving easily, all long arms and legs.

'This is getting silly,' I said. 'You've got grass stains on a perfectly good suit and I'm going to be sore for a week. It's clear we're both capable of hurting each other.'

That was for sure. The spook wasn't even breathing hard.

His eyes were cold. King shouted something. Wiggens hesitated, then made a noise that might have been a chuckle.

'Got any influence with the dog?'

'I'll deal with Butler. You deal with King.'

Then I went back to Butler. 'You OK?'

'Sure I'm OK.' The veins looked like snakes under his skin. I was afraid he would have a stroke.

'Where's Dicky?'

'Out with some tramp.'

'Can you get up to the house?'

'Sure.'

'You don't look too good.'

'I'm fine . . . Should have taken the goddammed money. Stupid.'

'I'll talk to him when he cools down.'

'No.'

'You need money.'

'Who don't?' He glared across at Henry King, who was glaring back, then doggedly picked up his saw again.

'Wait! You know your little upper woodlot near the top? Where it's real steep? Let me try and sell it.'

'I don't sell land.'

'It's steep as hell, there. You don't cut the wood and you don't farm it.'

'How much?'

'You could clear eighty thousand.'

'I don't know, Ben. You get city people and they start complaining about the fertilizer and tractor noise, and first I know I got Henry King problems on the both sides of me.'

'You're not farming near there. Except, what do you cut, hay twice a year?'

'Eighty thousand?'

'Clear. After commission.'

His mouth worked. He didn't like it. But it was a way out of a lot of problems for very little cost and less effort. He glared across the fence, again, where the Kings were trudging up the lawn towards the house. 'But swear you'll sell to good people. People'll leave a man alone.'

The couple I had in mind to buy Butler's acres were a pair of Price-Waterhouse lawyers living together in a midtown co-op they'd paid too much for. Which made them a little gun-shy about overextending themselves, again. But they really wanted to build a house in the country and when I walked them over the land the next weekend, they were suitably enchanted.

When I hadn't heard from them by Wednesday, I got nervous. I made a follow-up call. Turned out they'd been talking to one of our more larcenous builders who had quoted them a hundred and sixty bucks a square foot for quality construction, and they had begun to rethink in terms of two-week villa rentals in Tuscany.

'You'll never get rent back,' I said. 'Listen, I did a little research. Why not think of the house in two parts? One part is the necessary stuff – extra bedrooms, utility room, mudroom, offices, kitchen and garage. The other part is special: spectacular living room and drop dead fabulous master suite.'

'Which we can't afford to build.'

'You *build* in top quality the living room and master suite. You *attach* for the other rooms a log cabin or cedar post and beam kit. Thirty bucks a square foot for the kit – ninety turn-key – will buy you a handsome, solid wood house that opens into a living room of pure glass. And a marble bathroom,' I added hastily, because both had grown accustomed to five-star hotels on the client.

When I'm good, I'm good, and it worked. They were suddenly so happy that they were terrified someone else would buy the land out from under them before the weekend, and actually sped up from New York after work that night to give me a binder. I drove immediately up Morris Mountain, despite the late hour, to press the cheque personally into Butler's callused palm.

Dicky wasn't there. Mr Butler stood in the doorway, with the TV blaring behind him.

'Congratulations. I got a binder on that property we discussed.'

'Changed my mind. I'm not selling.'

'But you said you need money.'

'Let's see how we do with the false arrest suit.'

'But – '

'Warned you, Ben. I don't sell land.'

'Mr Butler, I gave my word to customers.'

'How do you know they aren't fronting for King?'

'I beg pardon.'

'Maybe King's paying them to steal my land.'

'In two-acre chunks?' I retorted angrily. 'At building-lot prices? It'll take him ten years and when he's done you'll be the richest man in Newbury.'

Mr Butler shot back a reminder that while maybe nuts, he wasn't stupid: 'At forty thousand an acre it would cost him less than five million bucks. He's got five million bucks, Ben. He'll just keep chopping away until I'm gone.'

'Mr Butler, I swear, these are ordinary people – a couple of lawyers who want to build a weekend house.'

'*Lawyers*? Lawyers working for Henry King.' He slammed the door in my face, and turned up the TV.

6

Spring came and lingered – warm and remarkably dry – a sensual spring that early on obliterated all memory of winter. It should have been a wonderful spring to fall in love, and had I had my wits about me I'd have abandoned the past to do so.

Summer got better, though not at first.

Despite our best efforts to warn the voters that Steve LaFrance stood for the supreme rights of the greedy, Vicky trailed in the first selectman primary. She had everything going for her, a solid record of hard work, rock-ribbed honesty and her cheery good looks. But Steve enjoyed the free backing of the radio and TV talkers who had learned that the appearance of a sense of humour could convince a worried electorate that cutting education, withholding food and shelter from helpless children and bulldozing environmental protections wasn't really short-sighted, mean-spirited and corrupt.

Then one day Vicky asked me to drive her to Hartford, the state capital, where she had lunch with a fellow of high estate in Connecticut's Department of Transportation. Lord knows exactly what transpired in Le Bistro: suffice it to say wine had flowed and she slept with her head on my lap all the way home.

Soon after, yellow machines repaved Main Street and the shoulders of Route 7 for miles in both directions with asphalt as smooth as a baby's bottom. Caravans of minivans set out for the Danbury Mall and within four days every man, woman and child in town owned Rollerblades.

Wrist sprains and road rash abounded, and old Doctor

Greenan was considering returning to Yale to brush up on fractures. But the voters were happy and Vicky, who conducted the rest of her campaign on tiny wheels, locked Steve LaFrance back in his Liquor Locker, where he could listen to talk-media to his heart's content. As Aunt Connie put it, 'Thank God for our school children, not to mention Victoria's ambition to get elected Governor of Connecticut.'

More good news was my commission for selling the Yankee Drover Inn. When school let out I could afford riding camp for little Alison. In my innocence, I even thought that I had defused the cat debate.

The couple of times I bumped into Dicky Butler, he was in town running errands for his father. He looked healthy: a ruddy tan suggested he was helping on the farm; only the deerskin gloves flapping from his pocket reminded me that he was marking time. He kept mostly to himself and didn't go looking for trouble. But trouble found him.

Some high-school dropouts jumped him in the only alley in town – a short-cut between the General Store and the Town Hall theatre parking lot – hoping to gain a name for themselves, losing teeth instead.

Trooper Moody bullied the victims into pressing charges. Tim Hall defended Dicky at a pre-trial hearing over in Plainfield, the county seat. Ollie had prepared his case diligently. Too diligently.

Tim, prepped by Ira Roth, asked Ollie to clarify the dates the incidents occurred. Then, professing astonishment that Dicky had assaulted all four men on the same day, he asked for the precise time of the incidents. The judge finished it for him, remarking acidly that a reasonable jury might conclude that the one man attacked by four had a right to defend himself. Then His Honor wondered aloud whether Dicky's false arrest suit against Trooper Moody might have influenced this investigation.

Fourth of July, a biker from Derby named J. J. Topkis sucker-punched Dicky in the White Birch Tavern. Wide Greg, proprietor, reported that Dicky was a real gentleman about it, paid cash for the window through which he threw the biker, who figured prominently in outstanding warrants and did not wait around to press charges. By the time Trooper Moody commenced his investigation, witnesses had called it an early night and Wide Greg was too busy sawing plywood to volunteer much information.

But Ollie went after Dicky anyway.

Late one night on the Morrisville Road I was driving home from dinner at the country house of Rita Long – a young widow who breezed in occasionally from New York or Hong Kong to thump my heartstrings like a heavy-metal bass player – when I saw Ollie's flashers strobing the night red and blue. I slowed down for a look. The cruiser's roof and search lights had pinned an elderly Ford pickup truck that looked like Dicky's father's.

Ollie levered his six foot five inches out of his cruiser, one hand near his gun, and in the other a long five-cell halogen Mag light that he had been known to confuse with a nightstick. Distracted by all his candlepower, or gripped by rage, he didn't notice my lights coming up behind him. In one swift fluid move he yanked open the pickup truck door, pulled Dicky out by the shirt, and threw him to the road. A wine bottle fell out after him and shattered on the pavement.

Dicky was drunk. Trooper Moody let him climb halfway to his knees before he kicked him. He lined up another kick. I blinked my high beams, about as stupid a move as interrupting a wolf in the middle of dinner.

Ollie motioned angrily to keep driving.

I stopped the car, turned on the dome light to signal I wasn't a threat, put both hands in plain sight on the steering wheel, and closed one eye before he could blind me with the Mag.

'Move it,' he shouted.

I turned off the ignition.

He strode nearer and recognized the Olds. 'Get the hell out of here, Ben.'

'The man's drunk. He can't defend himself.'

'Move it!'

'I'm a witness.'

'Say what?'

'You're beating up an unarmed citizen. I'm a witness.'

'I'm telling you once more, get the hell out of here.'
'Can't do that, Ollie.'

Handcuffed together in the back of Ollie's cruiser, charged with DWI (Dicky) and obstructing justice (me) we took the opportunity to review in low tones Dicky's father's problems with Henry King. Blizzards of paper had struck the Butler farm, courtesy of King, Inc.'s legal staff. For a while Ira Roth had shovelled him out, but now he was busy with a murder trial.

Worse than the paper blitz was King's helicopter.

'Son of bitch's buzzing the house,' said Dicky.

'You mean when he takes off?'

'He whips right over the house. You know what it sounds like to Pop? Sounds like he's back in Vietnam. Woke up last night screaming some door gunner's going to blow him away by mistake.'

'Does it happen often?'

'Too often. He's getting pissed,' said Dicky. 'He's got a slow fuse, but the helicopter's really bugging him.'

'Does he think they're still watching him?'

Dicky looked at me, his face just visible in the instrument glow from Ollie's dashboard. 'Nobody's watching him.'

'I wondered . . . What about the phone taps?'

'Maybe Pop's a little extra suspicious, if you know what I mean. Not his fault, the way that son of a bitch treats him.'

'Shut up back there,' growled Ollie.

'Fuck you,' said Dicky, which was even stupider than me interfering with a trooper on a dark road. Without even slowing the cruiser, Ollie whipped the Mag light around in a backhand sweep. It crunched into Dicky's head, scattering lens, batteries, halogen bulb and Dicky on to my lap. I felt for his pulse.

Ollie drove a couple of miles in silence. Finally he said, 'You jailbirds have gotten kind of quiet.'

'I think you killed him, Ollie.'

'Bullshit.'

But he stopped the car, turned the lights on and had a look. Dicky stirred. Ollie slapped his face. Dicky fended him off, groggily. A huge purple bruise was radiating from the point of his cheekbone.

'See that bruise, Ollie?'

'Looks like another assault charge for old Dicky.'

'I'll make you a one-time offer, Ollie. Take us back to our vehicles. Drop the charges. We won't file a complaint. But if you take us into Plainfield, you're looking at a year in court.'

Ollie had reptile eyes – dirty windows on a dull soul – but when warring with Newbury's resident state trooper, it paid to remember that reptiles have prospered long on the planet.

'You threatening me, Ben?'

'I'm threatening you with misery,' I said. 'You may beat it, but you're going to spend a lot of time in court.'

I could almost see him wince at the thought of all those days indoors. 'My sergeant'll back me all the way against a pair of jailbirds.'

'You watch this "jailbird" put on a suit and tie and smile at that jury . . . Besides, after a fight like that, will your sergeant back you next time? And let's not forget Dicky's false arrest suit.'

The reptile blinked.

Henry King got lucky too.

The dry spring made digging his lake a piece of cake. And then, in mid-July, just after they finished pouring the dam, Newbury got inundated with a week of rain that saved the farmers and filled King's twenty-acre hole in the ground to the brim. This called for a celebration: the first week in August, printed invitations summoned all who were anybody to a gala christening of 'Lake Vixen'.

I was surprised I got one. I must have been on the 'Newbury's First Families' list, because I sure hadn't made the distinguished service list – not after botching King's assignment to make peace with 'that crazy old farmer'. Surprised, but glad. I hadn't seen Julia Devlin since March and the one time I managed to dream up an excuse to drop by Fox Trot she and King had just lifted off in King's helicopter.

At our next Tuesday-afternoon tea I asked my Aunt

Connie if she would like to drive up to the party with me.

'I'm not going.'

We were ensconced – as we had been weekly since I was eight years old – in the alcove contained by the bay window of her dining room. A warm breeze tugged the sheer curtains and wafted perfume from her rose garden.

'You don't need an invite. Come as my guest.'

'"An invite"?' she echoed, a combative glint in her eyes.

Her eyes are clear as glass, and stony blue when she gets feisty, which is most of the time. 'I wonder,' she said, 'about a person who would kidnap a verb when there exists a perfectly serviceable noun. To encounter one in my own family comes as something of a shock.'

'Sounds to me like you're put out because you didn't get an invitation.'

Connie's manner, her bearing and her standards reflect the sort of breeding that lost currency when World War One turned the Republic into a superpower. In addition, she possesses an innate kindness – what she would call, in another person, Christian decency. But nothing obliges her to suffer fools gladly. Especially foolish nephews who forget that when men like Henry King court social acceptance in Connecticut, they had damned well better court Connie Abbott.

'Of course I received an invitation.'

'If you're worried about standing around in the sun, I'll run you home whenever you want. Though, from what I saw of the place, you can expect every comfort, including cool shade for the generationally-challenged.'

I looked for another thin smile. But she was through with word games, and suddenly deadly serious: 'I am not going to Henry King's party.'

'Why not? I saw people you know. Wills the younger asked for you, backhandedly.'

'That horse's behind.'

'So why aren't you going?'

'For the same reason that any decent American with a memory longer than two weeks would not go. Even that loathsome video couldn't conceal the fact that Henry King's prevarication, treachery and arrogance cost the lives of thousands of American soldiers and God alone knows how many Vietnamese.'

'You've been talking to Mr Butler.'

There are over a hundred Butlers in Newbury, but she loves the town the way a girl loves her dolls' house, and knew precisely which Butler I meant.

'Farmer Butler was wounded three times in Vietnam. Unless he suffered total brain damage – or is pathologically forgiving – I should imagine he'd like to punch his new neighbour in the nose.'

Should have talked to her before I went up there last March with my foot in my mouth.

'You know, King told me his feelings about the war and –'

Colour rose in Connie's cheeks. 'At best he was as out of touch with reality as the Soviets were in Afghanistan. At worst, he was motivated by a thirst for power.'

'Well, he admitted to doubts and –'

'He's a brilliant self-promoter, Benjamin. Don't be fooled. He saw years ahead of his competitors that the power that modern communications took away from the State Department would fall in the hands of an individual who spoke for the president. He was ready with a catcher's mitt.'

'I'm not saying I bought into everything he believes, and I don't know that much about the war, but I do think, relatively speaking –'

'I think it was Dr Johnson who said, "When a moral relativist comes to dinner, I count the spoons." '

I tried again the morning of the party. I found her reading the *Times* in her old-fashioned garden and I asked whether she had become a little more open-minded on the subject of Henry King.

'If I were that open-minded, my brain would fall out of my skull.'

'Let me ask you something. Would you prefer I didn't go?'

'I can't make that decision for you.'

'But what would you prefer?'

70

Connie thought about it. Finally, she said, 'Go. When children fight their elders' wars we get Bosnia.'

She did not go so far as to tell me to enjoy myself, though she did agree that King had lucked out with a perfectly beautiful day. A Canadian high-pressure system had slipped into the region under a crisp blue sky and the light was so pure that every painter in the state could dream of being Constable.

I banished the Olds to the barn and fired up the 1979 Fiat Spyder 2000 my mother had left when she moved back to her farm. The roadster, a rich Italian shade of British racing green, had been a love gift from my father. But Mom was too shy to drive something so 'flashy' around Newbury. So its body was in mint condition, the engine barely broken in. Top down, reflections of trees undulating darkly on its shapely hood, it conveyed me in splendour appropriate to a lake-christening at Fox Trot.

Julia Devlin was the first person I saw. She was guarding the gate with a guest list and party smile and made a vastly better first impression than the Chevalley boys.

She looked sleek in a sleeveless blouse. Her long arms rippled with a hint of muscle and her skin was tanned by the summer sun. A Liberty floral skirt fell straight to her sandals. The filmy cloth, slit to her knee, hinted at legs as sleek as her arms, and I found myself hoping it would be the sort of party where everyone threw off their clothes and jumped into the lake.

'I like your car,' she greeted me.

'Nice to see you again,' I greeted her.

She smiled welcomingly. 'And you are Mr . . . ?'

Oh, wonderful. 'Ben Abbott,' I helped her. 'Real estate. Last March?'

'Of course. Drive on up the drive. There's valet parking.'

'Are you stuck on gate duty all day?'

'I'm not stuck. I get to meet our guests while they're still sober.'

'How about I bring you a glass of champagne after everyone arrives?'

'Oh, that's nice. But I'm afraid they'll be dribbling in all afternoon. Have a nice time.' Her eye drifted to her clipboard. 'Mr Abbott.'

The phrase 'struck out' seemed inadequate.

Henry King's lake – first visible when the drive emerged from the gentrified woodlot – was big enough to be blue. It was a startling sight that tore the eye from the new house, taming that structure and somewhat reducing its enormousness. Yet another example of landscape designers pulling overblown architects' irons out of the fire.

A gigantic bright red hot-air balloon was soaring above the house, tethered to a windlass in the motor court. The high-school kids parking cars told me it was to show Mr King's guests Fox Trot's just-completed landscape design. A prancing fox adorned the bag.

'Ben!'

I looked up.

Newbury's first selectman leaned from the wicker passenger basket waving a champagne bottle, which, when our smiles met, she slipped between her lips. An on-again-off-again 'item', to use Henry King's word, Vicky and I were still off – thanks to transgressions on my part, and a new, less forgiving attitude on hers – and the tenderly ministered champagne bottle was a message: *suffer*.

'Let down your hair.'

Vicky had the hair for it, yards of beautiful Rapunzel tresses curled and heaped and framing her delicate features like a baroque picture frame carved of chestnut. But it was Tim Hall, my lawyer and Vicky's ever-hopeful beau, who instructed the balloon's operators. The winchman dragged the balloon out of the sky and I clambered into the basket. Tim looped a steadying arm around Vicky's waist. The burner roared and belched fire and we floated swiftly into the blue, whisking over the house's slate roof.

Fox Trot lay under us, the strict geometry of the house and gardens in orderly contrast to the sprawling farms and woods, and the whimsically natural shore of the lake. The field north of the lake had been planted in lawn, the lower ground to the south left wooded. The dam at the far end was still bright with raw concrete. Over the spillway bowed a bridge that looked like enterprising burglars had helicoptered it in from Central Park.

It was darned near perfect. The only flaw, if one could call it a flaw – and those who felt art must concede *something* to fate would regard it more benevolently than control freaks – was the long, narrow pasture that cut, to use King's word, into the manicured lawns like a knife. A rusty knife, as Mr Butler had been using it to dump old refrigerators and tractor tyres.

Seeking out my host and hostess, I bumped into friends from Newbury – Scooter and Eleanor MacKay, Ira Roth, Al and Babs Bell, and some of the country-club crowd, appropriately dazzled – and various megabucks New Yorkers, including a couple of wary erstwhile colleagues from the Street, who looked afraid I'd ask them for a job.

Bertram Wills, King's tame former Secretary of State, greeted me vaguely. He was hovering near Mrs King and looking grandly statesmanlike in a splendid linen suit. When Al Bell, whose namesake ancestor had married into social prominence after inventing the telephone, asked whether Henry King had negotiated the weather with the Pope, Wills gripped his side and chuckled, 'Very funny, Al. Very funny.'

King's retired CIA pet was there, too, muttering orders to the waiters from the side of his mouth. Sunlight wasn't kind to Josh Wiggens: Scotch was bloating his chiselled face. I gave him a nod and was not surprised when he snubbed me.

I *was* surprised, however, to see the handsome butler King had fired last March. 'Welcome back, Jenkins.'

I offered my hand. He returned his stiff bow. 'Thank you, sir, Mr Abbott.' With the caterers running things, he looked edgy as a general reliant on his predecessor's colonels.

'I'm a little surprised to see you here. That was a memorable exit.'

Jenkins gathered himself with brittle dignity. 'Madame insisted I return.' Tearing reverent eyes from 'Madame', who was flitting about prettily, he beckoned a waiter to refill my glass.

I climbed to the highest terrace, where Henry King was

surrounded by guests. He looked tired, pouchy under the eyes, and somewhat overdressed in a blue suit. He seemed nervous. His eyes were skipping everywhere, like an impresario counting the house. His champagne glass, filled with sparkling water, slipped from his hand. An agile waiter caught it and returned it gracefully, only to be chewed out for spilling a drop on the diplomat's sleeve.

King remembered me, if not fondly. His greeting, a pointed inquiry about Connie's health, made it clear that my invitation had come on my aunt's Blue Book coat-tails. But it was far too happy a day for my presence to blunt his pleasure. Everything he had ever worked for had come together in Lake Vixen. No expense had been spared to celebrate, no generosity overlooked.

Servants were legion, passing hors d'oeuvres in quantities to satisfy Catherine the Great and delicacy to delight Marie Antoinette. Had the July rains not filled his lake, it would have brimmed from spillage of champagne: magnums of Veuve Clicquot – no mere Moët at Fox Trot – poured liberally by staff wandering the terraces; more magnums stationed strategically about the walks in shaded ice buckets in the event a glass went suddenly dry while a guest was lost in a boxwood maze or deep in the sunken garden. But I do not suggest that my New England eye was offended by ostentation, for the choice of Veuve Clicquot, like the lovely food and the imaginative balloon ride, seemed determined by generosity more than display.

Mrs King proved to be generous, too, introducing me to her friends, including the wife of the British Ambassador, whom I had been coveting from a distance. Tall and slim, she had silver-grey hair and the level gaze of a woman who enjoyed what she wanted.

I think we surprised each other. We were both reading Trollope that summer – *The Way We Live Now* – I for the first time, Fiona for the third. She had children about to enter university, and when the subject of little Alison came up we discussed horses. Occasionally she checked that the Ambassador was happily occupied.

'Do you know the young woman talking to my husband?'

'Vicky McLachlan. Our first selectman. Would you like to meet her?'

'No. No. He looks content.'

Smitten was the more accurate word, but here I was smitten too, so who was I to talk?

Henry King bustled over repeatedly with guests in tow. He seemed miffed that I was monopolizing a star guest, and finally inquired, 'Has Mr Abbott sold you a house yet, Lady Fiona?' proudly stressing the very 'Lady' that she had invited me to abjure.

'Why ever would he?' she asked coolly.

'Didn't he tell you he's a real-estate agent?'

'Of course not.'

But King was persistent – and no slouch at the manners-as-power game – dragging personage after personage over to be introduced. The subtext, I began to scope out, involved British patents for a ceramic engine. The Japanese wanted to manufacture it. The British preferred to establish the factories in Britain, with Japanese money.

Aware that for the wife of the Ambassador this was a working party, I started to ease out of it, to make room for an Osaka industrialist accompanied by a New York publicist whose name had been synonymous with 1980s gluttony. Fiona laid her hand on my arm, and smiled a clear message that I was free to leave her if I cared to spend the rest of the afternoon with ordinary women.

The thump-clack of an old diesel Farm-all interrupted King's introduction of yet another industrialist. 'Oh look!' the publicity lady cried.

The bright red tractor came rolling down the long, narrow, sloping pasture that Mr Butler had leased from Mr Zarega. Mr Butler was driving, dressed in blue overalls and a dirty T-shirt, his long hair flying in the breeze. The flatbed trailer he was towing was piled high with green silage.

'Our local farmer,' Henry King explained in a hearty voice debunked by a tight smile. As Mr Butler drew near, preceded pungently by whiffs of exhaust, King walked towards the fence and waved, 'Hello, neighbour.'

Mr Butler never looked up. He stopped the machine,

tipped the trailer to dump the silage, blew three long, loud blasts on a horn, and thump-clattered back up the hill.

'Oh Henry,' the publicist gushed, 'it's so picturesque.'

Indeed it was. The tractor was red as kindergarten crayons, Mr Butler as long-haired as a nineteenth-century agrarian, his overalls as blue as the star field of the flag. The stink of diesel and silage weren't so picturesque but the breeze was dissipating it somewhat.

'I abhor flies,' muttered Fiona, 'and I rather doubt old Henry's thought to lay on insect repellent.' A country girl from Essex, the British Ambassador's wife saw what was coming long before King did.

'I've got a little in the car,' I said, 'Would you –'

'Quickly.'

We hurried around the house to the motor court and found my Mom's Fiat tucked among the Mercedes and Land Rovers, looking as bored as an Italian countess at a suburban country club. I got the minican of Deep Woods OFF! I keep in the glove compartment for swamp showings, and sprayed Fiona's arms and spritzed her fingertips so she could do her face. Then I sprayed my hands and did my face and rubbed a little in my hair.

Our eyes met. We were well protected now – excessively so for a minor fly invasion, a prejudiced observer like her husband might say – with one major exception that neither was inclined to ignore. I'd had just enough champagne to answer the dare in her gaze with, 'May I?'

'Please.' She lifted her skirt.

I knelt and sprayed. She eeked that it was cold, much to the amusement of the parking kids who seemed to think I was taking advantage of the situation. I asked her to turn around, then back again, and after awhile, she said, 'I think that's quite enough.'

I rose reluctantly and we walked back to the party, arriving on the terrace just as the woman who thought Farmer Butler picturesque cried, 'Oh look! Cows!'

Mr Butler was urging them through the gate at the top of the pasture. He needn't have bothered. Ordinarily they'd mosey in, slowly, while their leaders sampled the grass. But either the sniff or sight of the silage, or the chow-time signal of the horn, bore them down the long meadow like steeds of the Light Brigade.

Vicky drifted our way, eying the Ambassador's wife like a candidate for a flogging. I reached out quickly and whisked her cheek with my hand.

'What are you doing?'

'Fly,' I said, holding its body up for inspection. 'Here, put some OFF! on. And spray Tim, while you're at it. He's looking vulnerable.'

Vicky shook the can dubiously. 'I'm surprised there's any left. Her pantyhose are soaked.'

'Stockings.'

'What?'

'She's not wearing pantyhose.'

'You should not be allowed out with adults.'

'The British Ambassador seems to like you.'

'We were discussing the English roots of New England government.'

'*I* shouldn't be allowed out with adults? Benedict Arnold ran that line on Betsy Ross.'

Here and there around the terrace, conversation faltered and guests waved the air as a swarm sated on cow arrived to sample human. It was a minor annoyance, hardly noticed at first, even when a bare-shouldered lady ran indoors and others herded after her. But when the Osaka industrialist stalked towards the motor court, pressing an ice cube to a welt on his cheek, Henry King started yelling at the caterers.

I drained another glass of champagne and admired the cool waters of Lake Vixen. Fiona glided alongside, inquiring, 'Do you suppose that old farmer did that deliberately?'

'Very.'

'Poor Henry,' she said. 'Such a gift for antagonism. *What's that?*'

She had turned deathly pale. I had felt it too, an urgent thump up from the ground, like the shockwave of a distant explosion.

Fiona flung a frightened look at her husband, saw he was

all right, and recovered with a nervous laugh. 'I thought we were back in Beirut. Good Lord! Look!'

A cloud of spray was rising from the dam.

The concrete spillway gave a shiver as if it were made of Jello. Slowly, majestically, it slid into the waterfall. Angry white water tumbled after it, curling through the slot where it had disappeared – a fierce new waterfall unrestrained by concrete. It flowed hard and wide, tearing at the earthworks exposed by the vanished spillway, and roared dark brown into the valley below.

7

The explosion stampeded the cows back up the pasture and Henry King's guests on to the terrace where they stared in disbelief. In an amazingly short time, the water was gone. The gazebo towered on pilings like an oil rig, and Lake Vixen was an empty bowl of mud, seething here and there with puddles of stranded fish.

The scale of the transformation, the copious amounts of champagne already consumed, and an excellent desert-and-camel joke provoked laughter, which angry glances from Henry King stifled into hysterical snickers. All at once, everyone got the bright idea to go down for a closer look.

Bottles were snatched from serving maids, and forty or fifty of us trooped across a lawn blessedly free of the flies that the cows had taken with them. Somewhat looped on Veuve Clicquot, I found myself romping between earnest Tim Hall, murmuring, 'Poor Mr King,' and a seductively smashed Vicky McLachlan, who kept bumping into me with firm hips, soft breasts and giggled apologies.

I had a champagne epiphany: Vicky was my best friend in the world and I had really been stupid with her. As the insight further manifested as a deep ache in my groin, I began to pray that Tim would disappear in one of the many mudholes scattered about the lake bed.

Glancing back at the house, I saw Henry King shouting into a cell phone – calling the cops – while resisting the staffers who were urging him inside. Fiona and the Ambassador were disappearing in the direction of the cars, flanked by their uniformed chauffeur and a dangerous-looking young Brit with his hand in a shoulder bag.

Their SAS bodyguard, I realized, and felt a little silly for a moment, seeing the explosion through the eyes of people who had been targets in Beirut and Belfast.

When I looked again, Julia Devlin was at King's side, speaking urgently, guiding him indoors and ordering staff to secure Mrs King, who was wandering around the lawn in a daze. It never occurred to me there'd be more danger. I had assumed the instant I felt the impact under my feet that Mr Butler, fed up with lawyers and low-flying helicopters, had blown up King's dam exactly as he had threatened.

A terrorist attack was a sobering thought, and I felt my scalp tingling as we skirted the muddy banks, heading for the wrecked dam, which had blown into numerous large chucks of concrete tangled together with steel reinforcing bars. Then Vicky crashed softly into me again and I was back home in Newbury where feuds were comical by comparison.

'Mrs Ambassador ran away,' she whispered.

'So did Mr Ambassador.'

'Can you tell me what to do with Tim?'

'Beats me,' I said stupidly and regretted it a long time after. Vicky kicked off her shoes and stepped into the mud.

'What are you doing?' called Tim. 'You'll cut your feet.'

'I want to see. Who's coming with me?'

Up at the house, steel shutters were belatedly sliding over the windows, buttoning it up like a bunker. Over on the helipad, the Bell Ranger rotors began circling with a whine. While down the driveway roared the Ambassador's Daimler limousine, swaying through the turns the way cars do when they're weighted down with armour and bullet-proof glass.

I pulled off my shoes and socks and rolled up my trousers. Vicky passed me her bottle. 'Come on, Tim. Chicken.'

Tim warned we'd cut our feet.

'He's probably right,' I said.

'That's ridiculous. Before there was mud there was grass. There's nothing to cut our feet on.'

In fact, there *were* things sticking up out of the mud, including an oddly crooked thick root that reminded me of something. I started towards it for a closer look.

'*Ow!*'

I caught Vicky, saved her from falling flat in the mud. 'You OK?'

'No, it hurts.'

'Can you walk?'

'I can hop.'

'I'll carry you.'

Vicky was an armful in the best sense, and a very light armful at that. And an armful of intimate memories. I scooped her up easily and walked her back to Tim. Anyone with half a brain would have recognized lovers. But the vanished lake still had everyone's attention. I handed her up to him. Tim's a fair-size guy, but she looked heavy in his arms.

'Where you going?' they asked.

'Saw something. I'll be right back.'

The wind carried the approaching howl of Trooper Moody's siren. I forged back through the mud that had spilled from the lake, searching for the funny shape that had caught my eye just before Vicky cut her foot. I spotted it again, a muddy root or tree branch with a crook in it that made it look like a man's boot.

Closer, I saw why. It was a man's boot, a good-looking cowboy boot, the outlines of the tooling showing through a skim of mud. It was attached to a leg. I tugged. The leg came too easily. Then I saw a hand in a deerskin glove eight or ten feet away, and I realized this was going to be a lot worse than it looked.

8

I staggered back, frantic to look away. Green trees, blue heavens, puzzled friends lurching around the lawn. Anything that wasn't the horror scattered at my feet.

High on the horizon rose the rim of the Butler farm. Above it, silhouetted against the sharp sky, I saw Mr Butler standing on his Farm-all, watching. He was far away, but the sun shone brightly on the red tractor and the flicker of his wind-blown hair.

If I'd taken King's peacemaking assignment more seriously, if I'd gone back to Mr Butler one more time, could I have prevented this?

The state police siren got shrill.

I wished I knew a better candidate among the fifty or so people staring at the mud to tell the man that his son was dead. I forced another stomach-wrenching look. Enough details might keep him from coming down to see for himself.

The spillway had cracked like eggshells. Some of the pieces had burnt edges. I could guess the centre of the blast by the re-bars broken as if something very large had snapped the steel in its jaws. But all I could see of Dicky was that one booted leg and his gloved hand. God knew where the rest of him was – deep in mud, or sluiced downstream in the water path.

Far off I heard the exuberant horns of Newbury's fire trucks – young men and women exulting on powerful machines – and did not envy the volunteers their search.

Ollie arrived first. His big silver-grey Ford swung around the house, bounced down the lawn, headlights flashing, siren whooping drunks out of his way.

I slogged out of the mud, trying to step in the tracks I'd left coming in, sat on the grass beside a puddle, splashed the mud off my feet, and put on my shoes and socks. My hands were shaking and I felt sick.

Ollie came storming over just as I stood up.

'What were you doing in there?'

'Dicky Butler's dead.'

For a second the tension went out of the state trooper. His broad shoulders sagged and the anger that was the perpetual foundation for the structure of his face melted away, leaving it smooth and almost benign. Bye-bye false-arrest suit.

'You sure?'

'Blown apart.'

'You touch anything?'

'His boot.'

'Don't you know better than to keep your paws off a crime scene?'

I repeated the phrase that had provoked Ollie to hit Dicky with his Mag light and walked away. People had fallen silent, realizing something was terribly wrong. Vicky limped up to me. 'What happened?'

'Dicky Butler blew himself up.'

'Oh, my God.'

'I gotta tell Mr Butler.' I eyed the field and the woods beyond, scouting a route to the Butler farm, dreading arrival.

'Do you want me to come with you?'

She had not grown up in Newbury, and I asked, 'How well do you know him?'

'He came in to talk about his taxes.'

'Better not. I'll catch you later.'

I headed across the fields, and through the woods, up a steep incline, half hoping Mr Butler would have driven off before I got there. But no such luck. The Farm-all was right where I'd seen it. DaNang was stretched out in its shade. Mr Butler sat smiling like an old Indian watching settlers' waggons burn.

'What the hell happened?' he asked cheerfully.

I caught my breath. From Butler's field the devastation

83

looked spectacular, the lake bed raw brown, the land below it scoured by the escaping water.

'What happened?'

My courage fled. I looked past him, unable to speak the words that would change his life.

Behind this crest, which looked down on King's place, Butler's farm spread up a gentle rise. If on that mud-grey March day with Dicky I'd seen why farmers move to the city, this glorious August afternoon was the image of why they stayed.

Mr Butler's hayfields rippled orange-gold in the wind. The trees that traced centuries-old stone walls between the fields shimmered deep green. Maples in the distance puddled shade on the house. The house was far away, but it looked like they had painted it. And the main barn as well.

'You painted the barn?'

'Yeah, Dicky really got into it. Now he's doing the house.'

I hadn't expected this and it made it worse.

Mr Butler was watching me, mildly puzzled.

The next pasture over was dotted white. It looked like Scotland. 'I didn't know you raised sheep.'

'Yeah, we was supposed to sell the lambs, but I kept 'em. They eat that field down of bushes and weeds. And DaNang likes 'em, don't you, DaNang? Hey, you — sheep your buddies? . . . So what's happenin', Ben?'

'Looks like Dicky blew up King's dam.'

'Dicky? Dicky don't know shit about explosives.'

Based on the evidence, he certainly didn't.

'Mr Butler, I'm afraid –'

He looked at me sharply. 'Why you blamin' Dicky? He don't know dynamite. He don't know blasting caps. He don't know timers.'

'I'm sorry, Mr Butler. He blew himself up.'

'That's impossible.'

'It must have gone off early.'

'But I'm telling you, Dicky don't know to set a charge.'

I shut up. There was nothing else to say. Finally he said, 'You telling me you saw Dicky dead?'

'I'm sorry.'

'Oh, Christ.' He fumbled for the starter. The tractor clattered.

'Don't go down there, Mr Butler.'

'My boy –'

'You don't want to see it, sir. You really don't.'

He jerked his head sharply towards the sky. I thought I'd somehow convinced him not to go down. But then I heard what he had heard, a dull thud-thud. His eyes got wild. 'Jesus Christ, what's happening –'

His muscles bunched and he seemed about to dive under the tractor. 'Just a helicopter, Mr Butler. See?' I pointed out the dot coming from the north east.

He squinted, saw something about it that put him at ease, and sat back, rocking on the tractor seat, squeezing his arms around his body. His gaze returned to the mud where Dicky lay scattered. DaNang started whining. Mr Butler reached down to rough his ears.

The helicopter clattered on to the lawn beside the former lake. From where we watched we could see markings top and sides, big white letters, ATF. Alcohol, Tobacco and Fire-arms, the Federal bomb squad. Mr Butler cast dull eyes on the agents tumbling out in yellow windbreakers. He didn't seem to notice the second helicopter, marked FBI, which buzzed in swiftly from the west, spilling men and women who set up a perimeter and forced King's guests further from the explosion site than Ollie had. But when a third swooped in, an evil-looking, unmarked gunship, he muttered, 'CIA? Damned fools think it's terrorists.'

Glad to shift his thoughts from Dicky, I said, 'Yeah, well he was head of the Security Council.'

'Son of a bitch thinks he's such hot stuff only international terrorists can touch him.'

'Everybody's got a job, right? ATF for the explosives. FBI for an attack on the government. CIA for any possible espionage implications.'

Mr Butler looked at me like I was press secretary for President Nixon. Ultimately, of course, the bombing of King's dam would be a Connecticut State Police case. After a bundle of taxes was spent confirming that Dicky Butler was neither spy, assassin nor serial bomber.

'You sure it's Dicky?'

'Yes, sir. I'm sorry.'

He rubbed his battered hand over his face. 'Ben, leave me alone, OK?'

'Can I do anything for you?'

'Just split.'

'Maybe I'll drive up and see you tonight.'

'No.'

He started the tractor again and turned it around, DaNang scrambling from the wheels. 'Thanks for coming to tell me. You're a good kid, Ben.'

Head bowed, he drove off, the yellow dog trotting wearily after him. They skirted the hayfield and out through a cowbar opening in the stone wall – and disappeared in the direction of their house.

I stood alone awhile, watching the activity below. Fox Trot resembled a parking lot at a Public Safety convention. Four Newbury fire engines had responded. So had the volunteer ambulance. And a big square truck that belonged to the Frenchtown Rescue Unit. Pinkerton Chevalley showed up next in the Peterbilt wrecker, reasoning that by the end of day someone would need pulling out of the mud.

A fourth helicopter thudded to a landing beside King's bunkerized house. No markings. I decided to walk down to the dam for a closer look.

What I saw when I got there was that the senior agents of the various federal agencies that had descended from the sky had gathered up at Henry King's house. The second string, younger agents, hung at Ollie's crime-scene tape strung along at the edge of the dam site, noses to the window as it were. The ATF wore yellow, the FBI blue, the Secret Service jogging suits of many colours, and the CIA blue jeans and cowboy shirts.

Trooper Oliver Moody wore grey, and I must admit that for a sadistic, stupid local cop who ruled his turf by terror, Newbury's resident state trooper did the town proud. The Federal officers were all trying to order him around. But

Ollie had enjoyed a long career maintaining his independence from superior officers at the state police barracks, and his crisp 'Yes sirs!' resonated with hidden meaning.

Yes sir! to the ATF: nice work in Waco. Yes sir! to the FBI: is that short for Feeb? Yes sir! to the Secret Service: shame about the President straining his back crawling under White House windows. Yes sir! to the CIA: how are things in Guatemala?

He had help from old Dr Greenan, who shuffled around in rubber riding boots and a rumpled seersucker jacket that had seen many summers. Steve reminded the agents pestering him that as a Plainfield County assistant medical examiner he was in charge of a death scene until he ordered the body moved and it would move a lot quicker if they could kindly get out of his way. To an agent dumb enough to claim jurisdiction over the dam by right of national security, Dr Steve said, '"National security" lives up in that house. Down here's Connecticut. And it's going to stay Connecticut until we gather up the man who died here.'

I suddenly hungered for life and went looking for it in Vicky McLachlan. I had seen death, before. In prison. And once in the Service. But nothing like the scattering of Dicky's body. My family were all buried in the churchyard. I had grown vaguely in favour of cremation. Now I understood the mummy's hope of remaining intact.

I asked a pair of Frenchtown Rescue skin divers – the Meadows brothers, wet-suited, fin-footed, and be-tanked, with coils of orange safety line over their shoulders – if they'd seen Vicky and they told me that she was looking for me, too, and that I'd find her in the ambulance.

Ollie waylaid me halfway there and ordered me inside the perimeter he had taped. 'I want a statement, Ben. You the first to find the body?'

'I was first to find his leg.'

He wrote that down. 'How come you told me it was Dicky Butler?'

'I recognized his boot.'

'It's covered in mud.'

'I could still see the tooling. They were neat boots.' I didn't tell Ollie, but I remembered how Dicky wouldn't wear them in the mud.

'All you saw was his boot?'

'And his hand.'

'How'd you know it was his hand?'

'I recognized his glove. It was deerskin.'

'I didn't see any glove. You find a right or a left?'

I didn't want to think about it, but memory erupted. 'I found his right hand.'

'Yeah, well mine was a left and didn't have a glove.'

'His right hand had a glove. Jesus –' I'd been so thrown, I'd forgotten: 'You better warn Steve Greenan Dicky was HIV-positive.'

An emotion I had never seen before on Ollie's face – fear – flickered briefly. He was probably trying to remember if Dicky had bled last time he had hit him. 'Stay here!' He ran into the mud and spoke to Steve Greenan. Steve was way ahead of us. He waved thumbs up in surgical gloves.

When Ollie came back, I said, 'It *is* Dicky, isn't it?'

Ollie smiled. 'Yeah, it's him all right. Steve just found a tattoo.'

'Trooper Moody!' called an ATF agent.

'Yes, sir!'

'How much longer?'

'Soon as the assistant medical examiner says so. Sir!'

'We're going to lose the light.'

'Plainfield's sending lights. Sir!'

He turned back to me and, with a private sneer for the Feds, asked confidentially, one Connecticut Yankee to another, 'You knew the whacked-out bastard. Any idea why he'd blow Mr King's dam?'

'No, sir!'

As soon as Henry King reported the feud, many, many officers, including detectives from the state police major case squad, would be asking me that same question. I would answer, of course. But on general principles, and with no wish to advance his career, I was damned if I was going to rat Dicky out to Oliver Moody.

'Thought you two were buddies.'

'Jailbirds flock together?'

Ollie's jaw tightened like a cast-iron drain trap. Before he could threaten me, movement caught his eye and he turned angrily on a man in green who was ducking under the crime tape. 'Where the hell are you going?'

The man waved credentials. 'Department of Environmental Protection.'

'So?'

'We got a dam collapse, here, Trooper. Falls under DEP jurisdiction.'

Ollie jerked a thumb in the direction of the ATF, FBI, CIA and Secret Service agents glowering at him and each other. 'Get on line.'

'Trooper Moody!' called a clear, low melodious voice. Ollie spun smartly on his heel, saluting a handsome young woman with short dark hair and eyes as grey as Ollie's prowl car.

'Crime scene secured, Ma'am,' he said in his coldest, most correct, most dripping-with-contempt-for-female-superior-officers voice.

Major Case Squad Detective-Sergeant Marian Boyce raked me with a dubious eye. 'Then what's *he* doing inside the perimeter?'

'He found the body.'

'What body? I thought this was an explosives thing.'

'The jerk forgot to let go of them. Name's Dicky Butler. Just got out of Somers last March. Lived up the hill.'

Sergeant Marian turned to me. 'Friend of yours?'

'I knew him.'

'Figures. What were you doing here?'

'I was a guest at Mr King's party.'

'What were you doing down here in the mud?'

'Carrying the Newbury first selectman.'

Marian shot me a don't-screw-with-me look, and I added, 'She cut her foot. I was carrying her when I noticed Dicky's boot.'

Marian looked out at the mud, then down at her running shoes. Plain clothes, this Saturday afternoon, included pleasingly snug blue jeans and a soft polo shirt. She was carrying a baseball cap and I suspected the call had interrupted a day with her little boy.

'The mud's not deep,' I said. 'Except right below the dam.'

'Trooper, have you concluded your interview with Mr Abbott?'

'Yes, Ma'am.'

'Is that Dr Greenan down there?'

'Yes, Ma'am.'

'Would you please tell Dr Greenan I'd like a word with him when it's convenient.'

Ollie saluted and hurried down there. Marian said to me, 'What's this about?'

'Neighbour feud. King and Dicky's father were going at it.'

'About what?'

'Ostensibly a land thing. A lease dispute. But I think it was really about Vietnam.'

'Vietnam?'

'King helped run the war. Mr Butler got shot in the war. Three times. Also, it was a money thing – rich guy versus farmer. And a country–city thing – rich *city* guy versus farmer.'

'I assume we're talking about *the* Dicky Butler.'

'The farmer's son. Though, he was calming down a little.'

'Oh that's quite obvious,' said Marian, with a nod at the devastation. 'How do you happen to know all this?'

'King asked me to mediate.'

'Hope you got your fee up front.' She slipped on her baseball cap and said, 'Thanks for the help. Stay available please, and out of the way.'

She walked me to the tape and lifted it so I could step under. We had a lot of history, much of it pleasant. Right now I wanted to cling to something pleasant.

'Detective-Sergeant Boyce, may I ask you something?'

'What?'

'Did you like the flowers?'

'What flowers?'

'The roses? From my garden. Flowers I left with my note.'

'The note breaking our date.'

'Apologizing . . . I hope you liked them.'

Marian's eyes roamed the bomb site as she answered me. 'I figured the flowers were from a guy I'd been out with. That's how I usually get flowers. From guys who keep a date. They send them after the date. I guess it's their way of saying they had a good time. I mean, I wouldn't know, I'm not a guy, but do you think maybe that's why they send me flowers, because they kept a date with me and had a good time and maybe they're hoping we'll get it on again?'

'I had to go to New York.'

'Almost didn't make it.'

'What do you mean?'

'The road cop who wrote the ticket on 84 thought you were drunk, weaving like that.'

There were only about a thousand troopers and detectives on the entire state police force. Marian, in the vanguard of women officers, had made her share of enemies, but as her star had risen on merit she'd slowly become accepted as one of the boys. So dating her was like dating a woman with a lot of big brothers.

She gave me a moment to wonder what else the road cop had told her. Then, 'Did your passenger find that contact lens she dropped in your lap?'

'My passenger was my old friend Rita Long, unexpectedly and very briefly in town. In fact, I was driving her to the airport. She was flying back to Hong Kong.'

'I'll bet the pilots couldn't wait.'

Marian went to work down at the dam and I walked over to the Newbury ambulance where Vicky was sitting on the tailgate dangling a bandaged foot and surrounded by Federal agents going out of their way to co-operate with local government. She regarded me coolly. 'Are the state police grateful for your input?'

'How's your foot?'

'I need stitches.'

'Steve's tied up. I'll drive you to the hospital.'

'No way. These guys are giving me a ride in a helicopter.'

The various 'guys' showed their teeth. I left before they got into a gun fight over whose helicopter would perform the rescue mission, and wandered in a daze, up towards the house.

'Real-life' games with Marian hadn't helped at all. If anything, I felt worse, which surprised me. I had no claim to major grief for Dicky. We hardly knew each other. Maybe we had been drawn unexpectedly close, having reconnected at a turning point in his life. Maybe it was that we were mutual outsiders in our town – the 'jailbirds' who flocked together in minds like Trooper Moody's. Bad apples. Trouble.

'Halt!'

My way was blocked by a humourless Secret Service agent with a plastic earpiece in his ear and a hand on a bulge in his windbreaker. Suddenly, all I wanted to do was go home. I told him that, explained my car was around the front of the house in the motor court, explained that I was the local real-estate agent and a guest at the party and gave him my card and guaranteed that if anyone wanted to talk to me they could find me in the white Georgian on Main Street a couple of doors up from the flagpole.

He repeated all this into his lapel mike. I noticed a full magnum of Veuve Clicquot going to waste in an ice bucket, took a very deep slug, and slipped the still-bubbly bottle under my arm.

The guy gave me a look. I ignored him. I don't generally loot parties, but the bottle was open, and I knew damned well I'd need help sleeping tonight.

Josh Wiggens, grim-faced and stone-cold sober, came to escort me to the motor court. He didn't bother to hide the gun in his waistband.

'Do you know this man, sir?' the Secret Service guy asked.

'He's harmless.' The former CIA officer had the guest list on a clipboard. 'What kind of car, Mr Abbott?'

''85 Olds. Light green.'

'Mr Abbott, there is no '85 light green Olds parked in the parking lot.'

'Dark green Fiat, sorry.'

They looked at me like a Nazi spy claiming Babe Ruth played for the Dodgers.

'It's my Mom's car. I forgot, I borrowed my Mom's car.'

Wiggens walked me to the Fiat, checked the registration, and radioed the gate to let me out. The bottle I propped in my lap drew a glance of patrician contempt. I gave him one back. If, as I suspected, his permanent house-guest rent included responsibility for Fox Trot security, Josh Wiggens had screwed up big time and we both knew it.

The Secret Service had taken over the gatehouse. The Chevalley boys were nowhere in sight. Nor was Julia Devlin.

I drove slowly down the mountain, wondering if I should call on Mr Butler – grateful for his request not to – and marvelling at how capricious was an explosion that blew one glove off a man's hand and left the other.

9

Round numbers: ten billion pounds of explosives are detonated every year, ninety per cent in mining, leaving a hearty
billion for construction use. ANFOs – ammonium nitrate and
fuel oil mixes of Oklahoma City notoriety – are by far the
most common, being inexpensive and safe. But they don't
do well in damp. So at Fox Trot the honour had likely gone
to a water gel – ammonium nitrate mixed with aluminium
or TNT – or sticks of good old-fashioned dynamite.

Alcohol, Tobacco and Firearms chemists were determining
which. If it was a 'sold product', then traces of the explosive
might reveal 'flags' – molecular bits added at the factory to
track where the batch was sold and who bought it. That
person could expect bad-tempered visitors in flak vests.

I learned all this shortly after I woke up Sunday morning
to a ferocious champagne headache, the phone ringing and
the doorbell chiming. The phone was closer. I located my
watch before I picked it up. Business hours.

'Benjamin Abbott Realty.'

'Mr Abbott.'

'Speaking.'

'Special Agent Cirillo, Federal Bureau of Investigation.'

'Hold on, please. There's someone at the door.'

I climbed into jeans and slipped on a shirt and padded
barefoot downstairs buttoning it, to the front door where
two cop-looking guys announced they were from the Bureau
of Alcohol, Tobacco and Firearms and wanted a word with
me.

I invited them in, told them I was making coffee before
anyone got a word from me, led them into the kitchen,

started a pot and picked up the extension and told the FBI the ATF had arrived first; as I couldn't let them roam the house unattended, I would talk to them first and call him back. Special Agent Cirillo said he would come by personally within the hour. And that pretty much set the pattern for the rest of Sunday.

Henry King had fingered me as the failed local peacemaker. So when the Feds got done at Fox Trot, they sent physical evidence to their bomb labs, ordered their first-string agents back to Washington and dispatched the junior agents down the mountain for confirmation of the feud and any additional light Benjamin Abbott III could throw on the subject of Dicky Butler.

Concerning the land feud, I told them what I had told Sergeant Marian, minus my speculations on the Vietnam source of anger. About Dicky Butler I had less to contribute. It didn't matter. The life Dicky had wasted was very much part of the public record. Besides, all they really wanted was proof that the attack was personal, not political, so they could report back to Washington that the former head of the National Security Council had not been attacked by right-wing militia, left-wing radicals, or foreign religious fanatics. Who could blame them?

The Secret Service popped in as the FBI was leaving, a couple of little guys as trim and hyperactive as Jack Russell terriers. We went over the same ground.

Then the Connecticut State Police arrived in the persons of Sergeant Marian and her partner Arnie Bender, a short, tough city-bred detective. He and I had clashed on occasion, as I had with Marian, but without the boy-girl interest to ease our grievances. Arnie looked like he wanted to toss the house on general principles.

Marian demanded to know why I hadn't stuck around Fox Trot yesterday as instructed. I apologized, while reminding her that I had been extremely upset at the sight of Dicky Butler blown to smithereens. I got no sympathy. What could I add to what I had told her yesterday about the feud between diplomat King and farmer Butler?

I could honestly think of nothing.

'Tell you why I ask,' said Marian. 'Arnie and I were looking over Dicky's record. We didn't find anything about him being a loving son. You know, Ben? This kid was trouble. From day one in the incubator.'

'So how come?' Arnie asked, 'how come he's suddenly blowing up dams to please his father?'

'I can only guess,' I answered, belatedly alert to an unpleasant shift in the wind.

'Guess,' said Marian.

'As I informed Trooper Moody yesterday, Dicky was HIV-positive. He was scared of AIDS, scared of dying. Probably scared for the first time in his life. Plus, he was getting a little older, mid-thirties. And also, and I think this is important, for the first time in years he was out of prison and with no sentence hanging over his head. No parole. Free to take stock.'

'What are you talking about?' said Bender.

'Ben is suggesting that Dicky was becoming contemplative,' said Marian. 'Right, Ben?'

'Right. I think he was trying to patch things up with his dad. And from the way he talked to me, he was rethinking their entire relationship. He painted the barn. Was painting the house. I don't know, it's just possible he was finally going to straighten out.'

'Think the old man put him up to it?'

So that's where they were going.

While the Feds were clearing the national-security air, our local peace officers were looking to hang charges on poor Mr Butler. Conspiracy, if 'the old man put him up to it.' Accessory, if he helped. And, since Dicky was killed in the explosion, accessory meant accessory to murder.

I hoped that Marian and Arnie were only fishing, and weren't seriously bent on turning a stupid tragedy into a murder case. It wouldn't be easy to nail Mr Butler on accessory to murder. They would have to prove that he had participated – either by walking Dicky through the process, purchasing the explosives, or showing him where to detonate them.

But I'd have felt a lot better for Mr Butler if they weren't two of the brightest detectives in the state police with a conviction rate that would have impressed Spanish Inquisitors.

'Do you think that Dicky's father put him up to it?' she asked again.

I operate by two rules. I never lie. And I never rat. Gets confusing, on occasion, and this was one of those occasions. 'How the hell would I know?'

'You might have overheard a threat.'

While neither a licensed detective, nor a lawyer, I felt obliged to extend client–attorney–detective privacy to Mr Butler, who had trusted me to listen to his problems. Before he set his dog on me. 'What kind of threat?'

Bender looked at Marian. 'He's lying.'

'He hasn't said anything yet.'

'He's getting ready to lie.'

Marian sounded weary. 'Yeah, you're right.'

I said, 'The front door is this way. Let me show you out.'

Bender said to Marian, 'I think he'd rather talk to us at the Plainfield Barracks.'

Marian said, 'Why would he go to such trouble when he could just talk to us here in the comfort of his own home?'

I said, 'You guys are missing the point of good cop, bad cop. One of you has to be the good cop.'

'You'll want an overnight bag, Ben,' said Bender.

'Toothbrush, razor, clean towel,' said Marian.

'Telephone number of my lawyer.'

'The threat you might have overheard, you might have overheard while attempting to mediate between Henry King and Butler, Senior. Butler, Senior might have said something like, "If that son of a bitch doesn't stop bugging me I'll blow up his dam."'

'Mr Butler didn't blow up the dam.'

'Did Dicky do it for him? is what we're asking you.'

'Your guess is as good as mine.'

'Did his dad help him? is the other thing we're asking you.'

'Every Federal investigator I talked to – and it feels like I talked to them all – sounded convinced that Dicky did it all on his own.'

'That's their problem,' said Arnie. 'Your problem is, if Mr Butler turns around and confesses that you heard him threaten to blow up Mr King's dam, you're going to look pretty foolish. And a lot worse when we hang a conspiracy charge on him. We might find room in it for someone else he shared his plans with . . . You're familiar with misprision of felony?'

'Refresh me.'

'It's when you fail to report a serious crime you know is going down.'

'Oh come on, Arnie.'

'Goes back to old English law,' said Marian. 'They used to draw and quarter you. We'll just put you back in the slammer.'

'And maybe not just any slammer,' said Arnie, 'because if the explosives make Federal charges, we could ask our pals in the Feds to send you back to Leavenworth.'

Marian said, 'But you got worse problems than misprision, Ben. A man was killed while participating in the conspiracy. If Butler talked his plans over with you, you too could be looking at accessory to murder. Unless you help us wrap this thing up right now.'

'I've got work to do. I might even get a customer if you'll move your car from in front of my house. Anybody sees that unmarked cruiser they'll make the mistaken assumption that the police had good reason to be here.'

Marian's big hands strayed towards the pocket where she kept her handcuffs. 'Arnie,' she said after an ominous pause, 'I'll meet you in the car.'

Bender left without a word.

I said, 'There goes the good cop.'

'Listen, you. Answer me one question. Am I way off base thinking the father was mixed up in this? Honestly, Ben. I got a gut feeling. Am I crazy?'

She was very serious. What we occasionally enjoyed about each other rarely spilled over into the professional side of her life, and I knew it galled her to ask. I also knew that when she said, 'Honestly, Ben,' I had better proceed very carefully.

'Marian, you got a great gut. *My* gut tells me Dicky did it alone.'

'Based on what?'

'Based on two things: Dicky's rep for destruction; and Mr Butler's genuine shock when I told him Dicky was dead.'

'That's it?'

'It's enough for me. The man was stunned.'

'Grief or surprise?'

'Both. The man just lost his son. His only child.'

'How about fear?'

'Fear of what?'

'Prison, for killing his son.'

The doorbell interrupted whatever she intended to ask next. I stood up to answer it, saying, 'I'll tell you one thing Mr Butler told me.'

'What's that?'

'Dicky didn't know the first thing about explosives.'

'So?'

'It's one thing to shove a stick of dynamite under a stump and light the fuse. It's another to blow a dam. The ATF guy told me it was a real professional job.'

'Making a heck of a case against Butler,' Marian fired back. 'Young Dicky had professional help from his old man – a professional. Special Forces demolition, for God's sake. *And* a state-licensed pyrotechnician.'

'I'm aware of that implication. The reason I mention it is the ATF wonders who *else* might have helped him?'

'Yeah, right, we're combing Newbury for Arabs.'

'How about right-wing militia?' I asked, hoping she'd spill a little, and she did, shaking her head so that her short brown hair whisked her cheeks. 'Our intelligence says no way.'

'No one drilling in the woods?'

'In Newbury's woods? You got Jervises too busy stealing everything not nailed down. And your Chevalley cousins conspiring to wipe out the beer and deer supply. No, Connecticut's organized crazies are street and prison gangs and mafia, none of which would get caught dead in the woods. Give me a break, Ben. This is local and you know it.'

'Local, yes. Father, no.' The doorbell chimed again. 'Hold on, that might actually be business.'

It was a guy in blue denim and a cowboy hat. He was real friendly and gave me his card. An insurance investigator with World Wide Insurance. I invited him into the office. He leered appreciatively at Marian. Marian returned a look that could have fossilized a beetle.

'Detective-Sergeant Boyce, may I present Bud Smyth – that's Smyth with a "y" from the Central Intelligence Agency.'

Smyth looked embarrassed. As well he should have.

Marian ignored his hand. 'Call me if you think of anything else, Ben.'

I walked her to the door. On the front step I asked, quietly, 'Do you really want to badger that poor old guy with a conspiracy charge?'

'Not if I can nail him for murder.'

Bud Smyth was lurking near my desk, reading my mail.

'So how you doing, Ben?'

'Mr Smyth, until we have a proper introduction or become friends, consider me "Mr Abbott".'

'So how you doing, Mr Abbott?'

'I've had about one too many conversations on the same subject today. And how are you doing, Mr Smyth?'

'I was wondering what you could tell me about your Mr Butler.'

'Junior or Senior?'

'The deceased.'

'Dicky Butler was a talented brawler. He had a fast left jab most of us would be proud to call our best punch. He had great footwork. And a lazy right – his worst flaw.'

'Weapons?'

'Not his style – I suppose he learned a shank in prison, but he was primarily a fist fighter.'

'Did *you* learn a shank in prison, Mr Abbott?'

'Big difference between Dicky and me was I don't have a

lazy right. Which I will demonstrate, outside, if you don't watch your mouth.'

'Is that a threat?'

'Yes.'

He said, 'I should warn you I boxed in the Olympics.'

'You want to borrow gloves?'

Smyth looked like he wanted to change the subject. The telephone did it for him.

'Benjamin Abbott Realty.'

A soft and silky male voice I hadn't heard since I had served in the Office of Naval Intelligence said, without introduction, 'There is a very annoying fellow in your house.'

I felt my shoulders stiffen. At ONI, he had been one of those bosses that try to teach you how to maintain overview and tight focus simultaneously; the ball-busting kind that about five years later you begin to realize how lucky you were to work for him. Today, more than ten years later, if he announced an assault on Hell I'd probably suit up in asbestos and ask questions later.

'He is pissing you off.'

'Yes, sir.'

'You've probably threatened to take him outside.'

'It's heading that way, sir. Yes.'

'I asked him to have a word with you.'

I was surprised. It put Bud Smyth in a much better light than I'd seen him so far.

'This thing is local, sir.'

'I'm glad to hear it. Explain the details to the fellow who's annoying you and send him back.'

'Yes, sir.'

The phone died in my hand. I hung it up, contemplating that someone very, very highly placed was worried about Henry King.

'The Captain has vouched for you,' I said to Smyth.

'Admiral. He's been promoted. Tell me about Butler, Senior.'

'I met Mr Butler a couple of times when I was a kid. We had our longest conversation last March when Mr King asked

101

me to speak to him on his behalf, which I assume you already know.'

'Go on.'

'We had another conversation half an hour after the dam blew. I told him Dicky was dead.'

'Do you think he put Dicky up to it?'

'In my opinion, if Mr Butler wanted that dam blown he'd have blown it himself. He was Special Forces in Vietnam.'

Smyth nodded impatiently. He knew that, of course.

'And he's a licensed pyrotechnician. He could have done it on his own, if he wanted to.'

'Therefore?'

'Therefore he didn't put Dicky up to it. Conversely, if Dicky wanted to blow the dam, he would have done it without any encouragement from his dad.'

'So you think Dicky did it.'

I started to agree that it certainly looked that way. But I wanted to learn something, so I said, instead, 'I was talking to an ATF agent earlier.'

Smyth made a face.

'He said that the explosion looked like a really professional job.'

'I was talking to one who said it was a simple fuse a farmer could have lit.'

'The agent I talked to said it's more than how you light it, it's where you put it. Apparently it was well placed. So if it wasn't simple, where the hell did Dicky Butler learn that?'

'That's what I'm wondering.'

'What's your guess?'

'I'm not paid to guess, Mr Abbott.'

'You're not paid to operate domestically, either,' I reminded the pompous ass.

'Henry King is an American asset overseas. Makes his safety at home a matter of national security. Which is why I'm curious how Dicky Butler learned to blow dams.'

'The guy's life is an open book. Spent most of it in state prisons. Shouldn't be hard to trace his movements, such as they were. And his contacts. You'd be better talking to his wardens than a real-estate agent.'

'The Admiral said I could trust your take.'

'I already told him my take: this is local. A traditional Yankee land feud that got out of hand. Tell him I'll do anything I can to help, but unless the various investigations turn up something not obvious – like it was detonated by satellite – Henry King and national security have nothing more to fear in Newbury . . .'

'Except what?'

A miserable thought had occurred to me.

'. . . Except if Dicky's father takes it into his head to blame King for his son's death.'

'Son of a bitch.'

'On the other hand,' I said, 'King's got good security.'

'Sure did wonders for his lake.'

'Maybe the Secret Service should leave a couple of agents around a while till things calm down.'

Smyth gave me a funny look and for a second I thought he was going to tell me something important. But all he did was shrug. 'Let me leave a telephone number, Ben, case anything comes up and you want to talk.'

He offered his hand and headed for the door. 'Nice little town you got here.'

'How you happen to know the Admiral?'

'I was one of his boys. After your time.'

'How did you end up in the spooks?'

'Knew somebody.'

Sounded to me like the Admiral had infiltrated the CIA.

Late that afternoon, despite all my visitors, I actually sold a house. It was a sweet little cape in the borough, a starter home for a couple of young teachers at Newbury Prep. They were happy; they could walk to work. The seller was happy; she could move into a retirement condo at Heritage Village. I was happy, too, gratified that I could negotiate a deal that didn't end in people lobbing dynamite.

I did my paperwork and walked it over to Tim Hall's mail slot and Newbury Saving's night box. Walking home, with Alison Mealy bike-riding circles around me, it occurred to me that she was about the age Dicky Butler had been when he got himself committed to Manson.

I noticed there were still government cars in the Yankee Drover parking lot. The joint was jumpin' with a summer Sunday-night crowd clumped around pitchers of beer. Smashing Pumpkins was on the juke box. A big-screen TV with the sound off showed the Red Sox clinching the second loss of their doubleheader.

The Feds looked too busy trying to get lucky with maidens of the town to welcome being pumped for information that might discourage Sergeants Marian and Arnie from persecuting Mr Butler. I looked for Vicky, thinking she could smile us both into their midst. Friends said they hadn't seen her. I flashed on her and Tim at a candlelit dinner in her cottage behind the Congregational church.

I took the last empty barstool. The guy to my left was nose to nose with his girlfriend. To my right sat Julia Devlin, sleek as a cat in moonlight.

10

Her hair was swept back, gleaming like onyx, highlighting a profile that could have revived the American shipbuilding industry. She was wearing black leggings and a black sleeveless top. Muscle rippled under her smooth skin. She had hooked the heels of her laced half-boots over the rung of the barstool and she was drinking Rolling Rock from the bottle.

'Hello, Mr Abbott. I'm sorry about your friend.'

I didn't want to talk about Dicky Butler. So I said, 'Thanks. He wasn't exactly a friend. Sorry about your lake.'

'It wasn't my lake.'

'I'll bet it hasn't made your boss any easier to live with.'

She shrugged.

'Can I buy you a cold one? I'm sort of celebrating. I just sold a house.'

'Congratulations. Sure, I'd have one more. Thanks.'

She had a faint accent. It sounded a little Brooklyn, but not quite. It had another softer-sounding layer that I couldn't place.

'I'm going to have a burger, are you hungry?'

'I've eaten, thanks.'

I ordered a Rolling Rock for her, and a Red Stripe and a medium hamburger for me. We clinked bottles when the beers came and then I asked, 'How's the boss taking it?'

'He's sad.'

'Yeah, I gathered he really loves that place.'

'I feel so bad for him. I'd rather he was angry. He's easier to deal with angry.'

I asked how long she had worked for him. Six years.

'I guess you take a lot of flak.'

She bristled. 'He doesn't mean anything when he yells. He's under tremendous pressure. He works so hard. Most of his contemporaries are golfing around the lecture circuit, but Henry just won't stop. He's really easy-going, once you get to know him.'

I make it a policy not to argue with beautiful women I'm trying to get to know better. But there are limits. 'Nothing in that dumb land feud led me to think of Henry King as easy-going. If he were, he'd have made peace with old man Butler.'

'No,' she said, fiercely. 'You don't understand him. That house is like his *child*. He's never had children. To violate Fox Trot was to attack him deep in, in his soul. I'm sorry, I don't think you read him right, Ben. Not at all. He is a good and gentle man.'

She took a slug of her beer and stared moodily at the bottle.

I decided to get off the subject of her good and gentle boss. 'Did the explosion get in the way of his ceramic engine deal?'

'How do you know about that?'

'Party talk. I gathered he's brokering something big.'

She gave me a smile. 'Do I hear an old Wall Street warhorse neighing?'

'No way. But it did sound big.'

'It could be.'

'Lousy timing.'

'He's had better weekends,' she agreed. 'But if you want to understand him, Ben, you have to know that seeing his beautiful lake destroyed really broke his heart.'

'It's fixable. Mr Butler can't get his son back.'

'I'm not saying it's comparable. Neither would Henry. But it's not like Henry did it to him.'

'Is that proven?'

'Is what proven?'

'That Dicky blew the dam.'

'Of course he blew the dam.'

'I mean, have the Federal investigators worked out the details?'

106

'Unofficially – between you, me and the lamppost – this afternoon the ATF traced the dynamite to a batch bought from the Pendleton Powder Company down in Brookfield.'

'That was fast.'

'Priority Red, or whatever they call it.'

'Did Mr Butler buy the dynamite?'

'I hear he signed for it.'

It was my turn to stare moodily into a beer bottle. Sergeants Marian and Arnie would jump on that bill of sale like wolves on sirloin. 'And Dicky stole it?' I asked, hoping Mr Butler hadn't been stupid enough to blow King's dam with dynamite traceable to him.

'Maybe.'

'What do you mean maybe?'

'Maybe we change the subject?'

'I'm just wondering is the assumption that Dicky stole it from his father?'

'I don't know and I don't care.' She reached for her bag.

I said, 'Sorry. I'll bet you've had enough of this.'

'Enough to want a quiet beer a long ways from Fox Trot.'

'Understood. Stay. We'll drop it.'

Her hand wavered. Finally, she picked up her bottle. '. . . So what's your story?'

'Me?'

'Who's Ben Abbott?'

'Pretty much who you heard when you asked around for Mr King.'

'Excuse me?'

'Last March. King told me he'd heard that I was, quote, a pisser. It was probably your job to get that quote.'

Julia Devlin returned a teasing grin. 'Oh, right. Let me see . . . Small-town first selectman's son, Annapolis, ONI, Wall Street, Leavenworth Penitentiary, small-town real estate, first selectman's occasional lover . . . Any blanks?'

'Yes. Why'd you pretend you didn't recognize me at the gate yesterday?'

'I thought you were coming on to me.'

'You should see me when I'm not subtle.'

'Oh, you were subtle. At least you had me guessing.'

'Suppose I was?'

'I didn't want to encourage you.'

'Is your heart spoken for?'

She smiled again. 'That's a nice way of saying it.'

'Is it?'

'Let's just say I didn't need guys coming on to me.'

No surprise she was sleeping with the boss. Her eyes sparkled every time she said his name.

My hamburger came. Julia accepted my offer of a French fry and dipped several in ketchup. She ordered us a round of beers, surveyed the room in the bar mirror, and asked, 'Is this your local?'

'Two doors from my house. A very convenient crawl home.'

'That's great. The thing I hate about the country, you can't drink and drive.'

'Consider my guest room yours any time.'

'Yeah, right.'

'Where you from? Grow up in the city?'

'New York? No. My parents were divorced. I moved back and forth between New Orleans and Honduras.'

New Orleans. That explained her accent and bolstered a theory I've always liked that the famous Brooklyn accent was brought there by refugees from a New Orleans yellow-fever epidemic.

'My Momma's from New Orleans. Daddy's Honduran.'

'Devlin?'

'Granddaddy was Irish.'

'That's some mix. Who do you take after?'

'Momma, mostly. I guess. She's French. Daddy's kind of fair. I got his eyes.'

I was working hard at subtle. Otherwise I'd have observed aloud that she had inherited the best features of both sides. Daddy's blue eyes. Momma's raven hair and olive skin. Granddaddy's stunning body? 'I'll bet they're proud you're working for Henry King.'

'Daddy's proud. Momma wants me to get married. It's incredible. Like she's spent her life waiting on Daddy's support cheques and she still thinks I should get married. I tell her, no way, Momma, I'm ever going to depend on a man.'

'And that sends her up the wall.'

'Like, she thinks I'm *criticizing* her.'

Talk of home made Julia look and sound younger than what I had assumed were her late-middle thirties, and I realized that her manner and bearing were seasoned beyond her years by serving a powerhouse like King.

'I go, "Momma, I'm gonna pay my own way." She goes, "There's more to life than paying bills." I *love* paying my bills.'

'You do?'

'Yes! Twice a month I set aside special time to clear my desk and open all the envelopes and throw out the junk mail and put them in categories? You should try it. It's like a ritual. I close my door and turn off the phone. And I write the cheques with my favourite fountain pen.'

'Your Mont Blanc Meisterstuck?'

'How'd you know what kind of pen?'

'It was on the video.'

'What?'

'The A&E bio.'

'Oh, right. The bio. The director loved that. Anyway, Henry gave it to me – well, actually, he gave one to everybody.'

'Does he do that a lot?'

'Usually I buy staff gifts, but he bought the pens himself. That's why I say he gave it to me, because he surprised me.'

'You really like him, don't you?'

'Why do you say that?'

'You get all excited when you talk about him.'

'He's a very exciting man to work for. You wouldn't believe how we're at the centre of *every*thing. And the people who trust him for the most important things.'

She gazed into the back bar mirror, contemplating the miracle. I said, 'There's something I've never understood about Henry King. He's the world's greatest diplomat, the superstatesman. But he's not very diplomatic.'

'What do you mean?'

'When I think of "diplomat", I think of someone like Bertram Wills.'

109

'Bertram Wills?' Julia snorted, exposing the Fox Trot pecking order. 'He's a joke.'

'Well, King keeps him around for something, doesn't he?'

Julia backpedalled from her undisguised contempt. 'Bert's a good front man. He fills in when Henry can't appear personally.'

For the B clients, one would imagine. 'Well that's what I meant. Bertram Wills looks and acts like a diplomat. Smooth and charming and diffident. He doesn't offend. He's "diplomatic". Whereas Henry –'

'Henry King was not a "diplomat". He held the sceptre.'

'Beg pardon?'

'He was a warrior because he understood how he wielded the might of the American empire . . . He was a "superstatesman" because he knew that when Henry King stepped off Air Force One, he spoke for a nation that could deliver nuclear rockets in half an hour . . . I think I'm talking too much.'

Sounded like Henry King pillow talk. 'You're safe,' I assured her. 'I hold barroom confidences sacred. Tell me, if Bertram Wills serves as a good front man, what does Josh Wiggens do?'

'Josh consults on security,' she replied, with a distinct iciness that hinted at something personal.

'I kind of liked *Mrs* King.'

'Don't get me started.'

'Oh, come on. Private gossip is one of the great pleasures.'

'Private gossip?'

'Barroom confidences?'

'Excuse me a minute.'

She strode purposefully to the juke box and spent some time there. Boy, could she play a juke box.

Melissa's moody 'Shriner's Park' was among the more light-hearted she chose. Shawn Colvin cheered things up with 'Killing the Blues', and 'One Cool Remove'. And just in case Petrie and Callahan's 'The Dimming of the Day', hadn't put a stake in the heart of the evening, Whitney Houston's kiss-off song to Kevin Costner had taciturn ironmen pouring their hearts out to women who'd been about to tell the bozos to start sleeping in their trucks.

'Do you really want to know about Mrs King Incorporated?' said Julia.

'I liked her.'

'Let me put it this way: if you owned a television station and Henry King told you his wife gave great interview you just might find a slot for her.'

'Is there a thing between her and Bertram Wills?'

Julia looked at me sharply. 'You've got a good eye.'

'I thought I caught an adoring look.'

'Bert's or hers?'

'Bert's. She was very careful. Except once, when King yelled at her.'

'Yes, I noticed that too.'

'Does King know?'

Julia's shrug couldn't begin to conceal her delight that Bert Wills had Shanghaied her lover's wife.

Henry King and Julia Devlin.

Bertram Wills and Mrs King.

Josh Wiggens and God-knew-what.

I can't say I was surprised by Fox Trot's hot sheet permutations. King, the only *arriviste* in the multi-menage, seemed to have embraced – as enthusiastically as polo and buying land to the horizon – a grand old upper-crust WASP tradition of the sort revealed in biographies a generation after the celebrants have gone to their reward. The logistics, daunting to the middle class, were made manageable by constant travel, multiple homes and the privacy of mansions. All it took was money and enthusiasm.

Julia eased me back to the earlier subject. 'Actually, her television show is an asset. We can get people on that help us. No one dares say no.'

'Is King really still that powerful? I mean he doesn't hold that sceptre any more. He's just another well-connected business consultant.'

'Henry's more powerful than ever. I don't know of anyone on the planet who won't take his calls.'

'Except in Newbury.'

'That's the insanity of this whole mess. Here he's at the mercy of a struggling dairy farmer who happens to be his neighbour.'

'Beef,' I said. 'Mostly beef. He's getting out of dairy. Too much work, lousy return. Damned hard to make milk alone.'

Julia peered dubiously down the neck of her bottle.

'If you want another, the guest-room offer is legit. In fact, you can wander in any time you want. The house is never locked.'

'You're trusting.'

'What are you going to steal from me? You already got a great pen.'

'You know what I mean. Do you have a burglar alarm?'

'That's all I need. Trooper Moody barging in with a shotgun for a false alarm.'

'Guns?'

'Locked up in the cellar. I've got little kids in and out.'

'You have children?'

'No, no, no. A little girl lives in the stablehand's apartment in the barn with her mother.'

'I'd at least get a dog.'

'Alison, that's the little girl, wants a cat.'

'That'll be great protection. Sure, I'll have one more.'

I ordered for both of us. Julia insisted it go on her tab.

She drank about half. Then, up abruptly, she was signalling for her check. 'I gotta git. Nice seeing you, Ben.'

She left a generous tip, and carefully put the rest of her change in her bag, except for one single she kept in her hand.

'You OK to drive?'

'Fine.'

She certainly looked sober. And walked towards the door straight as an arrow. At the juke box, she slipped the buck into the slot and punched up her selection. She was out the door before the music began.

Bonnie Raitt.

'Nobody's Girl'.

Which, despite that old Henry King sparkle in her eye, I convinced myself might be a promising sign.

*   *   *

Dynamite sticks – we learned at the inquest over in Plainfield, the county seat – should be stored in a cool, dark place and turned regularly. Like bottles of port wine. If they weren't turned, the nitroglycerine settled to the bottom of the filler material, and leaked out the paper wrapper. Mopping up puddles of nitro was best done wearing a Kevlar bomb suit with ceramic chest and groin shields.

Mr Butler testified, in a low, beaten voice, that he kept his in a specially ventilated cellar of his outermost outbuilding, and turned them regularly. He admitted the shed wasn't always locked, explaining that he lived alone, most of the time, on the top of Morris Mountain, rarely left the property, and he had a large dog to discourage burglars.

Jurors rolled their eyes.

'And yet you claim,' said the Plainfield County medical examiner, who was conducting the inquest, 'that your dynamite *was* stolen.'

'Dog's getting old. I admit I shoulda locked it.'

He hadn't shaved or changed his clothes in a while and his face had aged ten years since Dicky had died. The ME was treating him gently, as if he were a very old man, and I saw that most of the jurors couldn't bear to watch as he rambled on about how Newbury was changing and you couldn't trust the outsiders moving in.

'Did you report the theft?' the medical examiner interrupted.

'They only stole it the day before they blew the dam. I didn't know until I went to check after Ben Abbott told me Dicky was killed. My stash was gone. Before I could report it, the cops were all over the place. Seized my licence, like they're afraid I'm going to run out and buy more.'

'How do you know it was stolen the day before?'

'Because,' he said, his voice rising, '*Two* days before – Thursday afternoon – I went up there and turned it. Like I just told you.'

'Tell us again, please.'

'Thursday's my day. Always turn it on Thursday. Otherwise you forget and before you know it, the floor's soaked in nitro.'

In the back of Plainfield's lovely domed courtroom, which was handsomely panelled and lit by stained-glass windows, Marian Boyce and Arnie Bender were taking notes. My friendly nod drew from Arnie a look he reserved for vagrants in the drunk tank and from Marian a glance to melt stone.

I had already testified how I'd found the body and had seen Mr Butler sitting on his tractor far up the hill. But a procession of Federal officers had confirmed what Julia Devlin had reported in the Yankee Drover: the explosion had been caused by Mr Butler's dynamite. An ATF chemist testified they had traced the dynamite to Pendleton Powder of Danbury and brandished computer printouts showing that it had been legally purchased by Mr Butler.

Yes, the farmer admitted, his son had lived with him since March. Yes, Dicky had access to the cellar. But Dicky didn't know how to set a charge.

Marian and Arnie smiled broadly at that admission. But their smiles faded as the ME pressed the issue, forcing the farmer to admit that what he meant was *he* had never taught Dicky how to set a charge. Detective-Sergeants Boyce and Bender were shooting grim and censorious looks at the medical examiner by then, and to my astonishment and great relief, I began to realize that the gist of all the testimony was that Dicky had acted alone.

The crowd smoking cigarettes on the courthouse steps during the end-of-testimony recess saw it that way too, predicting that the jurors would find exactly what the medical examiner had gone to great trouble to steer them to find. They were right: the jury returned a verdict that Dicky had blown the dam alone with dynamite he had stolen from his father; and recommended that for his laxness, Mr Butler's pyrotechnic licence be suspended.

The courtroom emptied quickly after the final gavel – it being an exquisite end-of-August afternoon ideal for a round of golf or a beer in the woods – and soon all the spectators were gone. Except for me and Marian and Arnie.

Mr Butler sat still, head bowed, long hair shielding his face. He didn't seem to realize that he was very, very lucky. The finding gave the Connecticut state's attorney absolutely no cause to indict him even on conspiracy, much less accessory to murder. But in his mourning, he still refused to believe that Dicky had accidentally killed himself.

'This ain't over,' he shouted. Marian recorded that in her notebook, and Arnie echoed, 'It sure ain't.'

They had recovered nicely from their earlier disappointment, and they watched him storm out with the bored expressions affected by patient cops and experienced vultures.

11

Two days later, Mr Butler surprised me with a visit.

I was in the kitchen, serving milk and peach pie to Alison Mealy, who looked cute as a *Saturday Evening Post* heiress in an old-fashioned riding habit Aunt Connie had found in her attic, and smelled strongly of horse.

'Look, Ben.' She removed her boots and raised her jodhpurs to show me bright red marks inside her knees.

'What's that?'

'I'm gripping with my knees, the way I'm supposed to,' she said proudly. 'Hey, someone's here.'

I said 'Hey is for horses,' as Connie had for me when *I* was eleven, and asked, 'Who?'

'Mr Butler. Oh, wow, he's got DaNang with him. Look! He's huge.'

Butler climbed down from his pickup, and knocked on the screen door.

'Gotta talk to you, Ben.'

'Come on in.'

'OK if he comes in the house?'

'Sure. Hi there, DaNang. Want some water?' DaNang shouldered me out of his way, and laid a head big as a crocodile's on Alison's lap.

'Oh, look at you. You're so big.' She started patting actively, and scratching ears. The yellow dog sank groaning to the linoleum and Alison went down with him, curling up to lay her head on his massive chest. 'Ben, you can hear his heart.'

If you hadn't spent the day on a sweating horse you could smell him, too. I told her that Mr Butler and I were going to go in my office and asked her to put down a few sheets of newspaper and on them a large bowl of water. Mr Butler trod heavily after me through the house. I sat behind my desk and gave him the near client's chair. I had a funny feeling he was going to sell the farm.

The poor guy looked worse than he had at the inquest. He still hadn't shaved, and I guessed he hadn't been eating because his cheeks were hollow. But what struck me hardest when he finally raised his head was the void in his eyes – black holes, dead with sorrow.

'You don't look too well,' I said.

'I'm not. Can't sleep. Can't eat. Tried drinking, it didn't work.'

I said, 'I'm sure you know, there's no rushing grief.'

'Drank a one-seven-five Jack in two days. All I got was a headache.'

I thought he was lucky he didn't get a stroke. 'That's a lot of bourbon.'

'He didn't do it, Ben.'

I contained a sigh. What the hell was I going to say to that?

'You hear me?'

'I hear you.'

'I'm telling you he didn't do it.'

'I know what you're telling me, but I –'

'The dynamite was stolen from my shed.'

I said, 'I heard you say that at the inquest. And I also heard the jury decide that you were lying to cover for Dicky.'

'State troopers said they was going to get me.'

'What do you mean, "get you"?'

'Hold on, Ben. I'm running ahead of myself. Just hear me out.' He hung his head for a moment, then flung it back, and pushed his hair out of the way. His eyes turned bright with anger.

'That dynamite was stolen from my shed.'

We had been here before. I pressed him for the same specifics the ME had, starting with, 'When?'

'Day before Dicky got killed.'

'Can you prove that?'

'No.'

'Well, do you have any theory,' I asked, 'about how Dicky got killed in the explosion?'

'Not a theory. It's a fact. He was framed.'

'By whom?'

'Same guy who stole my dynamite.'

'Who do you think stole your dynamite?'

'King.'

I looked out the window at Main Street, slumbering in the August sun. It was about four, traffic in a lull before people started heading home from work. He was getting worse. At least at the inquest he hadn't blamed King.

'You think I'm nuts.'

'Mr Butler. Why in hell would Henry King steal your dynamite?'

'To frame Dicky.'

'Do you really think that Henry King hates you enough to frame Dicky so elaborately?'

'I don't *think* it. I *know* it.'

'Enough to kill your son?'

'With Dicky out of the way, I'm next. If I die, he's got my farm.'

His jaw was set stubbornly. So I tried to stick to details.

'I don't see a sixty-year-old city man like Henry King sneaking into your shed and stealing your dynamite.'

'He's got hired hands. You saw that goddammed CIA agent lives there.'

'I don't see the man risking blackmail from hired hands. And I don't see him destroying his lake to frame your son in the hope that when you die he can buy your farm.'

'He won't wait. He'll kill me.'

I had heard enough. 'Mr Butler, I gotta tell you that I don't see Henry King cold-bloodedly killing for a piece of property.'

'I don't care if you see it or not,' he said sullenly. 'That's what happened.'

'If you don't care, why are you telling me?'

'The troopers are after me.'

'What?'

118

'I got a call from a buddy in Plainfield. A vet. He warned me they got a warrant.'

'An arrest warrant?'

'Yup.'

'What for?'

'Conspiracy to blow King's dam.'

'That's crazy.' I spoke automatically. In fact, it sounded as if Marian and Arnie had built a case despite the inquest. And *I* wondered if he *had* blown the dam.

'And accessory to murder.'

'That one's a lot harder to prove.'

'They're saying I killed Dicky.'

'We better call Tim Hall.'

'Ben, I didn't kill Dicky.'

'I know,' I assured him, although all I knew for sure was that he didn't deliberately kill him.

'I shoulda seen this coming. The troopers accused me to my face – said I gave Dicky the dynamite.'

'What do you mean?'

'They said it didn't matter if it was an accident. Told me it was accessory murder. They said if I owned up, they'd drop the murder charge. If I pleaded guilty to conspiracy.'

'But that's not what they said at the inquest.'

'The Feds wouldn't go along. The ATF agents insisted Dicky stole it, himself.'

'Let's go see Tim.'

'Yeah, but I had to talk to you, first. Tell you what really happened was –'

'Stop!' I said. 'Don't tell me anything. I can't keep your secrets.'

'You wouldn't rat on me. I know your rep.'

'Well, I goddammed don't want to get locked up for contempt for refusing to testify. Tell Tim. He's your lawyer.'

'I'm trying to tell you the reason I know that Dicky didn't blow up King's dam.'

'I don't want to hear it.'

'But you were Dicky's friend,' he insisted, an exaggeration of that relationship which exposed how lonely 'that crazy old farmer's' life had become.

119

'Tell Tim. Don't tell me. Please. I can't protect you. The troopers will have a field day if they think you talked to me.'

Suddenly, he stiffened and stared out the window at Main Street. I turned around just as Trooper Moody's cruiser screeched to a stop and backed up with a high-pitched whine. He swung into my drive, blocking Mr Butler's pickup truck, and got out of the car fast.

Butler was halfway to his feet.

'Don't,' I said. 'There's a child in the house. Just sit down and let's do this quietly. I'll call Tim.'

'Ben, I can't go to jail.'

'Don't worry. We'll get Tim on it, and Ira Roth. I promise you're not going to jail.'

'I can't stay indoors, Ben. I spend my whole day outside. I eat outside. Sometimes I sleep outside.'

I promised again we'd get him out real fast. Then I opened the door to Trooper Moody, who did it by the book: arrest, rights, cuffs, frisk and a lonely ride to the county lockup.

12

At the bail hearing the state's attorney argued that Mr Butler would blow Newbury off the map if allowed to roam free before his trial.

He dredged up the farmer's post-Vietnam emotional problems, which made him sound like a dangerous man, and produced Josh Wiggens – dubbed the 'Henry King Institute's Security Chief' for the occasion – to relate in tones of patrician outrage the morning Butler had driven up with a gun in his truck. Finally, the state's attorney reminded the magistrate that even if there weren't a very real risk to the public safety, the accessory to murder charge demanded very high bail.

Tim Hall had moved fast and elicited a quick evaluation from a friendly Plainfield therapist who testified that while on one hand Mr Butler was stable enough to be allowed to go home, he would very likely crumble under the stress of what she dubbed 'a jail situation'. Tim beat that drum hard, insisting that Mr Butler's emotional state – exacerbated by the shattering loss of his only child – was exactly the reason why the lifelong resident of the community should not be locked up before his trial. He even finessed the magistrate into demanding that the therapist put it in layman's language: 'He'll go nuts in a week.'

We lost anyhow.

The magistrate set bail at two million – about three times the value of his farm. Not surprisingly, no bail bondsman risked the two million.

Mr Butler was stunned. 'Ben, you promised.'

I couldn't meet his eye. Tim said, 'We'll get busy on your appeal.'

'What about my stock?' he pleaded. 'And my dog?'

I assured him I'd spoken with his neighbours. They were already pitching in to feed and milk his cows. But guess who got to keep DaNang?

Alison was thrilled.

I wasn't. I like dogs. Like them a lot. But I liked my house orderly and unhairy. Nor did I enjoy, while heading down to the liquor cabinet in the middle of the night, hearing a sinister snarl at the foot of the stairs. It was like living with one of those rent-a-cop security guards who double as a criminal when you turn your back.

DaNang didn't like the new arrangement either. The big yellow farm dog moped around the house and seemed to hold a grudge against me for a series of deodorizing baths. Though he cheered up when Alison visited him in the morning and again after riding camp. And of course at meal time. The dog ate like a carnivorous horse. Lugging sacks of dog food home from the Grand Union, I had to assume that Butler had stretched his limited budget by slipping him the occasional cow.

The dog practically wept when I returned from the county lockup bearing the scent of his master, who was sweating out the bail appeal and going downhill rapidly. When I asked the Plainfield therapist to have another look at him, she convinced his jailers to post a suicide watch.

She did not want him transferred to a prison hospital, since Plainfield was a fairly gentle surrounding, as jails went; the guards were sympathetic, as guards went; and he could have visitors like the middle-aged Vietnam veterans who trooped in to sit silent in the interview room. One was a prosperous Morris Mountain banker. The less fortunate included a guy who looked like he had arrived by boxcar and hung around the courthouse muttering to himself. I gave him money, wondering if that would be me one of these days.

I cornered Tim Hall at the closing on the teachers' Cape Cod, while everyone shook hands on the steps of the Newbury Savings Bank.

'Let me ask you something. Mr Butler swore to me that he knows for sure that Dicky *didn't* blow up King's dam. What does he know? Why's he so sure?'

'First I've heard this theory,' Tim admitted, anxiously. Lawyers hate surprises they haven't engineered. 'How does he explain Dicky's body under it?'

'I told him to tell you. I couldn't protect him.'

'He never mentioned it to me.'

'Probably doesn't trust you yet.'

Tim got very stern. 'Or suspects I won't swallow everything he swears to you.'

'I'm not saying I swallowed it. I'm just telling you that he swore he had reason to know that Dicky didn't do it. I don't want to tell you your business, but don't you think as his lawyer you ought to get him to open up to you?'

Tim asked, 'Did he ever tell you that King was spying on him? Watching him with binoculars? Or a sniper scope?'

'Dicky told me it wasn't true.'

'Of course it's not true. Which is why I'm not that impressed by Butler swearing he knows for sure Dicky didn't blow up the dam that fell on him.'

I didn't know what to say. Except that Mr Butler sounded spacier than ever.

'Happiness in your new home,' I said to the happy buyers. And Tim said, 'Happiness in *your* new home,' to the happy seller. They invited us to drink mimosas in the new home. Pete the banker accepted, happy with two new mortgages. There was something really uplifting about a closing, which resonated with beginnings, but I declined for Tim and me, apologizing that we had a meeting on another matter, and marched him back to his office.

He rented the same space his father had, former storage rooms above the General Store. Tim had modernized it by popping skylights through the slant ceilings and varnishing the pine floors. But you could still smell grain and lamp oil and candlewax.

Like me, he worked at his father's desk. Tim, senior, had

been a real force in the region, and Tim inherited a fine country practice – wills, trusts and real estate. He avoids divorce work, unless he can mediate for old clients, and argues the occasional criminal case, when the consequences aren't too severe, or the accused can't afford a heavy hitter like Ira Roth.

But Tim – broad and open-faced, with a gaze sometimes puzzled – has his work cut out for him if he's ever going to fill the old man's shoes. We share a bond, as I too peer into the mirror of Newbury's memories of my father. The difference is I do not expect to fill the old man's shoes. He was a pillar of the community. I was thirteen when I realized I was not pillar timber.

'Mr Butler is a mess. How's the bail going?'

'He's broke.'

'Show me a farmer who isn't.'

'I mean really broke. The farm is mortgaged up the wazoo and he's behind in his taxes.'

'Poor bastard. Are you going to stick with him?'

'Ira practically ordered me to represent him, pro bono.'

'Generous of Ira.'

'Well, he's acting as counsel. Strategizing with me.'

'Pro bono?' I asked. Ira enjoyed a very large income and was not famous for charity. Unlike *his* father – speaking of shoes to be filled – who had died broke and beloved by all he had given and lent to in his day.

'It's a heck of a deal for me. Like a free graduate course in the law.'

'If you need an investigator, count me in. But just remember I'm a real-estate agent.'

'Ira advised me to tell you, "Don't be coy." '

I had no intentions of being coy. If Tim and Ira Roth would defend Mr Butler in court, the least I could do was pitch in with some field support.

'I want client–attorney privilege. When the troopers hear I'm wandering around asking questions, the state's attorney can subpoena me to testify.'

Tim rummaged an employment application from his desk. 'Sign here.'

I signed. He took out a money clip and paid me with a tattered single. 'You are now an employee of Hall & Hall, with all the privileges that implies.'

'Health insurance?'

'Not while you're a probationary employee.'

'What do you want me to do?'

'Mr Butler asserts he was freeing a calf caught in his upper pasture fence when he heard the explosion. Find us a witness who saw him freeing a calf.'

'That's no alibi for conspiracy. Or even accessory to murder. He didn't have to be there.'

'You just admitted you're a real-estate agent, not an investigator. May I remind you you're also not a lawyer.'

'But I'm right.'

'Ira and I are attempting to establish that Mr Butler had absolutely nothing to do with the bombing and absolutely no foreknowledge it was going to occur. We like very much the picture of the father of the deceased calmly going about his daily chores at the moment his son was single-handedly bombing the dam.'

'Do you believe him?'

'Of course I believe my client. Find us witnesses who saw him that far from the dam when it blew up.'

'– I saw him far from the dam right after it blew up.'

'Grinning at the results is not exactly the kind of distance we're looking to establish.'

'If I were you I'd be worrying whether he could have detonated it by radio or set it on a timer.'

'He didn't.'

'Can you prove that – just in case I can't find a witness in a cow pasture?'

'The dynamite was probably detonated by a fuse.'

'That didn't come out at the inquest. I didn't hear any agents commit to what detonated it.'

'There's a lot didn't come out at the inquest,' Tim said quietly. If ever his father's son was sitting at the old man's desk it was now, with a foxy country-lawyer smile on his lips and lupine cynicism in his eyes.

'Says who?'

'The word is,' he answered, 'that some of King's pals slipped the medical examiner secret reports.'

'Which pals?'

'One was Secretary of State. Bertram Wills from Middlebury? My dad knew him.'

'And the other one is Josh Wiggens.'

'King's security chief. How'd you know?'

'He's ex-CIA.'

'Really? Any rate, they convinced the ME that the secret reports were genuine and "persuaded" him not to spill the beans. So he convinced the jury to report the obvious: Dicky Butler died while blowing up the dam, alone.'

'What beans?'

'National Security beans – investigative methods. Fox Trot security. King's enemies. Secret lab techniques the Feds would just as soon not blab to the media. All under the National Security blanket.'

'That's ridiculous.'

'Why? It's the nature of government to be secretive. You think Vicky tells Scooter everything? She tells him enough to keep the *Clarion* off her back.'

I didn't want to discuss Vicky with Tim. He used to come to me for advice about Vicky, which obviously he didn't need any more. In fact, the first time, he asked my blessing, which I had no right to give, but gave anyway, like a damned fool. I said, 'I know what you're saying, but it seems like a risky conspiracy to keep a few secrets.'

'Conspiracy is too strong word. This was more informal. Do you know the ME's background?'

I knew that before he had retired, young, to the pleasant sinecure in Plainfield – longtime seat of his family's summer home – the ME had been a superstar pathologist in Boston. Tim explained that meant he was connected to Harvard and all sorts of federally-funded institutions. 'Think of him as a national "old boy". Very Establishment, like the Willses have always been and Henry King's become.'

'What in hell is he doing back in Plainfield at his age?'

'What are *you* doing back in Newbury at *your* age?'

I gave Tim a back-off look. 'You know I'm banned.'

'Ira says you could get around it. Don't you want to?'

'Wall Street's all mutual funds now. It's a number-crunching kid's game.'

'They do more for the economy than the raiders.'

'You're right. All we did was pass the bucks upstairs. Now, Mr Butler –'

'That's why I wonder why you don't want to join them. They build. Look how they support high technology.'

'They're no "nicer" than we were, Tim. They live on fast growth. So if your business happens not to be high-tech, you have to do something to catch their eye, like fire half your workforce, hire temp workers, drop health care, and move plants overseas so they can pretend you're earning fifteen per cent profits.'

'Sounds like you stay in touch.'

I did keep up with the money world, which, despite knowing it too well to be dazzled, still fascinated me. And Tim hadn't asked me anything I didn't occasionally ask myself. But I didn't feel like wearing my doubts on my sleeve.

I said, 'You know how after swimming you dry off and don't want to get wet again?'

'Or are you scared to go back?'

'Dinosaurs don't get scared, Tim. They migrate. I'm damned lucky I had a place to migrate to. Now, could we get back to Mr Butler and ask why would Establishment "old boys" get mixed up in a piece of local silliness that just happened to turn fatal?'

Before Tim could answer, the answer occurred to me. 'Wait a minute. Does Henry King still work for the government?'

13

I should have guessed sooner.

Diplomats have always been spies. They live in the enemy's tent, accommodated for the sake of communication. Lovely Fiona and husband, domiciled in Washington DC to communicate British intentions, also observe and report. Whoever doubts this might read letters home by M. Paleologue, French Ambassador to the Czar's court during the Russian Revolution. (My honours thesis – to make up near-fatal shortcomings in physics – which propelled me into the clutches of the Admiral, then Captain, at ONI.)

Henry King, whose oh-so-public downfall and banishment from government office had supposedly reduced him to *freelance* diplomat, *private* consultant to corporate titans and high ministers, would make a hideously insidious spy.

What if all the while he was trusted by his clients as their personal diplomat, he reported to the National Security Council or the CIA or some new outfit no one ever heard of? It would explain the immediate response of helicopters, the Federal agents, the Admiral's personal emissary, and Julia Devlin's advance word on their investigations. And why they feared someone had tried to blow him up. Henry King was really nudging the envelope. With a spear. The word 'betrayed' might even spring from irritated lips.

'Ira wondered,' Tim said. 'Do you agree?'

'. . . Wait, wait, wait. If that's so – if they just wanted to make sure their "spy" was not under fire from a hostile nation – or a pissed-off client – then why stir everything up again by arresting poor Mr Butler? They were home free. Dicky's dead. Case closed.'

Tim and I stared out the window at tree tops for a while. 'We're forgetting something, here. We live in a democracy.'

'You're losing me.'

'A *federally* governed democracy. We have Federal government, and state government.'

'And state police.'

'What if the FBI blew it? What if they forgot to get the Connecticut State Police aboard? So your pal the ravishing detective-sergeant did what good cops do. She went looking for more suspects.'

'So let's convince the Feds to persuade the troopers to drop their investigation?'

'Ira and I batted that around. Problem is, by now, the troopers are too far into the case. It's one thing to shake hands behind a bush on the weekend. Much riskier to lean on an outfit as independent as the state police two weeks after the event. That *would* be a conspiracy. The kind that makes headlines. No, the only way we can get the troopers to drop it is to beat their case.'

'Wait. Let's ask Henry King to pay for Mr Butler's defence.'

'*Pay* for the defence of the man charged with destroying his lake?'

'If your spy theory works, then King has everything to lose if Butler goes to trial.'

Tim thought about that, didn't like it. 'No, it's too complicated.'

'Want me to ask him?' I could pitch it to Julia Devlin and let her talk sense to King.

'I'll bounce that off Ira. Meantime, you get busy. Find a witness who saw Mr Butler after he ran the cows into King's pasture and before you saw him watching from the ridge.'

I ran down the owner of the red balloon King had hired to show off his landscaping, but the guy had had his hands full operating the hot-air burner and keeping drunks from falling out of the basket and hadn't noticed any calf stuck in Mr Butler's fence.

He did recall that he was airborne at the moment of the explosion. But not being from Newbury, he didn't know the

129

names of his passengers. I pressed him for a description. But the best he could do was two guys in ties and two women in pearls.

At the General Store I found a hardworking high-school kid named Todd Gierasch bussing cups off the tables on the front porch. I poured myself a coffee and said, 'When you get a moment, I'd like to ask you something.'

'Sure thing, Mr Abbott. Be there one sec.'

Todd was a beef farmer's son, one of those kids saving for college with four after-school jobs and full-time work all summer. I knew him from my high-school career day real-estate workshop. Like a lot of the students, he hoped that my Wall Street years proved that the fast lanes promised on television were out there waiting for his diplomas.

'What's up, Mr Abbott?'

'That's what I was going to ask you. Rather, who's up. You were parking cars at Mr King's party.'

His face fell. 'Did they dent your Fiat?'

'No, no, no. Fiat's fine.'

'Oh, wow. You scared me.'

'Where were you when the dam exploded?'

'They gave us cokes after everybody got there. We were sitting under a tree. You could feel it in the ground. Like a kick. It was like, Oh wow, what's that? Then all the grown-ups started yelling.'

'Where was the balloon?'

'Up in the air.'

'You sure? It wasn't on the ground?'

'I'm sure. I was laying on the grass, looking up, kind of watching it.'

'I thought you were under a tree.'

'On the edge. I moved out so I could see the balloon.'

'Could you see who was in it?'

'No.'

'Not at all?'

'They were in the basket, hanging out the other side. I couldn't see 'em. Why, Mr Abbott?'

'I wanted to ask them what it looked like when the dam exploded.'

130

'I think it was Mr and Mrs MacKay.'

'I thought you couldn't see 'em.'

'I saw them get in the basket. Before they went up.'

Ask a leading question and you'll get the answer you deserve. The same goes for assumptions. I had assumed Scooter MacKay had shot the fine photograph on the front page of last week's *Clarion* by going up in the balloon *after* the explosion.

Well, perfect. My next-door neighbours might have seen Mr Butler freeing a calf from a fence. But Scooter and Eleanor had just left on a second honeymoon aboard the *QE2*. So I ran up the outside wooden stairs to Tim's office. 'Can I use your phone?'

'Make it snappy. I gotta meet Vicky.'

I dialled 'O' and gave Tim a reassuring nod as I requested, 'High Seas Operator.'

'High Seas Operator?' echoed Tim.

'I got to talk to Scooter.'

'But he's on the *QE2*.'

'Which is why I need the High Seas Operator – person to person to Mr Scooter MacKay on the *QE2*. . . Yes, he's a passenger.'

'How much does that cost?'

'Beats me.'

'It's not your phone.'

No kidding.

'Scooter . . . No, no problem. House didn't burn down. Newspaper's fine. Rupert Murdoch came by. We sold it to him. Listen, Tim and I got a question for you about the bomb . . . What? . . . I'll tell Tim – we caught them in their Jacuzzi. Scooter. Listen, the balloon? When you took the picture? At King's? . . .' I covered the phone. 'He wants us to know they're drinking champagne and eating caviar. Drunk as skunks.'

'I gotta take Vicky on something like that,' said Tim.

'Scooter. Listen up. Before the blast. Before the dam blew up? Did you see Mr Butler on his farm? . . . Down on his farm, from the balloon . . . You didn't? . . . Right, right, right.

The red Farm-all . . . Oh . . . OK, good talking to you. Kiss Eleanor.'

I hung up. 'They saw the tractor along a fence line. But they didn't see Butler.'

'Darn.'

'Well, it tells us he was up there, at least.'

'No. It only tells us his *tractor* was up there.'

'It strongly suggests he climbed off the tractor to free the calf, like he told us. There's trees along the fence. Scooter and Eleanor might have been looking right at him under a tree.'

'If my grandmother had wheels she'd be a Cadillac. They're not witnesses.'

'Guess who else called Scooter today.'

'On the ship?'

'Detective-Sergeant Marian Boyce. Connecticut State Police.'

'Why?'

'Breaking down Butler's alibi.'

I drove up to Fox Trot.

At the gate, a tight-lipped, very professional uniformed guard said that as far as he knew Albert and Dennis Chevalley had gone home for the day.

'I'm Ben Abbott. Would you call up to the house, please, and tell Julia Devlin I'm here.' While Tim and Ira debated, I'd hit King for Mr Butler's legal bills.

'She's away.'

'How about Mr King?'

'He's with her.'

I drove back down the mountain, and cut around Newbury to Frenchtown. On the outskirts was a hillside speckled with house trailers. Some were so old they were covered with vines. Some were newer and quite large. I knocked on a doublewide that belonged to Laura Chevalley, Dennis and Albert's Mom.

'The boys', as Laura called them in weary tones, had told her they wouldn't be home for supper because they were working late. Sounded like I'd find them at the White Birch.

Laura, round, red-faced and patient, insisted on making me a cup of instant coffee. She wanted to know when I'd last seen my mother. I told her I'd been out to the farm the weekend before last and that Mom was happier than ever that she had left Main Street. Which was exactly what cousin Laura wanted to hear, because no Chevalley, man or woman, thought a person could be happy living on Main Street.

Laura's living room was decorated with velvet furniture, ceramic lamps that *her* mother had acquired with Raleigh cigarette coupons, and one trillion knick-knacks. 'Couldn't have been weekend before last,' she called from the kitchen. 'I visited after Mass and she said she hadn't seen you in ages.'

'It was a couple of weekends ago.'

'She must be lonely at the farm.'

'She says she's happy alone.' In fact, it was my mother's holing up on the farm since my father died that had made me wonder if I'd inherited a lone-wolf tendency that would leave me muttering to myself like Mr Butler's visiting vet.

'The boys keep threatening to move out and get their own place. I don't know what I'd do if they did.'

I snuck a look at her end tables, which were fashioned of cloth draped over wooden boxes, and found bright red lettering, 'Dupont Explosives, Special Gelatin, 60% Strength'.

'Your Mom's not getting any younger,' she called.

True. But as she got older she discovered more and more links between my imprisonment and my father's death. I had been stunned when she first had edged around the subject in her characteristically tentative way. We had talked about it. Repeatedly. But no amount of talking pushed it from her mind for very long.

Laura stepped into the living room with instant and Oreos. 'You ought to get out there more, Ben.'

'Laura, she blames me for my father's death.'

'No, she doesn't.'

'That my going to prison killed him.'

'But she blames herself for you going to prison.'

'Herself?'

'For giving you her Chevalley blood.' Laura laughed, a

133

sound more wise than bitter. 'As if one of you upstanding Main Street Abbotts could never commit a crime.'

I left, with a promise to go out to the farm, soon.

Outside the White Birch, parked proudly among the chopped Harleys and flame decal-ed Cameros, was the slick black pickup with 'Fox Trot' on the doors. Inside, Dennis and Albert were revelling in the joys of steady money. They had stacked their pay on the bar and were buying rounds for anyone they could remotely call an acquaintance.

'Hey, Ben,' Albert bellowed, considerably louder than Butch Hancock on the juke box. 'Have a drink.'

'You remember my name.'

'Aw, come on. We're not working now. We know who you are. Right, Dennis?' He was half drunk.

'What's he drinking?' yelled Dennis. He was drunker. And his face was a mess, all scabbed and sporting bruises of fading yellow.

'What happened to you?'

'Nothing. What are you drinking?'

I said, 'Beer.' Wide Greg smacked down a Bud, *sans* glass.

'Good news about Dicky Butler,' Albert announced with an aggressive smirk.

I let that go. *I* hadn't gotten trounced last March.

Dennis chuckled, a sound reminiscent of DaNang in the night. 'Heard the fire department found his head in Fairfield County.'

They looked at me for a reaction.

'Guys,' I said.

They faced me, grinning in unison. 'What?'

Wide Greg moved towards the bracketed length of PVC pipe where he sheathed his baseball bat. He ran a tight ship at the White Birch – wise when you cater to bikers and your New England town fathers are itching to shut you down – and had a wonderful instinct for spotting trouble before it started.

'Guys,' I said. 'I want to ask you something.'

What fun was this? Egging the upscale cousin into a two-on-one fist fight, and instead he asks questions.

'Yeah, what?'

'Something about your pal Dicky Butler.'

'We heard he went to pieces,' Dennis snickered.

Enough. Their clowning sounded more vengeful than crude and not at all funny. 'I'm talking about the Dicky Butler who kicked your asses two by two.'

The brothers ducked, hoping none of the patrons hanging nearby for another free drink had overheard. Dennis got an ugly look on his face, more angry than embarrassed. 'Watch yourself, Ben.'

'Watch what, Dennis?'

'People don't have to know everything, you know what we're talking?'

'The man's dead. I'm not laughing.'

'Man's lucky he's dead. Dennis and me had a couple of axe handles with his name on 'em.'

'Did you see him?'

'When?'

'When the dam blew up?'

'You mean flying by?'

Albert roared laughter.

Dennis shook with giggles. But he was watching me closely with his small, dark eyes. Prodding. Testing. Or something deeper. I wasn't sure, but maybe Dennis wasn't as drunk as he seemed.

'How about his dad?'

'Huh?' The brothers sobered quickly.

'Did you see his dad?'

'When?'

'When the dam blew.'

'Hey, Ben, we're not supposed to talk about what happens.'

'What do you mean, what happens?'

'You know. Up at Fox Trot.'

'We got our jobs, Ben.'

'I didn't see you when I was up at Mr King's party. He give you the day off?'

'No way, man. We was working.'

'Oh, you were doing security?'

'You bet,' said Dennis.

'Undercover?'

'Yup. That's right. Undercover.'

'That's what I figured when I didn't see you.'

Albert beamed like Hubert Humphrey in the Vietnam part of King's A&E bio: pleased as punch!

Dennis looked wary.

'Where?' I asked.

'Whadya mean?'

'What cover were you under?'

They exchanged looks. Dennis grew dark. Albert blustered. 'Can't tell you, Ben. So stop asking.'

'Why not?'

Another exchange. Anxious? What the hell were they covering? Dennis answered, 'We signed a thing.'

A sidebar in the *Economist* article had explored King Incorporated's obsession with forcing employees to sign confidentiality agreements. But a paucity of imagination had prevented the reporter from interviewing King's tree-stump dynamiters.

'You signed a "thing"?'

'Yeah. A paper.'

'What did the paper you signed say?'

'I don't know.'

'Dennis?'

'It said we weren't supposed to talk.'

'About work?'

'We ain't supposed to talk about nothin' at Fox Trot.'

'What happens if they catch you talking?'

'Get our asses fired,' said Dennis.

'Who made you sign it?'

'Miz Devlin. She's the boss.'

'Isn't Josh Wiggens chief of security?'

'Yeah, but she's the *boss*, boss.'

'Ball buster,' said Dennis.

'Mr Wiggens's a ball buster, too,' Albert added, 'except when she comes out, he rolls over like an old dog.'

Sounded like the gloves came off at home.

'I'll bet Mr King's mad as hell you let Dicky get to that dam.'

'Not at us. He was yelling at Mr Wiggens. And Ms Devlin.'

'But he was yelling at them even before,' said Albert.

'At the party?'

'Before people got there. He was yelling and screaming.'

'About what?'

'Busted air conditioning.'

'Air conditioning? It wasn't a hot day. The doors were open.'

Dennis shrugged. And Albert added mournfully, 'They yelled at us.'

Chain of command. 'When you perform security undercover, do you patrol that perimeter road in the four-by?'

'Can't tell you, Ben.'

'I'm talking about that new perimeter road that circles the property just inside the fences. Except where the woods are really thick between King's and Butler's.'

'Can't tell you, Ben.'

'Well, you couldn't run the truck up the brook in the woodlots. Too narrow. And you'd need a tractor to climb that upper pasture.'

Nathan Hale was no more loyal to the American Revolution than a Frenchtown twenty-year-old to his truck. Dennis and Albert leapt to the Chevy's defence.

I said, 'You're not telling me you drove it up where King's upper pasture touches Butler's?'

'Damned straight,' said Dennis, and Albert blurted, 'We was up there the whole time. Up there the whole time.' Which earned him a boot in the shin from Dennis.

Time to pretend I knew something. 'Did Mr Butler thank you?'

'For what?'

'For helping him free that calf that was stuck in the fence.'

The brothers exchanged a long, long look. Finally Albert said, 'We didn't help.'

'You didn't offer to help a farmer free his animal?'

Why hadn't Butler mentioned seeing them?

'We was going to,' explained Albert. 'Before we could, the calf got loose.'

'How far off were you?'

Albert considered. Wet his lips. 'Quarter mile. We was way up there. The whole time.'

'How did you know it was him, so far away?'

'We got binoculars, Ben.'

'Thousand-dollar binoculars. Gotta turn 'em in when we go home.'

'So of course you didn't talk to him.'

'They told us not to talk to Old Man Butler.'

'But the real reason you didn't talk to him is you weren't close enough.'

'We wouldn'ta anyway, right, Dennis?'

'That's right,' said Dennis, eyeing me closely.

'What time was this?'

'Three-twenty-seven.'

'Exactly three-twenty-seven?' The dam had exploded around four-ten. Time enough for Butler to sneak down and light the fuse? Close. 'How do you know the time so exactly?'

'We got a clipboard in the truck. Supposed to write down anything we see.'

'We got a clock in the truck,' said Albert. The black four-by was probably the first vehicle he'd ever driven without a hole in the dash where the clock used to be.

'What time did you go up there?'

They answered in syncopation. 'Eleven,' said Albert. 'Noon,' said Dennis.

'Which was it?'

'Eleven.'

'Noon.'

'What does the log say?'

'Noon.'

'Eleven,' Albert snarled at Dennis. 'I wrote it. You was driving. I know I wrote eleven.'

I asked if they had shown the log to the state police. Albert said they turned it in each night with the binoculars.

'What did the troopers say when you told 'em you saw Old Man Butler with the calf?'

'Didn't tell her.'

'Her?'

'That plainclothes sergeant with the great ass? She was back again, yesterday, asking all this shit.'

'Yesterday?'

'Keeps coming around. Albert says she's hot for us. There's some women go for brothers.'

Albert said, 'I'm telling you she's waiting for us to hit on her.'

'Keep in mind she's armed, Albert. Why didn't you tell her you saw Mr Butler?'

'Told you. We got orders. Keep our traps shut.'

'But you just told me.'

'You're our cousin, Ben. Ain't nobody can make us not talk to our own cousin. Right, Albert?'

'Right.'

Albert draped a broad paw over my shoulder and pounded warmly. I uttered my next question vibratingly, like Robin Williams doing Ho Chi Minh Trail water-buffalo traffic reports: 'Was Dicky with him?'

'Nope,' said Albert.

Dennis said, 'He was down at the dam.'

'You *saw* him there?'

'*Heard* him there.'

'What do you mean?'

'*BOOM!*' roared Dennis.

Albert fell off his barstool laughing and landed with a crash that stopped the juke box. Dennis doubled over, whooping. I flashed on Dicky's leg and severed hand, and considered picking up a barstool. But in that moment, Gwen Jervis pushed through the door leading her daughter Josie by the hand.

Every guy in the joint straightened up.

Josie was home on leave, chubby, round and smartly turned out in pressed Army fatigues. She wore glasses and the scared smile of a teenager who was afraid people would stare at her. There was actually little danger of that. Not with her mother nearby.

Gwen Jervis was an angular redhead. Her long legs deserved her tight jeans. Her full breasts did wonders to her baggy sweatshirt. Sometimes she looked mysterious, sometimes she looked dark, sometimes bleak as granite, but today she was grinning triumphantly. And if I knew Gwen, her sweatshirt had an elastic inner liner and she had used her clean-cut Army daughter for cover shoplifting.

The guys in the White Birch greeted her respectfully. One of the more genteel actually tipped his Pennzoil cap. Then a stranger lurched out of the men's room, a biker from Bridgeport visiting rehab mates. His red eye fell on Gwen and he blurted an appreciative, 'Hey, Baby,' illustrating his sentiments by grabbing his crotch with both hands.

Jervis men, hunched over a corner table like kidnappers stuffing envelopes with body parts, looked up. The stranger's friends pounced from both sides and hustled him off, murmuring urgent warnings. 'Jervis . . . Old Herman's daughter . . . dead meat.'

Newbury's Jervis clan lived in housetrailers, deep in the woods. To tar all of them with the brush 'criminal' would be to slander fewer than five per cent. They stole cars, hijacked trucks, ran wholesale dope deals, and smuggled guns in partnership with their Canadian cousins.

Gwen's dad, Old Herman – a ferociously intelligent criminal, who with different connections would have flourished in corporate law and been president of his Park Avenue co-op – was clan leader emeritus. Her brother Bill, a multimurderer with an excellent attorney, had taken over day-to-day operations and by all accounts was proving quite good at it.

Once in a blue moon, some child escaped. Gwen almost did. Almost made it through high school in the teeth of small-town bigotry and family resistance. The good folk of Newbury despised Jervises as vehemently as middle-class city dwellers loathed crackhouse neighbours, while Jervises regarded the school system as a government plot to make turncoats of their children.

Her son never had a chance; already he was trucking cargoes the troopers would dearly love to inspect. But eighteen-year-old Josie was flourishing in the Army.

I went over and bent to kiss Gwen's cheek. She turned to catch me full on the mouth. Her lips were urgent, her intent

140

both erotic and mocking. (A subtlety I hoped was appreciated by the Jervis men who were now watching *me* like disembowellers on their cigarette break.) Gwen was a great mocker, particularly of Main Street pretensions. 'Benjamin Abbott III,' she rasped in a deep, husky voice just made for a bar. 'Cruising the White Birch.'

'Hello, Gwen. Hi, Josie. How's the Army treating you?'

Josie ducked her head. She looked terribly unhappy.

'Can I buy you a beer?'

'Sounds good to me,' said Gwen. 'Hon, you want a beer?'

Josie mumbled she wasn't thirsty. Gwen rolled her eyes at the ceiling, and I realized I'd stepped into a mother–daughter thing. 'Bar or a table?'

'Table,' said Josie, with a sullen glance at Albert and Dennis, who were swaying on their stools like the initial phases of an avalanche. The juke box had recovered and was thundering Hooty. There were few tables. Josie made a beeline for one in the corner farthest from the Jervises. Gwen and I followed.

'Is she OK?'

'No.'

'What's the matter?'

'I don't know. I took her shopping down the mall. Thought it would cheer her up. She's moping around like a goddammed teenager.'

'She *is* a teenager.'

'She's a high-school graduate and a corporal in the United States Army,' Gwen said with immense pride.

'How'd you do at the mall?' Maybe Josie resented being used as cover.

'Smell.' She pressed her wrist to my nose.

'Opium?'

'Poison.'

'Suits you.'

'Up yours, Ben Abbott.'

I grabbed beers for Gwen and me and a can of Diet Pepsi for Josie, who watched me covertly as her mother and I shot the breeze. Suddenly I remembered where I'd seen her last.

I tried to catch her eye. She looked away.

Gwen rasped on. Old Herman, she reported, had a bum knee with arthritis, which he had exacerbated by staying out in the woods all night poaching deer. Brother Pete was drinking like a fish. Brother Bill, the new clan chief, was in Canada. Gwen was vague about the purpose of his journey and one could only sympathize with our neighbours to the north.

After I made several failed attempts to draw Josie into the conversation, Gwen headed for the ladies' room, cutting a slow swath through the drinkers at the bar, leaving laughter and discreetly admiring glances in her erotic wake.

Josie sat as still and silent as an anvil.

I said, 'I thought I saw you at the funeral home.'

'Excuse me?' She looked scared.

I said, ''I thought I saw you at the funeral home.'' When Dicky was there.' She had been on the fringe of a small crowd of the curious, staring at the sealed coffin on which Mr Butler had wasted a lot of money he couldn't afford. I hadn't given it any thought at the time. People had gathered on the cratered sidewalk in front of the Empire State Building, too, to gape at the carcase of King Kong.

I said, 'Don't worry. I won't tell anybody.'

She whispered, 'Dicky said you were real nice to him.'

'Beg pardon?'

Josie glanced at the bar. Her mother was throwing her head back to laugh with Wide Greg. 'Dicky Butler. He said you were nice to him.'

'I didn't know you knew him.'

'He was my friend.'

'I didn't realize.'

'He was the only person in this lousy town who'd talk nice to me.'

'What do you mean?' As if I didn't know. Scooter MacKay's *Clarion* – arbiter of a Newbury social order that placed Jervises on a rung with rocks and toads – hadn't even published the Army's hometown press release that Josie had made corporal.

Tears welled behind her glasses. 'He was nice to me. Like you were nice to him.'

142

'Well, we had something in common.'

But Josie didn't mean prison. 'He told me about the bear.'

'Oh, jeez, the bear. God he was neat.'

'Dicky said he should have hung out with you more. He said he wouldn't have gotten into so much trouble.'

I said something noncommittal.

Dicky had been blowing smoke. Josie Jervis's uncles did their time for crime. Dicky, for sheer brutality. A Jervis would crack your head with the express purpose of hijacking your car, or to remind you of payment owed for delivery. Dicky Butler would slug a man to see him fall. That this chubby, childlike Jervis escaper had befriended him was terrifying.

What in hell was I going to say to her? Get a blood test? What else could I say to her? I owed it to the poor girl. And anyone she ever fell in love with again.

'How long are you home for?'

'I gotta report tomorrow. I never used to come home. I had all this leave racked up. So when I met Dicky, I've been home a lot.'

'When did you see him last?'

She blushed, bright red. 'The night before.'

'The night before?'

'Uhhh. The morning. I mean I drove him home in the morning and he was going to catch some sleep – he was drinking wine all night. So I told him, catch some sleep and I'll see you later. He wanted to go on a picnic.'

'*That morning* he wanted to go on a picnic?'

'He'd never been on a picnic. Neither had I till I went in the Service. When the kids did it in school, I couldn't get to town. The school bus only picked me up for school days and Grandpa wouldn't let me anyhow. I told Dicky how these friends of mine at Bragg invited me along. So he wanted to try it.'

I was damned curious how a guy would ask his girlfriend on a picnic the same day he was planning to blow up Henry King's dam.

Cover? Josie for an alibi? A good alibi, if he had laid a slow fuse.

'Where were you going to have this picnic?'

'Out by the covered bridge. There's a rock in the middle of the river when the water's low.'

'Great picnic spot.' Sergeant Marian and I had used it more than once. A big flat rock we reached by stepping stones. It was usually private. Although last time, when the Newbury Driving Club came trotting along the river's edge in their antique carriages and period costume, we had frightened their horses.

The covered bridge was to hell and gone from Morris Mountain so that if Dicky had been planning an alibi he'd have had to lay an unbelievably slow fuse.

'Josie? I have to talk to you.'

'Here comes Mom. Please don't tell her. She doesn't know any of this.'

Gwen glided up with a fresh Bud someone had bought her. 'What are you two so palsy about?'

'Talking about Fort Bragg. I used to have buddies there.'

'I thought you were in the Navy.'

'They're good soldiers at Bragg, but I never met one who could walk on water.'

Josie hid a grin and headed for the ladies' room. Gwen said, 'Thanks for cheering her up.'

'She's a nice kid.'

'How come you never come up for a visit?'

I looked at her, a little surprised, and more than a little interested. 'I guess I always got the impression Buddy wouldn't like it.'

'Buddy's in fucking Indonesia.'

'Is that an invitation?'

Gwen drank from her bottle and studied me carefully. 'Maybe.'

'Sounds like the beer talking.'

'So bring beer.'

I should have made a date right then. But I was worrying that I hadn't yet warned Josie that Dicky Butler was HIV-positive. And wondering, had it been Dicky's red wine talking picnic the morning he blew King's dam?

Josie came back and leaned a fist on the table and said with a firmness that surprised me and stunned Gwen, 'Mom, would you excuse us a minute? I have to talk to Ben.'

14

I said, 'First I have to talk to you.'

She said, 'Dicky didn't do it.'

'Do what?'

'Blow up Mr King's dam.'

'Yes he did. We'll get to that in a minute. There's something much more important.'

'What could be more important? Don't you realize what I'm saying?'

'Dicky's dead. You're still alive. Keeping you that way is more important.'

Josie shook her head and smiled a private smile.

'What?' I asked.

'We didn't really do it. You know?'

The private smile made her unexpectedly womanly. Not sexily womanly like her mother – though there was a sexuality to it – but brimful of the wisdom women take for granted and guys keep thinking we'll get when we grow up, despite the example of our older friends.

'You're talking about the HIV,' she said.

'He told you?'

'Of course he told me. He was my friend.'

'Did he protect you?'

'You shouldn't doubt him, Ben.'

I most certainly did doubt him. On his best day Dicky had been a selfish bully. On his worst, a sociopath. And while I too had fallen more than once under the blinding power of romantic love, I didn't have to buy into Josie's take on a Dicky Butler whom I'd known since Josie's mother was a voluptuous middle-school girl-woman with a long red braid.

'We didn't really do it,' she repeated softly.

We talked for a long time. Her mother watched irritably from the bar. Sometimes Josie blushed. Sometimes she cried. She was eighteen years old, a chubby child who had held herself in check her whole life trying to survive the chaos of the Jervis trailer camp. He had been in his thirties, going on a hundred. My friend, she kept calling him. My friend. How she missed him. Dicky Butler had lifted her eyeglasses off her nose, massaged the red marks, and told her she was beautiful. Because he had called me his friend, and she had no more friends in Newbury, she told me in frank and reassuring detail how he had introduced her to safe sex.

'Dicky had a pamphlet. From the prison?' She giggled. 'And I had mine from the Army.'

They'd had good fun comparing them.

'Don't tell anybody.'

'Of course not.'

'Especially her.'

'That's between you and your Mom.'

Josie glanced her way and announced, matter-of-factly, 'She's jealous I'm talking to you.'

I glanced at the bar. 'Well, she's going to have to get used to having a sexy daughter.'

'I'm not sexy. I'm fat.'

'Sounds like Dicky thought you were sexy.'

I'm here to report that goodly-intentioned foot in the mouth does *not* taste more like dancing pump than sewer boot.

'I can't believe I'll never see him again.'

I said I was sorry.

She cried harder. Thank God she had introduced earlier a change of subject.

'What's this about Dicky didn't blow King's dam?'

'He couldn't have. He was too drunk.'

The boot in my mouth smothered the obvious retort: Considering the results, way too drunk.

'Maybe he slept it off?'

'I didn't get him home till almost noon.'

That was cutting it close. 'How drunk was he? Too drunk to walk?'

'He was staggering.'

'And the last you saw, you put him to bed?'

'No! His father was there. No, I dropped him at the gate.'
She hesitated.

I asked, 'Did he go to bed?'

'I don't think so.'

'Did he go in the house?'

'No, his father was always ragging him about drinking.
Dicky said he was going to sleep in the woods. It was a
beautiful day. Remember?'

'Glorious.'

'There was a spot down the stream where he liked to hang
out. We'd go down there sometimes if his dad was out in
the fields. It was beautiful – all cool and shady.'

'Sounds buggy,' I said, considering the garment doffing
required to compare safe-sex manuals.

'Not really. There were dragonflies. Dicky said they ate the
bugs.'

'Did his dad know he was seeing you?'

'Sort of. We never came right out and said it, but he'd see
my Mom's truck and must have known something.'

'So you think Dicky slept it off in the woods.'

'The last I saw, that's where he was heading.'

'But, Josie . . . What did he do when he woke up?'

'He was *staggering*. He could hardly walk down the hill.
There wasn't time to get sober enough to do what the cops
say he did.'

When *I* drink way too much, I usually pop wide awake
about two hours after I hit the hay – up and roaring to go.
Several hours later, of course, I'm begging for death. But
immediately upon awakening I'm fairly sharp. Sharp enough
to sneak an armload of Dad's dynamite down to the neighbour's dam? . . . Possibly, provided I had such a dad and such
a neighbour. It might even seem like a good idea at the time.

'What are you thinking?' Josie asked.

Maybe the threat of death had mellowed Dicky. Maybe all
those regrets he had spouted about his father had presaged
major changes. Maybe. 'Did you tell this to Trooper Moody?'

'Are you kidding? He hated Dicky's guts.'

'How about the state police detectives?'

Josie stared hard. 'Told *her* to take a hike. Leaning on me about US Army responsibility.'

'I thought no one knew about you.'

'Bitch pulled me over the night at the funeral home.'

Busy, busy Marian. 'What did she ask you?'

'When did I see Dicky last? Did he say he was going to do it? All that stuff.'

'What did you tell her?'

'Nothing.' High-school diploma and corporal's stripes aside, she was still a Jervis. 'What do you think?' she asked again.

'I'm sorry. I think it's very hard to believe that he didn't accidentally kill himself while blowing up the dam.'

'You don't get it,' she said. 'I thought you'd understand, being his friend.'

'Understand what?'

'That it wasn't him.'

All I understood was that it certainly looked like it was him. And it was a Dicky thing to do. Or was it?

Maybe my mouth dropped a little. She demanded, 'What? What are you thinking?'

His girlfriend didn't think he did it.

His father didn't think he did it.

And actually, in one way it wasn't at all a Dicky thing to do. He wasn't a sneak-attack guy. He would punch you in the face, not in the back.

'If he didn't do it, how did he end up under it?'

'Maybe he was sleeping there instead of the woods.'

'On King's property?'

'He was drunk.'

'That's a bit of a walk for a drunk.'

'Maybe he took a swim in the lake. Then climbed out and fell asleep and it blew up on him.'

But he had been wearing boots, I remembered. And gloves. 'Assuming it did. Who blew it up?'

'His father.'

'His father?' My client, whose innocence I was supposed to prove. 'Why do you say that?'

'Who else? He's in jail, right?'

'The difference between jail and prison is the people in jail haven't been convicted yet.' A fine distinction, but one a Jervis child should appreciate. 'And he's charged with helping Dicky. Conspiracy for helping him, and accessory to murder for accidentally killing him.'

'He didn't help Dicky. He did it himself. Who else would have done it? He hated Mr King.'

'Mr Butler says he didn't do it.' Of course, he also said he knew for a fact that Dicky didn't do it.

Someone fired up the juke box. Josie got teary again. 'Dicky's favourite song.' She sang with it in the strong contralto she had inherited from her mother, ' ". . . Now I am guilty of something I hope you never do. 'Cause there's nothing any sadder than losing yourself in love." '

When it was over, and Megadeth started blasting a White Birch standard, I asked, 'Did Dicky tell you anything that would implicate his father?'

'Not exactly,' she answered carefully. 'But he did say how much his dad hated King.'

'What do you do with all this?' I asked.

'Nothing.'

'Nothing?'

'It was an accident. His father didn't mean to kill him. And if he did, knowing he did will be a horrible punishment.'

'Do you really believe this, Josie? Or do you just want to?'

'Hey, I don't care if Dicky blew up some rich bastard's dam. And I sure can't blame his poor father for an accident. He's dead either way.'

Chubby cheeks, eyeglasses and pressed Army fatigues notwithstanding, Josie was Gwen Jervis's daughter. Simultaneously cold and passionate. A great friend. Or a terrible enemy.

'Why are you telling me this?'

'I didn't come looking for you. You asked. You were his friend. Who else would I tell?'

'You could tell your mother.'

'What for?'

'Comfort. Don't underestimate her. She's one of the smarter people I know.'

'She's really hot for you.'

'Beg pardon?'

'I said my Mom is really hot for you.'

I thought she'd said that. 'Your mother and I go back a long way,' I answered, firmly. 'And there's been times we were special friends – times we stood up for each other.'

'Because you're screwing her?'

'What?'

Josie gave me a neutral smile. 'You heard me.'

Unexpectedly intimate with the young soldier, thanks to Dicky Butler, it still felt strange to say, 'I haven't slept with your Mom since I was fourteen years old.'

'Really?'

'Really,' I said, rocketed in memory to a hot summer night; an icy six-pack Pink had thrust grinning into my hands; a wild and worldly grown-up older girl, leading me into the dark, twining a long red braid around my neck, laughing at my excitement and mocking my fear. For which I would be forever grateful.

'I was sure you were.'

'What in hell gave you that idea?'

'Right after I went into the Service she got all silly. Started wearing makeup again and growing her hair like a teenager. I thought she was sleeping with you.'

'No such luck,' I said, making sure I smiled.

'Are you telling me the truth? Because I told you the truth. I told you stuff I never told anybody but Dicky.'

'I know that. And I'm flattered. I am telling you the truth. I don't lie. And if you think about it, I have no reason to lie.'

'Well, she was sleeping with somebody and it wasn't my dad because he was out in the Gulf.'

Buddy Jervis – he and Gwen were not-so-distant cousins – was apt to forget his mailing address while working oil rigs in distant fields. Particularly when it came to sending cheques. My sympathies and loyalties lay with Gwen. Nevertheless, it seemed a moment to be avuncular.

'Your parents have been together a long time.'

That was a big help. Josie started crying, again. 'I thought it would be like that with Dicky.'

Around my second boot in mouth I mumbled something brilliant like, 'I'll bet.'

'Some people are HIV a long time.'

More than are immune to dynamite.

Gwen came back to the table with a dangerous glint in her eye. I defused it with a private glance that things were better with Josie.

I went home and combed a salad out of the garden, which July's rains had choked with weeds.

DaNang didn't want any. I tipped several pounds of dry food in the washtub we were using for a bowl and freshened his water. He watched me with a baleful eye and made an angry sound.

'What the hell are you growling about?'

He stared. I stared. Suddenly his tail thumped for Alison in the doorway.

'That's his whine, not his growl.'

'Sounded like a growl to me. Why's he whining?'

'He likes a can of liverwurst on his dry food.'

'Since when?'

'Couple of days ago. I tried it. He liked it.'

'Liverwurst doesn't come in cans.'

She climbed on to a counter and opened a high cupboard door. 'Here.'

'That is *not* liverwurst. That is *pâté de fois gras*.' The remains of a Fraser-Morris care package from my friend Rita, whose generosity was exceeded only by her mobility.

'Well, you're almost out. You're going to have to get some more.'

The phone rang before I fed her to him.

'Yes!'

'Ben, this is Julia Devlin.' Wielding her used-to-being-obeyed voice.

'Hey. How are you?'

'Henry heard you called at the gate.' She made it sound like I'd been lurking there with a grenade launcher.

'I was in the neighbourhood. Had something I wanted to talk to him about.'

'Come up. We're having a little cookout.'

Orders roared by naval commanders dodging torpedoes cut more slack than that supper invitation.

'I'll bring the salad.'

15

I assumed that 'a little cookout' at the King manse meant barbecue for thirty. But little it was – family night: just Henry King and Mrs King; Josh Wiggens, half in the bag; Bertram Wills, holding his side and chuckling, 'Very funny, Henry,' at diplomatic intervals; and Julia; and me. And the reinstated butler, of course, Jenkins, dressed down in blazer and white flannels to shuttle ingredients to the aproned and chef-hatted master of the house who was presiding over an elaborate gas-fired brick grill.

Bob Dylan not withstanding, Fox Trot's architect should have had a weatherman tell him which way the wind blew. Or maybe he didn't listen. Most architects don't. Which is why savvy homebuilders keep them under house arrest and engage landscape designers to do the outside. King hadn't, and was paying the price.

Smoke billowed across his hungry audience into the house, instead of away from it. Flames leaped at his face. He had to retreat off the patio and, standing on the grass, lean over the backside of the grill to grope for the food somewhere in the conflagration. Oddly, it didn't seem to diminish his pleasure.

No clue, so far, about my presence. But while I waited, what a treat! A perfect summer evening. Two lovely women – blonde Mrs King camera-ready, every bit the trophy wife, and Julia, the great man's loyal retainer, demurely sexy in black cotton.

Ex-spy Wiggens sober enough to be wittily acerbic; former-secretary Wills a storehouse of insider stories, which he directed at Mrs King under the guise of entertaining the group. Excellent Pinot Noir, Calera, lightly chilled in deference to the temperature. Glimpses of a sunset to die for. And ample cold hors d'oeuvres, while things went to hell at the grill.

I leaned close to Mrs King and inquired, discreetly, whether her husband might want some help. Some guys do, some definitely don't.

'He would like to bond,' she whispered back, apparently in all seriousness. It's one of the ways women account for why men cook outdoors. So I let the butler refill my glass – asked quietly for a spray bottle of the sort used to mist houseplants – and dutifully rose to bond with my host. He greeted me with a game grin.

'The wind's in the wrong direction.'

'Usually is.'

'If it came from there' – he pointed east – 'it would be perfect.'

It would also be raining. Information I kept to myself.

King sacrificed the hair on his arm to paint a massive veal chop with an orange-coloured sauce. I knew damned well he didn't want to hear that it was time to turn it.

He turned to me, instead. 'What did you want to see me about?'

Talking to him was like facing a split-screen ThinkPad: Document One was a jolly gent enjoying late middle age as only the wealthy can – taking for granted that come evening's end he would wash the barbecue smoke out of his hair in a marble shower while his luscious wife scrubbed his back and bankers compounded his interest; Document Two, the shrewd operator who could gobble rewards all night and still wake up hungry.

I pressed '1' for the jolly-gent option. 'Mr Butler's in the Plainfield jail.'

'I know that. Conspiracy to dynamite my dam and accessory to murder.'

'I was wondering if you'd help spring him.'

'I beg your pardon?'

'There's no conspiracy. Dicky did it himself. And killed himself by accident.'

154

He didn't argue that. He only said, 'How would I "spring" him, even if I wanted to, which I don't?'

'Offer to pay for his defence.'

'*Pay* for his defence? Me? What good would that do?'

'It would certainly catch the court's attention. At least the judge would reconsider bail.'

'Isn't the community safer with him under lock and key?'

'He's a farmer, sitting in jail, worrying about his stock.'

'His neighbour's taking care of the cows.'

'And I've got his dog. And the neighbour's got his own farm to run. But that's not the point. The poor man just shouldn't be locked up. I saw him today. He's deteriorating badly.'

'Perhaps he should be transferred to a prison hospital.'

'The shrink feels he's better off in a local jail where he can have visitors. There's a couple of Vietnam vets have been stopping by. But she also feels he'll crack up in a week if we can't get him out.'

'Do you see down there, what they did to my lake?'

I saw a gathering of large yellow machines that rented for ten dollars a minute, each. '"They" didn't do that. Dicky did that. And died doing it. The poor guy's lost his only child. He's suffered plenty. Help me get him out.'

'You're crazy.'

'I know it sounds crazy. But look at it this way. You'll look like a hero. Rich man on the hill cares about the common man.'

King looked at me. The jolly gent of late middle age drifted off on the smoke. 'I'm not running for public office, Mr Abbott. I don't give a flying fuck what the common man thinks of me.'

'Do you want to testify at a public trial?' I asked the hungry diplomat.

'I'm not looking forward to it, but I'll do my duty as a citizen.'

'Do you really want to sit in a witness stand while Ira Roth picks through the details of your land feud?'

'Are you threatening me?' He got an angry, ugly look on his face.

I was angry, too. What was going on just wasn't right. 'I don't have to threaten you. I'm telling you what's going to happen.'

'And what's going to happen?' he demanded.

Julia Devlin stirred in the corner of my eye, watching intently, while pretending to listen to whatever Mrs King was saying to her and Bert Wills. Josh Wiggens noticed her interest, lowered his glass, and tracked her gaze towards me, his face hardening.

'Abbott, I asked are you threatening me?'

A newspaper reporter once told me he'd been taught to ask the hardest question first. I asked King, 'Do the people you report to want your business scrutinized in a public trial?'

Henry King did a beautiful job of covering his surprise. He'd have been hell across a poker table. And, in fact, I did not know for sure whether my spy barb had gone home. Until he started fencing.

'My clients are even less impressed by the common man than I am.'

'All of them?'

'Don't act naïve. You played this game before you ran home with your tail between your legs. Did you notice the man in the street for even one *second* when you plundered the financial markets?'

'His representatives noticed me,' I replied. 'It took them a while, but they caught on. And when they did, they didn't display much of a sense of humour about it. Or much tolerance. Something you might keep in mind.'

'Ah, but you committed the cardinal sin,' King smiled.

'You mean I got caught.'

'Much worse. You lost faith in yourself.'

He was an excellent fencer. He had struck home with that one and I was astonished how thoroughly he had had me investigated. You couldn't get what he knew by reading my trial transcript. Much less the newspapers.

'When *you're* caught I doubt that your "clients" will grant you a trial. They'll destroy you behind your back. They'll expose your . . . Gee, I'm a little speechless. The only word that comes to mind is "treachery" and it sounds so melo-dramatic.'

For a moment he looked like he'd run me through with his barbecue fork. Instead, he probed my guard. 'I'm told you refused to turn state's evidence. You could have saved yourself. Why didn't you testify?'

'I was taught not to rat.'

'In prison?'

'Prep school.'

'The word on the Street is you were too dumb to turn in the woman who set you up.'

'Always been a sucker for a pretty face.'

'She's running one of the hottest shops on the Street and you're stuck in Newbury.'

'And *you* have ordered Julia to go dredging up my past, again, to find something to use against me so I'd stop helping Mr Butler.'

King ignored that. 'I'm also told that the insider case sucked and you didn't really break the law.'

'I violated the spirit of the law. I got what I deserved.'

'Sounds to me like you spread your knees and took it.' Ira Roth had blamed an upbringing overly influenced by Aunt Connie's 'Puritan claptrap'. I didn't expect either high flyer to understand the relief it had been to admit the crime. To myself. And do the time. For myself.

'Paid in full, Henry. No debts. No guilt. Nothing to hide.'

'What is that supposed to mean?'

'It means you can't find anything to use against me. Clean slate.'

'Your "purity" gives you rights to hassle me?'

'I'm not threatening to rat you out. I'm only reminding you that you'll stand better with your clients by helping Mr Butler avoid a trial.'

'That's not a threat?'

'You want a threat? Here's a threat, you arrogant son of a bitch: find some other way to steal Mr Butler's farm.'

'Henry!' called his wife. 'It's burning.'

'Oh, shit! Now look what you made me do.'

Jenkins rushed forward. I relieved him of the spray bottle

157

and doused the flames, gently so as not to scatter ashes on the meat.

I cooled off, myself, in the process. King, too, seemed willing to back down a little and Gentleman Henry expressed delight. 'That's fantastic.'

Welcome to the country.

Jenkins stepped in to grill the vegetables – a skill even the most rabid outdoor cook will concede. King and I retreated to the wet bar, where he washed his hands and scrubbed his fingernails with a brush, while I dabbed my face with a wet paper towel.

'So I'm an arrogant son of a bitch?'

'I apologize. That was no way to talk to my host.'

'And you probably think I'm vulgar, too. And crude. And my house is ostentatious.'

'Actually, I kind of like your house.'

'Of course you'd never "insult your host". But you think it. I know that. All you people think it. All you people who don't know how great it feels. I remember President Nixon used to keep fires burning in the White House fireplaces all summer long with the air conditioning blasting about thirty-two degrees, the President standing in front of the fire rubbing his hands, saying, "They laugh at me because I burn the fireplaces. They don't know how great it is to wake up to all this stuff and say to yourself, I did it, Mister. I made it. I earned it. I came out of shit and look what I got." It was a great lesson, Ben. I used to be embarrassed about coming from trash. Took voice lessons so I'd sound like you or some English lord. Even hired over-the-hill socialites to teach me table manners. Waste of money. Nixon was right. I *like* being vulgar.'

He made it sound like fun.

We ate under the sky while Venus rose, warm and buttery as the veal, which Jenkins, in his wisdom, had marinaded so thoroughly that even strong men bonding couldn't dry it out.

'Julia,' King said suddenly. She was listening to Josh and didn't hear. 'Julia! Front and centre!'

'Yes, Henry?'

'Ben's asking me something really odd.'

Ben again, no longer Abbott, a good sign that our truce was holding. Still, Julia glanced at me warily. As did Josh Wiggens, who had been watching me with an expression I had seen occasionally in my own mirror. Could he be in love with Julia – obsessed with her – and wondering if I was competition? I looked over at King. If the musical beds were that complicated, one had to sympathize with Fox Trot's chambermaids.

King was saying to Julia, 'He wants me to pay for that crazy old farmer's defence. What do you think?'

'It might be a way to put a stop to all this.'

'Are you serious?'

'Well, yes. I mean –'

King shook his head. 'Christ, Julia, there are times I wonder about your judgement.'

She faced him bravely, betrayed by a little catch in her voice. 'It's not a bad idea, Henry. Provided Ben can talk sense into him and get him to agree to lay off and stop bothering us.'

Wills added, 'Sounds good to me, Henry,' and Mrs King nodded vigorous agreement.

'Can you do that, Ben? Get him to stop bothering me?'

'I would be delighted to try.'

'We would want that lease cleared up at the same time,' King said.

'What do you mean cleared up?'

'Cancelled,' snapped Josh Wiggens.

King looked at Julia, demanding her response. She looked down at her plate, then up, her face hardening. 'In exchange for paying his lawyers.'

'That's my girl. What do you think of that, Ben? I'll buy him the best lawyers money can buy.'

I looked at Mrs King, and guessed by her expression that she thought King's offer was as skeezy as I did. She glanced sidelong at Bert Wills. The diplomat dropped a hand to his side, but failed to produce any lockjaw laughs.

'That won't work,' I told King.

'Why not? It's a clear choice. Rot in jail or give me back my land.'

'He won't see it that way. You'll both be right back where you started.'

'Final offer, Ben.' He was joined in his cold expression by Josh Wiggens.

I found it easy to be cold, too. Nothing they were offering would save Mr Butler's sanity. 'You'll have to do much better.'

'I don't *have* to do anything,' King reminded me. 'You're the one asking favours.'

Mrs King shot an uncharacteristically demanding look at Bert Wills, who screwed up his courage to say, 'It's possible, Henry, that Ben is bearing favours as well. It would be excellent to put all this behind us.'

'Do not surrender!' said Josh Wiggens. 'Butler's a menace. Bail will only encourage him.'

'He was born on that land,' I said.

'That doesn't give him the right to torment Henry King.'

That pretty much ended all conversation. We got through salad and cheese. I passed on coffee and thanked Mrs King for a splendid cookout. Julia Devlin said, 'I'll walk you out.'

And once alone in the foyer, she said, 'Do you mind me asking why you're so involved with Mr Butler?'

'You two got me into this last March. I know he's difficult, but he's been abused all along. And right now, I'm trying to keep a foolish promise that I'd keep him out of jail.'

'How's he paying you?'

'I told you, he's not. Which is all right for a while. But if the charges go to trial, it's going to be more than Tim Hall can handle for free. So we really need help. And like I said in there, the act of Henry King supporting Butler would probably make the state's attorney lean on the state police to drop it.'

'Sounds awfully cosy.'

'Locally cosy, as opposed to nationally cosy.'

'What is that supposed to mean?'

'It means that just as your people leaned on the ME to quash the thing, we're trying to convince the state's attorney that Connecticut's state troopers have better things to do with their time and money than hound a poor old war vet who just wants to be let alone on his farm.'

'Henry wants that farm.'

'I already warned "Henry" if he wants to steal Mr Butler's farm, find some other way to do it.'

The scariest thing was she didn't bother denying the implication. All she said was, 'He really would relocate Mr Butler. I heard about a farm on Merry Mountain.'

'It's owned by Merry River Glen Ski Club. Old WASPs who started on wooden skis with a steam-powered lift. They'll never sell. Neither will Butler.'

Julia said, 'I feel sorry for Mr Butler. I'll do what I can to help.'

I was surprised. And grateful. Grateful because Henry King really was the key to Butler's freedom. Surprised, because Julia had offered the first crack I had seen in the monolith that was Henry King Incorporated. (Mrs King's opinion didn't count, while Bert Wills had mustered his tentative resistance only to please her.)

'I appreciate your bravery.'

Julia shrugged off the risk. 'Part of my job is to protect Henry from himself. I'll see what I can do.' She extended her hand and we shook. 'Good seeing you, Ben. Sorry it turned to hardball.'

'Can I ask *you* something?'

'What?'

'Tell me if I'm way off base, but why do you let him treat you that way?'

'You *are* off base,' she said coolly.

'Consider me stealing second. I think you deserve better.'

She wrapped her arms under her breasts. 'Yeah? Why's that?'

Now I had really stepped into it. '. . . OK, no one deserves to be bullied and embarrassed by their boss. How can you defend yourself?'

'Yeah, well maybe it doesn't seem like that big a deal to me. OK?'

'OK . . . Well, thanks for dinner. And for helping.'

'You're welcome.' She opened the door and I stepped into the night. 'Hey, Ben?'

'What?' I turned. She was struggling to smile. I waited. She stared at the dark behind my shoulder. 'What?' I moved towards her. She glanced back into the house and then the words came out in a rush.

'Hey, maybe I can call you for a beer at the Drover?'

'Terrific. I mean – I'd like that very much.'

'Well, OK. So . . . OK.'

'And the guest room is yours anytime.'

'Yeah, well, thanks, but . . . You know.'

'But I have to warn you, DaNang might crawl in with you.'

'Who is DaNang?'

'Mr Butler's dog.'

'No problem. I like dogs.'

I walked to my car, wondering where to rent a dog suit.

The car was parked in shadow at the edge of the motor court and I saw a shadow leaning on the trunk. Josh Wiggens, swirling the dregs in his glass.

'Come on down to the office. Let's have a drink.'

I didn't want a drink. But I did want to hear why he was so vehemently against helping Mr Butler.

We walked the lighted path to the old Zarega house, and entered through a side door into a panelled study he had appropriated for his office. It had an eight-line phone, a modemed laptop, and a mini fax-printer. All of which looked like it could be packed up and carried away in about two minutes.

Even his bar was portable, a neat little affair in a brass-trimmed teak box.

'You drink bourbon, I believe.'

Hardly a state secret, but he seemed to want me to know that he knew.

He was drinking Scotch. He poured generously. '*Slange*.'

'*Slange-va*.' (I had a client once who was trying to buy the Isle of Skye.)

We took comfortable easy chairs in front of a screened slider, open to the cool bug-song night, and we talked about the weather and Newbury and the prospects of a colourful fall. He said he was happy to be home to New England. Exeter, he explained. And Yale. No surprises there.

'I understand you were with Naval Intelligence.'

I gave him my standard answer: 'A contradiction of terms.'

He'd heard it before and didn't waste a smile. 'Did you know the Captain?'

'Dozens. We had them climbing out of the bilges.'

'This one became an admiral.'

'Reagan's six-hundred-ship navy made a lot of admirals. Most of them are on the beach now.'

'Not this one.'

'Did you know Aldrich Ames?' I asked.

Wiggens nodded. And gave me *his* standard answers when I asked, 'Was he as bad as they say?'

'Worse.'

'Was the damage that bad?'

'Much worse.'

'Are you retired?'

'Spit out,' he answered bitterly, drinking deep and rising to fill his glass. I watched his hand shake and thought how two of the easier covers to affect are bitterness and drunkenness.

'But you landed on your feet.'

'"Chief" of security for Henry King Incorporated?' he retorted gloomily.

'I don't get the impression that King is any less powerful than he was when he was official.'

'It's Henry's power, not mine. I'm just a hired hand.'

Yes, but after the explosion, he'd had a gun in his belt and Federal agents calling him 'Sir'.

I said, 'If Henry is doing what I think he is doing, you're in the thick of major events.'

'Like what?'

'That ceramic-engine deal sounds bigtime.'

Wiggens shrugged, noncommittally. A slant of wind bore chilly night air down the hill. He went to a bedroom and reappeared shrugging into a blue cashmere cardigan someone had matched to his eyes. 'You want a sweater?'

'No thanks.'

'Blood's thin. Too many years in the tropics.'

I said, 'Because King's "enterprises", shall we say, are bigtime, it would be simple to put an end to all this misery by helping Mr Butler. The man's had a hard life – served his country. Do you know, he was wounded three times in Vietnam?'

If Henry King displayed the arrogance of power, Josh projected a mafioso's insolence – the haughty arrogance of a man prepared to do violence. Here it came on a smile that gleamed like a knife: 'He's not the only man who went to war, Ben. Not the only man to serve his country.'

I felt my temper rise. The warrior class – better at starting wars than finishing them. Volunteer game-players who enjoyed privileges, and choices, not shared by the infantry.

'I don't mean to question *your* accomplishments, Josh. Or your bravery and patriotism. But if you suffered, then you know what he's been through. And if you didn't suffer, maybe you got close enough to guess.'

'Been there, done that, Ben. Which is more than I can say for your record.'

'I'm not going to apologize because my generation missed out on Vietnam.'

'What's your excuse for missing the party in Afghanistan?'

'I don't recall an invitation to the "party" in Afghanistan. And I can't say that looking at what's left of it speaks highly for the crashers.'

'We destroyed the Soviet Union in Afghanistan.'

'You bankrolled heroin networks and supplied every terrorist on the planet with Stinger missiles.'

'Ben, I'm going to give you some advice.' Suddenly I was facing a very sober man.

'What's that, Josh?'

'Stay out of it.'

I waited.

That was it. An icy threat – if it was a threat at all.

Ordinarily, I counterpunched threats. But Josh Wiggens had left me nothing to punch. He smiled. He knew it and I knew it.

164

I was particularly impressed by what he didn't say. He didn't say what would happen to me or who would do it. He didn't claim to command Company killers or government agents. He didn't remind me that my elderly aunt lived alone in a big house. Or that Alison rode her bike blithely home from horseback-riding lessons. He left it all to my imagination.

I was still sitting there wondering how the hell to impress him back when he revealed the chink in his armour that I had noticed earlier.

'And stay away from Julia.'

'Or what?'

'Good night, Ben.'

He smiled again. Still cool, but not totally invulnerable.

I said, 'You're really hung up on her, aren't you?'

His eyes flashed and for a second I thought he was going to stand up swinging. I said, 'I know the feeling. Been there, bought the T-shirt.'

'Good night,' he repeated, fully recovered and cold as steel.

Not a bad night's work, so far, I thought, as I headed down the driveway: I had Julia's pledge to try to persuade Henry King to help free Mr Butler; some new insights into the dynamics of the Fox Trot household; and a vague feeling I'd overestimated King's ceramic-engine dealings. But I still didn't know why Josh Wiggens was so against Mr Butler. Nor what made him feel so vulnerable that he had to threaten me.

The gatehouse was dark. Motion detectors turned on the floodlights and the gate opened to let me out. I drove a quarter mile, parked in a cow-bar indent in the stone wall, and let the air out of my left rear tyre. Then I sprayed my socks and cuffs with OFF!, took a cap from the trunk, and work gloves, which I wore to spread the strands of Fox Trot's electric deer fence.

When my eyes were used to the starlight, I skirted the gatehouse, climbed the meadow and joined the driveway where it entered the woods. When I saw the faint gleam of the road spikes, I swung into the woods again and emerged uphill from them.

A few lights still shone in the main house. Upstairs windows, mostly. The Zarega house was dark. I took a chance that the floodlights were not set to motion detectors, as the place would look like Times Square every time a raccoon strolled by, and headed towards dimly lit french doors.

They opened on the library. Henry King was sitting alone at a table, hunched over a book like a peasant eating porridge.

Over in the east wing, an array of windows suddenly went dark. Master bedroom suite: Mrs King had just turned out her lights. Overhead a single window went dark. Julia, possibly. Or maybe Bert Wills, though I thought his former eminence deserved a larger guest room.

I was standing outside the pool of light cast by the remaining windows, secure in the darkness behind me, when a telephone rang. King jumped up from his book and answered it. I glided closer, across a terrace and along the wall. I could hear his phony English accent had gotten stronger and guessed he was talking to a Brit. He didn't sound pleased. Nor did he sound in control of the situation.

I heard a noise behind me. Further down the terrace, a dark door opened. I pressed into the shadows. A figure in flowing white floated across the flagstones, on to the lawn and faded, silent and ghostly, towards the sunken garden.

King hung up abruptly. I heard glass clink and when I stole a look, I saw him pouring brandy into a snifter beside his book. He took a deep slug and sat heavily. I backed into the shadows and off the terrace on to the lawn where I angled towards the far side of the sunken garden.

When I saw the flow of white, I sank to the wet grass and crawled to the edge of the garden and looked down. Rose perfume lifted from its depths and waxy white impatiens lined the paths, glowing like footlights. On a bench in the middle sat Mrs King in a long, white nightgown. From the shadows materialized a low bulky shape. A dog, I wondered. No. It was human, creeping along the grass path. Mrs King gasped. It lunged at her feet.

'Madam!'

'Jenkins, get up.'

Head bowed in rigid silhouette, he asked, 'Can Madam forgive the intrusion? The grass is wet. I've brought Madam little boots. Shall I put them on for Madam?'

It was a while before she repeated, 'Get up!'

Jenkins sprang upright, only to bow again with the elaborate dignity of a functioning psychotic. Mrs King sounded used to it. 'Thank you, Jenkins. Go in the house.'

'Will Madam be safe alone here in the dark?'

'Perfectly, Jenkins. Good night.'

'Shall I carry Madam's shoes?'

'Yes, here. Thank you.'

'Madam.'

Clutching her shoes to his face, the butler backed into the dark, backed up the garden stairs, and marched stiffly towards the distant loom of the house.

Mrs King settled back with a sigh. She studied the starry sky. She cupped her watch. After a while, I saw a tall figure coming across the lawn. More footwear? Glancing over his shoulder, he scuttled down the stone steps, and made his way familiarly, cutting a dark silhouette against the glow of the white impatiens that lined the path to Mrs King's bench. They embraced. I heard whispers, then her voice, growing urgent, 'You must stand up to him. You must. For me. And for you. For *us*.'

To the muffled reply, she said, 'Be brave.'

Silence. Then she said, 'I can't wait that long. He's making too many mistakes. I want to settle before he's ruined.'

A muffled reply. It sounded like a plea.

Mrs King said, 'Yes. I love you, too. More than anything. You've saved my life.'

Stand up and kiss her, I thought. Let me see your face. But instead of him standing up, she sank back on the bench and tugged him on top of her.

I debated crawling closer; this was turning a bit voyeuristic for my taste. Mrs King saved me the trouble with a joyous, 'Oh Bert!'

I got out of there, retraced my route to the car, screwed a flat-fixer aerosol can to my alibi tyre, and drove home. Bert cuckolding his host and boss was no surprise. Jenkins worshipping her feet was. And though I couldn't see how the knowledge would get Mr Butler out of jail, it sounded like Mrs King had lost faith in her husband's career.

16

There were two messages on my answering machine. The first from Mr Butler: 'Ben? You there? *Ben?* Jesus. I gotta see you. I'm goin' nuts in here.'

The second was unusual. Connie didn't like answering machines. 'Benjamin. This is your Aunt Connie. Please call me the instant you get this message.'

I checked the front window to see if her lights were on and ran across the street. A china cup and saucer sat on the big, round wooden kitchen table – she won't use a mug, won't allow any in the house. 'Connie?'

She came shuffling down the pantry hall, dressed for bed in a nightcap, a high-necked flannel robe and slippers she'd gotten for free on an airplane.

'Are you OK?'

'Of course I'm OK.'

I sat down heavily, thoroughly spooked by the time bomb Josh Wiggens had lodged in my brain. 'Where were you?'

'In the facilities, where do you think I was?'

While direct, even blunt in important matters, she was raised genteelly early in the century. 'Difficulties' is her polite word for impending bankruptcy, 'festivities' for lovemaking. While a dog chasing a raccoon through her delphiniums would call forth a furious, 'Oh shoot!'

'Your message sounded important.'

'Farmer Butler telephoned from the jailhouse. He's terribly upset.'

'Why did he call you?'

'He said you didn't return his call.'

'I just got his message.'

'Then what are you sitting there for?' She levelled an imperious finger at the rotary dial telephone.

The night man at the county jail said it was way past lights out. Compared to most of the prisoners held for trial or sobering up, however, the farmer must have been a pleasant change, and the guard agreed to pass a message that I'd visit in the morning.

'Appreciate that. Just please don't wake him.'

'He's wide awake. He don't sleep none.'

'Maybe I could talk to him now?'

'Sorry. That I can't do.'

Suddenly I heard metal banging. Then Mr Butler shouting, 'That for me? That for me?'

'Pipe down in there,' the guard roared.

I said, 'Let me talk to him.'

'No way.'

'*Hey, is that for me?*'

I said, 'Don't hang up. Let me talk to him, I'll calm him down for you.'

'Hold on.'

It took a few minutes. I heard the cell door clang, and the guard warning him, 'Hold still!'

'You don't got to cuff me, man. I'm just –'

'Hold still! . . . OK. Two minutes.'

'Ben?'

'Right here, Mr Butler.'

'Ben. I gotta get out of here. I'm going crazy.'

I tried to talk him down, but our two minutes was soon up and I could hear him struggling with the guard. I called, 'I'll see you in the morning, I'll see you in the morning,' until the phone went dead.

Connie touched my shoulder. 'Your hands are shaking.'

'Got any more cocoa?'

She lit the stove, a Wel-Maid gas range she had installed the year they paved Main Street. 'Why is he calling you, Ben?'

'Mainly because he doesn't know who else to call.'

'Whom else.'

'Whom else. He was alone all those years, then suddenly he had Dicky back in a way he'd never had him before – working the farm. I think he was just getting over the habit of being alone, when suddenly he's really alone and in trouble.'

I settled on to a sturdy kitchen chair and tried to draw peace from the old walls. When, ultimately, Connie's home becomes the Newbury Historical Society's museum, about all they will have to do is hang out a sign that says, Museum. Any room in the house could establish a To-The-Trade-Only dealer on Bleecker Street: Chinese antiques plundered by Constantine Abbott's sea captains; European purchased by his canal-builder, whaler and railroad-tycoon descendants; Americana inherited as the bloodlines thinned, narrowing down to this last vigorous but childless old lady.

My house – my mother's house, that is – was actually much older, but events seemed bigger in Connie's mansion. And there's more continuity: Abbott House had twice passed out of the family when financial panics had driven merchant ancestors into farming or the ministry; no one but Connie's Abbotts had ever slept under this roof. At this table their countless cooks and housekeepers had planned a hundred thousand meals. Abbott women, their nieces and their neighbours had rolled bandages for the Civil War. The Newbury Hunt had gathered for stirrup cups and scones pulled fresh from the iron doors that studded the brick fireplace.

'Doesn't the insufferable Ira still handle his affairs?'

'Ira used to get Dicky out of trouble, which I never understood. He's not exactly Attorney Charitable.'

'Guilt,' said Connie. 'Ira Roth was a reserve officer after Korea. When he was called up for Vietnam, it would have meant sacrificing his practice, so he weaselled out of it, somehow. Helping a wounded war hero was his penance.'

'Ira's busy, right. He handed him off to Tim Hall.'

'Tim Hall is coming along, though hardly the man his father was.'

'Mr Butler embraces your prejudices. Darned fool keeps things from Tim.'

'It's a good thing *you've* stepped in.' Connie studied her hands a moment. They were wrinkled, of course, but

171

remarkably long and elegant. '. . . If raising bond is a problem perhaps I can help.'

'It's two million dollars, Connie. The bondsmen won't touch it with a rake.'

'*Two million*?'

'Accessory's a very heavy charge. Plus, the state's attorney convinced the magistrate he's dangerous. Which he isn't.'

'He *was* a Special Forces soldier.'

'He hasn't blown up anything since the war, except ledge and tree stumps.'

'But he knows how.'

'Whose side are you on?'

'I'm on the side of sanity,' she said tartly. 'And it seems to me you could use a devil's advocate.'

'I'll tell you what, Devil. Just between you, me and the lamppost.'

'I've not heard that expression in years.'

'Heard it just the other night at the Drover.'

'From Ms Devlin?'

'How?' Pinkerton Investigation Services and Kroll Associates combined couldn't match her sources when it came to keeping track of me.

'Lamppost . . . ?'

'When the dam blew? My first thought was Mr Butler did it.'

'You see?'

'I'm having second thoughts. In fact . . .' I studied the floor. The linoleum, laid shortly after the material was invented, was holding up nicely thanks to weekly waxing and a light tread. Even the Kitchen-Aid dishwasher was antique. The Smithsonian has offered Connie a new one if they could display hers in Washington.

'In fact what?'

'I'm not even sure Dicky did it.' I looked at Connie to gauge her reaction. Sceptical. Head cocked like a blue jay watching a cat yawn.

'What do you mean?'

'Something's felt off base to me from the second I found

172

Dicky dead. I still can't put my finger on it. But aside from that, when I add up how drunk Josie said –'

'Josie?'

'Jervis.'

'Good lord,' Connie shuddered.

'Gwen's daughter.'

'I *know* she's Gwen's daughter. I had blotted from my mind that they keep reproducing.'

'Josie's all right.'

'Yes, I take that back. She's doing nicely in the Army – what does she have to do with Dicky Butler?'

I explained – skimming over the nitty gritty – that Josie had told me he was dead drunk, how they had planned a picnic that afternoon, and that he was wearing his favourite cowboy boots.

'But if he was drunk, how did he do it? Can you imagine him lugging the dynamite all the way down the hill and around the lake? Those boxes run fifty pounds apiece.'

Connie thought on that. 'He could have moved the dynamite the night before, in the dark. *Before* he went carousing with Josie. That would explain why he wasn't seen. When he came home inebriated, he simply staggered down to the dam to ignite the explosives. Which would explain, also, the mistake that killed him.' She crossed her arms in minor triumph.

'Except for two things.'

'Which are?'

'One I can't put my finger on. Something about his body.'

'What's the other?'

'Dynamite wasn't Dicky's way. He was a violent brawler, not a schemer. He'd wade in swinging.'

'Not likely with all the guards Henry King has hired.'

'Guards wouldn't scare him. He'd run 'em over with his truck if he were hellbent to get his hands on King.'

'Benjamin, you've always been drawn to the worst crowd.'

'Besides, where were the guards when he staggered down to light the fuse?'

Connie thought a moment. 'I know that property. The woodlots connect. Or at least they used to.' She was a major

173

landholder, as well as a force in the Newbury Land Trust that snatched woods and hayfields from the jaws of developers. 'Unless Henry King has levelled his for a polo field.'

'They still connect.'

'Well, the woods would skirt the lower side of the lake, wouldn't they? Obviously, Dicky Butler *could* have done it.' She looked at the clock and covered a yawn. 'Give Mr Butler my best wishes when you see him tomorrow.' She had packed him a shopping bag with pickled sausage and jams and fruits from her garden.

'Incidentally, are you aware little Alison wants a cat?'

'Why don't you lend her yours?'

'That is not at all funny, Benjamin.'

Her last cat, Mehitabel, occupied a place of honour in her upstairs sitting room, thanks to the art of taxidermy.

It had been a while since Mr Butler had washed his hair, and it hung in lanky strands. His skin was grey, despite years of wind- and sunburn. In his county-lockup running suit he looked like some poor derelict the Salvation Army had trolled out of the gutter, and he welcomed me to the visitors' room with a grateful smile that tore my heart.

I told him about Scooter and Eleanor seeing his tractor from the balloon. And the fact that the Chevalley boys had witnessed him freeing the calf. He listened like a man whose mind was somewhere on a hilltop.

'I hope you don't mind, Mr Butler, but I took the liberty of asking Henry King to pay for your legal defence.'

I expected resistance and maybe anger. He only said, matter-of-factly, 'He won't.'

'My theory is he won't have to. The offer alone should be enough to make the state's attorney rethink his case.'

'I warned King,' Mr Butler said.

'Warned him? Warned him what?'

'If he wouldn't help then, he's not going to help for free.'

'Warned him what?'

'What I tried to tell you and you wouldn't let me.'

'Which was?'

'How I knew for sure it wasn't Dicky. I told him I'd tell the troopers if he didn't spring me.'

'You threatened him?'

'Blackmail. Which it was.'

'I don't follow you,' I said gently. 'Let's go back to how did you know for sure that Dicky didn't blow King's dam.'

'I put the dynamite in King's dam.'

Just like Josie Jervis had called it.

But I still had trouble believing my ears. And didn't want to.

He explained, drily, almost casually: 'Rigged it to detonate from the payphone in the Newbury General Store.'

I looked into his crazy eyes, and wondered what deal Tim and I and Ira Roth could work to keep the poor guy from spending the rest of his life behind bars. We had to keep him off the witness stand and we had to persuade him not to blab this lunacy to the cops.

'Mr Butler, you weren't at the General Store. You were on your tractor.'

'King took it out,' he said.

'What?'

'King's security people found my dynamite and removed it.'

'Wait, wait. You say you planted the dynamite and before you could detonate it King's people took it out?'

'Yup.'

'Mind telling me how you know they removed your explosives?'

'Because the morning of the party, when I got back from the General Store the lake was still there.'

For a farmer used to the sky overhead, daylight and weather, an independent man who never stood on line or waited in crowds, being locked up had to be particularly disorienting. 'Isn't disarming explosives specialized work? A bomb-squad job?'

Mr Butler pulled a face. 'I didn't *booby-trap* it. I wasn't trying to *kill* anybody. Besides, those aren't rent-a-cops protecting him. He's got top government security agents. Top.'

I gave him the benefit of the doubt on the security agents. If King could afford to keep a former Secretary of State and a retired CIA agent around the house, surely he could afford better than my numskull cousins. But even 'top' agents would call the bomb squad.

'Let me ask you this: why did it blow up at the party?'

'They put it back.'

'They put it back?'

'Rearmed it.'

'Why would they do that?'

'To cover up that they killed Dicky.'

Oh, boy, I thought. But ever the optimist: at least we had the makings of an insanity plea.

'You don't believe me?'

'No, I don't.' Actually, my problem was I might believe half his story. The first half. Maybe he did plant the dynamite. But the ATF hadn't found any wiring or remotes, which led me to speculate he had used some kind of slow fuse he'd learned in Special Forces. Then something went wrong, maybe water got in and delayed it. Whatever, his son had had the bad luck to pass out under the dam when it did go off. Just like Josie Jervis said.

'Why would I use a fuse? Why the hell would I take a chance lighting a goddammed fuse?'

'Why the General Store?'

'Nearest payphone. They could back-trace a call from my own phone.'

Play it as if he weren't nuts, I told myself, see what occurs in his alternate logic. 'Didn't you want to watch?'

'I didn't have to watch it go boom,' Mr Butler said scornfully. 'By the time I drove home the 'sucker's lake would be history. And another thing, do you seriously think I'd blow that dam during a *party*? What if somebody was walking on it?'

Or sleeping under it.

He had it all figured out. Most, if not all, wasn't true, of course. But if he had accidentally killed his son, then he had to have a story he could live with. A horrible coincidence – the Will of God, our Puritan fathers would say – but the man needed a story. Not to get out of jail, but to absolve himself of his son's death.

'Why would King kill Dicky?'

'I already told you that.'

'Tell me again.'

'To get my farm.'

'Sounds like he'll have to kill you next?'

'Might not have to,' Butler answered matter-of-factly. 'If they send me to prison, I'll lose the place to taxes. Either way, I got to settle this once and for all.'

'Settle? How?'

'Soon as I can bust out of here, I'm going to blow King's house off Morris Mountain.'

I could only pray that the guards weren't eavesdropping. 'Please don't even *think* about that, Mr Butler. You'll kill somebody and get killed in the process. Let Ira and Tim and me help you.'

'Best way you can help me is get some judge to grant bail. I'll take her from there.'

I gave him Connie's care package, which the guards had inspected. Stepping out into the sunlight, breathing free again, I had to admit I was less anxious to spring him. If his claim wasn't fantasy, then his threat wasn't either.

I exited the jailhouse just in time to see Trooper Moody empty his cruiser of a tall, lanky tattooed fellow in leg and waist chains. Guards surrounded the prisoner and Ollie, clearly very proud of himself, answered cheerfully when I asked what was up.

'J. J. Topkis,' he said. 'Outstanding warrants for assault. And robbery.'

'What'd he rob?'

'National Guard Armory. Major Case Squad's been after him six months.'

'Pull him over for speeding?' Moving violations and DWI were ever-popular ways to get arrested on old warrants.

'Nope.' Ollie was positively radiant. 'Went out and nailed the 'sucker. Heard he had a girl on Scudder Mountain. I

177

figured he'd get horny one of these nights. Caught him with his pants down.'

'Congratulations,' I said. I meant it. It was a good arrest, and Ollie had a right to be proud. 'Isn't he the guy Dicky Butler threw through the White Birch window?'

'Yup, real shame Dicky blew himself up.'

'How's that?' Ollie didn't look at all like he thought it was a shame Dicky was dead. If anything, he got even more cheerful at the memory.

'I could of turned this whacko to press charges.'

'Win some, lose some,' I said, and by then Ollie was in such a good mood that he actually chuckled, and accepted my invitation for a cup of coffee at the diner. We were settled in there, vaguely uncomfortable to be together, and chomping jelly doughnuts, when I filled the silence with a question.

'How'd you happen to hear Topkis had a girl on Scudder Mountain?'

'Got a tip.'

'Must have sounded pretty good to sit all night on Scudder Mountain.'

'Sounded like a pissed-off boyfriend.'

We cemented our unlikely camaraderie by agreeing that tips didn't come any better than that. A bailiff ran into the diner, warning his partners that the arraignment was about to begin and Ollie and I paid our separate checks and hurried back to the courthouse.

I was surprised to see that J. J. Topkis was represented by Greg Riggs, a swiftly rising star in the county, who was destined to become a very young judge. He was politically connected – admired by the entrenched crowd – and an active supporter of the up-and-coming. During Vicky's renomination battle Riggs had hosted a very profitable fund-raiser for her. Although I suspected that the hots for Newbury's first selectman had played as much a role as smart politics. Whichever, Greg Riggs was a very expensive lawyer for a raggedy biker.

And, it turned out, worth every penny.

He talked the magistrate into granting medium-low bail of forty grand, which Topkis's mother would guarantee with her house. Ollie left muttering darkly about 'pussy courts'. But it sounded to me like Topkis's hotshot attorney had him cut a deal to rat someone out.

Back in Newbury, Tim Hall had trouble with the concept that Mr Butler claimed to have tried to dynamite King's dam and maybe killed Dicky in the process. 'Do you believe him?'

I'd had more time to absorb it. 'I don't know. He sounds nuts. But he's very specific about planting the dynamite and that whole thing about detonating it by phone.'

'How do you detonate explosives by phone?'

'ATF guy told me you telephone a cell phone or a beeper to activate a radio transmitter, like a garage-door opener, that signals a receiver on the bomb. Little Alison could run one up for you in shop class.'

'Why didn't Dicky do it that way? A lot safer.'

'Because Dicky wasn't as imaginative as Alison. At least not when he was drunk.'

'But the ATF said they found no remote equipment. Come on, Ben, it's fantasy.'

'But Mr Butler sounded so definite – and so casual about it, so matter-of-fact. Really makes me wonder.'

'My next question is how did "they" get Dicky to stand next to the dynamite?'

'I don't know, for crissake.'

'Hey, I'm just asking the questions. You'd do the same for me if *I* came up with a cockamamie idea.'

'It's not my idea, it's Mr Butler's.'

'Assume for a moment that Butler's bomb went off late on a passed-out Dicky. How come nobody saw him stagger there?'

'The caterers and early party guests wouldn't have thought anything odd, seeing him at a distance. And the security people were busy with the caterers and temp help.'

'I think I want to confer with Ira Roth.'

'I already asked him to join us for lunch.'

Tim looked a little put out. Like I didn't think he was as smart as his mentor. I explained, 'I ran into him in the courthouse. He's worried about something.'

* * *

'A tattooed, redheaded ex-convict mingling unnoticed with the guests on his way to falling asleep under the dam?'

Ira Roth's sarcastic smile would have frozen Caligula's saliva.

'Drunk,' I added, before Tim could.

Ira tipped back his chair on the General Store's porch and surveyed Main Street like folk art he might purchase for his Morris Mountain tax-dodge horse farm.

'Drunk,' he echoed.

'According to Josie Jervis, who drove him home that morning.'

'You mentioned her already.'

Tim and I looked at each other. I'm pretty sure he felt the way I did – precisely the way Ira wanted us to feel – fifteen years old at Newbury Prep, in the thrall of serious adults.

'The insufferable Ira', Aunt Connie had always called him. I'd known him since I was a kid. Active in town affairs, and clever with land, he had been a regular at both of Dad's offices. I found him daunting. A glance at his pro bono acolyte confirmed that Tim did too.

Ira looked younger than his early sixties. Compact, medium height, radiating self-satisfaction, he appeared larger by dint of personality and costume – his trademark three-piece navy-blue suit, a pinstriped shirt, and a loud necktie that would stop traffic if most of it weren't covered by his waistcoat. He had a fine head of hair, remarkably black, though his active, bushy eyebrows were grey. The long cigar he would fire up after the sandwiches he had allowed Tim and me to pay for peeped from a waistcoat pocket like a surface-to-air missile.

I said, 'Ira, the question is do we believe Mr Butler's story.'

'No. The question is how do we keep the crazy fool out of prison.'

'That's right,' said Tim. 'And get him bail.'

'I'm having a problem with bail,' I said. 'I know he's going to pieces in there, but he's threatening to blow up King's house.'

'Talk,' Ira said. 'Just talk. He'll be OK as soon as we get him home.'

180

'What if he tried to blow up the dam like he claims? That's more than talk.'

'But not the same as blowing up a house. He's not a killer. He's just a farmer going nuts indoors.'

'It's possible he's also going nuts because he killed his own son. Accidentally.'

'Not in my book,' said Ira.

'Are you saying you're sure he didn't blow up the dam?'

'Dicky blew up the dam. Not my client.'

'Dicky used to be your client.'

'Dicky is dead. Our client is alive, in jail. We want him home.'

I said, 'Ira, I've been thinking. I'm also having problems with *Dicky* blowing up the dam. Why would he invite Josie Jervis on a picnic that same afternoon?'

'I don't care and this is the last I'll discuss it.'

'Then I'll listen real carefully, Ira. And I expect you to do the same.'

He didn't like that. Our relationship, daunting aside, was coloured by resentment: he was the leading criminal attorney in Plainfield County, a lion at the Superior Court, which was to say, a very big fish in a very small pond; he hated that I hadn't retained him to defend me when I got in trouble in New York, and even accused me once of not trusting a 'country lawyer' to get me off. Like Henry King, he could never understand that beating the charges had not been my main concern. As he saw it, I had robbed him of an incredible opportunity to prove himself in the Big Apple.

'Ben, you're asking the wrong questions.'

'And doing the wrong things,' said Tim. 'He went up to Fox Trot and asked *King* to pay for Butler's defence.'

To Tim's amazement, Ira turned to me with open admiration. 'You did? Now you're thinking, Ben. We'll end up making some money out of this thing. Did King bite?'

'Let's just say he's considering it.'

Ira got a crafty look on his face. 'If Butler's telling the truth that he planted the dynamite and King found it, King can't go back. Can't say to the troopers, "Oh by the way, we found Butler's dynamite and didn't tell anybody."'

181

'But that's the worst part of Butler's story,' I said. 'It sounds absurd. Why would King not tell?'

Ira wasn't listening. 'If King's in that position, he *has* to help pay for Butler's defence. To throw off suspicion. Jesus, we can bill him Washington rates. Tim, we'll make out like bandits. Even pay PI Ben, here.'

'Well, if he didn't he's in trouble now,' said Tim. 'He can't now. Because they'll ask, "Where is it?"'

'Ka-boom,' said Ira. Then he sighed. 'No. 'Fraid not. Ben's right. If our client – God forbid – did plant the dynamite, King's people didn't find it. It just blew up late.'

'I don't know that we should take Butler's word on anything.'

'Then who planted it?' asked Ira.

'Dicky,' Tim answered loyally.

'Unless somebody killed Dicky,' I said.

17

'*Killed* Dicky? You mean tied him to the dynamite and lit the fuse?'

Tim's laugh died in his throat when his mentor growled, 'Ben means before the dynamite.'

I could see Ira thinking, No pro bono ever went unpunished. He gave me a long, cool, I-don't-need-this-complication-in-my-life look. He surveyed Main Street again, gazed with satisfaction at his brand new turbo-charged Riviera gleaming in the shade of an elm. I hoped the car would act as a reminder that he could afford a little complication for a good cause. And might even enjoy it.

He waited long enough to make me uncomfortable. Finally, dripping reluctance, he asked, 'Suspects?'

'Suspects?' Tim looked from Ira to me and back to Ira, as anxious, suddenly, as a kid without his homework.

'Who?' Ira demanded. 'Come on! Who had motive and means to kill Dicky?'

I counted them off on four fingers and a thumb: 'Albert and Dennis Chevalley; Trooper Moody; a biker from Derby named J. J. Topkis; and Henry King, or someone who works for him.'

'Trooper Moody?' Tim blurted.

I spoke my answer to Ira. 'Dicky was going to sue him for false arrest – might have won, might have wrecked his career and cost him his pension. Plus he hated his guts.'

'Your cousins?'

'Revenge for kicking their asses.'

'King?'

'The obvious. Wants the farm.'

'The biker?'

'Same as Albert and Dennis. Dicky destroyed his rep. J. J. Topkis was the toughest, meanest son of a bitch east and west of the Housatonic until Dicky threw him through Wide Greg's window.'

'I love the law,' said Ira. 'I meet such wonderful people.' A glance put me in that category. I braced for him to tear my idea to shreds. Instead he said, 'What do you think, Tim?'

'Well, I just don't know about Ollie. Even for him that's going pretty far.'

'You didn't see the relief on his face when I told him Dicky was dead.'

'Relief or surprise?'

'Not necessarily surprise.'

'Albert and Dennis Chevalley, I don't think of as killers. You're talking about your cousins, Ben.'

'Distant cousins,' I said, mindful of when I saw them pummelling Dicky: if Dicky hadn't broken Albert's grip, and I didn't intervene, they'd have beaten him to a pulp. 'And if they're murderers, they're going to be a lot more distant.'

'I don't know the biker, except he's on the lam for something.'

'Felonious assault. With hand grenade. And robbery. And he's not on the lam any more. Ollie just caught him. Greg Riggs got him bail.'

'How could he afford to hire Greg?' asked Tim.

'Where did he get the hand grenade?' Ira interrupted.

'That's a matter of some contention. It came from a Hartford National Guard Armory. But Riggs made the robbery charges sound pretty weak. Maybe J. J. bought it from the thief. Maybe J. J. stole it.'

'Weak? Was that how Riggs got him bail?'

'J. J. might have turned.'

'What else was stolen?'

'Guns, ammo, a couple of mortars and some detonators.'

Tim nodded, ruefully. I'd done my homework, but he was still at Ira's blackboard. 'Henry King? I don't think so. What's the old song? "Some rob you with a six gun, some with a

184

fountain pen." We all know in the end King'll take Butler's farm with a fountain pen.'

'We don't know how patient he is,' I argued. 'It's likely, if Mr Butler goes to prison, King will get his chance to buy it now instead of ten years from now.'

Ira lit his cigar, and puffed reflectively.

'The whole idea is absurd. And your suspects are pitifully lame.'

His expression demanded an answer. But I reminded myself of all the lawyers' offspring that my fees had sent to private school back when I was a player, the German automotive products they had leased with my retainers, their summer houses and their concubines, and kept my mouth firmly shut.

Ira puffed harder. 'The least lame are Trooper Moody and Henry King.'

I sat silent.

'It's not impossible to imagine Ollie beating a man to death. I've always thought it would happen one day, but accidentally. Now you're suggesting a pretty strong motive. Did he grow up on a farm?'

Ira knew damned well he had. I let Tim answer. 'The old Moody place. Out by Scudder Mountain. His brother's got it.'

'So Ollie could know his dynamite, not to mention whatever bomb disposal courses the state police put him through . . .'

'Army,' I reminded Ira. 'MPs. Could have learned some there.'

Ira puffed hard. '. . . As for Henry King . . .' Smoke enough to screen a crippled destroyer. '. . . Henry King is the sort of arrogant son of a bitch who could justify anything.'

Tim and I glanced at each other – Ira calling the kettle arrogant? – and Tim made a valiant effort to strangle his snicker with a cough.

'What's that?' asked Ira.

'Ummgh, I was just – hummmgh.'

'And from what Ben tells me King's got at least one hard case hanging around the house. Ex-CIA, Ben?'

'Josh Wiggens.'

'What's that?' Ira shot back, with the litigator's instinct for the unspoken.

'Mr Butler told Tim he's seen someone, quote, "spying" on him from King's woods.'

'Through a sniper scope,' said Tim.

Ira shook his head. 'That poor lunatic – OK, so we'll assume King's got serious security people,' he continued aloud, warming to the possibilities. 'There's another thing about King. I don't know if either of you have seen the "Biography" show they ran on A&E, but back when he was a student he worked heavy construction in New York City. Those jobs include blasting. Could have picked it up. Worth checking out ... pretty complicated way to steal Butler's farm. But like you say, a hell of a way to steer the post mortem ...

'The biker, on the other hand, sounds too busy running from the troopers. And your cousins couldn't empty a bucket with instructions printed on the bottom.'

Maybe not. But the end tables in their Mom's trailer were fashioned from wooden boxes with bright red labels. Dennis's scabbed and bruised face could have come from a return match with Dicky. Albert had seemed overly anxious to convince me they had been up on Fox Trot's high pasture all day. And for all their impulsive bumbling, no full-blooded Chevalley had ever turned the other cheek.

Nor had Topkis looked like a guy to let a few arrest warrants stop him from causing bodily harm. Otherwise, Ira read my list the way I did. Ollie Moody and Henry King and his hired help topped my list, too.

'What about King's enemies?' protested Tim. 'Aren't we working on the assumption that he might –' Tim looked around. We were still alone on the porch and the kid inside at the cash register had Sony plugs in her ears. 'You know, still work for the US.'

Ira sighed. 'Can you check him out, Ben? If he's the official-unofficial double crosser we think he is, then it *is* possible that Dicky simply had the bad luck to pass out in the vicinity of an explosion detonated by disgruntled Germans.'

186

I supposed the Admiral owed me one for being polite to the jerk he'd sent to pump me. Maybe he'd see it that way, too.

'We're really reaching, here,' Ira said gloomily.

'Then why pursue it?' asked Tim. 'I thought the plan was to make the state's attorney cave before he goes to the grand jury.'

'Because,' Ira said, 'the state's attorney gave me bad news, this morning, very bad news, while suggesting I cop a plea.'

'Cop a plea!' Tim blurted, shocked into feistiness. 'He's got some nerve.'

'He's also got a very strong case against our client.'

'What happened?'

'Seems Ben wasn't the only person Butler "confided" in. Seems that a week before the event, he and King got into a shouting match in Mike's Hardware and he told King to his face he'd blow his dam.'

No wonder Ira was so willing to listen to my 'lame' theory.

'But that's just King's word against his,' Tim protested.

'Overheard by Mike, who was cutting keys.'

'Why the hell didn't Mike say this earlier?'

'Mike happens to be a Vietnam vet who sides one hundred per cent with Mr Butler.'

I asked, 'Who got Mike to talk?'

'State Police Major Case Detective-Sergeant Marian Boyce. You know her, Ben.'

'I've run into her.'

'Quite a comer, I'm told,' said Ira.

'That's my experience.'

The lawyer's smile was brief and grim. 'Understand, both of you. Our client's liberty is at stake. They've got that it was his dynamite. They've got the feud. They've got his son at the site. Now they've got an angry threat. And I'll bet before this goes to trial, the comely sergeant will round up additional witnesses to our client's emotional outbursts.'

'Are you considering an insanity defence?'

'You've seen him sitting there like a trapped animal. Institutionalize a man as unstable as he is, and he'll never get out. It would be worse than prison.

'Therefore: Tim will continue to concentrate on bail, and quashing the conspiracy charge. Find a legal precedent, new evidence, a friendly prosecutor, or some judge still beholden to your old man, I don't care which. But do it fast. He's not getting any more stable rotting in there.

'Meanwhile: Ben will check out his cockamamie suspects.'

The Long Island Sound sprawled pale blue in the muggy haze, dotted with sailboats and bordered by an indistinct coast.

Like most of the workers hired at Fox Trot – Albert and Dennis Chevalley being the exceptions who proved the rule, and had probably inspired the policy – King's caterers had come from far away. New York City, in the case of Party Box, although when I finally ran them down they were prepping a party on the back lawn of an estate down the beach from the Larchmont Yacht Club. The parking attendant gave the Olds a dubious look.

'I'm with the caterer.'

I was told next time use the service entrance and directed frostily to the kitchens. The cooks had coffee brewing and a radio on and were arranging flowers on serving trays. I asked for the boss.

'Out at the tent.'

Extremely attractive young men and women in white shirts and black pants were humping boxes across the lawn to a striped marquee. Under the tent, they were setting tables for a sit-down dinner for two hundred. I carried out a crate of flatware, and asked the prettiest woman I could find, 'Where's the boss?'

'I am. Who are you?' She was short, feisty and English.

'Ben Abbott. I thought you did a beautiful job at the King party up in Newbury.'

'The client from hell . . . Why are you carrying my lugs?'

'I wanted to ask you about the party.'

'Are you looking for work?'

'No. Not this party. I mean, I'll give you a hand if you're short, but –'

'*Who* are you?'

'Ben Abbott. From Newbury. Do you have time for a quick question?'

'Are you a cop?'

'Hell, no.'

'I talked to a lot of cops.'

'So did I.'

That got her attention, and jogged pleasant memories. 'I can't begin to describe,' she said, 'the fantastic pleasure – the absolute joy – when his lake exploded. I felt sorry for the fish, of course, and then later that poor guy who did it. But it was *fantastic*. I mean I have had clients. And I have had clients.'

'What did he do?'

'Bossing everyone around, *yelling* at us. Do this. Do that. Make sure you don't forget. Why isn't that man wearing a bow tie – because he's still setting up the bar, you nincompoop, which of course I couldn't say, but had to take time out to explain and promise that his party would be much better than the one we did for his close personal friend the maharajah. On and on and on.'

'Sounds like a miracle it was such a good party.'

'Thank God he didn't get there until right before it started.'

'What? What do you mean, right before it started?'

'That bloody helicopter brought him in. You'd think the president of the United States was landing. The whole house staff had to line up to greet him. Like "Masterpiece Theater"? They told me to line up too. I said, "Your party starts in two hours. You can have a line, or you can have food and drink for your guests – you choose."'

'What time did King arrive?'

'Late. One o'clock. He cut it really close. There was some problem with the plane.'

So much for former-construction-worker Henry King personally stuffing his dam with dynamite to bury a dead Dicky Butler.

'From where?'

She shrugged. 'I don't know. I think they said London. He looked like he'd been flying all night. All sweaty and disgusting and not exactly spiffed for a party. He was yelling at that

189

"personal" assistant that the client's chairman had taken the good plane and stuck him in one with broken air conditioning, and why the hell couldn't he buy his own plane. Bitch, bitch, bitch.'

'Who told you to line up? Ms Devlin?'

'The "personal" assistant? No, she was on the helicopter. It was that drunk talking out of the side of his mouth. I gathered he was a house guest. He'd been my main annoyance until Horrible Henry arrived.'

She and I bounced 'Horrible Henry' stories for a another minute or two. Then I asked her what I had driven two hours to ask: 'Did you lose any gear in the explosion?'

'That was the best part of all. The silly show-off insisted we use his own silver champagne buckets.'

'Even down at the dam?'

'That's where we really were lucky, thank God. I was going to put my best bartender at the dam, refilling glasses when the guests walked around the lake. But they just wanted a fancy bucket. Two-thousand-dollar silver antique – ka-plooy.'

'Lucky bartender.'

'Lucky Party Box. You know what it's like to find a decent bartender?'

'So he wasn't near it at all?'

'He was on *top* of it – replacing the magnum – *two minutes* before it exploded.'

I looked over at their service bar. A guy in a T-shirt was slicing limes. His white dress shirt hung from a nearby tent rope, protected by a clear plastic bag. 'Is that him?'

'Why?'

'Well, they've gone and arrested the old farmer who lived next door. The father of the man who was killed. They're blaming him too.'

'The old man on the tractor?'

'Mr Butler. He and King were feuding. Hated each other.'

'Oh really? Marshal!' she called to the guy slicing limes. 'Marshal. Come over here and talk to this man.' Marshal looked like he was in between jobs modelling Armani suits. Darkly handsome, almost sinister – until he smiled.

'Marshal, Ben,' said his boss. 'Ben, Marshal.'

We shook hands and Marshal asked, 'What's up?'

'Basically, I guess I'd be happiest if you could tell me you saw somebody put dynamite in Henry King's dam and light the fuse. Failing that, did you see anyone approach it who wasn't part of the party?'

'No, they asked me that. No. I only saw us and the guests.'

'Could you see the face of the dam when you brought fresh bottles?'

'No. I was above it. The bucket was set back a ways so nobody would fall over.'

'How far did the water drop?'

'How high was the dam? I don't know. About ten feet.'

'Didn't you lean over for a look? I'm usually drawn to the edge and I've got to look. Especially when there's water.'

'Oh, I looked. When I first went out there.'

'What did you see?'

'Nothing. It was kind of bushy and swampy. It looked like snake and mosquito heaven.'

'And the champagne bucket was next to the spillway?'

'Not next. A ways back.'

'How far?'

'Far. 'Cause first I set it up by that cute little bridge across the spillway. The contractor had blocked it off with saw horses.'

I'd last seen the replica of an Olmstead Central Park bow bridge washed downstream in the mud.

'But they came out yelling "Move it. Couldn't I read?"'

'Read?'

'The sign. "Danger! You'll fall off and die." You know. On the saw horses.'

'Did you see a red-headed guy about my size? Short stubby hair, tattoos on his arms.'

Marshal turned to his boss. 'That state trooper asked me that. Remember?'

The boss explained, 'She crashed a cocktail party we did at the Fortune Society. Arrested one of the guests.'

'Sounds like Detective-Sergeant Boyce.'

'Right. She recognized a fugitive, handcuffed him, and took him away.'

Seemed a funny coincidence. 'You mean she followed him to the cocktail party?'

'No. She came to ask us about what happened at Fox Trot. The fugitive just happened to be there.'

'What did you tell her?'

'I told her I didn't see the red-headed guy.'

'Did you see him?'

'Of course not. No way I'd lie to *her*, even if I had a reason to. No. No red-headed guy with tattoos. Sorry.'

'And no other party crashers?'

'No,' said Marshal. 'King had heavy security.'

'They demanded a final staff roster a week ahead,' the English woman added. 'No changes allowed. I said, "Give me a break. We've got actors working. Someone gets a job, someone else fills in." I guaranteed we'd have enough people. We always do. Can you believe they said, "Anyone not on the list won't get past the gate"? And you know the funny thing. Such tight security? Give me a break: someone stole two crates of champagne from our van.'

The entire time she was talking to me, her eyes were everywhere, checking the setup. Suddenly they gleamed with a smile. 'Would it be possible to make a small contribution to that farmer's defence fund?'

I drove back to Newbury with a generous cheque for Tim to deposit in his escrow account. I told him I'd learned that King had arrived barely in time for his party. Tim said Ira said that the word at the courthouse confirmed my impression that J. J. Topkis had indeed cut a deal with the state's attorney, but no one knew what. 'Greg's playing it real close to his chest.'

'How the hell can Topkis afford to pay Greg Riggs?'

'You can never tell with the bikers,' said Tim. 'Ira defended one last year who owned his own bodyshop. And sometimes they're doing drug deals. Or selling guns.'

I agreed that bikers sometimes scored big. But it was rare

they banked the profits for a rainy day. 'Can you find out how Riggs happens to be defending him?'

'Never.'

'Come on.'

'I wouldn't tell anybody how I'm defending a client. Why would he?'

'I gotta check Topkis out, anyway. Maybe *he'll* tell me.'

'Lotsa luck.'

I drove downriver to Derby, an old working town where the falls of the Housatonic used to power the factories and here and there the old races could still be seen to trap the water in stagnant pools.

J. J. Topkis was not hard to sneak up on. The sharp, hollow thunder of a Harley-Davidson motorcycle engine sounded like he had stolen his muffler from a lawn mower. His neighbours on the street of two-storey frame houses and battered old trees must have been counting the hours to his trial.

With others of his ilk, who had been caught earlier, he had formed a loosely knit gang of riders who called themselves the Derby Death. The Derby Death maintained a clubhouse in an abandoned factory, a place I had no desire to visit.

Much preferring to meet him home alone, and entertaining the vague hope that he lived with doting sisters and a mother anxious to protect her bail investment, I eased the Olds around potholes and past houses buttoned up against the heat and noise, checking for an address provided by a biker who had let me buy him a dozen Rolling Rocks at the White Birch Inn.

Number Forty-eight, which someone had dressed up with asphalt shingles after World War Two and aluminium storm windows during Vietnam, had a narrow driveway that squeezed between it and the house next door. At the end, in front of a sagging garage, I saw Topkis sitting cross-legged on the cracked cement revving a chopped Harley. His ear was cocked to subtleties I could only imagine as each twist of the handlebar produced noise reminiscent of the *Enterprise* launching F-18 Tomcats.

Two guys in cutoff workshirts were seated on garbage cans watching the operation with vacant gazes that grew sharper as they tracked my passage down their street. Exactly the clubhouse crowd I was trying to avoid. Well, maybe Mom was watching from the kitchen window. I drove past, turned around in a neighbour's driveway, and parked the Olds facing a getaway.

18

The Harley shut down. Silence descended.

Sometimes, certain types who have reason to expect the cops mistake me for the enemy. Maybe it's my general build, maybe some attitude. Sometimes, I don't disabuse them, though I never come out and say I'm the Law, which would annoy real cops greatly.

As the three of them tracked me out of the Olds and up J. J.'s driveway, it struck me this might be an excellent occasion to let them form the wrong idea about who the hell I was, what the hell I was doing there, and why the hell I was barking, 'J. J. Topkis.'

The two on the garbage cans looked mildly relieved. Topkis rose from the cement, uncoiling to his feet as effortlessly as a cobra.

'Yeah?' He looked me over, trying to place me. I was hoping he remembered me talking to Ollie at his arraignment.

'Drop the screwdriver.'

He laid it within easy reach on the bike's saddle.

If I wasn't allowed to say I was a cop, nobody said I couldn't act like one. 'On. The. Ground.'

He shrugged and knocked it off. It landed on its handle, with a dull thunk. I moved to where I could keep an eye on the other two.

J. J. looked me over, thought he could take me. 'What do you want?'

Had I found him alone I'd have tried the man-to-man approach – hear about Dicky Butler? Went out in a blaze of glory. That dynamite's full of surprises. But three-on-one made me a barking cop.

'Why'd you sucker-punch Dicky Butler at the White Birch?'

'Huh?'

'Biker bar in Newbury.'

J. J. just stared, trying to scope it out.

'June. A night to remember. He threw you through the window.'

'Oh, yeah,' J. J. answered slowly, stepping closer. 'I was shit-faced.'

'Did he start it?'

'You could say that.'

'Word is, you hit him first.'

'Yeah, he knocked my uncle's teeth out.'

That was news to me. I'd heard it was a simple one-on-one slugfest, over before it started.

'Coupla years ago in Waterbury. Tried to pick a fight. Uncle didn't want to fight 'im. Old guy, nearly fifty. Bartender and a mess a guys go, Get outta here. Leave the old guy alone. Dicky Butler heads for the door. Going by the pool table he picks up the eight ball and *blam*! throws it hard as he can, right in the chest. Uncle gets mad. What the fuck you do that for? Dicky punches him in the mouth. Teeth go flying across the bar. Guys are going, See that? Unbelievable. All his teeth, stuck together, flying across the bar. You know what?'

False teeth? A full set of uppers and lowers knocked out of Uncle's head?

I had forgotten that J. J. had sucker-punched Dicky. He sure was good at it. No clues, no telegraph hunch of the shoulder, no false smile to throw me off, just an engaging tale and, to use the master's word, *Blam*.

He was a tall man with exceptionally long arms and the punch had started down around his ankles. When it reached my jaw it was travelling like a FedEx truck late to the airport. One minute I was standing listening to his rap, the next I was flat on my back wondering how I got there.

Cops and bikers have one thing in common. They pile on. If a cop sees another pummelling a civilian, he doesn't saunter over wondering, What's this all about? Perhaps I should inquire whether that citizen is rightfully defending himself. No. It's, Gangway, Brother in Blue, let me hit him too. Same with bikers.

The nearest garbage-can sitter aimed his engineer-boot at my face, the other picked up a Stillson wrench.

I dodged most of the kick. His heel sliced my cheek half an inch from my eye. It probably hurt like hell, but I was too scared of the wrench to notice, trying to roll away from it as it came arcing out of the sky like the leading edge of a wrecking ball.

The wrench slammed into the drive and sent cement chips flying in my face. By then I was really moving, rolling halfway to my feet before J. J. hit me again.

His braced-and-ready punch made his sucker punch seem like a pleasant memory. He hit me hard and far and I saw shooting stars. The only good news was he knocked me clear out of range of his buddy's next kick.

Sky, tree tops and house and garage whirled. I was dead if I didn't get back on my feet. Three on one, how dumb could I be? Find my feet. Find the guy with the wrench.

I heard him yell like a Viking, a bad mistake. I was sufficiently frightened already, but now I saw where he was, swinging the wrench with both hands, a sight that focused my mind remarkably. I went down again, threw my shoulders at his knees, tumbled him over my back, and came up landing a right that his booted friend would remember to his grave.

For a moment I felt like Dicky Butler fighting my cousins – pure motion and deadly force. Until a punch in the back of my neck reminded me he'd been fighting two, while I had three of this Derby Death subchapter all to myself. I kept my feet, whirled, and brought up my guard.

J. J. was ready and waiting. I slipped most of his straight left, but not enough of his roundhouse right, and again I went flying, crashing into the Harley this time, which hurt a lot, and falling over it to the pavement in a kind of slow-motion sprawl that gave the three of them plenty of time to close the circle.

Boots was listing, but still dangerous. Wrenchman was flipping the damned thing from one hand to another like a demented drum major. J. J. took charge, co-ordinating their next attack.

I crouched into a boxing stance, and sprang at Wrenchman with a flurry of left jabs. All missed. But they were supposed to and by then I was churning into the middle, dropping my hands, and kicking J. J. Topkis in the balls.

It didn't work. He went down with a scream, but not definitively. The wrench whizzed past my head and clipped my shoulder like a ball of fire, deadening my left arm. Boots grabbed me from behind, clamped my arms, and urged his friend with the wrench to try again.

'Wait!' Topkis struggled to his feet, cursing me. He picked up his screwdriver, and approached slowly, holding the thing like a rapier.

The slowdown was killing me. I felt the pain where I'd been kicked and punched, felt the weariness in my arms and legs, the heat sucking up my strength, and fear gnawing my spirit. Again I thought of Dicky, exploding into motion.

I stomped Boots's instep. He let go howling, until I connected with a right cross that put him down, out cold. I tried to sprint for the Olds. But they blocked the driveway and backed me into the corner between the garage and the house.

Things got real quiet, except for the breath storming through my lungs. I was past fear now, into the stage where I knew I'd lost and all I could hope was to keep the damage below the fatal line.

19

I got my hands up and debated my options. Wrench in the skull? Screwdriver in the gut?

I deserved this. I was supposed to be a survivor, but somewhere along the line I'd stopped paying attention. Blundering into three-on-one fitted a pattern of royally messing up. Too solitary, unfocused, I was all over the place – lurching clumsily after three women at once – hoping to somehow connect with Julia Devlin, hoping Rita Long would come home from Hong Kong saying she'd suddenly known I was the one. While in the process, screwing up with Vicky. What a gorgeous trio they'd make, visiting me in Intensive Care.

J. J. cocked his head. The measured click of heels coming up the driveway. Get me out of this, I thought, and I promise I'll be good. Fat chance. It sounded like only one man – probably bringing beer.

The biker with the wrench turned to watch.

Thank you, Lord.

I knocked him down with a left hook to his ear, and eluded J. J.'s belated slash with the screwdriver.

Around the house came Detective-Sergeant Arnie Bender. Wrenchman got up, quickly. J. J. snickered when he saw that Arnie was not very big. Their booted colleague was waking up. I could almost see the Derby Death thinking, We'll throw both bodies in the mill race.

But right behind Arnie came Marian Boyce wearing running shoes, which hadn't clicked, and a mad-dog street face I had never seen before. She wasn't any less womanly – it would take industrious transsexual surgeons a long time to change that – but she looked ready, able and anxious to shoot someone and didn't particularly care who.

Their weapons appeared at some silent signal.

'State Police.'

For two people who disliked each other, Marian and Arnie put up a very convincing front. Neither biker questioned their solidarity, much less their jurisdiction within the city limits of Derby. Wrench and screwdriver thunked and clattered to the cement.

'Hit the deck,' said Arnie, gesturing with his weapon, a .357 Magnum, which looked enormous in his little hand.

The Derby Death lay down on the cement beside their awakening colleague. Old hands at this sort of thing, all three crossed their arms behind their backs and waited to be cuffed.

'Boy, am I glad to see you,' I said.

'You too, jailbird. On your face!'

If the prisoners were hoping to garner some advantage from jurisdictional discord, they were disappointed. The Derby Police provided the paddy waggon and seemed on excellent terms with their colleagues from the state. Marian stood by joking with a Derby uniform, while Arnie and a couple of local plainclothes frisked us and marched the Derby Death one by one into the van.

'What the hell's the charges?' yelled J. J. when his turn came.

'You were caught in the act of assaulting a tourist.'

This was my third time handcuffed in three months and I liked it even less than the night in Ollie's cruiser. My face hurt, so did the back of my neck and my ribs, not to mention the various parts that had collided with the remarkably sharp and pointy Harley.

The plainclothes cops hoisted me to my feet like a fence post. The Derby Death watched intently as they marched me to the paddy waggon.

'We'll take that one,' said Marian. 'He isn't worth the paperwork.'

'We need him for the complaint.'

Marian nodded the Derby plainclothes out of earshot. They

spoke awhile, then another nod, and my handlers marched me over. 'Ben,' said Marian, 'we'll need you to press charges against these guys who beat you up.'

'What guys?'

'You see what I mean?' she said to the Derby detective.

'Look, Abbott, we'll run you in and charge you right along with those whacked-out scum.'

'Charge me with what?'

'Disturbing the fucking peace, fighting and brawling.'

'There was no fight.'

'No fight? Where'd you get the face?'

'Tripped over a motorcycle.'

Marian said, 'He majored in Ethics at Leavenworth U.'

'Yeah, well if there's no fight maybe he wants to ride with his friends. Maybe we'll park it down by the river for an hour. Let you get to know each other even better.'

Nothing in Marian's expression suggested she would come to my rescue and not let that happen.

The Derby plainclothes grabbed me. 'OK, tough guy. Let's go.'

When your hands are cuffed behind your back, and you ache all over, and your face looks like Mike Tyson's speed bag, all you've got left of Main Street privilege is your voice. 'I know an excellent criminal lawyer. You'll want his number if a prisoner you're responsible for is ever injured while in your custody.'

Arnie and Marian stuffed me in the back of their unmarked cruiser. I said, 'They'll trash my car if you leave it on the street.'

'No problem,' said Arnie. 'Derby's impounding it.'

'For what?'

'Look for drugs. You'll get it back after they chop it.'

I said, 'Detective-Sergeant Bender. I know you've always wanted to see how fast she'll go. Now would be a good time. You have my permission to borrow my car.'

Arnie's eyes gleamed. The bored and stroked Caddy V-6 that a mechanically gifted Chevalley had shoehorned under the hood had some miles on it, but when the Olds lunched, Jags and BMWs went hungry.

Marian passed him their FBI light. 'You owe me, Little Boy.'

Bender fished my keys out of my pocket and started the engine, his weaselly face benign with ecstasy. He clapped the FBI light on my roof. He laid rubber all the way up the street, narrowly missing the only late-model car on the block, a shiny Ford Taurus which hadn't been parked at the corner when I arrived.

Marian followed, sedately, eyes straight ahead as we passed the Taurus and Josh Wiggens tossed me an ironic salute.

In the back seat, still handcuffed, I said, 'Can I ask you something?'

'Try.'

'How'd you happen to stop by J. J.'s?'

'We've got an assist thing going with the Derby cops,' she lied. 'In return, they were running registration checks on J. J.'s visitors. We heard about a certain light green Olds, and swung by for a look.'

'Amazing,' I said. 'Just in time.'

'Well, we didn't barge right in. Thought it best to watch what was going down.'

'You watched those guys trying to kill me?'

'What guys?'

'Marian.'

'You screwed up our surveillance, you jerk. We were praying you'd take them so we could maintain cover.'

'There were three of them.'

'I lost a buck to Arnie backing you.'

'Sorry.'

'My fault. Betting with my heart instead of my head.'

She drove in silence, for a while. Then she found my eyes in the mirror and said, 'I'm mildly curious. How'd you handle your no-rat policy at Annapolis? Don't they have an Honour Code?'

'I honoured the Code.'

'By the way, that was a neat strategy, letting those guys wear themselves out punching you. The dummies thought they were winning. I'm going to try that next time I fight three on one.'

'I really appreciate your saving my ass. Could you tell me again how you happened to come along in the nick of time?'

'Ben, I want you out of our faces.'

'*Your* faces? Every place I go, you've been already.'

'Like where?'

'Josie Jervis, Party Box, the *QE2*, Mike's Hardware, and now this jerk.' Was that a prideful shine in her eye? Was she toting up all the places she'd been to first? Or the others I hadn't even thought of yet?

She said, 'That's what the State of Connecticut pays me for.'

'We could be partners, except I'm trying to free my client and you're trying to hang him.'

'I already have a partner.'

'Unless he runs my car into a light pole.'

'I wish you'd get a private-detective licence,' she said.

'Why?'

'Then we could take it away.'

As if I hadn't thought of that a long time ago.

'Seriously, Marian. Want to trade a little?'

Her answer was along lines I'd been expecting. And she sounded a little weary. 'We're being dicked around from up above. I do not want to be dicked around by you below.'

'Oh yeah? Who's dicking from above?'

Marian stopped the police car, slammed it into Park, turned around, and stared. She had great cheekbones and they were red with a degree of anger that surprised me.

I spoke before she could.

'Let me guess who's yanking your chain . . . Henry King's mega-clients would like to get on with their lives. They don't care if Mr Butler helped Dicky blow the dam. You're in their way – threatening their privacy, with your highly imaginative investigation. So someone had a word with the Feds and now the Feds are slipping it to your bosses sideways. No actual threat. But if the Connecticut State Police don't lay off, there's suddenly a slight problem with funding for some nice little extras, like a DNA lab or GPS locators for your road cops. Nothing you could put your finger on, of course.'

'Basketball courts.'

'They're taking away your gym?'

'The kids'. The Feds were funnelling money through for lighted basketball courts in the neighbourhoods. Give teenagers something better to do than shoot each other, make us look good.'

'And of course no one is actually *ordering* you to lay off. But if you don't, everyone knows that Sergeant Marian and Sergeant Arnie let underprivileged children drift into a life of crime.'

'You're not very funny.'

'I'm on target.'

'This is the kind of thing they wreck you on,' she answered quietly.

No woman rose as swiftly in the state police unless she was very ambitious. Marian was that. Like Vicky, she had an agenda, which, ironically, was political too. She was working on a law degree and planned to retire in her mid-forties to run for state office. But she was burdened with high standards.

I said, 'I feel for you. You're standing in front of people who get what they want. Is that why you're playing footsie with Josh Wiggens?'

'Who?'

'The guy who tipped you I was getting my head handed to me.'

'Never heard of him.'

'The guy sitting in that Taurus on the corner.'

'Friend of yours?'

'No.'

'Then why would he tip the police that you were getting beat up?'

'I have no idea.'

'It makes no sense, right?'

'No sense at all,' I agreed.

'Ben. If you can't tell me why such a thing would happen then it didn't happen.'

'What's he offering? Is he helping you somehow?'

204

'Who?'

'Josh Wiggens. He works for Henry King.'

'Oh, yeah. King's security man.'

'I'd be very careful of him, if I were you.'

Marian turned around and drove. I asked, 'Is Arnie pushing to sell out?'

'As a matter of fact, no. He's got his dander up.'

'So you'll do the right thing.'

'Yeah, right.'

'Except,' I said, 'it's the wrong thing.'

'How's that?'

'There was no conspiracy. Mr Butler did not put Dicky up to it and did not help him.'

'Says the real-estate agent.'

She headed north on 34, along the river.

My whole body ached. I'd been taught how to take a punch and I was not horribly wounded. But I still wanted a hot bath and to close my eyes in a cool, dark room for a while.

'You wouldn't want to uncuff me, by any chance?'

Silence. For miles. Finally, crossing the Stevenson Dam, she said, 'What do you have to trade?'

'You first.'

'Up yours.'

Silence, again. More miles. Deep into Plainfield County, on back roads even I didn't know. My turn: 'Mr Butler did not conspire with Dicky to blow King's dam.'

'Sure of that?'

'Positive.'

'Why?'

'You first.'

'Up yours.'

There was a fork in the road ahead that I recognized. Right led to Plainfield, the State Police Barracks, and jail. Left to Newbury.

I said, ' "Up yours" was essentially what Josie Jervis told *you*. I'll tell you what she told *me*. If you'll tell me what the Derby cops get out of J. J. Topkis.'

'Everything she told you?'

'Every fact,' I promised, damned if I was going to share

Josie's lunatic theory that Mr Butler accidentally killed his son.

'Deal,' said Marian, and veered left. 'When Derby's done with Topkis, I'll decide if it's worth a trade.'

'Would you take these goddammed handcuffs off, please?'

She tossed the key over her shoulder. 'You didn't mind them last time,' she reminded me.

'Last time was different.'

I found a note under my kitchen door. 'I'm at the Drover, if you feel like a beer. Julia.'

20

I felt like many beers. After some bourbon, a bath and an ice pack. Many beers.

It was nearly an hour before I limped into the Yankee Drover's cellar bar, scrubbed and dressed in a clean shirt and pants, with Jack Daniels beginning to numb the pain. (Aleve might have worked as well, but I'd miss the side effects.)

Julia had been at the juke box again.

There was a kind of a bittersweet pall hanging over the place, not exactly melancholy, but a lot of people not normally given to reflection appeared to be re-examining their lives. God knows what she had played first – *Deus Irae*, maybe – but Bob Seeger was just finishing 'In Your Time', and his promise that peace lay across the 'unbroken void' did not seem to cheer those hoping things would straighten out sooner.

I cranked in some Smokey Robinson and made for the bar on a tide of 'Since I met you baby'.

Julia had reserved the stool next to her with her bag. Blue jeans, tonight, blue as her mood. Snug, sleeveless stretch top. Her hair long and loose. She saw me and a tired smile wavered uncertainly. 'What happened to you?'

'Slipped in the shower.'

'Seriously, are you OK?'

'Yeah, I'm OK.' I sat carefully, nodded at her Rolling Rock. 'You did say beer?'

Annemarie, one of the new owners who turned the Drover into a much friendlier place than their surly predecessor, hurried over.

'Slipped in the shower,' I explained, adding that a beer would make things much better.

Julia seemed too preoccupied to ask questions, which was fine because I was not in an answering mood. So we listened to the music. But when I suggested another round, she said, 'I've a better idea. You're getting swollen. Let's go to your house and put ice on your face.'

It was a better idea. In fact it would have been perfect, if we hadn't run into Vicky as we were walking out. 'Ben, what happened to your face?'

'Slipped in the shower. You remember Julia Devlin, from Fox Trot?'

'Nice to see you again,' said Vicky. Her pretty, lively face was framed by her curls like a ruby in a filigree setting.

Julia nodded, a cool diamond on black velvet.

'Ben, are you OK?'

'Yeah, I'm going to do ice. Come along and watch, if you like. Thought we'd sit out back and have a beer.'

She hesitated for an instant. Then the light drifted from her face. 'No, I can't. I'm meeting someone.'

Julia, who had stood by noncommittally, said as we stepped outside, 'Am I causing you a problem?'

'No, I'm pretty good at that on my own.'

'Ben, if you want to do ice with her, feel free.'

'Don't worry about it.'

I took her in the kitchen door and opened a couple of Amstel Lights. Julia filled a plastic bag from the freezer and wrapped it in a towel and we went out to my cutting garden, where the day still lingered in the sky.

I eased into an Adirondack chair and held the cold cloth to my face. Julia wandered the narrow paths, exclaiming at the lush colours. I enjoyed looking at her. She was a fitting addition to the garden, an ornament in fine-lined opposition to the extravagant, jungly end-of-summer foliage.

She cast off her blues. 'I love this,' she kept saying.

I credited the seeper hoses buried under the mulch that had kept the flowers from wilting in the August heat. Coreopsis were hanging in, daisies, black-eyed Susans, zinnias and cosmos exploding into their own. My tea roses had just caught their third wind.

'This is what Captain Jack dreams of at sea.'

Of our beloved Patrick O'Brian novels. Jack Aubrey, a red-blooded fighting man and the scourge of Napoleon's navy, had a black thumb ashore, where his often-bankrupt estate was host to every cutworm and weevil in the British Isles.

'How do you do this?' she asked. The awe in her voice made me inordinately proud.

'My Aunt Connie taught me, "Put a fifty-cent plant in a five-dollar hole."'

Julia really did seem to love flowers, so I winced up out of the chair, filled a coffee can with water, and cut her a bunch. She followed me to the mulch pile where I stripped excess foliage and arranged some semblance of a bouquet, highlighted with blue spikes of salvia. 'Change the water and trim the stems every few days.'

She studied them bloom by bloom, then surprised me with a warm kiss on the cheek. 'Oh. Oh, God. I hope that didn't hurt. Your poor face.'

We sat down and drank beer.

'Need more ice?'

'No, it's fine. Tell me, how's the King–Butler defence fund coming along?'

'I don't know, yet. He may go for it. I can't promise.'

'Is he making your life miserable about it?'

'No.'

King couldn't be happy. The dilemma's horns I'd sent his way would scare the gonads off a matador. If he were involved in *killing* Dicky Butler, then Mr Butler's conviction for accessory to murder would end all investigations; but the trial could get awful messy if Mr Butler repeated his claim that he had set charges that King had defused. But if he or his people *didn't* murder Dicky Butler, the horns took on triceratops proportions: a trial that exposed King's secrets would anger betrayed clients; yet Butler's incarceration would let him snap up his farm.

I said, 'His best bet is to move quickly to get the charges dropped.'

Julia changed the subject. 'What are you doing to get his bail reduced?'

'Tim's hunting precedents back to Governor Winthrop's administration. And tapping old friends of his father.'

'That's a lot of work pro bono.'

'Ira Roth, mentor from hell, is encouraging him.'

'And what are you doing?'

'Going around asking questions.'

'Is that how you got the black eye?'

'You shoulda seen the other guys.'

Julia smiled, a startling flash of white against her olive skin and midnight hair. 'How many were there?'

'Three. But I had some help from the cops.'

'Cops? What were they doing there?'

'I got lucky. A concerned citizen tipped them off.'

'That *was* lucky.'

'Yes,' I said, wondering if any of this was news to her. 'They showed up in the nick of time.'

We talked about luck as the evening fell. Patrick O'Brian wrote about it as a serious commodity. Henry King taught his acolytes that they needed three things to succeed. Talent, hard work and luck. 'He says we can't make it big with only two.'

'Are you lucky?'

'In waves,' she answered. 'I was lucky to meet Henry. Got me out of a dead-end job.'

'Doing what?'

'I could see down a long life of civil service like a tunnel. Suddenly there was light.'

'A train.'

'In a way. Henry came roaring through and I jumped aboard. Never looked back.'

'Sounds like you left somebody lying on the tracks.'

'In the station.' She tried to smile, tried to make a joke. 'Please. I'm not that bad.'

'Josh Wiggens,' I said.

'Excuse me?'

'The concerned citizen. Who called the cops.'

'Josh? What was Josh doing there?'

'Beats me.'

'Are you being deliberately mysterious?'

I was, but I denied it. 'No. Maybe you could tell me what Josh was doing there.'

'How would I know?'

'Well, you work together.'

'That may be, but I don't – where was this?'

'Derby. It's a river town.'

'I know Derby. We were down there buying stained glass for the house.'

'Then you know it's a long way from Fox Trot.'

'Ben.' She shook her head and looked baffled. 'I don't know what to say. He goes off on his own . . .'

'Well, when you see him, tell him thanks. Saved me a trip to the emergency room.'

'I have no idea what he was doing there.'

'Maybe he was visiting his girlfriend or some old CIA buddy. There's a helicopter plant near there. At any rate, it was lucky for me . . . Are you still lucky?'

'Hope so. How about you?'

'I think your friend Josh cashed in most of mine today.'

'Henry says you should make your own luck.'

'Lucky people say that. Makes them feel less afraid they'll lose theirs. Am I right that you're a little down, tonight?'

'Just work.'

'OK.'

'Maybe I'm a little depressed.'

'Something happen?'

'It was just – he was just . . . he screwed up and then . . . I don't know.'

'And then he blamed you.'

'I guess that's what happened. Why do you keep pushing that button?'

'In New York I had a woman like you work for me. And I saw plenty others. Big business, small business, there's always a glorified go-fer stashed in the back room to keep the boss on track. Always a woman. Job description includes be cool, be calm, think ahead, cultivate contacts, cover the guy's ass, and take abuse. It's a hard life. The only happy ones go up and out.'

'Did yours go up and out?'

'Like a Saturn rocket. Nothing left but cinders on the launchpad.'

'How did you feel about that?'

'I survived. And so will Henry.'

'But how did you feel? Were you scarred? Did it take for ever to recover? Have you recovered?'

'Yes. Mostly.'

'Do you hate her?'

'On my good days I tell myself I can look back in fifty years and say, "Better she got out, than got old and tired carrying my bags."'

Julia bristled. 'Well, Henry would be the same way. He'd support me if I wanted to leave. He'd . . . do everything he could to help me. Ben, why do you make me doubt him?'

'I'm sorry. I have a big mouth sometimes. I get very opinionated. And, to be honest, I like you. I'm fascinated by you. If you told me you were dumping him, I'd say, How about a date?'

Julia regarded me for one of the most serious seconds I've ever experienced. 'You know what I like about you?' she finally asked. 'I like that you're not afraid to annoy me.'

'Why should I be afraid? I don't need anything from Henry King.'

'*Everyone* wants something from Henry King. All those bloodsuckers feeding off him.'

'You mean like Josh and Bert?'

'*You* want Mr Butler's lawyer paid.'

'That's a decision I can't influence. I've done my job. I've brought it up –'

'That's not what I mean.'

In the fading light I could see a little pout shape her lips and cloud her eyes. 'What did I say? You look hurt.'

'I wasn't talking about Henry King,' she answered quietly. 'I was talking about me. You don't know it, but when I'm not with him, I'm a very strong person. Most men are afraid

212

to annoy *me* regardless of the boss I happen to work for.'

'The boss who happens to treat you like a very weak person.'

'Maybe you're just like him.'

'Me?'

'Maybe you're bullying me under a guise of telling me how terribly he treats me?'

'Why would I do that?'

'Maybe you want me to betray him.'

'Better than betraying yourself,' I answered, with no idea whether we were talking about Mr Butler or sex or love. Or, with luck, all three.

An unlucky mosquito chose the moment I was leaning closer to land on Julia's knee. I killed it and said, 'Let's go inside. They're beginning to bite.'

21

The kissing started on the wrong side of the screen door. It was long and hungry and when we finally got inside, we were kind of bitten up. Rubbing alcohol occasioned rubbing.

Our fall into bed was the culmination of a slow tumble that had started last winter at that lunch at Fox Trot. It was worth the wait.

If you tumble into a fall, what happens next? Fling? Swoop? Dive. Plunge. Immerse. Emerge.

'Don't stop!'

We left the lights on. We drank a little beer. Deep in the night we got hungry and we went down to the kitchen and I made omelettes. I doubt we tasted them any more than reconnaissance jets refuelling in the air.

Partway up the stairs – old friends by now – we grew impatient, and acrobatic. DaNang, who had taken a shine to Julia, thumped his tail enthusiastically. I asked him to go out and hunt rattlesnakes. Back in bed, I told Julia she was the strongest woman I'd ever known. Her sleek arms and ripply legs were hard with muscle. She bench-pressed me to prove my point, and told me she worked out to burn excess sexual energy. I told her how glad I was the regimen hadn't worked. While she rested, I turned us over and practised curls.

Birds woke us and we slipped together like we'd known how since the Ice Age. I was gone after that, like a skydiver minus chute, who had enjoyed every second of the trip. Suddenly, I awakened, thinking how wonderful life was, and only gradually realizing that something was wrong.

Julia was curled on the far side of the mattress, her body tight, and shaking with sobs.

I reached for her. She stiffened. I went to hold her. She pulled away.

'Don't.'

'What's the matter?'

'Please don't.'

I climbed out of the bed, walked around it, and sat on the floor where I could see her face. I kept my hands to myself and said, 'If it helps at all, you've made one person very happy.'

'Great. You're happy. That's just wonderful.'

'Well, I am.'

'How do you think I feel?'

'Up until just now I thought you felt great.'

'It was great. Thanks a lot.'

'I've heard sweeter tones from sergeants of firing squads.'

'Would you please just leave me alone. I'll be OK in a while. I really will.'

I retreated to the kitchen – figuring, OK, she's feeling guilty about King, or mad at herself for betraying him, or mad at me for seducing her into it. I brewed some coffee and brought it upstairs, hers in a covered mug. She had curled under the sheet, small as a child. When I eased back into bed, she took the sip offered, then tentatively pillowed her head on my thigh and closed her eyes. Her face was streaked with tears and new ones kept creeping from her lashes.

I think if murdering someone would have made her happy I'd have done it on the spot. She let me stroke her hair. After a while, I asked, 'Can you talk?'

'I don't want to.'

I waited some more. 'Mind if I guess?'

'Yes, I do mind.'

'It might help.'

'Just because I slept with you doesn't give you the right to know my whole damned life.'

'I don't want to know your whole damned life. I just wish you could be happy right here and now.'

'This isn't about you.'

215

'I was hoping it was about us.'

'Well, it's not,' she snapped angrily.

'So it's about him.'

When was I going to learn to keep my mouth shut? She sat up, bundling herself in the sheet, and glared. 'It's about my wasted life. OK? Not yours. Not his. *My* wasted life. OK?'

'OK.'

'Your face is bleeding.'

'Just from washing.'

'I'll fix it.' She stalked to the bathroom – a sight to sizzle the retinas – ran warm water on a washcloth and dabbed my cheek. Then she rummaged in the medicine cabinet and scampered back with Band-aids and gently covered the cut. Being busy had stopped her tears, and when she was done with the Band-aid, she kissed around it. 'Hurt?'

'No.' In fact, I told her, our night had done wonders for my aches and pains. Better, much better, than Aleve or Jack. Although in the interest of medical science, I wondered whether more testing was in order.

'Could we do it without talking?'

I nodded.

When next she woke, she said, 'You're smiling.'

'Yup.'

She sat up and inspected the Band-aid. 'I hope you don't have plans to get punched before this heals.'

'I'm planning to spend the rest of the year in this bed with you.'

'Tell me it's not past nine.'

'Eight-thirty.'

'I gotta go.'

'That door is barred.'

'Oh, I wish.' She spotted the covered mug. 'For me? . . . Oh, God. Thank you. You even make coffee.' She looked around my bedroom. 'Do you know where my clothes are?'

'Burned 'em,' I said. I showed her the shower and gave her a towel and a toothbrush and had fresh coffee ready when she came out. This was one house guest I wanted coming back.

I was surprised, considering the time, that she accepted my offer for breakfast. Coffee, toast and Aunt Connie's strawberry preserves.

'So what are *you* doing today?'

'Reminiscing.'

'You sweet thing. No more fights?'

'I think I'll make it phone and paperwork day.'

Ollie was on my list. I had to build up a timeline for the hours the state trooper could have killed Dicky and dynamited the dam. No way to get a look at his log for the weekend of the Fox Trot party. But I could read the police reports in the *Clarion* to find the various miscreants Ollie had nailed speeding, cited for failure to maintain control of their vehicles – his standard diagnosis for highway accidents – and arrested for beating up their wives.

And while I was in, check out Henry King's government status with the Admiral, which would entail waiting around for return calls.

Julia stroked the head DaNang had dropped on her lap. 'Real estate or Mr Butler?'

'There isn't much real estate in late August. I've got plenty of time for Butler.'

'Well, I'll push Henry today. Can I tell him what you're doing?'

I'd been wondering about that all night. '. . . There's a couple of theories going around that maybe Dicky Butler didn't blow the dam.'

'Isn't that the state police theory?'

'The cop theory says Mr Butler helped Dicky, which makes him an accessory. Another theory says Mr Butler blew the dam alone – and had the incredibly bad luck to accidentally kill his son in the process.'

'Coincidence aside, that has a logical ring to it. Is there another theory?'

'Neither of them did it.'

'What?' She stopped patting. DaNang groaned and nearly turned over the table as he tried to get his head under her hand again. Julia asked, 'Who, then?'

'It's just possible that Dicky was already dead and his killer blew it up on top of him to get rid of the body.'

'Are you serious?'

'They could count on a favourable post mortem.'

'Is this your theory or the cops' theory?'

'I *thought* it was my theory. I worked it up with Tim Hall and Ira. But every place I go to ask a question Detective-Sergeant Boyce and weaselly sidekick are there ahead of me.'

Assuming the worst – King killed Dicky, and Julia reported everything to him – he'd at least have to wonder whether the sudden death of an unarmed real-estate agent would solve all his problems.

'Is the weasel Bender?'

'You've met.'

'They were up at Fox Trot.'

'When?'

'Well, the day of the explosion, of course. And several times since.'

'What did they ask?'

Julia shrugged. 'Josh dealt with them. He said they were following up on the explosion.'

'Speaking of Josh. He warned me off you, you should know.'

'You didn't listen.'

'Does he do that often?'

'You're the first,' she smiled. '. . . He knows me too well.'

'Are you safe around him? I mean, is he obsessed or something?'

'Don't worry about me, Ben. If I didn't feel safe Henry would fire him.'

Julia looked at her diamond-crusted watch. She had carried it in her bag, last night. It would have been ostentatious in the Yankee Drover. And scratchy in bed. But I recalled my years of sending ladies Rolexes instead of roses, and couldn't help but notice room on her other wrist for a Cartier bracelet.

'Gotta go. Thanks for a great time.' She kissed me on the mouth. 'Many great times.'

'I'll call you,' I said.

'Listen, I'm sorry about before.'

'Don't be. You've got a lot of balls in the air. Oh, Jeez, that sounds – I meant –'

Julia laughed. 'You're blushing.'

'I'm sorry.'

'No, I am. You deserve better. I'm really mad at myself for taking it out on you.'

She scooped her flowers off the kitchen table and cradled them to her breast. 'It's like there's two of me – rational and irrational. I'm caught between them – and so are you.'

One last kiss. Then another, interrupted when Alison banged on the screen door. 'DaNang? Walk time! Oh . . . Ben, what happened to your face?'

'Slipped in the shower. Come in. Come in.'

She came, downcast eyes taking in the flowers and the breakfast dishes.

'Alison, I'd like you to meet Ms Devlin. Julia, this is Alison Mealy, my neighbour.'

Alison extended her hand, as I had taught her, and said, 'How do you do?'

Julia shook her hand and said, 'Oh, I've heard so much about you. How are your riding lessons coming along?'

Alison shuffled her sneakers and mumbled that they were going to start jumps today.

'Good luck. It's very nice to meet you. Bye, Ben. We'll talk.'

Alison watched her hurry down the drive. 'Is she buying a house?'

'If I'm lucky.'

'She's kind of skinny.'

'She works out a lot.'

Alison's gaze swept again the toast plates for two. 'Do you trust her?'

'I beg pardon?'

'She wouldn't look me in the eye.'

'Maybe she was surprised to see you just then.'

'I don't like her.'

'She's very nice,' I said, gently.

It had taken her ages to cotton to Marian and then only

219

because she adored Marian's five-year-old, Jason. She was polite to my friend Rita, but never warm, though a ride in Rita's Jag convertible had melted her some.

'You haven't said anything about my hair,' she said.

'I noticed it's longer.'

'You did?'

'Sure.'

She laid a hand partway down her shoulder. 'When it gets to here, Vicky's going to make me curls.'

'Excellent,' I said. 'There isn't anyone who knows more about curls than Vicky.'

She was loyal to Vicky. Vicky who did her hair for her. Vicky who let her watch her make up. Vicky who Aunt Connie said Ben ought to marry before he lost an excellent woman.

She tugged at her hair as if to accelerate the growth. 'Can I ask you something, Ben?'

'Sure.'

'Why do you trust her?'

'Julia? Because we're very similar. We think alike.'

'Oh, that's a great reason.'

'DaNang likes her.'

'She probably fed him behind your back. Let's go, DaNang! You traitor.'

'Hey, Alison! Where's that *Clarion* I was saving?'

'Under his dish.'

The Police Report indicated that Trooper Moody had had an unusually busy weekend, even before the biggest dam in his territory was blown to bits. There'd been a slew of traffic accidents and several break-ins. On top of that, Plainfield Barracks had issued him a new laser speed detector, which he had put to enthusiastic use. Scooter had published a photograph of him pointing the damned thing at the camera like a Klingon death ray. It had worked so well that I was going to need help tracking down everyone he'd nailed.

I telephoned Aunt Connie and read her a list of speeders starting with Mildred Gill and ending with Al Bell.

'I read all that in the *Clarion*,' she said. 'Are you aware that none of these people are younger than seventy-five?'

'I'm giving you the older ones.'

'People our age don't speed.'

'The laser doesn't lie,' I said. 'And apparently it allows him to get you coming or going, which you might remember next time you unleash your Lincoln.' (Her thirty-year-old Continental was powered by a pre-pollution-control, pre-guzzler-tax engine Lincoln had built to compete with NASA's moon shots.)

'Just ask what time were they stopped? How long did it take Ollie to write the ticket? And what was his mood?'

'Triumphant, I'd imagine.'

'Please don't put words in people's mouths. Just get their impressions.'

'They'll get the impression that I'm the biggest busybody on Main Street.'

I then got on the phone to several younger ticket recipients whom I knew personally. Indignation ran high, shame low. Steve LaFrance's 'Thirty-two fucking miles an hour in a thirty zone', pretty much capsulized their mood. As to Ollie's mood, smug and gloating were repeated frequently.

All remarked, too, on the briskness of the encounter. He had wasted no time on unnecessary registration checks and less on his famous lecture that concluded with an ominous, 'I don't want to have to pull you over again,' when you both knew he just couldn't wait to pull you over again.

I phoned my condolences to a couple of Danbury Hospital patients recovering from a River Road head-on. Ollie, it seemed, had proved Solomonic in an attempt to hasten the investigation, slapping both colliders with 'excessive speed for conditions'.

A Jervis had been nailed for DWI. Abe, a half-breed – Jervis father, Chevalley mother.

The telephone company has never run lines into their woods, knowing full well they'd be pulled down for copper. And while, like any respectable modern criminals, they used cell phones and beepers, these numbers were guarded closely. So I drove out to the River End Bar – a dirt-road juke-joint in the deep north woods that made the White

Birch look like the Rainbow Room – hoping to find Abe bonded to a barstool.

He wasn't. Working, I was told. I bought a six-pack from Matthew Jervis, who owned the dive, being among the very few of the clan without a record. Then I drove rut tracks and lumber roads for an hour or so, and finally found Abe hard at work in an open-air bodyshop chopping some poor guy's Toyota four-by.

It was a clearing in the woods about the size of a suburban backyard, littered with skeletons of cars and trucks rusting in the bug-infested sunlight. Noise from their gas-powered compressor for the air tools masked my approach and I was inside the clearing before they noticed.

Skinny teenagers ran into the trees.

Abe stood up with a resigned expression that turned to relief when he recognized me. Pushing fifty, hard, he had a Willie Nelson ponytail, the scars and broken teeth of a fearless man who'd lost more fights than he'd won, and eyes used to groping through a chemical haze. It was even money whether he remembered he owed me a favour.

While his clansmen crept back suspiciously, debating whether it was worth trying to strip my car, I asked him about his arrest.

'How late we talking?' I asked, after we had popped a couple of Buds and established month and day.

'Hell, I don't know.'

'Midnight?'

'Yeah, midnight.'

'Newspaper said Ollie released you on your own recognizance.'

'Yeah.'

'How'd you get home?'

'Hitched.'

'Lucky he didn't lock you up.'

'Yeah, I figured I'd be sleeping in Plainfield. 'Stead he just lets me go.'

'Why?'

'I don't know.'

'Did he beat you up?'

222

'Naw. Slapped me around a little – I could tell his heart wasn't in it – confiscated my keys and sent me walkin'.'

'I wonder why?'

'You know what I think?'

'What do you think?'

'I think Ollie's gettin' old. If he weren't gonna lock me up, he shoulda kicked my ass, 'steada just letting me go. Shoulda happened, right? A man used to know he gets caught alone by Ollie Moody, he's gonna get his ass kicked. Now, a man don't know if he's coming or going.'

'Where'd he go when he left you?'

'Whole goddammed world's going to hell.'

I passed him another warm beer. 'Which way did Ollie go?'

'Morrisville Road.'

'East?'

East to Morris Mountain, Fox Trot and the Butler farm. 'Midnight?' I asked again, and Abe Jervis said that sounded right to him. Though it could have been one or two. Or maybe three.

Back in civilization, I found Connie in her rose garden. She'd fallen asleep reading the *Wall Street Journal*. My shadow crossed her as I reached for the paper and she awakened with a puzzled smile. '. . . Loveliest dream . . . Hello, Ben.'

'Like some tea?'

I brought tea pot, hot water, china and shortbread out to her. She put down the *Journal* with an indignant snort. 'I cannot understand why this otherwise excellent newspaper puts the comics on the editorial page.'

'How'd you make out with your fast-lane friends?'

Connie snorted again. 'No shame. They're *proud*! Trooper Moody spiced up their lives.'

'What did they say about Ollie?'

'His usual holier-than-thou self. A bit short. Very little time spent on lectures. What did your friends report?'

'The same. Except they're not proud. They're mad as hell.'

'What's this about, Ben?'

'Trying to figure out how he spent his time that weekend.'

'I wrote it all down.'

He had been very busy in the hours between the Thursday that Mr Butler had turned his sticks and the Saturday afternoon King's dam exploded. Twenty-seven speeding tickets in three days – how his new laser toy missed me I'll never know – six accidents, traffic control at two fires, domestic disturbances, a scuffle of teens in the Grand Union parking lot, burglary investigations.

Eventually, I could account for his waking hours. Except for one long, three-hour gap between ten o'clock Saturday morning and one o'clock when he issued an octogenarian a speeding ticket on 349, fifteen minutes from the Butler farm.

Waking hours. But while normal humans slept, Ollie could have snuck up Morris Mountain and transferred Mr Butler's dynamite to King's dam. Then, Saturday before one, killed Dicky Butler after Josie dropped him off, and carried his body to the lake? But where had he hidden his cruiser? The big grey Ford stood out like a lion on the prowl.

I was getting nowhere.

Mike's Hardware was between the dry cleaner and the Grand Union.

If there's a happier man in Newbury I've never met him. Mike came home from the Vietnam War with medals he'll never discuss and a GI Bill accounting degree. For years he had commuted up to Pratt and Whitney's financial office. Then one day he seized his dream and leased the old hardware store.

In the teeth of the shopping mall warehouse home centres he kept it personal. You can buy a wing nut from Mike, a single cotter pin, or three lock washers. He'll beat Ag-Way on seventeen-gauge deer fence wire and NAPA Auto Parts on windshield wipers, and he discounts Makita power tools. You'll pay more than elsewhere for your wheelbarrow, but it comes assembled by the scads of relatives he's got working for him, and if it won't fit in your car they'll drive it home for you. On slow mornings, after the contractors have bought their supplies, Mike can be found crouched on a stool sorting his nuts and bolts drawers, happy as Silas Marner.

Happy, at least, until I asked him about his encounter with Sergeant Marian Boyce of the Connecticut State Police. 'Ben, I swear I wouldn't have told her a thing, but she found some old biddy who'd heard it too, told her I was there and heard the whole thing. Which I did. She leaned hard, she knew she had me.'

'Who was the old biddy?'

'Edna Crampton.'

'Oh, no.'

Miss Crampton had branded the English language on fifth graders' brains for forty years. Steel bear traps were slower and gentler than her mind. And her hearing was as acute as a grand jury would expect of the choirmistress of the Newbury Episcopal Church.

'Did Mr Butler really say he would blow King's dam?'

'Among other things.'

'Like what?'

'The only thing Miss Crampton heard was the dam and that's all I'm repeating.'

'I'm trying to get him out on bail. Can you help us?'

'Trust me, man. It won't help.'

'Trust *me*. Let me decide what'll help.'

Mike reached into the five-sixteenths hex nut drawer and extracted a three-eighths that some barbarian had returned there by mistake. 'If I'm the only one who heard it, it's safer with me.'

'Mike. Give us a break. We're beating the bushes for anything. What else did he say? Look, did King hear it?'

'If he didn't he was deaf.'

'What'd he say?'

Mike sighed. 'I hope you know what you're doing, Ben.'

'If I don't, I've got Tim Hall and Ira Roth backing me up. I have client–attorney privilege. You can talk to me and it doesn't go any farther. What did you tell the detective?'

'Just that Richard threatened to blow the dam.'

'What else did he threaten?'

'He told King to buy a bag of clothespins.'

'Clothespins? What for?'

'He said his party guests were going to need them.'

'Did he say why?'

'Not to King.'

'What did King say?'

'The whole damned thing was King's fault. And lousy luck. I mean how often does a farmer come in here, right? He finds what he needs in his junk pile or he makes it. So that damned day had to be the one day Richard's in here trying to buy a Swiss Army knife.'

'A Swiss Army knife? What for?'

'Dicky's birthday.'

The knife display was next to the key-cutting machine. I'd peruse it occasionally, wishing it were as exciting as it had been when I was a kid.

'He told me, first time he'd bought a birthday present in twenty years. He was really getting into it. Anyway, King's in the next aisle raving to somebody about how he's going to buy his neighbour's busted-down farm for back taxes. I mean, how stupid can the guy get?'

'He probably didn't realize Mr Butler was in the next aisle.'

'Even if he didn't know Richard was listening, it's pretty dumb to go around Newbury bragging he's going to rip off his neighbour. What kind of a jerk is he? It's gotta get back to the guy you're badmouthing.'

'Apparently he's not the most diplomatic diplomat.'

'Yeah, well anyhow, Richard goes postal down the aisle, so mad he's spitting, "It's not for sale. Not for sale." That's when he said he'd blow the dam.'

'What did King say?'

'He sounded kind of scared, like he believed him. He said, "That's a very serious threat, Butler. I should report it to the police." ' Mike plucked an offending washer and restored it to its proper place. He looked up at me, a reflective expression on his face. 'Richard seemed to catch hold of himself. I thought he was going to start screaming more, but he backed down a little. Mumbled something I couldn't hear. Then he said, "There's more than one way to skin a cat." That's when he told him to buy the clothespins. Came back and stood staring at the knives until King left. Just blinking at them. You know, like when a kid's trying not to cry?'

'What's the thing about the clothespins?'

Mike looked around, confirmed we were alone in nuts and bolts and whispered, 'I asked him, soon as King left: "Richard, what's with the clothespins?" He said if worst came to worst he was going to order a tank truck of liquid pig shit and spread it on that field he leased from old Zarega. You know the field I mean?'

'Oh, yes.'

'I'm not a farmer, but I hear it really, really stinks.'

'I smelled it once. It was a long time before I ate another BLT. But who keeps pigs around here? Enough for a tank truck? That's some kind of factory operation.'

'Over in New York. Columbia County.'

An hour drive. 'Do you think he meant it?'

'Sounded like he'd already talked to them. Said he just had to call and they'd send a spreader truck right to the field. He said it cost almost nothing. They're glad to get rid of the stuff.'

'What did he mean by worst comes to worst?'

'I don't know.'

'I guess it didn't. Because he didn't do it . . . You hear about the flies?'

'Al Bell was telling me. It must have been funny as hell, till Dicky got killed.'

'Pig manure would have been a lot worse than flies. Wonder why he changed his mind?'

I walked back up Church Hill, thinking I'd grab breakfast at the General Store. Ollie went by in his cruiser. When he saw me on the sidewalk, he pulled a tyre-squealing U-turn and shoved the passenger door open. It was amazing how he filled the big car.

'Get in.'

Very curious, I obeyed.

22

The trooper was wearing his mirrored sunglasses, so God knew what was churning in his brain. The new laser speed detector sat on the seat between us. A nightstick was clamped within easy reach and a locked clip held a stubby shotgun. Handy for fighting his way back to his main arsenal in the trunk. It occurred to me that the UN was missing a bet dispatching mere armies to enforce the peace.

'Hear you been checking up on me.'

Excellent. I said, 'You were a busy man the weekend Dicky died.'

'Why?'

'You tell me.'

'Why are you checking me out, you son of a bitch?'

'I've been trying to figure out where you were between ten A.M. and one P.M. that Saturday.'

The sunglasses didn't hide the tightening of his mouth. He covered quickly. 'Stay out of my face, Ben.'

'Are you saying stop asking questions?'

'I'm warning you. Stay out of my face.'

"Cause if you are, just tell me now where you were between ten and one.'

He amazed me by answering, 'Traffic control.'

'Could I see your log?'

'You get a goddammed court order you can see my log.'

'Why not save us both the trouble?'

'Why you asking? What do you want?'

Instinct said now was the time to get out of his car. I opened the door. He stomped the gas. The cruiser leaped forward, shutting the door.

I counted the fingers I'd almost lost and said, quickly, 'Ira Roth and Tim Hall are also curious. They told me I was taking a chance of riling you, but I said, "No, Ollie surely has some perfectly legal explanation for how he spent those mystery hours."'

'I don't owe you any explanation.'

'"Besides," I told them, "a sworn peace officer isn't about to assault a law-abiding citizen who's already turned over his meticulous notes to the two lawyers who employ him."'

'You think you're really smart, don't you?'

'No, Ollie. I don't. But I don't think you're that stupid.'

Maybe not, but he sped up. Which reminded me that one could go wrong forgetting that Ollie was a sociopath in uniform. I had a feeling I'd just gone wrong.

The big Ford took the turns like a train on rails. We went through Frenchtown at sixty-five, passed Chevalley Enterprises, the garage where Pink fed my Oldsmobile money, and north into the woods and farms.

I had turned pretty wild as a kid around the time I realized I wasn't going to be the upstanding and proper citizen my father had been. In a small town like Newbury, 'wild' meant challenging the turf controlled by the resident trooper.

Ollie had tried to tame me. I had resisted. Pain and suffering had been shared about equally and it was largely a draw. My biggest win was the time I chained the rear end of his cruiser to a large tree, with enough slack to guarantee we would stay at each other's throats for ever.

'You can slow down, Ollie. I won't jump out even at thirty.'

'You sure of that?'

Scooter would headline the front-page story, 'PROMINENT LOCAL REALTOR FOUND DEAD ON FRENCHTOWN ROAD. . . "Thought it was some poor deer at first," reported Newbury's Resident State Trooper Oliver Moody. "Saw what was left of the face and realized it wasn't."'

Ollie swerved on to a dirt road. After a couple miles, he slammed on the brakes. The big Ford stopped fast and straight.

'Out!'

'Let me tell you what's going on.'

229

'Get out!'

'I think Dicky Butler was murdered.'

'Bull. He blew himself up.'

'I think somebody blew his body up.'

'You're dreaming.'

'I'm trying to clear suspects. Obviously, you're a prime one when it comes to motive.'

I waited. He said nothing. I couldn't see a thing through his glasses.

'On the other hand, you're a police officer. I don't think you go around murdering people.'

'Well, you're right about that, Ben.'

'So what I'm saying is, help me and I'll help you clear this thing up. You're vulnerable. You help me. I'll help you.'

'Out!'

I climbed out, wishing I had the brains to run and knowing pride would stop me. Ollie outweighed me by a hundred pounds and in the long run I didn't have a chance, even if he left his stick in the car. He knew it too. He sat there, making me wait for it. It would have been nice if someone drove up, but that wasn't likely in the middle of nowhere.

'Any more questions, Ben?'

'Same question. Where were you between ten and one the Saturday Dicky got killed?'

'Traffic control,' he repeated. 'Any more?'

'Yes. What makes you think I'm not going to find out?'

'When you do you're going to feel pretty stupid. Could have saved yourself a long, hot walk.'

He stomped the accelerator. The Ford threw dust and gravel and a moment later was a loud roar fading fast.

'Son of a bitch.'

It would have been a pleasant walk without the humidity, the heat, the swarming gnats and biting deer flies. A hat would have helped a lot. So would bug spray. I got to Cheval-ley Enterprises in about two hours – mid-morning there hadn't been a damned car going my way – my clothes soaked with sweat, my arms tired from waving off the gnats.

Pink thought it was the funniest thing he'd heard in weeks.

I got a free Diet Coke and doughnut in the customer waiting room while waiting for him to give me a lift, and had a chat with Betty Chevalley, my cousin Renny's widow, who was making a go of the business in spite of Pink's help. I asked if she were seeing anyone, yet. She told me she didn't have the time. 'Besides, who's going to go out with a working Mom?'

'You're a pretty cute working Mom.'

She was a redhead – a Butler girl, distantly related to my client. I assured her we had high hopes and that I was heading over to the Plainfield jail to see him now. She bagged him some jelly doughnuts.

A sly smile started to light up the prisoner visiting room, when I asked Mr Butler about his pig manure plan. But it faded as if wind had snuffed a candle.

'Damn truck never showed.'

'Is that why you ran the cows in instead?'

'My last shot.'

He chewed mechanically on the doughnuts, polishing them off one after the other after I swore I'd had lunch on the way over. 'Pig shit would have been better. Or the other thing.'

'The "other thing"?'

'You know. What I told you about. What you said don't repeat.'

I'd been hoping he'd forgotten.

'So now what?' he asked.

'Tim's plugging away. And I'm going around asking questions for him.' No way I'd share my Dicky-was-murdered theory. He had too many theories of his own.

'Right now, I've got an appointment to pump Detective-Sergeant Boyce.'

'Yeah, you do that.' He tucked his chin to his chest. His hair curtained his face, and he curled inside a hopeless stare.

I hurried across the street to the State Police Barracks.

Major Case Squad Detective-Sergeant Marian Boyce looked lovely through the bullet-proof glass, dressed for court

231

in a pleated skirt that brushed her knees and a loose blazer that covered her gun. 'You can buy me lunch.'

'How about the Hopkins Inn?'

'Room service? I don't think you're going to feel up to it.'

We found a booth in the courthouse diner. Lunching troopers eyed us curiously. After we ordered, I said, 'I'm surprised you're hungry. You look like you've had the canary special.'

'For breakfast.'

'Tell me.'

'We had a deal: you tell me what you got from Josie Jervis. If it's not smoke, I'll tell you what I got from J. J. Topkis.'

I said, 'Josie told me that Dicky was too drunk Saturday morning to *walk*, much less dynamite King's dam. He'd been drinking all night.'

Marian's grey eyes complemented her basic bored-and-cynical-law-officer look. 'She's trying to protect him.'

'From what? He's dead.'

'Go on.'

'You want more?'

'Damned right I want more.'

'Josie and Dicky were planning a picnic that afternoon. He was going to crash for a couple of hours and then they were driving out to the picnic rock. By the covered bridge?'

'I remember it.'

'Fondly?'

'Right up there with First Communion. Is that all you have to trade?'

'That's a lot.'

'What's it supposed to mean?'

'It casts very strong doubt on the idea that Dicky blew up the dam. And even stronger doubt on your conspiracy case against Mr Butler.'

'Oh really?'

'If they'd teamed up Mr Butler certainly wouldn't have left Dicky holding the dynamite.'

'You're reaching.'

'Your turn.'

'I already knew that Dicky was drunk.'

'How?'

'His drinking buddy told me.'

'Who?'

'J. J. Topkis.'

'No way! J. J. hated Dicky.'

'They shook hands and went drinking.'

'You believe Topkis?'

'I believe the witnesses I interviewed who confirmed that J. J. and Dicky were very friendly.'

I couldn't believe I was hearing this.

Marian said, 'J. J. says they told each other all their secrets.'

'What did Dicky tell J. J.?'

'Dicky got downright confessional.'

'What did he confess?'

'Oh aren't we excited? Big real-estate deal pending?'

'Marian.'

Marian licked her lips. 'Dicky Butler told J. J. Topkis that his father – your client – taught him how to make a detonator timer out of a wristwatch.'

'What?'

'And your client also taught his son how to guarantee that the bomb squad would never find the watch.'

23

I threw money on the table. 'I gotta run.'

'Oh, come on. Stay for lunch. Don't be a sore loser.'

'It's not a game. The poor man's dying in jail.'

J. J. Topkis's story made Mr Butler a perjurer for testifying that Dicky knew nothing about explosives. Worse, it made him a participant and accessory to murder.

I said, 'Wait. J. J. nails Dicky's dead hide to the wall – not to mention Mr Butler's – with an uncorroboratable lie that conveniently eliminates himself as a suspect.'

'Did I say J. J.'s a suspect?'

'Can he prove it?'

Marian smiled. 'Did I say it's "uncorroboratable"?'

'Is it?'

Silence.

'Come on, Marian. I'm running around in circles. It wouldn't be a big deal to tell me if you've eliminated Topkis as a suspect.'

'Running in circles? Ohhhh. Did it ever occur to you that your circles keep *you* out of *my* way?'

'Thanks a lot. How did this supposed timer disappear?'

'A little watch. Coated with a nitro paste, so when it blows, there's nothing left to find. Isn't that interesting?'

'Bull. They always find something.'

'Not always. Especially when an entire lake washes away the evidence . . . Ben, where you going? Aren't you hungry?'

'You're that sure?'

'Believe it, fella.'

'J. J. could have read that in the library. So could Dicky.'

Marian grinned. 'You really disappoint me, Ben.'

234

I disappointed *myself*. I was falling way behind. I had to do something to catch up. '. . . Look, do me one favour.'

'Maybe.'

'Get me a copy of Trooper Moody's log for the Saturday morning before the explosion.'

Marian stopped grinning. And in case I'd forgotten who she was she gave me a dose of cop eyes, bleak as a January midnight. 'Out of some damned good memories, I'm going to pretend I didn't hear that.'

'I apologize,' I said.

'You have some nerve.'

'I never should have asked.'

Our tuna sandwiches arrived just in time. I chomped into mine to hide a smile that an unfriendly observer might have called a smirk.

I never expected her to hand me state police documents. But if I knew Marian, she'd be poring through Trooper Moody's reports the second she got back to the barracks, wondering what the hell I was getting at. I gave her two days of frustration before she finally came out and asked.

A minor victory, however, compared to the damage J. J. Topkis had sown. Unless Tim could find some way to keep the biker's testimony out of the trial, Mr Butler would end up wishing he was back in Vietnam.

I didn't believe him. A banger who took pride in his sucker punch was exactly the kind to shake hands and hoist a few with an enemy he was about to blow to Kingdom Come. But why stick it to Mr Butler, too?

I burned up the roads back to Newbury and ran into Town Hall. The first selectman's door was open, her receptionist off somewhere. I knocked on the frame.

Vicky looked up and pushed her curls from her face. 'What?'

'Can we talk?'

'Zoning and Planning are down the hall. Tax Collector across the lobby.'

'Vicky, every time I turn around I see you holding hands with Tim.'

'You've never seen me hold hands with him.'

'Well, I've seen him put his arm around you.'

'Take it up with him.'

'Look, this is kind of important and I –'

'Sorry,' she said. 'I thought we were talking about something important.'

'Vicky, I'm sorry.'

'Hey, you don't owe me apologies.'

'But you're acting like I do.'

'No, I'm acting like I'm hurt. Which I am. Even cheerful Vicky gets hurt, sometimes. When I see you with somebody.'

At that moment, seeing the hurt in her face, I wished I could say that Julia was just one of those things.

'What do you want?'

'Can I close the door? It's private.'

'Oh, this wasn't?'

'OK if I close the door?'

She nodded. I closed it and came in and sat in the chair beside her desk.

Vicky rounded on me, 'Did it ever occur to you that if I screwed around the way you do you'd think I was a *whore*?'

'No. Because, as you darned well ought to remember, when I get involved I get deeply involved.'

I felt pretty proud of the depth and clarity of my answer until she shot it down with a scornful, 'That's worse! You talk yourself into that romantic fairy tale and make yourself so damned believable that you end up hurting every woman who falls for you.'

'I get hurt, too, Vicky.'

'Oh good. I feel better already.'

Several minutes into a silence less pleasant than assisting at an amputation, I ventured, 'Let me say that this doesn't come as totally new information. It's been on my mind, too. I will think about what you said. But right now, I need a favour.'

'If I can.'

'Can you chat up Greg Riggs for me?'

'Why?'

236

'He's defending a biker named J. J. Topkis. I want to know who hired him.'

'Well, didn't Mr Topkis hire him?'

'I doubt he could afford him. There are bottom-feeders who specialize in bikers.'

'You want me to ask him?'

'It's for Mr Butler.'

'Oh . . . What makes you think he'll tell me?'

This was delicate. If not distasteful. 'Remember the fundraiser party he threw for you?'

'Gratefully. Greg Riggs was very good to me. I owe him.'

'Well, I knew it made political sense. But I had the feeling he might not go to such an effort for an ugly candidate.'

Vicky stared long and hard. 'Greg Riggs is engaged to be married. And if you're trying to flatter me by pretending to be jealous, it would work better if you had ever earned the right to be jealous.'

I slunk home and settled in with the telephone.

My third call to the Admiral got another promise that he would receive the message and get back to me.

A call to Fox Trot elicited the information that Ms Devlin and Mr King were 'out of the office'.

At Fort Bragg, everyone I spoke to called me sir. I finally got through to a barracks with the background sound of women laughing. 'Yo, Jervis!' cried the woman who answered and Josie came on the line, crisp and proud.

'Corporal Jervis.'

'Josie, it's Ben Abbott.'

Her breath caught. 'Is my Mom –'

'Fine, fine. No problem. I gotta talk to you.'

'I can't. I'm on duty in a minute.'

'J. J. Topkis told the troopers that Dicky said his father taught him how to make a time bomb.'

'He did?'

'Did you hear Dicky say that?'

'No.'

'But you were drinking with them.'

'Not really.'

'Is he lying?'

'Well, no. I mean, when I got there, we left. Dicky and me.'

'You mean they were drinking? Just the two of them? Then you came.'

'I didn't get there till midnight. My Mom had the truck. They were pretty far gone by then. Ben, I gotta go.'

'I'm curious why you didn't mention J. J. when we talked.'

'We went off by ourselves. Dicky was just killing time waiting for me.'

'Did he say how he happened to get friendly with Topkis?'

'Not really.'

'I was surprised to hear it.'

'Dicky didn't hold a grudge. He was kind of happy . . . You know what he told me?'

I waited, but she had started crying.

'What?' I asked, and when she told me I thought, again, What a waste, just when he was getting his miserable life in order.

'He told me . . . he told me he never used to think what would happen next. But now he'd wake up in the morning and think, Hey, I'm going to see Josie today . . .'

I had to make another trip to Derby. But I was really worried by how low Mr Butler had seemed that morning. So I drove back over to Plainfield. He shuffled into the interview room, confused and distracted.

He had botched a shave, which had left his face raw and flecked with small cuts and clumped with stubble he had missed. When I handed him a Coke and a cheeseburger, he fumbled open the wrapper and chewed slowly.

I told him what J. J. Topkis said about the detonator.

He finished the burger, before he looked up. 'I told you already, I never taught Dicky anything about explosives.'

'I remember. But I had to ask. I know you wouldn't lie to me.'

He threw back his head and chugged the Coke, and remained in that position, staring at the ceiling. 'Well, I did lie to you, once.'

'About what?'

238

'There was no calf.'

'What do you mean?'

'No calf caught in the fence.'

'What? Why?'

'I thought I better say that to fill in the time.'

'Where were you?'

'I was up there, but there was no calf.'

'But Albert and Dennis Chevalley said they saw you with the calf.'

'They're lying.'

'Why would they lie?'

'Maybe *they* need an alibi.'

One lie at a time. Derby. But not alone. I telephoned Betty Chevalley and asked to borrow my cousin Pinkerton.

'You can keep him as far as I'm concerned.'

'What did he do now?'

'Since you were here this morning? He threatened to break my best mechanic's hands, told Reverend Owen to you-know-what himself, and mounted drag slicks on Mildred Gill's Dodge.' Mildred was eighty-four and her Dodge wasn't much younger.

I promised to keep him till dark, loaded the car with beer and ice, and swung down the hill to Frenchtown. His mood could be read on his black T-shirt, in letters stretched wide across his enormous chest,

> WHEN IT ABSOLUTELY,
> POSITIVELY, HAS TO BE
> DESTROYED OVERNIGHT!
> *****US MARINES*****

No one knows if Pink was in the Marines – he did disappear for a few years when I was a boy – but I've yet to see anyone demand his credentials to wear that shirt.

'Pink, let me buy you a beer.' I opened the cooler in the back seat of the Olds, packed with Bud.

He licked his lips. 'I'm kinda busy.'

'I cleared it with Betty. Hop in.'

'Hey, I don't take no shit from no women.' Women – except his mother, with whom he still lived at the ripe age of forty-something – he regarded as a subspecies poorly adapted to deliver food and sex, in that order.

'Where we going?'

'Derby.'

'I'll drive.'

There was no arguing. He powered the seat all the way down and back to accommodate his giant frame, and tromped the accelerator.

No one can drive like Pinkerton Chevalley. For years he dominated the New England dirt tracks, racing Renny's souped-up stock cars to victory from Rhode Island to Maine. His fingers, thick as a girl's forearms, played lightly on the wheel and stick; his size fourteens skipped like ballet shoes between brakes and gas and clutch.

'You know Ollie got a new laser thing.'

'What's in Derby?'

'The Derby Death. Ever hear of 'em?'

'Weenies. That's who gave you the black eye?'

'J. J. Topkis.'

'That dude Dicky Butler nuked Wide Greg's window with. Shit, you can take J. J. Topkis.'

'He had a couple of friends.'

'So we're going to kick ass.'

'Uh, no. I'm going to talk to him.'

'Weenie.'

Pink drove and drank in silence for awhile. Every time he lowered the window to toss a bottle I'd grab it out of his hand and explain I was saving the deposits. Lower down Route 34, traffic thickened up until, to my relief, it was impossible to maintain Warp speed.

'Let me ask you something, Pink. What do you think of Albert and Dennis?'

'Dumb as rocks.'

'Can you imagine them killing anybody?'

'Not if they had to think how.'

'Let's say they did it accidentally.'

'Yeah?' He looked over, mildly curious.

'Could they get away with it?'

'Not if they had to think how.'

'What about Dennis?'

'What about him?'

'Is he maybe smarter than he seems?'

Pink thought that over. 'Could be. 'Course, it wouldn't take a lot.'

Derby was hot as last time. But the neighbourhood was quiet, and only J. J.'s mother was home. 'J. J.'s at his club,' she informed me. Her directions took us to an abandoned warehouse beside an ancient mill race diverted from the river.

Six bikers were hanging in the shade of the shed roof. Pink parked the car facing out. 'Sweet Jesus, look at that man's bike.'

J. J. was sitting on a brand-new custom Harley – the kind that comes chopped from the factory – with red enamel tanks, red leather seat, and everything else but the tyres made of chrome.

'Where the hell did he get the money for that?'

'Now's your chance to ask him.'

J. J. stepped off his new bike, his hand extended in a friendly manner. 'Man, did you piss off the cops. They couldn't do squat without you ratting.'

We shook and I said, 'That was the general idea. This here's my cousin Pinkerton.'

Pink solemnly enveloped J. J.'s hand in his and waited for a wince before he let go.

'Fine-looking machine.'

J. J. acknowledged the compliment and answered a few technical queries Pink put to him.

The biker in the engineering boots whom I'd laid out cold was watching me sullenly. His wrench-wielding friend, however, was barely paying attention, deep in conversation with three others who were passing a bottle of Jack.

Somewhere in the rundown neighbourhood of struggling machine shops and vacant factories, the state police might have a surveillance team. Or might not.

'Were you banging the cops telling 'em you were drinking buddies with Dicky Butler?'

'Naw. I figured, truth can't hurt, right? The 'sucker's dead meat already – no offence to your friend.'

'Where were you drinking? River End?'

'White Birch – how'd you hear?'

'I figured you two for duking it out.'

'Me too. 'Stead, he goes, "Hey, you want a beer?" First I didn't believe him. Then I noticed he was carrying those gloves, you know he wore? Carrying 'em in his pocket. Last time, he puts 'em on before he hits me back. Funniest god-dammed thing. Guy picked himself up off the floor, put these gloves on like he's one of them tuxedos dancing in a movie. Long as he didn't put them gloves on I knew we wasn't gonna fight. Everybody's weird one how or another. Right? How'd you hear?'

One glove on and one glove off.

When the dynamite exploded, he'd been wearing only one.

Because when he was murdered – I finally realized – he had been in the midst of putting his gloves on. Had one glove on and was reaching for the other.

Suiting up to slug it out.

Off balance while trying to protect whomever he was about to beat up from contracting AIDS through a split lip or blood-ied nose. Off balance while he was doing the right thing, for the first time in his miserable life. Guard down long enough for his victim to turn the tables.

J. J. was growling in my ear.

'What?'

'I said, "How'd you happen to hear we was drinking?"'

'Dicky's girl.'

'Oh, yeah. Little fatso.'

Pink had sort of drifted back, waiting near the Olds like the Atlas Mountains. I saw that look I'd seen last time in J. J.'s eyes, that belief he could take me.

'J. J., you've had a heck of a week. First you get arrested on an anonymous tip. Then you get bailed out by a hotshot attorney you can't afford. But I'm thinking maybe he's not such a hotshot, maybe you got bail because you ratted Dicky's dad to the troopers.'

'Say what?'

'You told them that Dicky told you his dad taught him how to detonate a bomb with a disappearing timer.'

'Bullshit. I never said that.'

'Cops make it up?'

'You been talking to 'em?'

'I figure you did what you had to do to make 'em go away. Like you said, Dicky's dead, so who cares? Except it's a pretty elaborate story just to get the cops off your back.'

'It worked.'

'Except you're really hurting his father. What do you get out of hurting that old farmer? . . . Well, you did buy yourself a brand-new twenty-five-thousand-dollar factory-customized Harley-Davidson motorcycle. So I wonder where you got the cash, J. J.?'

'You wonder all you want.'

'Or did you jump Dicky later that night?'

'Are you kidding? The dude had the AIDs.'

'How'd you know that?'

'Told me. He said, No more fighting. I said fine with me, man. I didn't want to get his blood.'

'Why didn't you tell me this before?'

J. J. Topkis's sucker punch rocketed from the deep nowhere. So fast that Pink admitted later it had caught even him by surprise.

I'd seen it before.

The Derby Death wasted a millisecond gaping at their fallen hero. And another putting down their bottles. By then I was passing Pink at a dead run.

'You drive.'

24

With five motorcycles swarming after us like a squadron of Messerschmitts, what remains most clearly in my mind is Pink's attempt to put my Oldsmobile into a power slide to cross the Stevenson Dam.

Lake Zoar lay dead ahead. The road hooked sharp left on to the dam. The flimsy fence that was supposed to keep vehicles that missed the turn from flying into the water had been torn down so they could build a better one, which they hadn't done yet.

The lake I'd been watching grow rapidly large in front of the car was suddenly visible through the passenger window. The view out the windshield was a green blur of roadside. The motorcycles formerly manoeuvring in the rear-view mirrors, now appeared in the driver's window – hazily through a cloud of rubber smoke. Pink downshifted to second, turned on the radio and reached back for a beer.

Six inches before the turn, he released the brake, popped the clutch and bore down hard on the accelerator. The Olds shot left on to the dam. Three Harley-Davidsons Knievelled into the lake.

It was well after dark when we pulled into Frenchtown.

Pink opened his fourteenth Bud. 'Did J. J. do Dicky Butler?'

'No. But he sure did a number ratting out his father.'

'What for?'

'That was a hell of a Harley. Maybe somebody paid him to.'

'Who?'

'Beats me. But I know one thing – whoever killed Dicky did it in a fight.'

'You better make an appointment to get your wheels aligned.'

Next morning, the Admiral still hadn't returned my calls. When I telephoned Fox Trot, Jenkins reported that Henry King and Julia Devlin were in a meeting.

It was a day early to expect inquiries from Sergeant Marian about my interest in Trooper Moody's log.

I telephoned the county jail. The guard who answered said Mr Butler was, quote, 'a real mess', and offered to bring him to the phone. But the farmer wouldn't come.

Tim reported no progress swinging a bail deal with the state's attorney.

Then Vicky called. 'I had drinks with Greg Riggs last night.'

'That was fast.'

'You said it was important.'

'What'd you find out?'

'Something weird.'

'Want to meet for coffee?'

'I don't want to see you.'

She said it with a crisp golden-spike-through-the-vampire's-heart finality that didn't leave me room to say more than, 'OK . . . So what happened with Greg? Did he tell you who hired him to defend Topkis?'

'He was practically bragging to me.'

'Gee, I wonder why?'

'I did too, pretty talkative for a lawyer.'

'Who hired him?'

'He was so proud of himself. He kept saying, "I hit the bigtime."'

'Who?'

'He swore me to secrecy.'

'That doesn't help Mr Butler.'

'I crossed my fingers.'

'Excellent. Who?'

'You won't believe this.'

'Who, for crissake?'

'Bertram Wills.'

245

'You're kidding.'

'Ben, why would a former Secretary of State hire Greg Riggs to defend biker scum?'

'Beats me.'

The phone was quiet. Then Vicky said in a small voice, 'Ben?'

'What?'

'Is Mrs King the kind of woman you dated when you worked in New York?'

'Mrs King? I'm not sure what you mean.'

'Fancy clothes and jewellery and that incredible hair.'

'I had a standing order at Elizabeth Arden, and a discount if I picked them up at the door.'

'She came in to see me, yesterday.'

After a longish silence, I asked, 'Can I assume that Mrs King paid you a visit with a purpose beyond making you feel like mud?'

'I feel so stupid. I don't care about that stuff. I really don't. Then all of a sudden she's looking me in the face and I'm thinking, What is she, fifteen years older, but I'm the one who looks like roadkill? . . . Tim just doesn't get it. He's, like, "Oh, you're so pretty."'

'Maybe you caught Tim on a busy day. What did Mrs King want?'

'She paid Mr Butler's back taxes.'

'*What?*'

'She made an appointment to meet me. Asked how much Mr Butler owed. And wrote a cheque.'

'Did she say why?'

'She said he had suffered too much. She didn't want him to worry about the farm.'

'Did you accept it?'

'Of course. The town needs the money.'

'Were there any strings attached?'

'No strings. I told her that up front. I even had Don Darbee explain that Newbury had no immediate plans to seize his farm – in case she was thinking to buy it for taxes.' Don was town attorney.

'Did she agree to no strings?'

246

'Absolutely. I don't think it ever occurred to her to ask anything back. Except, she made me promise not to tell anybody.'

'You're telling me.'

'You're different. I thought maybe it meant something for Mr Butler. Besides, I trust you.'

'Well that's an improvement.'

'To keep it to yourself. Anyhow, I thought you should know . . . Does it mean anything?'

'I don't know . . . How did she pay?'

'Personal cheque.'

'Joint checking account?'

'No, her own.'

'Interesting . . . I had the impression she's not comfortable with King bullying Mr Butler. Sounds like she decided to do the right thing.'

'You know what else she did?'

'No.'

'She asked me to have lunch. Like just the two of us. Like ladies lunching?'

'Do it. She could be a good friend. Somebody to know when you run for governor.'

'I thought of that right away and hated myself. She seems a little lonely. Anyhow, she said they're real busy wrapping up something and then she'll be free and let's have lunch. Isn't that nice?'

'She's a nice lady.' How nice? Mr Butler had been about twenty-five grand in the hole. A lot of money, even for a woman who could cover it with her personal cheque. And I'd seen all sorts of possible agendas five nights ago in Fox Trot's sunken garden.

There was no one around the Butler farm, the morning milking long done by the neighbours. Someone had mowed the grass around the house. The beds where Dicky's mother might once have nursed flowers were choked with goldenrod and black-eyed Susans. The heat still hadn't broken. Yet a lowering angle of the light presaged autumn creeping down from the north, and a fuzziness in the sky threatened rain.

As I got out of the car I realized it was almost the same time of day that Josie had dropped Dicky off to sober up for their picnic. I stopped and reoriented myself, and tried to imagine it through Dicky's bleary eye: climbing down from Josie's pickup truck; reeling uncertainly. He sees his father's truck. The tractor is nearby, so he knows the old man's having lunch.

The stream funnels down a gully lined with brush and trees and drops into the woodlot that was always too steep to plough. The sun is hot. His father's in the house. He heads for the cool trees.

I found his path.

The animals had made it. Big-hoofed fat cows beating a surprisingly narrow track that hugged the rim of the gully, then sloped down to the stream bed at the easiest descent – a route as mathematically correct as if civil engineers had surveyed it with transits – to a pool where they drank. Hundreds of hoof-prints pocked the mud. Beyond, the track forked. A furrow of beaten earth rose from the watering hole back up to the field. While a narrower deer path that paralleled the stream continued down into the woodlot that separated the Butler and King properties.

Dicky had cleared obstacles. I could see sawn stubs, and dead leaves still clinging to the brush he had flung into the woods. Here and there, where the path criss-crossed the stream, he had placed stepping stones. A shaft of sunlight, penetrating the leaf canopy, gleamed on a red Marlboro box he had tossed.

I followed the deer path nearly a quarter mile, the ground sloping with the stream, which tumbled over rock falls where it was steep and pooled where it was level. Path and stream entered a glade where a giant silver birch had fallen, providing a comfortable bench. The opening it had left in the canopy admitted a circle of sky and sunlight.

He had constructed a rock dam across the stream bed, lined with black plastic, forming a deep swimming hole fifteen feet across. Two sights spoiled the otherwise magical setting: a pile of broken wine bottles and a high seven-strand deer fence, hung with yellow electricity warnings and NO TRES-

signs that marked the property line of Henry King Inc.

It layered a kind of industrial meanness on to the mood of the sylvan glade. The heavy-gauge wire was strung tree to tree on plastic insulators. The bottom strand cleared the ground by less than a foot to prevent enterprising deer from lying down and sliding under and the ground had been recently cleared so brush and weeds couldn't sap power from the lines. Only crossing the brook had the fence builders fallen short. A deer willing to get wet could slip under where the stream bed dipped.

I lay down on a shaded bed of pine needles, looked up at the sky, and listened to the water rushing on the stones.

Dragonflies swooped. Dicky was right. No mosquitoes.

There weren't any pines nearby and I realized that he had carried the soft needles down here to make this love nest with its view of the swimming hole. Through the fence, I could see King's half of the woodlot descend with the stream. It was too thick and far to see the Fox Trot lawns and mansion, but I could sense, if not quite see a sunlit opening to the right – the leased pasture that penetrated the King property.

Yet if I lay back and stared at the sky or turned to gaze at the still pool, or let my ears drink the sound of water falling over Dicky's plastic dam, I could easily imagine I was a hundred miles from my nearest neighbour. With a bedazzled, sweet-natured Josie Jervis on the pine needles beside me and state prison a distant memory, and the HIV quiescent, I might be a very happy man indeed.

I shivered. Something cold passed through me. Puzzled and a little apprehensive, I propped up on my elbow to look around. The pool, the jagged wine bottles, the fence, the warning signs, the distant sunny grass, the deeper woods downstream. Light glinted like a sliver of the sun, and I realized I wasn't alone.

25

Every blood cell in my body wanted to dive for cover. Every brain cell screamed that if I moved I'd get shot by the spy sniper scope that Mr Butler had supposedly hallucinated. I did the sensible thing out of sheer paralysis, and lay stock-still. But my spine was tingling and my skin crawling and I craved cover like a sinner craved forgiveness.

Cover beckoned beside the stream – midway between Dicky's swimming hole dam and Henry King's deer fence – a man-high boulder dropped by a friendly glacier seven thousand years ago. Behind that boulder, I could slide down the bank and crawl away in the stream bed.

Slowly, I stretched my arms and rolled over, slowly, hoping to put a couple of trees between him and me. I wished I carried a gun. Preferring not to live that way, I could end up dying this way.

I spotted the glint again. He was moving, clearing his field of fire. I stood up and opened my fly.

As I did, I edged nearer the boulder. I stopped. I inspected the ground like a poodle picking hydrants. I moved behind the boulder, dropped into wet moss, zipped up, and plotted a quiet escape upstream into Butler's woods, until I was out of range with hundreds of tree trunks between me and the stalker.

How long would he sit staring at the boulder?

Not as long as I would like him to.

I slid down the bank, crawled into the stream on all fours. The gully was deep. If it stayed deep and I stayed quiet and he stayed where he was in the trees, I just might be able to get away.

I started crawling upstream. Adrenalin flooded my heart – sucking strength from my limbs. I dragged leaden arms and legs through the shallow water, scraping rocks and gravel and broken branches.

Suddenly, I stopped.

In my weak-limbed, numbed-skull panic, I had forgotten Dicky's dam. Five feet high, it blocked the stream bed entirely. Either around or over would expose me to a clear shot.

I turned around, and crawled back the other way, under Henry King's deer fence and his NO TRESPASSING signs. I considered standing up and sticking my hands in the air. But that trusting an act might be taken as an invitation to target practice. Best to keep crawling down into the open and run like hell to Henry King's house.

A hundred feet downstream, I raised a cautious head to get my bearings and saw a glove.

It was lying on the right-hand bank – inches from my face. A shrunken, dead-skunk cabbage leaf covered it partly, and it looked like it had been rained on.

I pushed the leaf off. Then, with a stick, I raised it slightly and peered underneath. The leather had stiffened. Pale white weeds were curled under it, starved of the sun. A couple of them had escaped and were sending out green shoots.

It was deerskin. One of Dicky's deerskin gloves – the glove that hadn't been on the hand Ollie had found. The glove he'd lowered his guard to put on.

A bright red dot suddenly hovered on it like a shiny red bug. I stared stupidly. It looked transparent. I jerked my hand back just in time. An eight-inch bolt thwacked through the glove, pinning it to the ground.

It was a crossbow bolt, guided by the red dot of laser light. Twentieth-century technology married to medieval. Dead silent. Deadly accurate. It woke me up in a way I had not been awake in a long time.

I yanked it out of the ground, stuffed Dicky's glove in my pocket, ran down the stream bed and stopped, suddenly. Crashing sticks and leaves sounded behind me. My cue to vault the bank and into the woods. As I did I glimpsed a flicker back in the stream. A swift black figure, black from head to toe.

I slowed, moved more quietly, and stopped again, on the far side of a fat red oak. Again I heard him, out of the stream too, into the trees about fifty yards behind me. I debated attacking, reasonably sure that he didn't have a shotgun, the one weapon I feared in the trees. His crossbow was near useless in the dense growth, until he got right next to me.

Ten yards to my left stood an enormous lightning-blasted silver birch, an ancient tree nearly as big around as my oak. I knelt down to pry loose a rock that the oak roots had heaved from the ground. As I worked at it, I steadied my breathing and calmed down a little. I was, after all, in my element.

Despite their propensity for mayhem, Chevalleys matured into wonderful uncles when they got older. My father had been a very busy man, so my mother had steered me towards her long-gun- and chainsaw-toting brothers and cousins, men who thought it their natural responsibility to teach little boys how to shelter, hunt and hide in the trees. I'd dressed my first deer when I was old enough to hold a knife – several weeks before the season, if memory serves. By the time I was ten I could start a fire in the rain, sleep in the snow, and eat almost anything that wandered my way. I had lost the cold eye for hunting years ago, but I'd been taught by masters.

I bowled the rock hard and low. It crashed through the brush like a Main Street real-estate agent tromping leaves, while I Chevalleyed left on my belly, towards the silver birch. As I had expected, half the tree stood hollow and, rejuvenating itself, had reinforced the break with a shield of new bark.

The cavity was like a chimney. I squeezed inside and wedged my way in and up, climbing nearly ten feet on toe-holds of crumbling heartwood.

Had I time I'd have checked for snakes, weasels, rabid raccoons and bees, all of whom might regard my hidey-hole as home. But a rustle nearby told me I'd cut it close as I could. A convenient knothole would have been nice to watch his progress. But there were none and I waited, blind in the dark.

He entered the tree so quietly that he was inside, blocking the light and peering up through weird goggle eyes, before I realized he was there. I let go all holds and dropped like a stone.

He leaped back.

I kicked, and connected, hard.

For a second I thought his head had fallen off. But it was some kind of helmet and as it fell away I glimpsed a military crewcut and a very thick neck. Then I got my legs all tangled under me, and before I'd squeezed out of the tree trunk, he was gone, a distant crashing in the trees. I started after him.

I wanted to ask why he was stalking me. Had he tried to shoot me or Dicky's glove? Who gave him his marching orders? And, while we were at it, where was he the afternoon Dicky got blown up with King's dam?

A crossbow bolt smacked into a nearby hickory. I took a serious look at the carbon-fibre shaft quivering a foot from my face and reconsidered my options.

I already had quite a haul for a walk in the woods: Dicky Butler's glove, a real treasure, albeit holed palm and back; two hi-tech crossbow bolts; and the helmet. Which turned out to be a black skullcap of cotton-lined neoprene fitted with night-vision binoculars and sound-enhancing Big Ears – as they were called by low-life, high-tech deer hunters – so sensitive they could hear an animal's frightened breath.

It hadn't been bought in a sporting-goods store. There was no brand name. It looked like a piece of highly restricted military hardware, and very expensive. I headed back upstream, ducking under King's deer fence, to return it to its rightful owner. Via his front gate.

I telephoned Fox Trot from Mr Butler's kitchen. King and Julia were in another meeting. I said, 'I'll be by in a half hour.'

The receptionist bridled. 'You need an appointment.'

'Tell Mr King that one of his employees lost valuables in the woods. I'm returning them.'

I hung up before she could argue.

Magneted to Mr Butler's rust-pitted refrigerator door was a business card for A&D Piggery, Route 7, Gallatinville, New York. I took it and charged down to Fox Trot.

Albert and Dennis were back on the gate.

'Name!'

'Sun Tzu.' I held up the helmet. Jaws dropped. 'I'm expected.'

'Where'd you get that?'

'Open the gate.'

They opened the gate.

The driveway spikes were up, gleaming like serpent teeth in the shady light. 'Ben Abbott.'

'You may continue.'

The spikes sank.

The helicopter parked on the lawn down from the house was whining, and as I parked, its spinning blades speeded up. I ran up the steps and pounded the front door. Jenkins opened up. 'Is that King leaving?' I yelled.

'No, Mr Abbott. They're down at the office. You're expected.'

I walked the garden path to the old Zarega house, carrying the helmet like a gorgon's head. Julia came for me, greeted me with a handshake. I thought at first it was for the receptionist's benefit. But there was no private smile for me.

She looked beautiful in a skirt and blouse of pale and paler green. Her hair was up, her neck exquisite. Her hand trembled a little. So did mine. It went with the dry mouth and the accelerated heartbeat.

She glanced at the ceiling, a clear warning that the joint was bugged.

'Where'd you get that?' she asked aloud.

'I'll explain to the boss.'

King's office was a blandly, expensively furnished room – the old main parlour, if I recalled, repanelled and decorated by the sort of interior designer who spends money on touches like a marble surround for a fieldstone fireplace.

King was on the telephone. He flashed me a fairly friendly nod and motioned me to sit, while raising an inquiring eyebrow at the war prize dangling from my hand. I sat on the couch Julia indicated, and placed it on my knee. Julia took a chair opposite and we waited quietly for him to finish his call. No one, not even the butler, had commented on my wet and muddy clothes.

King's voice was imparting high-priced wisdom in a low register – something general-sounding about the new climate in London, the words less important than the tone. When he hung up, he made a note on a pad beside, read it, then looked up expectantly.

'What is that?'

'Night-vision and sound enhancer. It fell off one of your employees.'

'Thank you,' he said, reaching across his desk.

I held on to it. 'Not good enough.'

'What's wrong?'

'The son of a bitch shot at me.'

'I didn't hear any shots.'

I took the crossbow bolts from my back pocket. 'Neither did I.'

'But I'm sure no harm was intended if you walked into his target practice.'

'I was the target.'

'Were you on my property?'

'Trespassing is not a capital offence. Your people have no right to try to kill me if I stray over a property line.'

'Well, I can see how you might be upset, Mr Abbott.'

I had not come in upset. If anything I was exhilarated to have some leverage in the house. But his arrogance was getting to me – his bland assumption of might makes right.

'Not as upset as you're going to be when I report this to the police.'

'Now, now, now. I see no need to go off half-cocked.'

'I came near getting killed. I'm already half-cocked.'

'I'll have a word with the person in question.'

'So will I.'

King shrugged. 'All right, if that will make you happy.' He pressed an intercom button. 'Josh. Front and centre.'

To me, he explained, 'Josh is our security chief.'

'I know. He testified at the inquest.'

255

We waited in silence. Josh Wiggens hurried in, elegant in a grey suit. 'Yes, Henry.'

King nodded at the helmet. 'Ben, here, is upset. He claims that an employee wearing that, shot those' – he indicated the bolts in my hand – 'at him.'

'Had you breached the perimeter?' Wiggens asked.

'Josh,' I said, 'I owe you one for Derby. But cut the crap.'

'Julia mentioned your gratitude. No problem. Lucky I was nearby.'

'Lucky? Or were you following me?'

Josh regarded me with an expression of pity. 'A former colleague has become an antiquarian book dealer down in Derby. Dumb luck you happened by.'

'Then I'm grateful to both of you. But that was Derby. This is Newbury. Your guy shot at me. I want to talk to him.'

'Not possible.'

'The boss says it's possible. Don't you, Henry?'

King waved a benevolent hand. 'Put his mind at ease.'

'I'm afraid that the employee in question just left.'

'When's he due back?' I asked.

'Early next week.'

I said, again, loudly, 'Not good enough. He shot at me twice.' I tossed a crossbow dart on King's desk, the mud-crusted one that had pierced Dicky's glove. King grimaced, as if the dirt it scattered on the immaculate rosewood upset him a lot more than the weaponry. 'Get him,' I demanded. 'He hasn't gone anywhere.'

'I'm afraid he has.' Wiggens nodded to the window as the helicopter took off, rattling the glass. I headed for the door.

'Where are you going?' cried King.

'Cops.'

Josh Wiggens started to protest. King gestured him to be silent. 'You're not going to the cops, Abbott. If you intended to go to the cops, you'd have gone directly. You came here, instead. You obviously want something. Tell me what you want and we'll see if we can give it to you. Sit. Down. Sit down. Julia, dear, ring for Jenkins and let's have a cool drink. What would you like, Ben? Iced tea? Lemonade? Something harder?'

'Iced coffee,' I said, just to be perverse.

'Iced coffee it is. Me too, Julia. Josh? Your usual?'

Julia picked up a phone. King mused over the bolt in a deep, professorial voice, 'The crossbow changed warfare by making the footsoldier the equal of heavy horse. The first long-range hand missile. It could be fired accurately by an illiterate peasant and pierce the armour of the noblest knight. Comparable to today's fedayee with his Kalashnikov. A weapon so atrocious that popes banned it.'

'Except,' I reminded him, 'against infidels.'

King nodded. 'I know. And you're thinking, What of the English longbow?'

I was thinking, What did I want from him? Other than his mistress. What did I want for Mr Butler? And I was wondering, would Henry King blow up his lake to protect an over-zealous security employee? Throw in trespassing and Dicky's tattoos, and it wouldn't amount to more than accidental death.

'But the English yeomen were not peasants in the European sense of rabble. Nor could they fire longbows from concealment. Crossbows, massed, devastated Saladin's forces at Arsuf.' He held up the bolt, and studied it by the light of the window pouring over his shoulder. 'What's this quarrel made of?'

Son of a bitch even knew the correct word for the bolt.

'Carbon fibre, it looks like.'

'Don't they make sailboats out of that?'

'And stealth planes.'

'A similar world-changer. Imagine an enemy –'

'We're not at war in Newbury, Henry. Why'd your man shoot at me?'

'*You* may not be at war, Ben. But Fox Trot was attacked.'

'Come on.'

'*And* I will defend it.'

'Dicky Butler's dead. His dad's in jail. Who the hell are you defending against?'

'Why were you on my property?'

'I fled on to "your property" when your employee started stalking me on Mr Butler's property.'

'Do you expect us to buy that?' Wiggens interrupted.

King gestured for silence. 'Ben, is it possible you panicked? What made you think he was stalking you?'

'I felt him tracking me in the trees.'

'It sounds to me like an awful misunderstanding. How are you so sure?'

'Some sort of sixth sense?' asked Josh. I glanced at Julia. She looked away.

'I saw the sun glint on his sights.'

'Is it possible he was merely watching you?'

'Henry, would you like me to watch you through a telescopic sight? Maybe at night, when you're ready for bed and you stop in the window to look at the stars?'

'You have a peculiar imagination, Ben.'

'Call that helicopter back.'

King looked at Wiggens.

Josh nodded at the window. 'The pilot said there's a front approaching.'

The sky had gone steely and a dark, anvil-topped thunderhead was looming from the west. 'If he doesn't get around that now, he'll be socked in for a day . . .'

'I don't care if he's socked in for a week.'

King said, 'Julia. Bring me the Institute chequebook. And send in what's-her-name – the one who takes dictation.'

I hated the way she jumped to obey him. She hurried out and returned with a leatherbound register. As she opened it for him, she glanced defiantly at me as if to say, If you don't like my life, tough.

King took a gold Mont Blanc from his shirt pocket and wrote with a flourish. He tore the cheque from the page, blew on the ink, and pushed it across his desk towards me.

'What's that, a bribe?'

'Read it.'

I got up, still holding the Big Ears, big-eyes helmet, and picked up the cheque. The Henry King Institute of Geopolitics had just contributed twenty-five thousand dollars to the Richard Butler defence fund.

The receptionist hurried in with a laptop and typed what King dictated: ' "In my opinion my neighbour Richard Butler has suffered far too much from the loss of his son. I see no good purpose pursuing a shaky conspiracy case against him and therefore I contribute this twenty-five thousand dollars for his defence in the event the state's attorney refuses to drop the charges.'' Print that up and bring it back immediately.'

There are bribes no decent person would accept. And there are bribes no decent person could refuse.

'Leave the helmet,' said King. I put it on his desk, and again he grimaced, this time at the earthy sawdust from the inside of the silver birch. I had a pretty good idea what was coming next. So I turned to the window, and concentrated on the first raindrops splashing the glass in order to collect my spirit.

When I was a boy, Connie taught me that lying was the worst sin on the planet. On the rare occasions I do, I still have to brace myself.

'And the glove,' said Josh Wiggens.

'I dropped it when I ran.'

'Where?' asked King.

'In your stream.'

26

I'd come up with too little too late.

I delivered King's cheque and letter to a delighted Tim Hall. But when Tim called Ira, Ira scotched our hopes for bail, much less dropping the charges. The J. J. Topkis testimony about the timer had convinced the state's attorney to prosecute Mr Butler. Detectives Marian and Arnie were wrapping up the case for the grand jury.

I slunk home, wolfed gloomily at a late lunch of pesto and beefsteak tomato on Portuguese bread, and wondered what the hell to try next. Alison Mealy burst through the kitchen door, scattering rainwater from her yellow slicker.

'Aunt Connie says get over there right away.'

'Is that how she put it?'

'She said to ask you if it was convenient to stop by her house.'

DaNang had lurched stiff-hipped from sleep. 'Care to join us?' I asked, and the three of us trooped across Main Street like the tag end of a modest circus.

Connie was studying her television, an ancient nineteen-incher, which she kept in the old cook's parlour off the pantry. The King A&E 'Biography' video was shivering – freeze-framed – on the tag-sale VCR that Alison had repaired with a thirty-cent part. She looked puzzled.

'Ben, look at this.'

Alison interrupted. 'Connie? DaNang's on the porch. Can he come in the house?' Connie looked puzzled. 'Has some meteorological event transpired I'm unaware of?'

'Huh? I mean, I beg your pardon?'

'A change in the weather? A sudden blizzard, perhaps.'

260

'It's raining.'

'Would you call it a nor'easter?'

'No.'

'Then DaNang will be perfectly dry and happy on the porch. And *not* on the chaise longue. Ben, look at this . . . What do you see?'

Same thing I had seen at our earlier viewing, a shot of King and four former State Department poobahs exiting a helicopter at a luxurious Aspen, Colorado non-profit think-tank mountain ranch maintained by our tax dollars.

'What else?'

'Five middle-aged guys enjoying the rewards of public service.' By some remarkable coincidence, each was attended by an aide in her early thirties. Julia was by far the most attractive, but none had to fear being kicked out of bed.

'What else?'

I studied the scene, rewound it when it stopped, and played it through. Connie said, 'I don't understand, but I think I've discovered an odd pattern. Move the picture, ahead, Ben. Stop at any travel scene that has your pretty friend in it.'

I fast-forwarded to where the group got back on the helicopter. I stopped the tape again when King's entourage bustled into Heathrow, and again where he was greeted by Arabs looking princely on horseback. In Beijing, he bowed to a cadre of bloody-minded old men.

'Henry King carries his own bags,' Connie marvelled. 'The others have loaded their young women like pack animals. But he carries his own. Don't you find that unusual?'

'Why?'

'An ill-mannered, ill-bred, unprincipled lout, globetrotting on the public dollar, who carries his own bag? He treats your Ms Devlin like a lady.'

'*My* Ms Devlin?'

Connie's blue eyes cut like glass. 'How lovely she looks, striding beside him.'

'Lovely,' I agreed, long stretches of our night permanently burned in my memory's eye, even as I wondered about my cool reception at King's office.

'Look at that other girl struggling like a porter, for pity's sake. Why do you suppose he carries his own bag?'

I rewound to the beginning. A&E had resurrected a snippet of Kinescope eight-mil. home-movie film that showed a burly seventeen-year-old King pushing a wheelbarrow on a Manhattan construction job. His friends start ragging him, the way kids do for the benefit of the camera, and King had waded in and put a headlock on the ringleader. The next old shot showed him alone in Harvard Yard, hurrying by with a load of books. He barely nodded at whatever relative was recording the moment, and it was clear his heavy-lifting days were nearing an end.

And indeed, from the mid-Vietnam era into the late 1980s he sprang from aircraft and limousines – bag-toting acolytes scrambling after him like apprentice machine-gunners with fresh bandoliers. Until, as Connie had noticed, Julia entered the moving pictures. With her King carried his own bags. Only after he had 'retired' to private life.

'Perhaps he carries his own bags because he's in love with the woman,' Connie ventured, dubiously. 'Though the thought of King in love makes one shudder.' She smiled at her jibe, then turned seriously to me. 'Be careful, Ben. Henry King would make a vicious enemy.'

'Beg your pardon?'

'Alison, cover your ears.' Alison did. Connie whispered, very seriously, 'Jealousy.'

'Did she –'

'No, Alison did not "rat you out". You're staring at that film like a slack-jawed orang utan.'

Alison, who had not covered her ears very well, fell over giggling. And suddenly I could explain to Connie why King treated Julia like a 'lady', when they travelled.

'She's his bodyguard.'

'Bodyguard?'

'A real professional. She keeps her hands free.'

'That little thing?'

'She's not that little. And she's in terrific shape.'

I sat down and talked it through. 'She said she had been a civil servant. But she was really Secret Service. She's either been detached to him officially, or she resigned and works directly for him. But that's why she doesn't carry anything. She's there to protect him.'

'How strange you must feel, Benjamin.'

To put it mildly.

I was sleeping with a woman who could kill me with her bare hands. Bodyguards had a long and honourable tradition of rising in their charge's estimation. Patty Hearst had married hers. Julia was bright. Why wouldn't she gradually become one of King's confidantes? And finally his runner.

A handy woman to have around. Confidante, travel companion, manager, protector and loyal defender.

Assassin? asked a little voice. A little voice that next asked why, when any sensible man would be making a play for a perfectly lovely woman like Vicky McLachlan, I was pursuing an already-involved woman who happened to be a trained killer.

'Alison, dear,' said Connie. 'Would you please run out to the kitchen and put on water for tea and lay out a platter of cookies? Thank you, dear.'

She watched Alison clump reluctantly down the hall and when she was out of earshot asked, 'May I ask, seriously, are you involved?'

'You'll like her. She's a solid person. Lot of depth. And from what you've figured out, an interesting background.'

'Is she "involved" with King as well?'

'Looks that way.'

'Be careful.'

'I can handle him.'

'I mean, of her.'

'I feel a connection with her. It feels special.'

'She has to protect him.'

'If that's her job.'

'I mean in *addition* to her job. Benjamin, forgive me, but look at your past. You are so stupid about women. Particularly when they have long dark hair like your mother's.'

'Come on, Connie. That's such a cliché.'

'*You* act like such a cliché . . . Ben, you understand people so well, most of the time. Try and understand this woman.

263

If she is giving herself to that married man – being his servant and assistant and doormat – she will do anything to prove to herself that she's not wasting herself on him.'

'I think she wants to change.'

'I should hope so. But don't you understand that she must hate herself for everything she gives to you?'

'Maybe giving to me helps her break away.'

'The only person she will never hate is Henry King.'

I passed on tea and cookies.

Back in my office I stared at Dicky's glove. After a while, I fished A&D Piggery's business card from my pocket and telephoned. I got an answering machine. I left my name and number and said I wanted to discuss a manure delivery.

I put the glove under my desk lamp and snapped a few photographs, top and bottom, with my Polaroid property camera. Then I went down to my workbench in the cellar and sliced small pieces of deerskin from inside the palm with an Exacto knife.

Back upstairs, I telephoned the Admiral, again. Again, they promised my old boss would call back. Twenty seconds later the phone rang.

A silky voice, no preamble. 'What can I tell you, Ben?'

It was not a rhetorical What can I tell you. He was cautioning, Don't ask the wrong question. The category of wrong question might include the password to enter the computer that controlled Spy In The Sky Satellites, the name of our woman in Cairo, or more than he cared to spill about Henry King.

I knew this and he knew I knew this. 'Tell me where King returned from the day of his party.'

'London.'

'Tell me his route.'

'Heathrow to Bradley International by General Motors corporate jet. Bradley to Newbury in his helicopter. Arrived 1300.'

As said the Party Box lady.

'Tell me who his client was in London.'

'No.'

'Tell me what he did in London.'

'Fouled up.'

That I hadn't expected. I wasted a moment coming up with my next question. 'What kind of fouled up?'

Silence.

'For us?' I asked, 'us' meaning US, and doubting he'd answer.

But he did. 'No. For our offshore-island friends. Both of them.'

Britain and Japan. GM supplied his free transport. 'The ceramic engine! He blew the deal with the Brits and the Japanese?'

'Royally. The ceramic engine was only the beginning. He was supposed to herd them into a long-term techno-industrial agreement.'

'They were talking about it at the party.'

'He'd been planning a big-splash announcement – the Fox Trot Accord. The man has an ego the size of Mars.'

'And an eye on the IRS,' I added. 'To write off the party and a good hunk of his construction costs.'

'I wouldn't know about that.' The Admiral affected a patrician disdain for commerce. 'More your line.'

Not any more, I thought. I'd been off-line so long that I had mistaken blown-deal-blues at King's party for a deal in progress.

'Anyway,' the Admiral volunteered, 'instead of signing contracts, Henry King was scrambling around trying to pick up the pieces when one of your yahoo friends blew his dam. Any more questions?'

'King keeps a drunken ex-spook around. Josh Wiggens. Is he for real?'

'Josh Wiggens served his country,' came the cold reply. 'He was a fine officer, in his time. Any more?'

'Yes, what made him a fine officer? What's he like?'

'He was a hell of a fighter.'

'An infighter?' I asked.

'Very imaginative.'

I listened to silence, while the Admiral reflected more upon the ex-spy. 'Loyal,' he said after a long time. 'If I had to choose one attribute to describe Josh Wiggens, I would say it was loyalty. A rare asset, loyalty, when everyone's got their own agenda. And their own morality to justify it.'

Josh Wiggens had testified against Mr Butler at the inquest. He tried to scare me off helping Butler. Then he turned around and saved my bacon from the Derby Death. Loyal to whom? To King? To Julia? To the United States government?

'Anything else?'

'Yes. Is Josh Wiggens still in the loop?' Meaning the CIA loop.

The Admiral sighed. 'Anything else?'

'How does he happen to work for Henry King?'

'Needed work.'

'How about Bert Wills? Did he need work, too?'

'Everybody needs work, Ben. Anything else?'

'Is Julia Devlin currently employed by the Secret Service?'

'Anything else?'

'Were Julia Devlin and Josh Wiggens "involved" before they worked for Henry King?'

'I figure that's nobody's business.'

'Sir, I'm working for an old farmer, a Vietnam vet, who's rotting unfairly in jail.'

'Anything else?'

'No, sir. Thank you.'

'Let's not make a habit of this,' was his goodbye, and it stung.

I still didn't know whether Henry King worked for the United States government. But he had indeed been far away the night before the explosion. Anticipating triumph, he'd come home in defeat. I had to marvel at his composure. He had looked tired and drawn, but only his caterer knew of his misery. For his guests, he had acted every bit the proud squire of Fox Trot – happy homeowner and generous host, at least until Mr Butler's fly attack.

One hell of an act. What else did it hide? But corporate statesmen of the new world order didn't kill farmers to get their farms.

I still hadn't heard back from A&D Piggery.

I telephoned. Got a machine.

I stared some more at Dicky's glove.

I stepped outside to rescue flowers and tomatoes from the rain. I recalled Mr Butler's tomatoes rotting on the vine. I telephoned again. Got a person. He didn't apologize for not responding to my message. All he said was, 'We don't deliver to Newbury, Mr Abbott.' And hung up.

'What?'

I dialled again. 'What'd you hang up on me for?'

'I told you, we don't deliver to Newbury.' And hung up.

I dialled again.

'If you hang up on me again, I'm going to drive over to wherever the hell you are and throw a brick through your window. OK?'

'Try it, Buddy.' He hung up.

I got in the Olds, and headed west. It was a slow drive in the rain, up through Sharon and across to Millerton, New York, up 22 and west on a short-cut to County 7 I remembered from visiting a Millerton shopkeeper I'd once fallen for while she was between husbands. Her farmhouse was freshly painted and framed with flower gardens and – yikes – a bright new slide and swing set.

West of Ancram started signs for Gallatinville, which billed itself, A GREAT LITTLE TOWN.

I had my doubts. Even with my windows up I could already smell A&D. A smell that got stronger and stronger until, when its barns and stock pens hove into view, I feared for the Oldsmobile's paint.

One side of the road were stock pens, crowded with large, rounded pink animals with active snouts and calculating eyes. Like a herd of Dennis Chevalleys. A nicely kept farmhouse was on the other side, a rambling building added on to over the years. It had a little front porch, and on it sat a white-haired guy in a rocker. He had a view of the pigs, and a B-B gun across his knees.

I pulled into his drive, which was bordered by a spectacular perennial garden – as good an advertisement for pig manure as one was likely to see. The wind – and I assumed they had planned it that way – blew the pig smell away from the house. Most of it.

'You the guy with the brick?'

267

'Left it home.'

'Lucky for your windshield.'

'I've got to ask you something. Why didn't you make a delivery you promised to Richard Butler?'

'You have driven all the way from Newbury, Connecticut to remind me of a town I never want to hear of again.'

'You're mispronouncing it. It's "New-brie", like the cheese. Why didn't you deliver?'

'Do you know a state trooper named Oliver Moody?'

Ah. 'Trooper Moody and I have been mortal enemies for twenty years.'

The old gent smiled. 'Can you stay for dinner?'

'I'm under the gun. What did he do to you?'

When I got home an unmarked Connecticut State Police car was waiting in my drive. In it, Marian Boyce was drumming her big fingers on the steering wheel and drinking coffee from a paper container.

'You win. I'll bite. Why do you want to know Trooper Moody's whereabouts between ten and one the day of the explosion?'

'I already know 'em. Come in the house, I'll make you some real coffee and trade you Trooper Moody's whereabouts for J. J. Topkis's.'

She said, 'No way,' but followed me into the kitchen.

I said, 'I won't accept any Trooper Moody "facts" you can't back up with witnesses who were wearing clothespins on their noses.'

Marian's very pretty mouth dropped open. 'You bastard.'

'Let's not be a sore loser.'

'I keep forgetting how much time you have on your hands. Tell me, do you ever sell a house?'

'Sold a cute little cape, last week. There's an even cuter one coming up right here in the borough if you'll bail out of that condo. At a price you could handle.'

'Thanks. Would that make your second sale for the year?'

'Sold the Yankee Drover in May.'

'Really?'

I said, 'Trooper Moody spent those three hours that morning on traffic patrol. He pulled over A&D's fertilizer tank truck for a broken tail-light, charged it was overloaded and commanded the driver to follow him to Plainfield where he wasted an hour setting up the portable scales. It was not overweight by much, but he ticketed it anyhow and threatened to impound it if the driver didn't go straight back to New York State. Where, quote, "They may not care about overweight vehicles threatening the lives of law-abiding motorists." Now, can you add anything to this that might interest me?'

'Why do you believe pig farmers with a grudge?'

'They're not exactly your average pig farmers. They sold A&D Communications for a ton in the late 1980s, became lady and gentleman farmers and bought two pigs. The rest is history. Now come on, pay up. Give me something back.'

'Why, Ben? *Why* did you want to know about Trooper Moody?'

'I'll give you a hint. The manure truck was headed to Mr Butler's farm.'

'So?'

'It never got there.'

'I don't get what all this has to do with Trooper Moody.'

'Well, it tells me that Mr King has probably tapped Mr Butler's telephone.'

'What are you talking about?'

'But mainly it tells me that Trooper Moody took a bribe.' Marian looked suddenly unfriendly. 'From whom?'

'Henry King.'

'To do what?'

'To stop that truck from dumping pig manure at his party.'

'That son of a bitch.'

I figured she meant both of them.

'Mr Butler had threatened to do something to King's party. The reason I think King tapped Butler's phone is that Ollie was waiting for the truck on the Morrisville Road. The pig guy thinks Ollie broke his brake light when he pulled him over. You know damned well King didn't bribe him with a cheque. But add it up and it's clear he paid Ollie to keep that truck from getting through.'

'Goddammit.'

'I suppose Ollie could tell himself he was bribed to enforce the law – as opposed to the more traditional looking the other way.'

'You think that's any different?' Marian shot back. Her father had been a Bridgeport beat cop, shot and on disability for his pains. Lord knew his conduct in a city suffering dying industry and middle-class 'Abandon ship', but Marian was as straight an arrow as Robin Hood ever fletched.

'It's not as bad as what I thought he did.'

'Which was?'

'I thought he killed Dicky.'

'Dicky killed Dicky,' she snapped back, a little too fast.

'Sure of that?'

'Positive. With his father's help.'

'Oh, get off the party line, Marian. You had to consider Ollie. Dicky's lawsuit could have got him fired.'

She gave me a bleak road-cop stare. But I wasn't speeding. 'It's pay-back time. Fair trade, not to mention gratitude for confirming Ollie's "alibi".'

'What do you want?'

'What's the status of your other suspects?'

'There aren't any.'

'You're sure it wasn't somebody else.'

'Who else?' she asked with elaborate patience. 'Henry King was three thousand miles away –'

'Ohhh, you were wondering about King too?'

'Of course, you jerk. We're clearing every "obvious" suspect Butler's lawyers would wave in our face. God, I hate amateurs.'

'Then you've looked into Josh Wiggens, who was not three thousand miles away.'

'None of your business.'

'How about Bertram Wills?'

'What about him?'

'What if he had a thing for Mrs King?'

'I hate amateurs.'

'I just told you a lot of good stuff. Tell me, have you put any thought into Dennis and Albert Chevalley?'

270

'You saved me a drive to New York State. Big deal.'

'The least you could do –'

'They're your cousins, Mr Real Estate.'

'I'm not a blood-thicker-than-water person when it comes to murder.'

'You've got a self-esteem problem, Ben. Too much of it.'

'You've got worse problems.'

'Like what?'

'While you grace my kitchen with your pretty face, Tim Hall, Mr Butler's lawyer, is depositing in the Butler defence fund a cheque for twenty-five thousand dollars. Guess whose cheque?'

'Twenty-five *thousand*. Who can afford – you're kidding. *King* is backing Butler?'

'He wants an innocent man set free.'

'He wants me and Arnie off the case.'

'He wants me off the case, too.'

'*Too*? That "too" reminds me of a five-dollar hooker parking her ass on a Cadillac to improve her image. Anyway,' she confirmed Ira's gloomy prediction, 'he's too late. No way we're dropping the case.'

I poured the coffee, wondering what I could pry out of her about Josh Wiggens. 'You still owe me.'

Marian gnawed her lip. 'Here's your pay-back: J. J. Topkis is not a suspect.'

'Thank you, Marian . . . Do you happen to know how he paid for his new chopper?'

'I'd guess drugs or the armoury job. Just a guess. But his alibi on the King dam is iron-clad. From midnight the night before, when he and Dicky parted company at the White Birch, until the day after the explosion, J. J. was with that welfare witch at whose residence Trooper Moody arrested him.'

'Isn't she protecting her boyfriend?'

'I let her believe she was selling him out on something else. She's pissed he gave her crabs. Speaking of which, how's it going with Ms Devlin?'

'Huh?'

Marian showed her teeth in a semblance of a smile. 'Neat

271

thing about being an amateur detective is you get to sleep with witnesses and suspects. If *I* started sleeping with witnesses and suspects, my bosses would get real mad. You know how distrustful those old cops are. They'd think if I slept with witnesses and suspects I might get confused.'

'Cynics.'

'Of course it's probably different for a guy. Guys don't get confused. I wouldn't know. I'm not a guy. But what's to get confused if you don't have feelings – Hey! I'm a police officer. What are you doing?'

'Groping you, officer.'

'She any good?'

'Very.'

'Better than me?'

'No one's better than you.'

'You had to say that.'

'No, I mean it. You're so beautifully endowed, gun, cuffs – Ow!'

I'd completely forgotten teeth, and there was considerable heavy breathing going on before I recalled the promise I'd made to stop lurching around like this and get my life in order. Whatever hopes I had of starting up with Julia Devlin deserved a clear eye and tight focus.

'Hellooo?' said Marian. 'Where'd you go?'

'Sorry. Sorry, I just got confused.'

'About what?'

'Uh. About your boyfriend.'

Marian looked at me, more than a little suspicious for breaking the rules. 'You know darned well I am not playing pocket pool with *you* to hear about *my* boyfriend. Oh, no, have you really fallen for that broad?'

Before I could utter some irrevocable reply, she said, 'Have you gone and gotten yourself another Rita?'

'What do you mean?'

'You know what I mean. Conveniently unavailable.'

'Hey, I didn't –'

'When are you going to grab a woman who can grab back?'

I took too long forming an answer. Marian looked at her

watch. 'Actually, I don't have time for this anyhow. Rain check?'

'Rain check.'

She gave me a friendly goodbye squeeze. We disentangled. A gleam in her eye hinted that her boyfriend, whom she described as low-maintenance – a nice former professional tennis player turned Pratt and Whitney jet-engine sales engineer – was in for a real treat tonight.

I stepped into a real cold shower.

I was closing in. I'd earned J. J. Topkis for Trooper Moody. Two for one, not bad. Particularly, if over in Frenchtown, Dennis and Albert would make it three.

'Don't jump,' a voice said.

27

I jumped anyway – practically out of my skin – as Julia Devlin drew back the steamed-up curtain.

'*Where did you come from?*'

'I stopped at Happy Hour and snuck into your guest room to nap it off – well, look at you. Do you always take cold showers?'

'Only when I'm lonely.'

She reached back to bobby-pin her hair into a bun. My bathrobe fell from her shoulders and yes, I confirmed, she had the panther musculature to be a bodyguard.

A sliver of fear was a remarkable aphrodisiac.

Later, in my arms, she whispered, 'I have to tell you, I heard you two talking downstairs.'

'I'm . . .'

'I'm a little jealous. I mean I don't have any right to be . . . I envy you and Marian – you sounded like such good friends.'

She seemed very sad and I debated saying that she was friends with Henry King. But she touched my lips and said, 'No. Don't say it. Just let's be.'

'Did you hear me say I'd fallen for you?'

'You can't do that, Ben.'

I finally had my answer to Marian's question: women who weren't free to grab back couldn't break promises they couldn't make. But though it was freshly minted, and straight from the heart, it sounded like death.

Maybe if Dicky could learn to love life, I could learn to

take chances again. In fact, I suddenly felt this was my last chance. 'Leave Henry,' I said. 'You deserve better.'

'No I don't.'

'You do.'

'Ben, you don't know.'

'I know you're way too young for him. You're bright and special and something tells me you're ready to break out.'

'I love him, Ben.'

Wondering was one thing. Hearing it was like crashing the Olds into a tree. I must have flinched, because she reached out to comfort me. 'He saved my life.'

I had heard those words before, Mrs King uttering them lovingly to Bert Wills kneeling before her. 'Saved your life?'

'Yes. He gave me purpose. A chance to make something of myself. I'm with him in everything.'

'Do you really want to play handmaid to an arrogant, unprincipled . . . He's a taker, Julia. That's all he'll ever be. And you're not. You can't win with him. You're an object, you're like property. He has you because he assumes he's entitled to a lovely young woman on the side. It's not love. It's power.'

'I like power.'

'For what?'

'I want it. I don't want to be helpless. I don't want to be afraid. I don't want to be dependent.'

'But you are dependent.'

'Not like my mother was.'

'Oh, come on. You're miles ahead of your poor mother.'

'Don't tell me, "Oh come on." I tried it the other way. I spent years propping up a man who needed too much. It's my turn. Henry King's a great man.'

'At least you didn't say he's a good man.'

'Are you better?'

I asked myself if I was any 'better' than Henry King. I wanted to take her away from him. But would I treat her better than he treated her? Better, for instance, than I had ever treated Vicky?

'Wasn't this what you meant about wasting yourself?'

This time she flinched. And I could have cut my tongue

out for the pain I had flung on her face. I reached to her as she had reached to me.

'Please,' she asked. 'I can't think now. Just hold me. Just let's be.'

And we were, again and again. Although she never opened her eyes.

We woke up early.

Julia left in silence.

I hurried out to Frenchtown to see whether my ridiculous cousins were murderous, too.

They were already out. So was their Mom. Figuring Aunt Laura had gone shopping and wouldn't find it too amiss to discover me in her trailer claiming I'd found the door unlocked, I pried her spring lock with the flat blade of my penknife. It wasn't much of a lock, but with Albert and Dennis in residence, she had as much to fear from thieves as the owner of twin pitbulls.

I waved up the Chevalley hillside as if hailing an aunt, just in case other relatives were watching from their trailer homes, and stepped on to the wall-to-wall carpeting inside. The rain drummed on the roof. Laura Chevalley's kitchen and the living room were neat as a pin. But I could search Albert and Dennis's little bedrooms with a backhoe and no one would notice.

Their beds were unmade, their clothing heaped strategically for third and fourth wearings. Reading material lay open on the floor – glossy magazines devoted to the female body, motorcycles, guns and oriental weaponry, often simultaneously. Tools stood propped in corners. Towels hung from doorknobs. Mail – reminders of missed motor-vehicle court and 'free-introductory-offer' CD club demands for payment – was scattered like a sore loser's poker hand.

None of this smelled as bad as it might have. Testament to their mother's efforts to at least keep it clean – a hypothesis supported by the absence of pizza boxes, empty beer cans, and the worst species of used sock.

Nothing I found stuffed beneath their mattresses bears telling. The shotgun and rifle collections under their beds, how-

ever, deserved life member
backs of their closets were
handguns they'd probably negl

The Holy Bible looked out of pl
But slipped between Revelations a
a dog-eared E. I. Du Pont pamphl
Dynamite'.

The jacket photograph of a long lin
the ground like a Mohawk haircut did
King's dam exploding. But the instructio   plete,
everything from primers to blasting caps,   idling so-
called safety fuse.

'Important: As soon as the fuse is lighted, the blaster should
hasten to a place of safety.' (They just don't write manuals
like they used to. My new Rollerblades instructions
demanded, 'Never skate in traffic. Observe all traffic regu-
lations.') *Hasten*. Copyright, 1944. Very curious why Dennis
had hidden Grandpa Chevalley's blasting manual in a Bible,
I searched on.

The wall next to his bed was panelled with imitation wal-
nut. I noticed a horizontal seam where there shouldn't have
been, discovered a little door. I worked my knife into the
crack. The panelling and the full thickness of the wall swung
inwards. I peered inside, thinking I'd find a stash of some
sort and finding instead a portal to Albert's room.

Finished with their bedrooms, I checked the front door.
Still alone, the Olds agleam in the slackening rain. I started
on the living room. Here I had to be a lot more careful. It
was a normal human-being living room, fair-sized in the
doublewide, and absolutely packed with the knick-knacks
that junk shops dub collectibles, all of which were breakable.

I doubted Aunt Laura had heard of Tennessee Williams's
Laura, but she could match her glass menagerie in a walk.
China cats roamed her coffee table. Dog-painted plates
covered the walls. Shelves were dense with Hummel-like
figurines.

I went through her hutch, bright full of Fiesta Ware that
might be worth more – according to a woman I knew who
collected the stuff – than the entire trailer. Nothing to indicate

...ky Butler. The same, when I opened ... her bookcase. No more 'Ditching with ...nuals, only a pristine set of the *World Book* ...*a* purchased before she had got to know her chil-...well.

I closed the bookcase, stymied.

Having poked shamelessly through her personal belongings, I wondered why Aunt Laura had allowed Albert and Dennis to put the wooden end tables in her living room. Obviously, the boys themselves were not allowed in this place of pride. They had TVs in their rooms and if they wanted to watch their mother's huge colour set, they did it from the hall or the kitchen door. While her tastes were not my tastes, the room had a certain consistency that the dynamite boxes seemed to violate.

They were actually pairs of boxes, stacked two-high on either side of the velvet couch. I started to remove a lamp so I could open the top. Then I noticed that the front had duct tape along the bottom edge. It made a hinge, in fact, allowing the front of the box to swing down like a door. I slipped my fingernails into the joint and started to pull, when I felt the floor move under my knees.

The rain had stopped. A heavy man had stepped into the trailer. And a loud metallic clatter sounded exactly like a big-bore shotgun shell being chambered.

'What the hell are you doing?'

Dennis. Albert was behind him, still on the steps, *his* shotgun pointed skywards. Dennis's – a semi-automatic pump job – was pointed way too close in my direction.

'Hey! Dennis, don't point that gun at me.'

'What are you doing, Ben?'

'I'm looking what's inside this box,' I said.

'Ben, don't do that,' he said, and his shotgun drifted closer.

It was a little early in the morning for them to be drunk. Albert belched and I realized that for them it was still late last night. Worse, they looked scared. What the two of them high as kites, scared and armed might egg each other into, I didn't want to guess.

I said, 'I am standing up, carefully.'

'Don't move.'

'I won't move.'

Dennis said, 'Check out if he took anything.'

Albert squeezed past him, gun now pointed at the ceiling, and lumbered down the hall to the bedrooms. He came back almost immediately. 'Naw, he didn't go in there.'

'So what's he doing here?'

'I don't know.'

'Let's ask him.'

'What are you doing here, Ben?'

It was difficult to see them as comical while they were holding pump shotguns.

'Guys, I really think you ought to put down the guns before somebody gets hurt.'

'You!' Dennis bellowed. 'Not somebody.'

'You can't shoot me in your Mom's living room. You'll mess the whole place up.'

Dennis proved a strategist. 'Yeah, but what if we thought you was a burglar?'

'Your Mom would still be pissed. And so would the cops. You're not allowed to shoot burglars. Come on, guys. Whatever you got in that box isn't worth killing me for.'

Albert said, 'I don't want to get caught.'

'You *will* get caught,' I told them. 'Count on it.'

They looked at each other, then stared at the dynamite boxes. 'They'll fire us.'

'Why will they fire you?' I asked.

'They'll take back the truck,' Albert said mournfully.

'Why would they take back the truck?'

'You son of a bitch,' said Dennis. 'It's all your fault.' He cocked his gun angrily and the shell he had chambered previously went flying across the room and knocked a knock-off Hummel from the shelf.

'Jesus Christ! Mom'll kill us.'

'Ben made me do it.'

'It didn't break,' I soothed. 'Look! It landed on the rug. It's OK.'

'Where?'

'Rolled behind the couch,' I told them.

279

They lumbered into the room, crouched down on hands and knees like hippos in mud, and felt behind the couch. 'Oh, no.' Dennis held up a coyly smiling fisherman's head. 'It busted.'

'I misled you,' I said, engaging the safety as I picked up the shotgun he had laid on the carpet. Albert reached fool-ishly for it. There was no talking sense to them, so I popped him in the forehead with the muzzle, and smacked Dennis lightly on the rebound.

Then I retreated to the far side of the living room where I sat on Laura's Lazy-boy, pointed both shotguns – safety secretly on – their way, and waited for them to accept the situation.

It took a while. But time was on my side. Their heads hurt. Dennis was rubbing his right sideburn. Albert had a nickel-sized indentation in his forehead. Far worse, I was sure, were the hangovers closing in fast.

'Aw come on, Ben.'

'Don't "Come on, Ben" me.'

'We was only kidding.'

'Like you were kidding when you killed Dicky?'

'Huh?'

'What?'

'Killed Dicky? Dicky Butler? We didn't kill Dicky Butler. You nuts, Ben?'

'Where were you between noon and two that day?'

'We was working.'

'Bull.'

'We was. We was. We told you, Ben.'

'I know what you told me. But I also know you were lying.'

'Ben, don't turn us in.'

'You admit you did it?'

'Did what?'

'Killed Dicky.'

'No,' they chorused.

'Then why did you lie about seeing Mr Butler with the calf?'

'We didn't lie.'

280

'There was no calf. He made it up.'

'He did?'

'And you guys went along because you needed an alibi – Dennis, your face is all scabbed. Looks like somebody really did a number on you a couple of weeks ago. Dicky kick your ass, again?'

'No one kicked my ass,' he said sullenly.

'What happened? Who hit you?'

'No one.'

'Then what happened to your face?'

Albert started snickering.

'Shut up,' Dennis growled.

'He was doing airbags.'

'What do you mean, "doing airbags"? You mean *stealing* airbags? From cars?'

'Jervises'll pay a hundred bucks for 'em. But they're kind of tricky.'

'The airbag blew up in your face?'

'Yeah, kind of – I was getting pretty good at it.'

Albert snickered, again. 'He got an Allen wrench stuck in his head. I had to pull it out with pliers.'

'Come closer, Dennis – not too close! . . .' I peered over the shotgun barrel. Damn. 'OK, back where you were.' The Allen wrench had left a distinctive right-angle blue scar.

'If you weren't killing Dicky, where were you? What's in the box?'

They traded another long look and some resigned nods. Albert spoke. 'Don't tell nobody, OK?'

'That depends on what's in the box.'

Dennis wrung his hands. 'We didn't kill Dicky.'

'Show me!'

Albert lurched to his knees and opened the dynamite box. I was praying it didn't hold bloody axe handles; my cousins were just dumb enough to hide them instead of burning them.

I was not expecting Veuve Clicquot champagne.

'Don't tell Mr King, he'll fire us,' groaned Albert.

Dennis explained, 'That's why we lied about seeing Mr Butler and the calf. We were afraid they'd find out we took the bottles home. So when you asked about Mr Butler, we figured we were covered.'

'What did you steal it for? You jerks. You got good jobs. You got a neat truck. He's paying you regular. What'd you steal his champagne for?'

'He wouldn't let us run the gate during the party,' Albert explained sullenly.

'And the stuff was just sitting there in the back of a van,' Dennis furthered the explanation. 'Sat there for an hour. We figured, they got so much they ain't going to miss it.'

'How much you got left?'

'All of it. We ain't touched it.'

'Well, why don't you take it back? Say you found it in the woods. Like maybe somebody stashed it to steal later, then couldn't come back with all the new security after the explosion.'

'We went to the Liquor Locker. Steve says the stuff costs like sixty bucks a bottle?'

'That's what Steve would charge.'

'We was wondering like maybe we could –'

'Take it back.'

'OK, Ben. If you say so.'

They were very contrite. But when they actually apologized, I got suspicious. 'Wait a moment, guys.'

'Hey, we're late for work, Ben.'

'This'll just take a minute.'

'What'll just take a minute? We gotta go. What are you doing? Careful!'

I opened the box again and lifted out a bottle of champagne. And another. And a third. And there in the bottom was an unpleasant-looking stash of dynamite sticks.

'Well, what do we have here?'

'Dynamite.'

'Hidden dynamite,' I corrected. 'Have you been turning this?'

'Yeah.'

Thank God for small favours.

'Let's walk it way outside and then you'll tell me where it came from.'

I carried it myself after offloading the Veuve Clicquot. They shambled after me like arthritic hounds tracking their dinner plates. I made several trips on to the wet grass and noticed something peculiar. There was a variety of dynamite types. Some was ditching dynamite, 50 per cent strength. Some was marked Special Gelatine 60 per cent. Other sticks were labelled Extra, at 40 per cent. I didn't know much about dynamite, but clearly the sticks, which varied from five to eight inches in length, had not all been purchased in the same batch.

'OK, guys. Where did it come from?'

'I don't know. We had it around,' said Albert, and Dennis volunteered, 'I think Grandpa left it.'

'Your grandfather's been dead twenty years. I'm going to call Trooper Moody if you don't tell me where it came from. Did you rob another highway job?'

'No.'

'Where'd it come from?'

'Found it up at King's.'

'King's?' How had such a motley collection of dynamite ended up at Fox Trot?

Dennis claimed they'd found it in a construction shed. 'Figured, what the hell, you can always use some dynamite around. Right?'

Henry King's imported house builders had not been the country-casual sort to leave explosives behind.

'I'm calling Trooper Moody.'

'No!'

'Why?'

'You're lying.'

'Tell him,' said Albert.

'Shut up.'

'Tell me.'

'OK, OK,' and opened up with what sounded at first like an even bigger whopper. 'Mr King sent us up to Butler's to steal his dynamite and we –'

'What?'

'He said Butler was going to blow up Fox Trot if we didn't take his dynamite away so we snuck up there and stole it.'

'Oh really? What'd you do with it?'

'Stashed it where Mr King showed us in the shed we told you about.'

'And kept some for yourselves?'

'No! Not his main stash. Just these little extras.'

'They was loose in a little box,' Albert chimed in. 'And we was all out. Nobody'll miss 'em.'

'Boys, if I could just recapitulate . . . You robbed Mr Butler's dynamite for King, except this dynamite which you kept from King? OK? Couple of questions. How'd you happen to get past DaNang?'

'The dog wasn't there.'

'And Mr Butler?'

'He was gone too.'

'Convenient, seeing as how he rarely left his property.'

'Mr King told us the coast was clear, they was in Newbury.' At the General Store, telephoning his detonator. 'How about Dicky?'

'Didn't see him.' Sleeping it off in the woodlot.

What the hell – 'Could I ask you guys a question? Did you ever wonder about a connection between the dynamite you stole from Mr Butler and the bombing of Mr King's dam?'

'Sure, Ben,' said Dennis. 'We're not stupid. What happened was, me and Albert was too late. Butler set his charge before we stole his dynamite. Weren't our fault,' he added, little pig eyes brimful of honesty, and I knew he believed that Henry King had taken precautions, too late.

If my cousins had just joined Trooper Moody and J. J. Topkis in the pantheon of the somewhat innocent, I still couldn't believe that a twenty-million-dollar-a-year diplomat to the stars would kill a man to steal his farm.

I hurried back to Newbury.

Josh Wiggens, maybe, thinking he was doing Henry a favour. Or Josh could have set King up for a fall, hoping to catch Julia on the rebound.

Bert Wills sticking it to Henry, to avenge old insults and land Mrs King and all she'd reap in divorce? Great motivation, except Bert wasn't brave enough.

I found Alison weeping in my office.

'What's the matter, sweetie?'

'Mr Butler took DaNang.'

'He's out?'

'DaNang just jumped in the truck. Like he never said good-bye or even looked back. Mr Butler whistled and it was like he was never here.'

'We'll visit him.'

'I want a cat.'

I dialled Tim. 'Hey, congratulations.'

'For what?'

'For springing Mr Butler.'

'I didn't spring Mr Butler.'

'He was just here. He got the dog.'

'You're kidding. Ira must have – I'll call you back.'

Typical Ira, I thought, grandstand Mr Butler's bail approval and neglect to inform Tim, who had done all the work.

'If I can't have a cat I want a belly ring.'

'No, you can't have a belly ring. You're not even old enough to have a belly.' I had to figure some way to lean on Henry King.

'I really, really want a cat.'

The phone rang. Tim, sounding a lot more hysterical than I liked my lawyers.

'Butler escaped!'

'How?'

'Blew the door right off his cell!'

'With what?'

'They think his vet buddy slipped him C-4. I don't believe it. I'm now representing an escaped prisoner old enough to be my father. Blinded the guards with a flash bomb, hotwired a truck, and took off.'

'I don't believe it either. Where'd his buddy get plastic explosive?'

'You don't need much – they could have smuggled it in a cupcake.'

'Who was this buddy?'

'That old homeless guy who kept visiting? The guards said he always calmed him down – I can't understand how that crazy old farmer got past the roadblocks. The troopers sealed off Plainfield. He still got away.'

Tim didn't understand that his client had been a warrior.

'He took the guards' guns.'

'Jail guards don't carry guns.'

'Blew open their weapons locker.'

I ran for the door.

The troopers hunted armed quarry by stricter rules – hardly news to the kindly soul who had slipped Mr Butler his C-4.

Alison scrambled after me. 'What? What?'

'Where's your Mom?'

'Cleaning.'

'Go over to Connie's. Tell her I told you to stay with her.'

'Why?'

'Mr Butler escaped from prison. Cops'll be here any minute.'

'He did?'

'Go. Now.'

'OK. OK.'

'Wait. Did you talk to him?'

'No. He just whistled. If I didn't open the door DaNang would have jumped right through the screen – Ben, will the cops hurt DaNang?'

'What was he driving?'

'His truck.'

'His *own* truck?'

'Old Blue. The Ford 1500.'

'You sure? You actually saw the truck?'

'Yeah, it was all loaded up with wood.'

'Wood? Firewood?'

'Boards. It was really full. DaNang had to ride inside.'

Last I'd seen it had been parked empty in the barn.

'OK. Tell Connie Mr Butler escaped from prison and I don't want you in this house if the cops come looking for him here.'

'Where are you going?'

'To find him first.'

28

Josh Wiggens was probably hoisting a celebratory Scotch.

Tim might not understand warriors, but the CIA man did, and I was willing to bet blood that he had arranged the 'homeless vet buddy'. Set up to seize weapons, the old farmer would fight until the troopers gunned him down and ended, for ever, the investigation that would expose Dicky Butler's murderer.

But Josh was in for a big surprise.

He hadn't heard Mr Butler promise to blow Fox Trot off Morris Mountain.

And the old farmer could do it, or die trying. Thirty years since Special Forces didn't matter. More dangerous than creaky fighting skills was attitude.

Obstacles were opportunities.

To win was to survive.

Win by any means.

Thank God he had told me. It gave me a brief leg up over the troopers. Which made me the only person in Newbury with a hope in hell of saving the poor lunatic.

I threw gloves and a wire cutter into the car. Ollie Moody's grey cruiser screeched into the driveway, blocking me.

'You seen Butler?'

'I just got here.'

A rusty pickup roared in behind him, decanting a grizzled old woody, Frank LaFrance — father of Steve of failed-first-select-challenger fame — and Frank's eager bloodhound, Ike, who, hired out to the troopers, would follow DaNang's scent like an Interstate highway.

'You don't mind if we search the house,' said Ollie, clearly intending to search it and give Ike a sniff whether I minded or not.

'Move your vehicles first, I'm going to work.'

'You sit tight.'

Ollie ran in the kitchen door, trailed by the tracker and his dog. My father used to call Frank 'Guns and Dogs' for proclaiming at town meetings, 'What this country needs is more guns and dogs.' Frank was in his glory today, Ike slathering on the trail, gun rack loaded for bear.

I drove across my lawn and through a perennial border.

Short-cuts up Morris Mountain didn't help. The troopers had beat me to the Butler place anyway. A blue and yellow Crown Victoria straddled the driveway. The uniformed road cop sheltered behind it with a shotgun looked young and nervous. I didn't even slow down enough to make him wave me off, but kept going up the mountain, glimpsing, as I passed, another car and cop stationed at the house. But if they thought they had him covered, they were wrong.

Resident troopers like Ollie never would have made the mistake. But Plainfield Barracks, stretched thin, had been reinforced by suburban-bred road cops who couldn't know that farmers with winter time on their hands built roads. Three generations of Butlers had riddled their sprawling property with farm and lumber tracks, which were hidden in late summer by sumac and goldenrod.

They were ready for me when I raced back. The trooper had manoeuvred his car broadside across the road, he and his partner behind it, sidearms drawn.

'Out of the car! Hands on the roof.'

One stayed under cover, the other patted me down after checking inside the car. 'Open the trunk, sir.'

'Mind telling me what's the problem?'

'Escaped prisoner, sir. He's armed.' They levelled their weapons at the trunk, according me the honour of standing in the line of fire with the key.

When neither DaNang nor Mr Butler jumped out, they sent me on my way. I drove all the way down to Fox Trot's gatehouse. The heavy, ornate iron gate was locked.

Albert Chevalley lumbered out of the gatehouse, yawning. 'Hey, Ben. You seen all the cops?'

I turned the car around and headed back up the mountain.

Mr Butler had had long nights in the Plainfield Jail to hatch his plan. There was no way he could breech Fox Trot's main gate. Even if he did somehow manage to blow it off its posts, the driveway spikes would shred his tyres. Whereas, their adjoining woodlots were a natural base for an attack on King's house. If he had any sense left at all, he would wait until dark.

After several false trails, I turned on to dirt ruts that veered between a couple of Mr Butler's fields, then snaked around to parallel Fox Trot's deer fence.

I found a cow bar overgrown in blackberry, and backed the Olds into the briars. Then I put on my gloves, squeezed out of the car, and draped more briars around it. I climbed the stone wall which was topped with the deer fence and clipped the lower strands. The tension in the wire whipped them left and right, crackling where electricity pulsed in the grass. I slipped under, crossed the dirt perimeter road that paralleled the inside of the fence, and started jogging across a hayfield.

I was high above King's house. The distant woodlots blocked sight of all but the furthest corner of the lake, which the heavy rains had partially refilled muddy brown. I crossed another stone wall and another hayfield. The rain had settled dust and pollen, or I'd have been kicking up clouds and sneezing my head off.

Across a third field, steeper than the first, a final stone wall, and I was inside King's woodlot. I stopped to get my bearings. I was still high on the property, near the Butler boundary. The stream should be less than a quarter mile ahead. I headed for it, navigating by the sun glimpsed through the tree canopy and the slope of the land.

I thought I heard voices.

I stopped, listened intently. Wind sighed overhead. A cardinal was whistling. Woodpeckers drilled. Squirrels chattered. A flock of jays swooped by, screaming.

I glided forward again, slowly and quietly, eyes in the

distance, looking for the flicker of movement through the trees.

I smelled the water.

Voices again.

I veered upland, to come at them down the stream. I reached the deer fence first, lifted a strand with my gloves, and slipped through, with only one stinging shock on my back. On Butler land now, I climbed a ways inside the fence, then continued towards the stream, certain I'd heard voices. Then, suddenly, my own voice – in a loud, startled yelp – as the ground collapsed under me and I pitched face forward into a hole deep enough to bury a coffin.

29

I fell with King and Butler jungle-warfare bamboo spikes in mind. I crashed, instead, on plywood, crunching my knee-caps and skinning the heel of my hand.

The sides of the hole were plywood, too, forming a three-by-three-by-six-foot underground box, which was empty, except for me. I remembered I had yelled out loud when I lost my footing. I raised my head to see who'd heard me.

Thick brush had grown on three sides – thicker than the surrounding vegetation, which was stunted by tree shade. Whoever had dug the pit had transplanted wild mountain laurel on to the mounded diggings – not the easiest landscaping project, as the mountain laurel resists mightily attempts to separate it from the rocks and roots with which it has entwined.

How many lies had Mr Butler told me in order to protect his secret dynamite stash? The fourth side, which faced up the slope, away from the King property, opened on to a long-unused lumber track. Long-unused, that was, until a few hours ago when he had backed his truck right up to the rim of the hole. The tracks of bald tyres were fresh in the mud, but there were no puddles in the ruts. They'd been laid after the rain had stopped.

Peering in the opposite direction, through the laurel, I could see the deer fence, thirty feet downslope. Beyond the fence, down on King's property, I sensed motion in the trees.

I climbed out on to the lumber track and crawled.

Somewhere to my left was my old friend the stream that emptied on to the King property and eventually fed Lake Vixen. I jinked left into the woods and headed for it.

I heard it roaring before I saw it. The rains had gorged the bed. Where I had crawled puddle to puddle last time, now several feet of water rampaged over the rocky bottom. Excellent. If Butler was down there he wouldn't hear me until I swarmed him. If it was King's guard, the brook would roar in Big Ears like Seventh Avenue expresses passing Columbus Circle.

The water was so cold it almost froze my heart. I had expected to sort of wade hunkered down chest-deep. But it was deeper and moving a lot faster than I had estimated. I was plummeted from rock to rock like a woodchip, wishing I had a life vest and a motorcycle helmet.

In seconds, it sluiced me into Dicky's swimming hole. The dammed-up pool was brimful, the water lapping over the banks. Anyone looking my way would spot my head above the banks. I scrambled over Dicky's dam as fast as I could, scraping down the waterfall like a crippled otter, and crunched on to the rocks below.

King's deer fence loomed, plastered with threats of electrical shock and penalties for trespassing. Swept on the current, I saw the fence's logic: come late winter, when hunger made the deer more aggressive, the brook ran higher; the lowest strand over the stream wasn't low at all. It skimmed the rain-swollen surface at a point between my nose and neck.

I ducked my face in the water, but not fast or deep enough. My wet hair brushed the strand, I felt a sharp kick in the back of my head and a startling pain that snapped my mouth open with an involuntary gasp into which icy water poured. Coughing – drowning – I slammed rock to rock as the current accelerated down the steepening descent. A root I grabbed tore loose in my hand.

I seized another and clung for my life.

'What the hell are you doing on my land?'

And there was Henry King, shoving through the brush like a Cape Buffalo in a territorial mood.

The master of Fox Trot wore Eddie Bauer gardening trousers, a Ralph Lauren 'British county flannel' shirt, and a jaunty Navy VIP visitor cap, which was embroidered *USS Iowa* in shiny gold and heaped with more scrambled eggs than the Church Hill diner served all weekend. His face was red.

'You're on my land!'

'I'm in your brook. You want to give me a hand out of here?'

'You're on my land!'

I climbed out on my own, gasping and shivering. 'Get out of my face! This is not eighteenth-century Poland.'

King's trousers were soaked and mud-stained to the knees.

I took a not-so-long-shot in the not-very-dark.

'Did you find the glove?'

'What?'

It had rained continuously since I had claimed to drop it. This afternoon was his first opportunity to conduct a thorough hunt.

'The glove I told you I dropped. The glove your security zealot shot holes in.'

'I've had the man fired. And I've already apologized to you for that incident.'

'The glove you asked for when I returned his helmet. *Dicky Butler's glove*. What are you doing in the woods?'

'They're my woods.'

'You're looking for the glove. It links someone in your woods to Dicky Butler.'

'It does not! It proves that Dicky Butler was trespassing on my land when he dropped his glove.'

'How badly do you want the glove?'

'What?'

'Assume I lied the other day. Assume I have it. Hidden, stashed away safely. What's it worth to you?'

Sheer hell across a poker table. Not a flicker, not a twitch of bushy brows, not even a change of light in his eye. And this time, he didn't bother fencing.

'Shop your blackmail elsewhere, Abbott. You surprise me. I read you wrong. I didn't think you were that sleazy.'

'I read you wrong, too,' I replied. 'Maybe that's why I still can't figure out why you killed him.'

King laughed the way you laugh when a crazy corners

you at a party. '. . . Just out of curiosity, how'd you read me wrong?'

'You have a great motive – you want Mr Butler's farm – but I can't see you killing him for it.'

'That's a relief.'

'And I also can't imagine you destroying your new lake to get rid of the body.'

'Another relief.'

'But everyone else who might have killed him, didn't.'

Henry King laughed again. 'Good thing you're not a cop. It would cost me a fortune in attorney fees for a false-arrest suit.'

'Trooper Moody didn't kill him. My lamebrain cousins didn't kill him. J. J. Topkis didn't kill him.'

'Who the hell is J. J. Topkis?'

'J. J.'s a biker with a hotshot criminal attorney who was hired by your man Secretary Bertram Wills.'

'Bert Wills is from a patrician Connecticut family known for helping the less advantaged.'

'J. J.'s become more advantaged since Josh Wiggens bought him a brand-new twenty-five-thousand-dollar factory-customized Harley-Davidson motorcycle –'

'How Josh spends his money is his business. I know he came into some recently when his mother died. As for the "company" Josh keeps' – he wiggled his hand in the gay-slur gesture – 'his young friends are his own business, too. He is always welcome in my house.'

'Your "house guests" have been working real hard to use J. J. to hang Mr Butler. Josh tipped Trooper Moody where to arrest J. J. Bert hired him a hotshot criminal attorney who cut a deal for ratting out Mr Butler. Josh bribed him with a new Harley to keep his mouth shut. He even stopped J. J.'s gang from stomping me to death – against his fonder desires I am sure – in order to keep him out of jail on murder charges. My guess is next time J. J. steps out of line he's going to end up dead.'

'If you could prove this nonsense you'd have turned Josh into the police.'

'Except you're the one looking for Dicky's glove.'

'I'm not looking for the glove.'

'Your knees are all muddy. You've been crawling around looking for Dicky's glove.'

'I tripped and fell. I was enjoying a walk in my woods. It's very peaceful, here. Usually. I often stroll here, collecting my thoughts. I'm a city boy. Nature's new to me. I find it very relaxing. Don't you?'

'Not when I run into hostile neighbours.'

'That's because you're walking in someone else's woods. Try your own, sometime. You'll find them much safer.'

'Let me make you an offer,' I said.

'I'm not interested.'

'I'll give you the glove for free.'

'I don't want it,' he said.

The mud on his knees said he did.

'This whole thing is driving me crazy. I'm rooting around like a pig with a ring in his nose. I'll give you the glove in exchange for the answer to one simple question.'

King looked bored.

I asked, 'Do you want to be the star attraction at the second glove trial of the century? Is that why you are hunting the glove alone?'

'That's two questions.'

The plywood hole in the ground, Mr Butler's balding tyre tracks leading up it, and the motley collection of dynamite sticks the Chevalleys had stolen from Fox Trot, made it three: 'Is it true that your security people found dynamite in your dam the night before it blew up?'

King's smile turned reflective, his gaze opaque. He reflected for a long moment. Then he shrugged, still smiling. 'May I frisk you, Ben?'

'I'm not armed.'

'For a tape recorder.'

'Be my guest.'

He patted me down, clumsily, but thoroughly.

'The glove is in my Olds. Nearby.'

'Do I have your word?'

'I will give you Dicky's glove,' I promised, but I was getting a queasy feeling that Henry King was playing more games with me than I was playing with him.

He rubbed his chin. He removed his *Iowa* cap, ran cooling fingers through his silvery hair, and put his cap back on. 'The answer to your question is, Yes.'

'Your people found dynamite in your dam the night before the party?'

'Yes. Now go get the glove and bring it to my house.'

'But they didn't tell the cops.'

'I was in London. The party was scheduled the next day. My staff made a decision to leave it there, disarmed.'

'Is that why you roped off the area?'

'Of course. And a good thing we did. The goddammed stuff went off.'

'With Dicky Butler under it.'

'He was drunk and fell asleep. Understand, Julia made a command decision based on all sorts of variables there's no point in going into. It wasn't her fault.'

'You mean the ceramic-engine deal.'

King said, 'You've been busy, Mr Abbott. What a shame you didn't put such effort into the job I hired you to do. Yes. That fucking engine. Julia and I were in constant communication, of course, and when they found the explosives, it still looked like I was going to forge an agreement I could announce at the party. Julia decided we could not have a police bomb squad swarming over the grounds. A decision I support fully, regardless what went wrong.'

'How'd you know Dicky was drunk?'

'I assume –'

'You spoke like you saw him.'

'I assumed –'

'You said it like you knew it. You saw him drunk . . .'

King looked around the woods. Then down the stream.

I pushed him. 'You got back from London late. Eight hours in a cramped aircraft with broken air conditioning. Julia picked you up in the helicopter. You were upset. You had botched the negotiations . . .'

'You're absolutely right. I had had a ghastly week in London. And a hellish flight home. No sleep. And I had two

296

hundred people coming to a party where I had to pretend that Henry King was a winner. So I walked up here and sat under a tree. That tree.'

He pointed out a pleasant-looking ash near the stream. 'I have a Victorian walking stick that opens into a shooting stool. Quite comfortable. I had already discovered that Connecticut ground is cold and wet even in summer.' His voice trailed off.

'Your back to the fence?' I coaxed. 'Looking downhill?'

'Everything I saw was mine. I could look downstream into my woods and listen to the water. Birds. Little animals I couldn't see at first. But I had learned that if I stayed still they'd come out.

'All of a sudden I heard glass break. I turned around and just across the fence was Dicky Butler – drunk. He was trying to smash the neck off a new bottle.

'He saw me and he called out, "Hey, King. Got a corkscrew?"

'I could smell his sweat and breath twenty feet away. I tried to ignore him. I truly did. But he started taunting me. "Hey, big man, you got a big party today? My dad's having a party, too, down in the pasture."'

'The pig manure.'

'I must remember to hire you next time I need some ferreting.' His intelligent eyes probed mine. 'Seriously, come up to the office. I'm going to put you on retainer. I've got projects all over the world you could help me with. Did you keep any decent suits?'

'They smell of mothballs.'

'I'll have Bert take you shopping. Of course I knew what Butler was threatening and I wasn't worried. I'd already dealt with the pig problem.'

'By bribing our resident trooper.'

Henry King said, 'I enjoy negotiating with moralists; they're so inflexible that they're predictable.'

I didn't care if he meant Ollie or me. 'Then what happened?'

'I folded up my stool and started to go. "Hey, big man!" He kept calling me that. Big man. "Hey! I'm warning you.

No more helicopter. My old man's really hurting. Leave him alone.''

'I know you warned me not to get into it, but I couldn't stop myself. I went up to the fence. I said, ''Tell your father I'll buy him any farm in Newbury he wants. Tell him he can have money, too. You can start over, no debts, modern equipment, new breed cows.''

'He just grinned at me. Filthy, yellow teeth. I felt helpless, like I was back in grade school. You know, when some slum kid leans on you because he has nothing else in his life but to make you hurt. And you can't do anything about it. And keep in mind, Abbott, I had just been informed that his father had tried to blow up my dam . . .

'But I stayed cool. I turned my back on him. I walked back to my house, took a shower, and dressed for my party. And just as I was easing into the swing of it, Dicky Butler blew up my dam, destroying my lake, and, since he blundered and killed himself in the process, turning a vicious act of vandalism into an ongoing annoyance.'

'No. You didn't go back to the party until *after* you killed him.'

'I didn't kill him. You just went through it yourself. I had neither the motivation, nor the means. For Christ Sake, Abbott, how could I kill a jailhouse brawler half my age?'

Killer question. King was in pretty good shape for his age, solidly built, but shorter than Dicky, who must have out weighed him by fifty pounds. I'd seen King's temper. But how could he take a man so much bigger, stronger and younger? What anger had super-charged his strength?

King's deep-set, hooded eyes shifted towards the stream, again. This was a man who yelled that a coffee cup with a spot on it was 'filthy'. At his cookout I'd seen him scrub his fingernails as fastidiously as a surgeon.

I got it at last.

The wolf had marked his territory.

'Dicky pissed in your stream. He opened his pants and pissed in the stream.'

King stared off into the trees for a full minute. Then he stared at me. Then he looked around, confirming that we were alone in the woods. He sounded detached, at first, like a man narrating a movie, but soon righteous with passion.

'The stream was low. Just a trickle. It had been a while since the rains . . . I saw this ugly yellow stain spread down from his property into mine. These backwoods *scum* were destroying everything I had worked for. I threw myself through the deer fence. It stung like bees, which made me madder, and I threw a wild punch. He fell backwards, laughing at me.

'Then he stood up and I thought, This monster's going to kill me. I was terrified. I'm sixty years old. I hadn't been in a fight since I was sixteen. I was going to die in the woods, beside a pile of broken bottles. Then it was like a miracle: he stopped to put on a glove.

'It was the best chance I'd get.

'I grabbed his wine bottle and hit him in the head. I didn't mean to kill him. I figured the bottle would break and stun him and I'd run. But it didn't break. It caught him right in front of the ear and crushed . . . his head split, like I'd dropped a cantaloupe or something. *I only meant to stop him from killing me.* Can't you understand that, Ben?'

I could imagine his fear at the moment a brawler like Dicky Butler climbed menacingly to his feet. Had I got my hands on the bikers' wrench I'd have easily accidentally killed one of them down in Derby. 'You could plead self-defence.'

'I'm not pleading anything. It's over. He's dead and buried and it's time for the rest of us to get on with our lives.'

I recalled a line from a Mary Chapin Carpenter song Julia had played on the juke box: 'The world is kinder to the kind who won't look back.'

That depended on what they were not looking back on.

'So you had a body on your hands,' I said.

'As you've guessed.'

'With its head bashed in.'

'He would have killed me.'

'And a nearby dam set conveniently to explode.'

'In that I was damned lucky.'

'The famous luck of the Silver Fox?'

'Not the first time it's rescued me.' He smiled in gratitude to the Higher Power that arranged such things.

'But this time you stretched your luck,' I said. 'You over-reached. You weren't satisfied with lucky and convenient. You got greedy.'

30

Henry King looked at me like I had lurched from the gutter to shake an empty cup in his face. He had unburdened himself. He would deny anything repeated by the real-estate agent with the chequered past. My word against his, no corroboration.

'Greedy? What did you want me to do, wreck my life by confessing to the cops? Forget it.'

I said, 'You know that's not what I mean. You got greedy.'

'You promised to return the glove, Abbott.'

'Butler's dynamite wasn't booby-trapped. Your people removed it immediately. There was no way Julia would take a chance leaving it in place. But when you had to get rid of the body, you got this great idea to put the dynamite *back* and blow the dam.

'Except somebody noticed there was a variety of dynamites. All different types. And it occurred to them what Mr Butler had done.'

'What had he done?' asked King.

'He didn't want to get caught any more than you want to get caught. He used untraceable dynamite. Leftovers he picked up from jobs here and there – not hard for a guy with a licence. That's when you got greedy. You figured if you had to lose your lake in the process of covering up your murder, you might as well turn a profit.'

'I don't follow you.'

'Two birds with one stone. You sent my stupid cousins up to Butler's farm and stole his legitimate dynamite – traceable explosive he had purchased at Pendleton Powder – and used it to blow the dam on to Dicky's body.'

'You're nuts, Abbott.'

'That's how Mr Butler knew the instant the Feds traced the dam explosion to Pendleton Powder that you had switched loads and killed his son. Got to hand it to you. You thought fast under all that pressure. It was a great plan. Butler got interrogated, harassed and jailed. At best the poor guy'll be locked up for ever, at worst, you'll drive him crazy. Either way, you'll get his farm.'

'Then why did I pay for his defence?'

'That was my idea and you loved it. For twenty-five thousand dollars, you looked innocent. Cheaper than half a million to buy him another farm. Dollars to doughnuts, while you pretend to pressure the state's attorney to drop the case, Josh Wiggens'll keep tossing raw meat to Detective-Sergeant Boyce.'

I turned away.

'Where are you going?'

'I'll bring the glove up to your house. I'm done with it.'

'What do you mean?'

'I've already photographed it, and scraped samples of Dicky Butler's sweat. Detective Boyce can get a DNA match out of his coffin.'

'So what?'

'The glove alone won't convict, but it sure will scare the hell out of the people who covered up for you. I'll turn them if it takes me all year.'

King sighed. 'I can only hope that you'll get bored and stop slandering me after six months.'

'I'll start with Josh Wiggens.'

'Do it before lunch, if you want coherence.'

'How about Bert Wills?'

Henry King took off his cap, ran his hand through his hair, and jammed it on again. Then he looked me straight in the face. 'You'll find Bert in my wife's bedroom. Or on warm nights, in my sunken garden.'

I tried to look shocked – *shocked*. 'You know?'

'Of course I know, you idiot. He keeps her off my back until I can work out an affordable divorce.'

302

Sounded awfully like Julia would be registering at Tiffany's.

I said, 'If that's so, then Bert has lots to lose. And more to win by selling you out. Even if he didn't help you carry the body, he probably knows who did. Josh would be my guess. But I don't have to guess. My friend Detective-Sergeant Boyce is a smart woman with political ambitions. And a real bear of a confessor. You know how she breaks people down? Once she knows what to ask, she says, "Bert, Josh, whoever, the door to immunity from accessory to murder is here. First one on line gets through." Before you know it, Bert gives up a piece. Josh gives a piece and my friend E-mails your name to the state's attorney.'

Henry King plunged a hand into his pocket and whipped out a flip phone. 'Front and centre!'

Josh? I prayed to see him saunter from the forest. Or Bert Wills? Even Jenkins hugging Mrs King's shoes? But no such luck, and no surprises. I saw Julia Devlin moving through the trees.

She walked past me, eyes down. I'd expected defiance, or anger at me, or a look of love for King, but she just stared at the leaf-strewn ground. Yet something easy in her stance spoke of pride or resolve. It was very puzzling.

'Julia,' King said, 'Ben has the glove in his car and he claims to have taken photos and scrapings from it. We'll want them from his house.'

I said to Julia, 'You didn't find it in my house last night because I put it in my glove compartment. And I am willing to believe that you were looking for more than the glove.'

She said to King, 'There is nothing he can prove.'

'He'll push, and push, and push until someone falls. I can't allow it.'

Julia gathered herself, and yet couldn't seem to raise her head. 'I'm sorry, Ben.'

When I looked back at King, he was smiling the bored smile of a victor anxious to get on to other things.

And when I turned to Julia she was already airborne, lofting at me like a panther.

31

Aunt Connie was sitting down to afternoon tea, miles away, but she saved my life. Thanks to her sharper eye than mine, I knew why Julia Devlin never carried Henry King's bags. And remembered it in time to take her flying kick on my chin instead of my throat.

I picked myself off the ground, confident that I outweighed her by enough. She knew too, of course, and was standing easily with a pretty little gun braced professionally in a cross-wrist grip.

'Don't.'

It never crossed my mind. Here was the warrior woman I'd imagined last March at Fox Trot – the grandee's daughter fighting Moors. If it was any consolation, I was an accurate judge of character, only slow on the uptake.

'Sorry, Ben,' she said again. She looked like she meant it and I answered from my heart, 'Not half as sorry as I am.'

King looked over sharply. 'What the hell's going on? Julia, is there something I should know?'

'No,' I said. 'She's very loyal.'

I'm not that self-effacing, or even that gentlemanly – it would have taken the spirit of a punching bag to be so after what Julia had done to me – but as there were two of them and one of me and she had the gun, I thought it best to confuse him a little, and her a lot.

'Did I mention that Josh Wiggens also helped Mr Butler escape from jail?'

'We heard on the police scanner that he had escaped. He won't run far with the entire Connecticut State Police force after him.'

'My guess is Agent Josh figured, Let the cops shoot him down and get it over with.'

King shrugged. 'Josh,' he said, 'always had a gift for the details.'

'Josh figured wrong.'

'What do you mean?'

'Mr Butler is not running . . . Who's guarding your front gate?'

King looked at Julia.

'Chevalleys.'

'Jesus Christ, Julia, get somebody out there with a brain.'

'The gate is locked,' she said coolly. 'The road spikes will stop him dead even if he gets through. Which he can't.'

'Goddammit, do I have to do everything? Give me that radio!' He snatched the VHF handset she produced and started shouting, 'Chevalley boys. Chevalley boys. Are you there? Goddammed numskulls.'

'Yes, sir! We're here, sir.' It was Dennis, sounding reasonably sharp, considering he'd been drinking all night and whacked in the head by me this morning.

'You looking out for Butler?'

'He just got here.'

'What?'

'Yeah. Sir. He just drove up. Boy, he's got something weird hanging off the front of his truck – Albert, go see what the hell that 'sucker – SHIT!'

'What?'

I heard a sharp bang in the distance. King cried out and whipped the radio from his ear and we all heard Dennis shouting, *'Run, Albert, run!'*

'Don't run!' King screamed.

'The thing in front blew the gate right off the hinges! He's throwing bombs.'

Staccato banging on the radio was echoed by explosions in the valley. Then deep, deep silence.

'Chevalleys? . . . Chevalleys? . . . Answer me!'

'He got in, sir. We couldn't stop him.'

'Get him!'

'He bombed our truck. The son of a bitch bombed our truck.'

305

'The spikes will stop him,' said King.

Now I knew why Mr Butler had loaded his truck with boards.

Julia drew her cell phone, dialled without moving her gun enough to tempt me to try anything, and spoke urgently with the house. 'Button up. Don't let anyone in.'

'Tell them to get out of the house,' I said.

'They're safer inside.'

'No, they aren't. Get them out – Julia, listen to me. Get them out of the house.'

'He'll never get past the spikes,' said King.

'He will,' I said. 'The house is his target. Tell them to run.'

'The house?' King cried. 'Tell them to stay and fight.'

'Julia. They're maids and gardeners. Tell them to run.'

Julia spoke into the phone. 'Close the shutters and get everybody out. Everyone. Now!' She looked at me. 'I'm not a killer.'

Choosing to ignore a kick that almost killed me, and not wanting to hear the answer to a stupid question like, Did you sleep with me to keep tabs on my investigation, I contented myself with an angry, 'But your boss is. And you know it.'

'*Henry!* Stop!'

Henry King was already a hundred feet downstream, running like the wind.

Julia took off after him.

She was fast and agile. I was slowed by my wet clothing and not quite so nimble. She whisked through the trees with that panther ease of hers, screaming for Henry to stop. Once she fell, sprawling. I gained ten yards, before I tripped over a root and went down, too.

Back on my feet, running flat out, dodging trees and shrubs and granite ledges, I could see sunlight down the slope as the trees began to thin. I tripped again, but caught my balance and kept running.

They broke out of the woods into a hayfield. Amazingly, King was still pulling ahead of Julia, fuelled by the sight of Mr Butler's old blue truck drawing into the cobblestone motor court.

Fox Trot servants were streaming from the terrace doors
– a cook and sous chef in white, maids in black, a plumber
in overalls. Jenkins, last out, counted heads and ran them
towards the woods.

The farmer climbed out and began unloading planks. He
seemed to be moving slowly, such was his deliberation.
Working at a smooth and steady pace, he constructed a ramp
of boards up the front steps. Just as earlier he had laid a
wooden ramp over the driveway spikes.

Josh Wiggens came lurching up the slope from the old
house, waving his pistol. He passed Mrs King and Bert Wills,
who were emerging from the sunken garden, and fired a
wild shot. DaNang streaked from the cab and charged him
like yellow lightning.

Wiggens braced and fired, again. The shot kicked dust from
the cobblestones. The dog kept coming. CIA man drew a
bead.

A sullen boom. Wiggens ducked. Another, echoing loudly.
Josh slewed away and joined the servants running for the
woods. Mr Butler propped his rifle against his truck and
unloaded another plank.

Henry King ran pell-mell down the fields and on to the
lawn that sloped towards the house. Julia was catching up
now. I put on a burst of speed. I caught her in my arms, and
wrestled her to the ground. 'Let me go,' she screamed. 'Let
me go! I have to stop him.'

'Too late.'

She doubled me over her knee and started after him again.

In that moment I could see exactly what was going to
happen as clearly as if a pilot had skywritten it in chalk-white
letters overhead. And the only thing that made sense to me
was to save one soul less guilty than the others.

Butler climbed into his truck. He whistled. His dog jumped
in back, standing high on the cargo. The farmer drove up
the ramp, up the front steps, building speed, aiming at the
front door.

The Ford was an old three-quarter-tonner with heavy
bumpers. It crashed through the double oak doors like a
battering ram and disappeared into the dark of the centre

foyer. The last I saw of them was DaNang, barking like a Dalmatian on a hook-and-ladder.

'*Henry!*' Julia screamed. 'Henry!'

I took my last shot, lunged after Julia, hit her legs and staggered her. She fell on the grass a yard from the motor court as King reached the front steps. Julia twisted around with her gun. 'Don't!'

'Leave him. It's too late. Live your life.'

'He is my life. I told you. I love him.'

'Why'd you hook up with –'

'I thought you'd rescue me.'

All I could do was offer my hand and whisper, 'Please.'

It slowed her for a moment. But she turned towards the house, and was surging to her feet, when Butler's truck bomb exploded with a roar that blew the shutters off and knocked us to the grass. Dust and fire poured from the windows. The house trembled.

The mighty portico fell first, tumbling as the pillars shattered. Then the entire centre collapsed, the roof descending in one huge piece, slates smashing musically, until all that remained was an empty space framed by the opposite wings.

Through that void, I could see a patchwork of woods and hayfields – Fox Trot's and the neighbours' beyond. They were fenced by ancient walls, stacked stone by stone by the families who had farmed and logged these hills. And loved. And hoped, like the weeping woman raging bitterly at me. 'I'd have caught up if you hadn't stopped me.'

'If I hadn't stopped you, you'd be under that too.'

Sirens howled. Julia turned her tear-stained face to the ruined house. 'At least he's better off than in prison.'

I doubted Dicky Butler would agree.

But she would need to believe that for a very long time. Her heart was broken and the troopers were coming.

32

A week after Mr Butler blew up Fox Trot, Henry King, himself and poor DaNang, I was waiting at my kitchen door
when Alison came sadly up the drive.

'Hey, you. How was school?'

'OK.'

'Glad to be back?'

'No.'

'Want to see something?'

'What?'

'A new friend?'

She looked at me, warily. 'What do you mean?'

'Someone to play with. Want to see?'

'Where?' she breathed, trying to look past me into the
kitchen, hope kindling in her eyes. She looked surprised
when she saw Vicky, and asked what I usually asked when
I saw Vicky outside of Town Hall. 'Who's running Newbury?'

'I just stopped by for coffee.'

'It's next door,' I said. 'Over at Scooter's.'

She looked dubiously at the thick hedge that separated
our yards. 'Naomi didn't have a litter.'

'Let's have a look.' I led her through the hedge where it
grows thin in the shade of our side-by-side barns – mine red,
Scooter's bigger and white. Her eyes got big at the sight of a
new split-rail fence.

I passed her a carrot. She stared at it, afraid to look up and
be disappointed. When she did, she gave as satisfying a gasp
as I'd ever heard from another human being.

'His name is Redman,' I told her. 'He's a little big for you,
but you'll grow into him.'

'Oh, wow!'

'Need help getting aboard?'

'I can do it.' She passed the carrot over the fence. Redman demolished it with teeth like piano keys, and nuzzled her palm for more. She stroked his nose and let him smell her. When she climbed the corral fence, the stallion stood like the patient middle-aged thoroughbred he was, although he skittered a little as she scrambled into the saddle, causing Vicky to tense up beside me.

With the quick physical ease with which she was blessed, Alison leaned over and adjusted her stirrups.

'Connie! Look at my horse!'

Connie was negotiating cautiously across the lawn on Scooter's arm. She waved her silver-headed walking stick. 'What a handsome horse!'

To me, in hushed but stern tones, she said, 'Benjamin, have you any idea how much these animals eat?'

'Worth it.'

Scooter remarked that when you added up the stall I'd built secretly in his barn while Alison was at school, and the corral, and the hay I'd humped up into the loft, no one in Newbury had ever gone to so much trouble not to get a cat.

'Worth it.'

Redman's ears got suddenly sharp and swivelled towards Main Street. Around Scooter's house came Ira Roth from whose tax-shelter horse farm I'd acquired Redman in exchange for a promise of too many hours of free investigation. He was carrying a liquor box under one arm, and wearing a Stetson hat, which he removed with a flourish for Connie.

'Hello, Miss Abbott.'

Connie's 'Good afternoon, Ira', would have caused an Eskimo to button up her sealskins.

'Hello, Vicky. Hello, Scooter. Hello, Redman, how are you getting on here? Little girl, you got yourself a crackerjack. He was a heck of a racehorse.'

'Ira,' said Connie. 'He looks high strung, Ira. Is she all right on him?'

'Perfectly safe as long as Redman's got his pet.'

'Pet?' I asked. 'What do you mean, his pet?'

'Race stallions generally have a monkey or rabbit that lives with them to keep 'em on an even keel.'

'Are you telling me this horse comes with a monkey?'

'No,' Ira laughed. 'You're such a kidder, Ben. No monkey. Just Tom.'

'Tom?'

'Here. My groom forgot this when you picked him up.' He pressed the liquor box into my hands and backed away.

'What's in the box, Ben?' asked Alison, her hands suddenly full of excited horse.

'He smells him,' called Ira. 'You can let Tom out now. Don't worry. He won't run away.'

'I'm not worried.' I put the box down. Scooter opened the flaps. A grim eye peered up. Redman gave a delirious snort. The occupant of the box climbed out, stalked to the corral, and let the horse stroke his back with his huge nose.

'Wow!' yelled Alison.

'Looks like a cat,' said Scooter.

He was 'Tom' as in 'conspicuously-unaltered tom', with a long lanky body and a hunter's head that surveyed his surroundings as mercilessly as a praying mantis.

'At least he'll live in the barn.'

Ira Roth, still backing, called, 'Most of the time.'

'If he's the horse's pet, it stands to reason he's going to live with the horse.'

'Except when they have their little tiffs.'

'Tiffs?' asked Vicky. 'What sort of tiffs?'

'They're like a couple of old bachelors. Good friends, until they get bent out of shape over some darned thing and Tom stalks off to the house for a couple of weeks.'

'Whose house?'

'Not mine,' said Scooter. 'We got our hands full with Naomi.'

'Mom's allergic,' Alison called down from Redman.

'Mine's too far,' said Vicky. 'Besides, I'm sure Tom would prefer the company of someone who sits around the house all day waiting for the phone to ring.'

Connie's house was right across the street. With any luck,

311

while crossing one night, Tom might encounter a huge truck barrelling through town and hop a ride to Massachusetts and Redman would make friends with a squirrel.

'I'm so sorry,' said Connie. 'But, as you couldn't resist reminding me the other night, I already have a cat.'

An April Shroud
Reginald Hill

After seeing Inspector Pascoe off on his honeymoon with a few ill-chosen words, Superintendent Dalziel's holiday gets off to a damp start, then, rescued by a bunch of singularly cheerful mourners he accompanies them back to Lake House to recuperate.

Bonnie Fielding – seemingly more troubled by the half-finished Banqueting Hall that was to have rescued the family from penury than by her husband's sudden demise – and her ample charms stir feelings that the obese Dalziel had forgotten existed, and when he discovers that her first husband died in murky circumstances, he is inclined to take the news lightly. But before long the rundown mansion is littered with fresh corpses and it looks as though Pascoe will have to save his normally hard-headed boss from making a complete fool of himself...

'Always original, never boring and strongly recommended'
Independent

ISBN 0 00 649860 4

A Grave Talent

Laurie R. King

Kate Martinelli, a newly promoted Homicide detective with a secret to conceal, and Alonzo Hawkin, a world-weary cop trying to make a new life in San Francisco, could not be more different, but are thrown together to solve a brutal crime – the murders of three young girls.

As Martinelli and Hawkin get nearer to a solution, they realize the crimes may not be the sexually motivated killings they had seemed, and that there is a coldly calculating and tortuous mind at work which they must outmanoeuvre if they are to prevent both further carnage and the destruction of a shining talent...

'If there is a new P.D. James...I would put my money on Laurie R. King'   *Boston Globe*

ISBN 0 00 649354 8

An Image to Die For

Mike Phillips

Independent TV producer Wyndham Davis unearths crucial evidence that could overthrow Leon Ross's conviction for the brutal murder of his wife and children on a tough London housing estate. Invited to attend an interview on the estate where a mystery witness is being questioned, black journalist Sam Dean is sickened by the vicious stabbing of one of the programme's researchers. So when Wyndham offers Sam the job of tracking down Amaryll Johnson, Helen Ross's lover, he isn't wild about taking it on... but emotional pressure is brought to bear by a figure from Sam's past.

As he embarks on his search for Johnson, Sam realizes there's more than one agenda here. There are secrets from Wyndham's life influencing events and Sam is getting sucked right into the dark heart of the mystery. Tough, vivid and shocking, *An Image to Die For* is a disturbing and compelling read from one of Britain's foremost crime writers.

'This is Mike Phillips's best novel, brutal and caring, totally authentic'   *The Times*

ISBN 0 00 649671 7

Giotto's Hand

Iain Pears

General Bottando of Rome's Art Theft Squad is in trouble: his theory that a single master criminal, dubbed 'Giotto', is behind a string of major thefts has aroused the scorn of his arch enemy and rival, the bureaucrat Corrado Argan. He needs a result, and the confession of a dying woman may just provide the vital clue.

In pursuit of the elusive Giotto, Bottando's colleague, Flavia di Stefano, sets off hotfoot for Florence, and English art dealer Jonathan Argyll is dispatched to London and then on to rural Norfolk...only to discover a body and a mystery which could lead to the greatest art find of his career.

'An elegant and amusing book, perfect for those who love a clever puzzle'   *Mail on Sunday*

ISBN 0 00 649026 3

Clean Break
Val McDermid

Manchester-based private eye Kate Brannigan is not amused when thieves have the audacity to steal a Monet from a stately home where she'd arranged the security. She's even less thrilled when the hunt for the thieves drags her on a treacherous foray across Europe as she goes head to head with organized crime. And as if this isn't enough, a routine industrial case starts leaving a trail of bodies across the North West, leaving Kate with more problems than she can deal with.

Cleaning up the mess in *Clean Break* forces Kate to confront harsh truths in her own life as she battles with a testing array of villains in a case that stretches love and loyalty to the limits.

'Tough, funny and intensely topical, McDermid stands out as one of the few contemporary writers actually nourished by the here and now'   *Literary Review*

ISBN 0 00 649772 1

The Mermaids Singing

Val McDermid

You always remember the first time. Isn't that what they say about sex? How much more true it is of murder...

Up till now, the only serial killers Tony Hill had encountered were safely behind bars. This one's different – this one's on the loose.

In the northern town of Bradfield four men have been found mutilated and tortured. Fear grips the city; no man feels safe. Clinical psychologist Tony Hill is brought in to profile the killer. A man with more than enough sexual problems of his own, Tony himself becomes the unsuspecting target of a battle of wits and wills where he has to use every ounce of his professional skill and personal nerve to survive.

A tense, brilliantly written psychological thriller, *The Mermaids Singing* explores the tormented mind of serial killer unlike any the world of fiction has ever seen.

Winner of the 1995 CWA Award for Best Crime Novel of the Year

'Truly, horribly good'   *Mail on Sunday*

ISBN 0 00 649358 0

The Killing Floor
Peter Turnbull

A motorist's error leads to the discovery of a decomposed headless and handless corpse in the garden of a house in a prestigious Glasgow suburb. For Glasgow's P Division, the first task is to identify the body – an identification which reveals a person with a talent for making enemies.

Then there is another killing – a murderous stabbing in an east-end housing scheme – and the police investigation takes on an added urgency. The whiff of corruption is in the air, and soon they are unravelling a thirty-year-old fraud of massive proportions, which, if made public, would shake the city to its very foundations.

'Few can rival Turnbull for dire authenticity'   *Observer*

0 00 647976 6